OBERON'S CALLING

The Birth of Nick Jones

KEITH MCINTOSH

This is dedicated to my friends and family.

ACKNOWLEDGEMENTS

I'd like to thank Aaron Nash and Pete Chaffe. All those hours playing a certain turn-based Alien invasion game on playstation while wondering, "What would Nick Jones do here?" were not wasted.

I continue to be thankful for my wife, Renee, for her love and support in this endeavor. She's my favorite editor. Even though, I'm about as welcoming to critique as a hungry bear is to a slap in the face.

Another special thanks to Kathy Carter. My first fan. The Annie Wilkes to my Paul Sheldon. She is the first one to read anything I write, and usually the last one to say anything bad about it. Maybe that's why we get along so well. Hmmm.

And of course, my readers, a big thanks goes out to all of you who dared to pick up one of my books. I hope you are enjoying this journey as much as I am.

FOREWORD

Surprise! I'm doing science-fiction now. A few people who may recognize my name from my Ronin of the Dead series might wonder why I decided to suddenly publish a completely different book, in a completely different genre, half way through my zombie action series. Simply put, because I can. More importantly, because it's profitable. Some might be surprised to learn the zombie-apocalypse genre has a limited, but devout, fan base. For reasons I can't even fathom, some people don't like zombies at all. I know. Weird, right? So, in an effort to reach more people I sat down and plotted out two completely different series. One Science Fiction, and the other is a modern day Cosmic Horror. This is my foray into the Science Fiction genre. I am looking forward to continuing this series, I had a lot of fun writing this book. Hopefully it works out with the readers. On the plus side, this book has the longest fight scene I've written to date, and it involves two supersoldiers. So, there's that to look forward to. All joking aside, I sincerely hope you enjoy it.

PROLOGUE

Captain Val Biggs

"Captain?" Rat's nervous voice came over the intercom.

Val Biggs, captain of the Poseidon. A dated class 'B' waterhauler, that maybe in its prime was an impressive ship, but now had more replacement parts than original. But it was his, kind of. It was a special corporate lease job. Those Corporate fucks still get to squeeze him until his balls turn blue, but he got to pick his contracts. If it was up to him, he would haul for someone else. Maybe the colonies. God knows they could use the water. Maybe even Earth. He had bills to pay though, and nobody paid better than The Corporation.

"What is it, Rat?" He replied absently to the still air of his quarters. His next shift wasn't for another couple hours and Val was still looking over the maintenance reports from the last shift. "Hey," Val perked up his tone. "What the fuck is going on with the heat shielding on booster three? Trevor recommends a total refit at next dock?" He asked with a certain amount of indignation. He couldn't help it. These guys just didn't appreciate how expensive running a hauler of this class was. If they wanted to make *real* cash, they had to keep costs down.

"It's those high-G burns, Cap." Rat said quickly. "A ship this old isn't meant to run so hot for so long."

Fair enough, Val thought bitterly. They *had* burned a hot streak across the solar system to get here. Time is money, that's the guiding principle of water haulers. They were a strange breed that ran the razor's edge between shipping schedules and maintenance costs.

"What's the reactor running at?" Val asked gruffly and stretched his back in his chair. Even in Zero G his back ached. At sixty-three years old, he wasn't the oldest ice hauler in the system, but he was close.

"Ninety-three percent." The silence that followed told Val everything he needed to know.

"What the hell? Why am I just finding out about this now?"

"Trevor wanted to nail down the cause before he came to you with it?" *Reasonable.*

"And?"

"Nothing yet."

"Does he think he'll have it fixed before we ship out?" Val asked feeling like he already knew the answer.

"Dunno. You'd have to talk to him. I'm not the engineer." *Fucking typical.*

"Fine, I'll call him when we're done." Val pinched the bridge of his nose. *Fucking ship is falling apart.* At this rate, he and his crew were probably only looking at a fifteen percent profit margin. *Fuck sakes,* Val cursed silently. This quarter was beginning to look like a total write-off.

"He's sleeping right now." Rat informed him coldly. "He pulled a triple shift, Cap." There was a pause before he added, "You should probably let him sleep."

"Why'd he pull a triple?" It was a knee-jerk question. Val felt he already knew the answer to that as well.

Trevor Aquila was one of the best engineers in the system, for the money. But even as skilled as he was, he was still just one man. A ship this size should have an engineering staff of at least five.

"This old girl just keeps breaking, Cap. He's running around trying to plug up all the holes. It's not his fault." Val silently nodded his agreement to that statement as he keyed up the work schedules for the next shift. Maybe he could wrangle some bodies to help out.

"What about Ramirez and Kupa?" Val asked absently as he looked over the schedules. Rat answered him a second before he found the information for himself.

"Nope. Ramirez is on Drone team two, and Kupa is out with the flu. *And* even if he wasn't, he's needed on drone team four."

"Fuck."

"Yeah." Val could hear the sympathy for his dilemma in Rat's tone. "Anyway, I actually called you about Cube Two. Something strange came up on the preliminary scan."

The Poseidon was capable of hauling ten, half-mile long cubes of ice within her storage bay. All neatly lined up in a row along her length. It was hard, dangerous work that promised long hours and a big payday at the end. If, they all did their jobs right. They were two months into an eight-month haul.

Their ship was currently in a geo-synchronised orbit over Europa, so the small ice moon was shielding them from the massive amounts of radiation that came off of Jupiter. Val was lucky enough to secure a mining claim to Gamma-twelve. The solar economic trade treaty cut Europa's icy surface into a grid. His grid cell was near Europa's equator where some of the most favorable mining conditions could be found. It made the job easier, but it was still a long way from easy.

"What? Contamination?"

The cubes they cut out of the moon's surface were usually pure ice, hard as granite. But sometimes they had terrestrial contamination in them, rocks mostly. It was a problem because every ounce they carried that wasn't pure water, was essentially dead-weight. Every ton they didn't get paid for, was another tonne they were paying for. If the contamination was too bad, the cube would have to be abandoned. Which was a disaster.

"Yeah, we have a single, small solid mass in the top quadrant. Nothing too bad." *Well, that's good.* "But I'm getting some weird density readings from it."

"Oh?" That piqued Val's interest. A couple years ago another ice hauler, The Tiburon, found a chunk of pure gold in their grid cell. They could definitely use a payday like that. "Mineral deposit? Iron maybe?" He offered, secretly hoping it was something more lucrative.

"That's the thing, Cap. It comes up as crystalline." It was then Val started to hear the excitement in Rat's voice. "If I'm reading this right, I'm looking at a diamond that's as big as a damned commercial shuttle."

***

"Up chute! Make a hole!" Val shouted as he quickly drifted up the maintenance chute towards the bridge. The chute only had room for one body and he didn't want anybody else jamming it up. The bridge was four decks away and this was the quickest way there.

The Poseidon, because of the G-forces during thrust, was organized like an office building, or maybe like one of the Corporation's stacks on Mars. If the rumors were to be believed. The bridge was at the top, followed by ten personnel decks. Then came the expansive five-and-a-half-mile long storage compartment, and at the back of the ship were the engineering decks. If Poseidon had been an office building from the ancient times, it would almost breech earth's troposphere. And she wasn't even the biggest ship out there.

Val eased his ascent to a slow stop at the bridge level. He gently kicked off the ladder to orientate himself to a standing position, then he clicked his heels together to engage his mag-boots and stepped down onto the deck. He walked with practised grace through the entranceway to the bridge. Each step highlighted by the telltale clicks of the mag-boots engaging and disengaging on the metal deck.

"Captain on the bridge!" Rat yelped dutifully into the empty space. He was the bridge's sole occupant, and was seated at his usual station. The wiry young man was responsible for the ship's operations while on the drift.

"Fuck off, Rat." Val waved off the formality as he approached the crewman's station. Nigel Ratborn was born with an unfortunate name, but he was a talented pilot, given his age. His addiction to certain narcotics is why he came so cheap. Most former corporate pilots found themselves addicted to the low-end chems they dump into their systems during the high-G burns. Luckily, he still had most of his teeth. "Let me see it."

Rat tapped a few keys and swiveled his monitor so Val could see the full-screen scan for himself. Val lowered himself down and had a look. He moved his hand over to the directional ball on the console and panned the scan around so he could see all angles of the shape. The scan was in poor resolution, it *was* just the preliminary scan, but even so he could still make out an angular profile to the shape. It was like a knife's point at the one end, sharp and angular, and spread out towards the other end. It was a strange shape for a simple rock. At its longest point, the shape was exactly 35 meters long. At its widest point, it was exactly 18 meters long. Again, strange. Rocks usually didn't measure in exact values like that.

"Can you clean this up?" Val turned to Rat who just shrugged apologetically.

"That's the best I can do. Claire might be able to run it through a few filtering programs, but if you want a better picture than that we have to shoot a deep-core probe into it." Val turned the image one way and then another. He couldn't shake the feeling that somehow it was familiar.

"Where's the OES report on it?" Val asked and Rat promptly tapped a few more keys on his console and the image on the screen was replaced with the Optical Emissions Spectrometry report concerning the object.

"What the hell." Val couldn't help himself. Rat had been correct to be concerned. According to the scan, the outer surface of the object is so dense the scan couldn't penetrate it. It came back as a crystalline structure that was fused with an unknown alloy that didn't reflect light.

"Right?!" Rat cut in. "You see what I mean. Look at the weight ratio. It's all fucking wonky too." Val did indeed look at the object's mass to volume index and it didn't match. *It's hollow. Like a ship.* Val absently allowed his gaze to drift back to Rat and the kid just stared at him with wide eyes. "Do you think it's an alien spaceship?"

"What?" Val snapped out of his thoughts. "No. Don't be stupid." He straightened up while still eyeing the report and scratched his chin. *It couldn't be. Could it?* "Where are we with the cubes?" Rat pulled his screen back and went back to his console.

"Umm. Cubes one and two are locked and stacked away. Three is still being fitted with the orbital thrusters. E.T.A? Three more hours according to the last shift log. Drone crew three and five are currently cutting Cube four out of the icefield."

"Okay," Val said. "Wake up Trevor, get him to shoot a probe into Cube Two, and let me know as soon as he gets the results. And, raise up the communication array. I need to make a call." Val issued his orders and absently turned away, his mind still reeling from the possible implications of his hunch.

"What?" Rat complained idly behind him. "What about the triple? I can just get the cargo crew to shoot the probe and do the scan."

"No!" Val turned back and pointed angrily at his crewman. "Fucking wake him up and get him to do it personally." Nobody else would have seen the preliminary scan except Rat, which was good. The cargo crew were just responsible for locking the cubes away in the hold. They wouldn't know anything. "I want to keep a lid on this. So, until you hear from me you keep your mouth fucking shut about this, Rat." Val leveled the man with a hard gaze. They both knew he had a habit of gossiping with other crew members. "That's an order."

***

Three hours later, Val was nervously waiting in his quarters. His tight-beam request was accepted and he waited for the response. With galactic distances being what they were, the only feasible way to communicate was by tight beam laser. It requires line of sight, and in a moving system where each location is hurdling through the universe at a velocity that was in the five-digit range, that was tricky. To minimize time, and maximize signal strength, the Shipper's Union set up a communication array network that was neutral. All factions could use it. It was set up to save lives. Space travel was dangerous business, after all. Even with the signal bouncing around all those relays, there was still an eight-minute delay to Mars.

It felt like an eternity to Val.

Stay calm, Val told himself as he rubbed his hands together waiting for the response to come through. *You're the one holding all the cards here.* Val couldn't believe it himself. Trevor had done the deep core scan. Val was hoping the weary engineer would just do it and insist on going back to bed. But once he saw the composition of the outer hull of the craft in the cube, he knew. Material engineers had been trying to replicate that alloy for centuries. *Mythrial.* That's what they called it. Now, Trevor was wide awake. He knew the biggest obstacle the Corporation R&D guys had was that they didn't have a sample to study, to reverse engineer. That was because there was only one place to procure such a sample, and it wasn't like The Council was going to just hand it over.

The Council, the former governing body of the human race. Seven immortal superhumans with genius level intelligence who took it upon themselves to rebuild the human race after The Shattering broke Earth and scattered the species throughout the galaxy. It was a monumental task, nobody blamed them for their failure. Later, during the Great Reclamation War, The Council sided with Earth and pushed back the Corporate Armada all the way back to Mars. The Corporation was set to fall, the whole galaxy felt it. Then the impossible happened, The Corporation changed its stance and sought out peace. Humanity held its collective breath as the first peace summit was to be held in neutral space. An emissary of The Council was even sent to oversee the proceedings on the Corporate flagship, the Titania. What happened next is still one of the biggest controversies in the galaxy. The Corporation insisted someone from Earth sabotaged the ship's drivecore. Earth labeled it as a Martian betrayal. People still argue about it. When the Titania's drivecore erupted, it vaporized all the neighboring ships in a fireball that looked like a small sun before it winked out. The whole system saw it. Every news telescope was solely aimed on that tiny patch of space. One second, every major military ship was posed in a tense stand off, with the Titania in the middle. The next moment it was all gone. Every ship was reduced to atoms.

Except one apparently.

Val knew it was crazy. That happened hundreds of years ago. The exact number he didn't even know. The Council

Member, Ares, was assumed to be among the vaporized. Yet, Val was staring at his ship. His mind was still reeling with how he was going to get that craft out of that cube without every eye on the ship on him.

First things first, he told himself. First, he had to make the deal. Something like this was a real game changer. This was the greatest technological discovery in...*Fuck sakes, in like centuries. Maybe since the dawn of space travel.* Val forced himself to take a deep breath. *Aim high. Don't be afraid. This is the only time you'll ever have the upper hand on this prick, and you'll only have it until you say 'yes'. Then it's gone. So, aim high and let him try to talk you down.* Val struggled with what even to ask for. The lease on the ship, obviously. That was the starting point, but what to ask for after that. *This guy is over a hundred and fifty years old, he has the money. Don't be afraid.*

Boop-beep

Val jumped at the sound. On his monitor that connection opened and he saw the smooth features of Lucien Malum, another upper-echelon Corporate ladder-climber. Truth be told, Val didn't really know what that asshole even did. All he knew for certain about the man was that he was older than dirt, held the lease on The Poseidon, and had more money than God. *Fucking asshole still looks like he's thirty,* Val thought bitterly as he thought about all the gene therapy this guy must have had over his countless years. By the annoyed, and disheveled look on his perfect face, Val figured he woke the man up.

"Who the fuck is *Val Biggs*? And why the fuck are you calling me at such an ungodly hour?" He complained into the camera and then his image froze, indicating the end of the transmission on his end. Val sighed in annoyance. He would have thought these corporate types would be a little more considerate of the time delay. Regardless, Val put on his best face.

"Yes, sir. Val Biggs, I own the Poseidon. It's a water hauler. Anyways, I'm out here on Europa and I think I found something you might be interested in." Val sent the message and waited. He looked at the side portion of the monitor where his information packet was queued up and ready to send.

"Okay, first off, you don't own shit. That's *my* ship," Lucien gently corrected. Val should have known better. Corporate doctrine doesn't allow the recognition of ownership until the debt is fully paid. Even though, Val's dad had secured a generational clause that allowed Val to retain ownership after his passing, regardless of default. Problem there was, Lucien would probably just have him killed at that point. Val was sixteen when his father saddled him into this contract. He said it was an opportunity of a lifetime. Technically, he was right. It was an opportunity to spend a lifetime hauling ice around the galaxy in an ancient, dilapidated ship. "Second, *Jerome* Biggs is on that lease. I don't know a *Val*." The image froze.

"Fucking guy." Val's father passed away thirty years ago when he stroked out from a high G burn. Val had personally spoken to Lucien Malum three times since then. Before he could respond the image came alive again.

"Sorry, sorry. I have the lease agreement in front of me now and I see you're signed on as the secondary. Also, it has been amended after your father's passing. Sorry for your loss," Lucien added like it was a tedious formality he had to include. "So, you're the Captain now. Good for you, moving up in the galaxy." On the image, he could see the young man's face studying something on his monitor. "Looks like you were late with a payment last year, the first quarter." Then Lucien looked grimly at the camera. "I would be very disappointed to learn this call was just to inform me of another late payment." The image froze with Malum's perfect blonde-haired, blue-eyed stern expression staring him down.

"If I remember correctly you were some director in the R&D branch in the Corporation, is that right?" It was Val's turn to completely ignore what Lucien said so he could continue on with his spiel. "I think I have something you're going to want?"

Eight minutes later.

"I'm the Vice Director of Special Projects in the Research and Development Sector," Lucien said with a certain amount of indignation. Like it mattered. "Get it right. Now, what could you possibly have that I might find of value?" Val smiled.

My turn, asshole!

"I have something here that is going to cover the remainder of my lease, and then some. And then a lot more actually." Val ended the message with the ridiculously high number he came up with, he attached his informational packet to the message, and sent it.

Then he waited. It was a long eight minutes. He went over everything in his head. The alloy's composition of the hull. The object's profile he matched against the ship's database. He even had the ship's dated AI work out the possible trajectory the craft would have had to make to finally get sucked into Jupiter's immense gravity field which pulled it down into its ice moon. It was real. He had the proof. Val breathed out and thought again of the insane credit amount he gave the man, that was on top of The Poseidon's lease. *I went too far,* he thought rubbing his hands together.

Then the image moved, and Lucien was once again gravely looking at him. For the first few seconds the man said nothing, and just stared at the camera. Val would have checked the connection but he saw the image blink. When Lucien finally spoke, he said the five words Val knew would change his life forever.

"When can you get here?"

CHAPTER 1

Eve

Eve rocketed through the system in her ship, Nike, like an ebony bullet. She'd been on a steady 5G burn for about a week now, chasing after the Poseidon. A normal human being would have stroked out long ago. The crushing weight would have reduced a normal body to a sack of lumpy paste by now. She could take it, though. The nanomachines that were permanently bonded to her body protected her from the gravitational forces. Hell, after all this time traveling the solar system, she barely felt the single digit G's anymore.

Countless lifetimes ago, she was born Eve Carter. She still remembered the city she grew up in. Red Deer. In the Northern part of the American confederation, where the winter months still had a bitter bite to them. Back when she still felt temperatures. She brought herself out of the slums and became a Navy pilot. A damned good one too. She even met the living god, Oberon, the last wonder of the human race. The one person, at the time, who was implanted with a strange piece of alien technology and became the first superhuman in recorded history. He was a marvel. The guiding light that would usher humankind into its next era. Then the gravity bomb exploded somewhere on Earth and the shockwave wiped the earth's surface clean. The blast wave sent trillions of tonnes of debris into orbit. It destroyed any hopes of a unified planet as it sent humanity into the stars. The fortunate ones moved on to greener pastures and left the survivors on Earth to die.

It was then, in humanity's despair, that mankind's last hope came to her with an offer she couldn't refuse. *Help me fix this. Help me fix mankind,* he said. After that, after the implantation, the solar system knew her as Athena. Honestly, at the time she felt the codenames were silly. After all these centuries though, she had to admit. She felt less and less like Eve Carter, and more like Athena. The solar system needed Athena after all. It didn't need a woman of low birth from some forgotten low-end city in the frozen wastelands of the Americas. It needed her to be a pinnacle of wisdom and strength. A moral light that guided humanity forward. At least, that's what Oberon would have them believe. After they lost Thomas though, that guiding light had dimmed considerably.

She was Athena, Council member; she knew that. She accepted who she was, and she hadn't lost sight of their mission like some others. She still allowed herself to be Eve, though. To let that golden, godlike façade fall away and expose the vulnerable woman on the inside. She did that with Thomas. Allowed herself to be Eve Carter. Not at first, of course. At first, she thought he was just another pompous asshole who was high on his own self-image. In the beginning he infuriated her to such a degree she refused to call him anything other than his codename, Ares. He wore her down though. It was bound to happen. People who worked in such close proximity like they had, couldn't help but develop a sort of intimacy. It was the little things he thought went unnoticed that caught her attention the most. Like how he would hold a baby. It was the little pieces of Thomas that Ares let slip that made it so easy to fall in love with him.

Then he died.

Even now, when she thought of her beloved, she couldn't help but see that incredible fireball that just swallowed up everything in her life and turned it to ash. That was the day Athena's façade broke and Eve Carter's scream let loose from within. She didn't even know she was capable of making such a sound. All the pain and hurt just erupted from her until her lungs were empty and her throat was raw. It was the last time she could say she truly felt something. Since then, she felt like the endless blackness she was currently rocketing through. A cold, unforgiving void.

Eve felt the weight pressing down on her begin to lessen.

"We are approaching the target as specified, Eve," Nike spoke softly to her over the intercom.

Eve opened her eyes. Council Members don't sleep. It was a drawback of the Motherbot implantation. The best they could hope for was a deep meditative state where time just seemed to slip by unnoticed. This is when she roamed her thoughts, which lately had almost exclusively been focused on Thomas and the Poseidon's recent discovery.

Ahead of her, through the crystalline canopy, she could see the twinkling light of the Poseidon's drive plume. At this distance, it looked like a bright star. As ordered, her ship's AI brought them in behind the ancient waterhauler's wake and matched its velocity. Nike settled them into a comfortable 1G burn at the edge of the targeted ship's radar range.

"Thank you, Nike. I guess it's time to wake up," Eve responded and a second later the displays in front of her came alive. "Have they pinged us?"

"No, ma'am."

Eve was just being overly cautious as she looked over the transponder data from the ship in front of them. Nike's outer hull was a strange composite Oberon invented that absorbed all known forms of radar. As far as the Poseidon's Threat Detection System was concerned, Nike was invisible. She still had a heat signature, of course, but it should be masked by the Poseidon's massive heat plume shooting out the back of it. If she did this right, the only way she could be detected was if the occupants of the Poseidon physically saw her ship. That would be next to impossible, even if commercial ships had exterior windows. Which they didn't.

"Would you like me to bring us in to docking range, Ma'am?" The AI politely asked while Eve adjusted her seat.

"No," she said with a smile has her hands slipped around the familiar controls. "That's the fun part."

Eve kicked their velocity up a notch and it nudged her back into her seat. After the week long 5G burn, it could hardly be considered pressure at all. Nike steadily crept forward towards the icehauler. The tiny star of its drive plume grew to the size of a small sun. Eve slowly drifted the craft up and over the massive fiery plume of the ship just as Nike's exterior temperature started to slip into the four digit range. The ship's AI already provided her HUD with a vector to follow, it took some of the fun out of it as she navigated the ship past the massive engines of the giant six mile long, boxy-looking vessel. *Fucking ugly bitch,* Eve thought bitterly as she brought the ship in low and cut the main engines. She didn't want to melt the hull of the ship after all. Eve switched to maneuvering thrusters as she began to navigate the surface of the Poseidon.

"I assume your scanning the interior, Nike," Eve said before adding. "Quietly."

"Of course, Eve," the AI responded back, even managing to sound hurt by it. "The craft is only partially loaded, I show only three large cubes of ice in a storage bay that is large enough to hold ten. From the design schematics, I've located a small maintenance airlock on deck nine, Ma'am." On her heads-up display, Eve could see the spot Nike pinged off in the distance.

"Crew?"

"I see thirty-two life-signs, Eve. All located in the crew compartments." *Probably locked down into their thrust chairs.* Most commercial ships didn't want crew walking around haphazardly under thrust.

"Put the crew manifest on one of the screens." *Never go into a ship blind.* It was one of her personal rules. Eve already had the layout of the ship memorized, she had a lot of time to kill on the trip out here. She easily located the key crew members and memorized their faces and names as she drifted up the body of the massive ship like a mosquito approaching its target. "Okay, Nike, take over and bring us in." As talented as she was, Eve still couldn't land on a ship as quietly as the AI could. No human brain could make the thousand micro-bursts of thrust required to land on the metal hull of the craft without it sounding like a bell being struck inside the ship.

"A mother's touch, Ma'am."

Oberon, when he first presented the council members with these ships, warned each of them the ship's advanced AI would develop a personality that would be unique to the pilot. At first, Eve resisted the idea of treating a ship as anything more than a thing to be used. In those days, Nike's electronic voice was distinctively feminine. Eve didn't like to admit it, but when Nike changed its voice to a more masculine one, it made it easier. *I did it for you, Ma'am,* Nike said when Eve inquired about the change. It was also the first time Nike started using the formal title. Slowly, AI crafted a personality that was akin to an executive assistant. Which Eve didn't hate. Though, she had to remind herself on a few occasions that Nike was just a ship, despite the fact she was probably closer to this ship than any other living person in the system.

"Do you really think Hera is down there, Ma'am?"

"That's what we're going to find out."

"I hope she is. I miss her terribly," Nike said with a cold detachment. Eve suspected the ship was being sincere, though. It wasn't a stretch of imagination to think Nike would have an affection for Ares's ship. Hell, the pilots cared deeply for each other. Why not their ships? "Though, I have to admit I would feel terrible if she was. I was the one who calculated the possibility of Hera surviving the blast from the Titania. It was my input, and I was wrong. All this time on that cold rock, do you think she will blame me?" Nike asked like it was some idle curiosity passing through its quantum brain and wanted to ponder it.

"We all made mistakes that day, Nike. Don't feel bad," Eve said absently as she prepared for her departure. "The main thing is we confirm it for Oberon, and then we can focus about getting Hera back home. *If* Oberon is right about this," she said it like there was a distinct possibility the system's smartest man might be wrong about something. It was then Eve felt an all too familiar tingle in the back of her mind.

Do you doubt me? Oberon's voice said playfully inside her head.

"Ah, speak of the devil." Eve didn't have to say the words out loud, but it was just easier that way. She was still tweaking the infiltration program on her datapad.

I'm not sure I like the inference there.

"If the shoe fits." She didn't have to finish the saying to get her point across. "You *are* inside my head from across the solar system." Eve was going to continue but Oberon cut her off.

Besides that, it wasn't me who sent you on this... He paused, searching for the words. *Whatever it is you're doing out there. I don't need any sort of confirmation from you. I know what's there, and where it's going.*

"You've been wrong before," Eve said as the soft thud of the ship touching down on the icehauler's surface reverberated throughout Nike's hull. An instant later the landing gear's mag locks engaged.

"I'm secured to the surface of the Poseidon, Eve. I've begun prepping the airlock for departure. It's time," Nike declared. *What exactly is your plan here?*

"Simple," Eve said with a bit of a growl in her voice. "I'm going to see if *Thomas* is down their, *John*." Eve said their birth names with a bit of venom. They weren't really gods after all. They were people, no better than anyone else. "And if he is, I'm going to bring him back home and I'll kill everyone of these motherfuckers if they try to stop me. Now if you'll excuse me, I have work to do." Eve shut the flimsy door in her mind and cut Oberon off from herself, for the time being. It wouldn't last.

Eve pushed her seat away from the pilot's station and swiveled it back to face the tiny crew compartment of the small ship. She rose off her seat and walked a few steps through her quarters to the airlock. She walked past the collection of firearms that were neatly secured to the bulkhead without a thought. This was an icehauler with a skeleton crew, not a military ship, she didn't need anything more than the sidearm that was already secured to her battle suit. Eve engaged the helmet as she entered the airlock, and after a series of sharp clicks, the helmet formed at the back of her neck and quickly rose to envelop her head. The visor fell down in front of her field of vision and formed the pressure seal at her collar. A moment later, the signature hiss of her air supply came as her suit pressurized before the heads-up display came to life. The suit ran through its system check and displayed its findings on the HUD. Eve saw that each status bar was green.

Satisfied, Eve queued the airlock door and stepped out into the void.

She slowly climbed down the ladder and stepped onto the expansive hull of the icehauler. Eve felt the maglocks of her boots engage before she dared to let go of the ladder. The massive vessel was still under thrust, and would be for another eight hours. Their velocity was in the middle of the six-digit range, and it was still increasing with every second. Looking around the rusted expanse of the ship and the endless void all around them, it was impossible to judge their speed other than the slight pull she felt towards the back of the ship. If her magboots were to inexplicably release from the ship, Eve knew the ship's velocity would continue to increase. In an instant, the ship would pass below her in a blinding speed, and if she didn't impact some outcropping of the hull like a missile, Eve would get caught in the drive plume and be reduced to atoms before her brain even had time to register the heat increase. The laws of motions were not especially forgiving at these velocities.

Eve swiftly moved towards the airlock door and crouched down to the access panel. She gently touched a clawed finger of her suit to the screen and allowed a small amount of nanomachines to bleed onto the display. When she felt that the connection was made, Eve ran the infiltration program which would allow her to open the airlock without setting off about a dozen different automated alarms throughout the ship. Eve cycled the airlock door and stepped into it amidst flashing lights. She knew the airlock's klaxon would be sounding off by the entrance. It couldn't be helped. Some safety systems couldn't be overridden.

The airlock quickly pressurized and the entrance into the Poseidon opened.

"Ma'am?" Nike opened a channel to her suit. "I have a lifesign approaching your location. Apparently, someone was alerted by the airlock's alarm."

"Thank you Captain Obvious," Eve said with a smile as she stepped onto the ship and disengaged her magboots with a simple click of her heels. She wouldn't need them while the ship was under thrust.

"Ma'am?"

"Nevermind." Eve had to remind herself that certain expressions were lost on the AI. "How long?"

"Less than a minute."

"Okay. I'm going to be off the comms for a bit. Continue with standard protocols until you hear from me."

"They'll never know I'm here, Ma'am."

Eve keyed the battlesuit's release and the front of it simply folded open, allowing her to step out of it. She was wearing dirty grey coveralls underneath the suit. It wouldn't match the crew's, but she could explain that away easy enough. With a few audible clicks the suit closed itself off behind her, and then the empty, black helmet regarded her.

"Stealth mode," Eve ordered. "Stay close and stay out of sight." A second later the Mythrial battlesuit shimmered slightly before it faded from existence. Only the soft sounds of its boots shuffling away were the only indication she got it was even still there.

Eve concentrated hard on the face she had in mind. Euro-Asian descent, mid-thirties, dark eyes with matching shoulder-length hair. Slight build, of course, space farers rarely had extra weight. Maybe a little taller than five feet, not too tall. But not too short either. She wanted to create a person that was easily forgettable and hard to describe. When she had it in her mind, she let out a slight groan as the nanomachines in her body went to work and created her vision. Her bones shrank and repositioned themselves throughout her skeleton as her body readjusted to fit her new frame. Eve's facial bones shifted painfully as she took on the woman's face. The nanothreads that served as her hair lengthened and the pigment darkened as it flowed down past her ears.

Behind her, the airlock door cycled closed and the Klaxon abruptly ended. Eve could hear the rapid drumbeat of the footfalls approaching her. As the nanomachines were darkening the pigment of her skin, Eve dropped down beside the airlock door and removed the access panel beneath the controls. She yanked the diagnostic panel out and pulled out her datapad and hooked it up to the unit just as the crewman was rushing around the corridor's corner.

"Sorry," Eve cried out nervously. "Sorry. That was me." Eve looked towards the greasy-looking man as he rounded the corner and waved to him apologetically. "I'm sorry," she said again looking at the man with a sweet face.

"What the fuck?" The man said slowing to a stand still in front of her. "What the sweet fuck are you doing? Who the fuck are you?" The man shot off his questions in rapid-fire succession.

Eve quickly disconnected her datapad and stowed the panel back away before she stood and faced the man with a remorseful expression.

"I was just doing a diagnostic on the door, and I guess I must have set off the alarm by accident. I didn't mean to," Eve said while internally commanding the nanomachines to make it look like she was blushing slightly. She ignored his other question. Eve quickly read his nametag. *Kupa,* she remembered him from the crew manifest. He was listed on the drone crews. So, why was he here wandering the halls during a burn?

"What the hell are you even doing down here? You're suppose to be in your chair while we're on the burn." The man looked at her with a certain amount of indignation. "What's your name?" He asked finally after he scanned the front of her coveralls and didn't see a nametag. Completely overlooking her coveralls were a different color than his and didn't have the ship's logo on it.

"Jane. Jane Hirono," Eve said politely and wiped the imaginary grime off her hand before she offered it to him. "I don't think we've met yet." The man's shoulder settled slightly.

"Bijan." The man took her hand and shook it firmly. "Bijan Kupa. Drone crew." He added automatically.

"Geology," Eve replied quickly and watched as his expression changed. Eve knew on ships like this, the science staff rarely mingled with the rest of the crew.

"Geology? What are you doing messing with an airlock?" It was an obvious question, so Eve was prepared for it.

"I'm working on the Airlock Module for my maintenance supplemental," Eve said with an innocent smile and shrugged.

"Oh yeah?" Kupa perked up. "You working on your engineering certificate too?"

"Yeah. I'm trying to." Eve motioned to the opened compartment. "Having a few problems with this one yet." Eve pouted slightly. "I guess."

"Hey, don't worry about it. This old bitch is touchy. You probably just inadvertently triggered the system check. Which is why the alarm went off." Bijan then pointed to the door's panel. "You mind?" He asked and Eve stepped back as she shook her head.

Kupa squatted down next to the opened compartment and pulled the diagnostic panel out again. He pulled his datapad out of his pocket and hooked it into the door's computer. Eve looked on over his shoulder from a polite distance. She didn't have anything to worry about. Her program would have wiped any trace of her entrance from the door's logs. The man's dark locks flowed down around his head as he pulled up the maintenance subroutine of the door and checked the system status. Green status lights, all across the board.

"Oh," Eve said with an enlightened sort of disappointment as she continued to play her part. "That's what I did wrong. I did a system check, when I wanted to check the system *status*." Eve smacked her forehead audibly. "Man, I feel stupid. Shit!" Eve cursed loudly and took a dramatic step away from the man. "I don't know why I'm having such trouble with this."

Eve spoke softly, like the comment was just meant for her ears, but still making sure the man heard it.

"Hey," Bijan said smiling at her sympathetically. Eve quickly noticed he was missing a few teeth. "Don't beat yourself up about it, you're just starting out. This is a new field for you. These things take time." Bijan rose up and reached out and gave her arm a gentle squeeze. Eve just smiled innocently while thinking about how easy it would be to shatter the bones of the hand that was touching her.

"You're sweet," Eve cooed while slightly tilting her head. "Thank you." The man wasn't entirely unattractive, but his face featured a few blemishes, and his nose was crooked. Probably from being broken at some point in the past. There was also a prominent scar from a chemical burn of some kind that ran down his neck. It disappeared underneath the fabric of his coveralls.

Kupa waved her off with his rough looking hand and went back to the diagnostic panel. He returned it to the compartment and put the panel back in place.

"There, good as new." He looked back to her. "Seriously though, you should be in your chair until we're on the float. Then, if you want, come find me and we can go through some maintenance procedures. Maybe get some food while we're at it?" The man stood over her and smiled again while he leaned against the bulkhead. Eve heard the soft padding noises of the battlesuit moving in behind him. Luckily, the man's attentions were squarely focused on her as he ran his gaze over her body with approval. Eve just smiled innocently, knowing full well the nanotech shell would rip the man into pieces if she gave the command. "Us engineers have to stick together, right?"

"I thought you said you were on the drone crew." Eve watched with some amusement as the man visibly deflated. She continued before he could respond. "I'll probably be confined to the science deck when Claire finds out about this. She doesn't like it when I work on this stuff during shift. But fuck, when am I not on shift?"

"During thrust," they said in unison. Bijan just nodded sympathetically. "I get it. Listen, we'll keep this between you and me. There's no reason to ruffle a bunch of feathers over a minor ship infraction. Right? Just head back to your quarters, and when we're on the float I'll see if Val can coordinate our off time." *Gee, how lucky of me.* "That way we could work on getting you up to speed on some of these systems. Shouldn't take long." Bijan wet his lips before he smiled at her again.

"That would be amazing," Eve lied sweetly and with a big smile as she tucked a strand of hair behind her ear. "You'd do that for me, *Bijan*?" She asked and softened her tone when she said his name.

"Sure, no problem. Just get to your quarters, and watch out for the other guy on duty on deck four. That guy is a real prick, he'll write you up in a heartbeat." Kupa winked at her like it was some inside joke they shared.

"Sure, of course, I just have to run a few core samples on the cubes for Claire." Eve thumbed down the corridor in the direction she needed to go. "Something about the last ones didn't add up and she wants another one done before the float." It wasn't an unreasonable thing to be ordered to do. Unlikely, on most ships, but Eve was banking on a few safety protocols being overlooked on the Poseidon. Kupa just frowned.

"What?" He said confused. "The cargo hold is on lockdown."

"Oh?"

"Yeah, the coolant pipe from reactor three sprung a leak and flooded the compartment with radiation. Which is why we're heading to port," he said looking at her like this was all information she should already know. "There was a ship wide announcement about it." Bijan took a step back as his expression changed. Eve didn't wait to find out what he was thinking.

"Sedative," Eve said coldly.

"Whu-?" It was all the man got out before the invisible battlesuit grabbed him. Eve didn't see the suit, of course. She saw Bijan's head wrench to the side unnaturally, the expression of raw terror that bloomed across the man's face, and saw the dimple in the man's neck where the syringe went in. Then Kupa's eyes rolled up into his head and his body fell gracelessly to the deck.

Eve sighed.

That went well, Oberon's voice rang clearly in her head.

Shut up, Eve growled in her thoughts. *How was I supposed to know that?*

"Take the man, and place him someplace safe and out of the way," Eve commanded to the battlesuit, even though she wasn't exactly sure where it was. "When you're done, meet me by the entrance to the cargo hold." Bijan Kupa's body rose into the air by its abdomen. Eve imagined that the suit reached its arm underneath the still man and picked him up. Bijan's limp arms and legs swung freely as his body floated down the corridor and disappeared around the corner.

So, now we have a witness. Your level of interference is becoming unacceptable, Athena.

Eve snorted.

"Please," she said dismissively. "The sedative will erase any real memory he had of our interaction." Eve smiled before she added, "If it makes you feel better, I could stuff him in a recycler and we can be done with it." The silence in her head was the only answer she got.

Eve turned down the corridor and headed towards the crew lift.

I'm struggling to see any benefit from this endeavor of yours.

"I have to know," she said quietly as she entered the lifted and keyed the cargo deck. "Besides, I'm struggling to see the benefit of letting The Corporation have the ship."

I have no such intentions.

"Kind of looks like it from where I'm standing. Not to mention, the insane idea that you think I'd let them have *him*."

Again, I have no intention of letting them have Ares.

Bastard! Eve thought secretively to herself.

"Not him, Thomas! You arrogant asshole. I won't let them have Thomas!" She couldn't help it. Her voice echoed within the confines of the lift.

Thomas is gone. Once again, there was silence inside her head.

"That's what I'm here to find out." She was determined to find out for herself. It was a visceral need she had to satisfy. Eve needed to know for sure that Thomas wasn't coming back to her. She couldn't explain it, but if she didn't at least try, she would spend the rest of her days waiting for him to return.

Eve reached the cargo level and quickly noticed the other lift was in operation. She strongly suspected who was following her down to this level. Or more precisely, what. Eve moved deeper into the space and found the cargo hold airlock easy enough. She wasted no time taking the panel off, pulling the door's diagnostic panel out, and hooking up her datapad to the link connector. Eve again uploaded her infiltration program into the door's processing unit. She deactivated the door's alarms so her intrusion into the bay would be unnoticed, and for good measure, she even locked down the other lifts. Eve waited until she heard the lift's door open in the distance before she locked that one down too. A moment later she caught the subtle sounds of her battlesuit's approach. Eve disconnected her datapad, pushed in the panel, and then replaced the cover for the compartment. When she was done, she stowed her datapad back into her pocket and sighed.

Might as well get this over with, she thought.

"Open." Behind her, a few inches to the left of where she suspected, her battlesuit shimmered into existence. It promptly folded the front plates back and Eve expertly backed into the open shell. The suit quickly adjusted to her new body with a series of clicks before it closed in around her, wrapping her in its warm skin before it sealed closed with another series of muted clicks. Eve confirmed the seals were good before she reached out and cycled the airlock.

There is no real up or down in the void of space. There is only the direction that thrust pulls you. In this case, by the design of the ship, the crew lift descended into the depths of the impossibly large cargo hold. In order to preserve the giant cubes of ice during the journey to port, the designers of the ship kept the hold in a zero-atmosphere environment. The drone crews cut the cube to be almost the exact dimension of the hold. With only a little room on the sides to compensate for the massive cargo clamps that extend out from the bulkhead to secure the cube. After all, you didn't want a half mile long cube of ice bouncing around in your ship's hold under heavy thrust.

The hold wasn't meant for crew members. The only light was from the crew lift. Eve could turn on the light in her visor, but the lift's lights illuminated everything she would need to see. In front of her, a wall of ice slowly, and continuously rose up from the ground and disappeared above the canopy. To the sides of the lift, utter blackness.

It was a slow ride, and she had a long way to go yet. According to the information packet Oberon intercepted, the second cube in the bay was the one that she wanted. If Thomas was here, that's where she would find him.

As the lift sank deeper into the belly of the ship Eve couldn't help thinking of the paradox of being immortal. Oberon had explained the dangers of implantation. That's what he called them. *Dangers.* The nanomachines in their systems allowed the Council members to survive just about any wound, and quickly recover from it. They could survive just about anything and keep fighting, as long as the Motherbot remained intact to put them back together. *However,* Oberon cautioned them, *there are some things you may not wish to survive. And yet, you will.* Like being frozen solid in a cube of ice on some remote moon in the void of space. *So, be careful.*

Eve descended into the blackness and tried not to think of Thomas trapped under a mile of ice. Oberon insisted that there was no way Thomas could have survived the blast, and that he and his ship had been reduced to atoms when it was caught in the massive explosion.

Yet here Hera was, neatly preserved in ice.

Eve feared Thomas was inside, in some horrible condition. The nanomachines, either damaged by the blast, or maybe frozen in some form of stasis in the ice, but whatever the reason, they were unable to repair the damage to his body. He was trapped inside his broken and charred body for all eternity. Just awake enough to feel the pain from his injuries, and to be tortured by the helplessness of his situation. Immortality could be cruel if you weren't careful.

Here.

Eve slowed the lift to a stop shortly after she passed the boundaries of cube two. She quickly spotted the hole for the probe they would have used to scan the interior of the cube. A few dozen meters into the ice, her love had been waiting for her all this time.

"Better late than never," Eve said apologetically to the featureless sheet of ice in front of her.

Eve, please. He's gone. You need to accept that.

Eve ignored the voice in her head as she placed her hand against the exterior of the giant ice cube. She closed her eyes, and reached out into the darkness behind her eyelids. Her eyes watered when her faith was returned with a cold, unfeeling blackness. Eve clenched her free hand tight into a fist as she felt a sob well up from the depths of her being. *He has to be here. Please! Please, be here.* Eve strained internally, pushing until she felt the familiar needles behind her eyes poking her.

"No," Eve said composing herself. "He's not." There in the distant blackness was a single pinprick of light. It took an immense strain for her to sense it, and she was practically right next to it. She didn't blame Oberon for not feeling it. But it was there, *he* was there. Just a faint whisper of a consciousness, crying out in the darkness, *I'm here.* "I feel him. He's here."

That's not him, Athena. Oberon said gently inside her mind; as if he was consoling her. She then felt Oberon switch gears inside her head. *Athena, you are jeopardizing any chance we have of recovering Ares. If you continue on this path, whatever is left of Thomas will be lost to us forever. I promise you* Eve, *if you stay the course I have laid out for you, we will get back everything that was taken from us, including Ares. Your love will be returned to you.* There was a moment of silence before he added, *you will have your revenge for what they did to us. For now, however, you are needed elsewhere.*

Revenge? Eve questioned what she just heard. Oberon didn't speak of revenge, ever. He preached about maintaining a safe distance and keeping the miniscule amount of peace that was left in the solar system. Since they lost Ares, Oberon had been all about *not making waves.* Now, he was promising revenge. But that wasn't all he was promising, which she didn't take lightly because in the time she had known the man, she had learned he didn't make promises lightly, and he always delivered. Always.

Eve weighed her options.

She could kill everyone on board. It was surprisingly easy to kill people in the depths of space. Right off the top of her head, she could hack into the ship's ancient AI and override the safety protocols. Then it was just a matter of opening all the airlocks and evacuating the atmosphere to the void. All the automatic blast doors would remain open, and during thrust, nobody would get to their Vac suits in time. Simple. She could, just as easily, walk up to each crewmember and pop each of their heads with her bare hands. If she wanted to. The crew wasn't an issue. She would have to locate and disable the ship's transponder. Eve could use a series of short burns to avoid someone detecting her drive signature as she moved this behemoth sunward. She might have to go as far as inside Mars' orbit before Eve could dump the cube into the void and let the heat of the sun's rays sublimate it away to nothingness. But then what? Eve had to admit, she feared what was inside of Hera if all that remained of Thomas was a tiny pinprick of consciousness. What if it was just a pile of dust inside a battlesuit, with a tiny nanomachine control unit buried within it? The system may respect and/or fear her as Athena, unstoppable warrior of the Council, but she was only Eve Carter. She wasn't Oberon. She couldn't make the promises he could, and he was promising to bring Thomas back. She wasn't a naïve girl, she knew there were caveats to that promise Oberon wasn't mentioning. She knew it wasn't Thomas that concerned Oberon, it was Ares. It was the Motherbot that had bonded to Thomas. That's the thing that turned Thomas Ferguson, into Ares. But the Motherbot can only bond with one person, or so she thought. *Whatever is left of Thomas will be lost to us forever,* that's what Oberon had said. *Your love will be returned to you.* So, does that mean there's a chance she could save a part of him?

All she had to do was have some faith.

Fuck!

"Fine," Eve said bitterly and removed her hand from the frozen wall. "Nike?" Eve opened the comm channel as she reached out for the lift controls.

"Yes, Ma'am." Nike responded obediently.

"Prep the ship. I'm on my way out." Eve sent the lift back to the cargo deck and sighed heavily as the ice wall began to slide down from the canopy of the lift. Eve wasn't sure this was the right thing to do, but Oberon always delivered.

Always.

CHAPTER 2

Lucien

Lucien Malum stepped off the spacious, lavender scented interior of the executive Corporate shuttle with its plush, velvety thrust chairs accented with the corporate colors and the dark fabricated wood paneling. He then stepped into the stale-smelling recycled air of Russo Station. He had, thankfully, secured a corporate dock that avoided the calamity of Port Security and Customs the rest of the riffraff of the universe had to put up with. He was an executive of The Corporation, hasd been for a generation. Such nonsense was simply beneath him.

"Jesus Christ!" Lucien complained loudly to his personal assistant and bodyguard Brock, who loomed menacingly behind him in the airlock. "Look at the state of this place," he exclaimed with muted disgust.

Russo Station was a Corporate entity until the terrorist attack that destroyed the Titania. Wild accusations had all eyes cast on the weakened Corporation with suspicion. At the time, the pristine station was the pinnacle of everything

The Corporation had worked so tirelessly to achieve. An actual commercial foothold. They could control all trade throughout the system. Everything that could be bought or sold would go through Russo Station. And The Corporation would get a piece of all of it. With that station, they didn't need earth anymore. There wasn't a need for the war any longer. The Corporation had already won. The Council-supported terrorists blew up the Titania, managed to rupture its drivecore and ruined everything.

The station was a gift, from The Corporation to the mewing masses scattered throughout the solar system that cast their suspicious eyes on the Corporation and cried foul play. The single most expensive public relations measure ever taken by the Corporation in its long history. The move was ordered by the CEO himself. It was the one mistake his opponents had been waiting for, but they were wrong. It wasn't a mistake. The entire system forgot about the war, all the ugly transgressions that allegedly happened, the Titania, all of it. The masses even forgot about the proposed peace agreement between Earth and Corporate Mars. The bleeding hearts had their station, a spot in the system where all parties could come together for their mutual benefit. The Corporation gave up their station, and instead, leased an entire armada of commercial space craft to a new generation of space farers who were excited to head out into the void in search of their riches. All the while, Corporate entities, like himself, made a tidy profit.

"It seems every time I come here this place depreciates more and more." Lucien held his hand up and covered his mouth as a collection of offensive odors wafted into his nose. He also didn't particularly like the awkward sensation that came with the station's centrifugal gravity. Spin Gravity, the locals called it. It has been decades since he had last been to this place. He didn't remember it being so...grimy. "Look at these filthy pigs," Lucien said in disgust and waved to the river of people moving along the concourse in front of him. All dressed in shabby-looking clothes that didn't match.

There were a few Corporate members here as well, sporadically dotting the never-ending flow of people in front of him. They were easy to spot. Clean, pressed uniforms with the proper attention being made to personal grooming. Lucien couldn't even imagine what it would be like to be assigned to such a place with all these...*animals.*

"Let's go," Lucien called back to Brock. He checked to ensure his tie was straight and smoothed out the front of his tailored suit jacket before he entered the rabble. "Try not to touch anything."

Lucien snorted angrily as only a few steps later he had to walk around a piece of litter that was on the deck of the concourse. *We're not even at the main promenade yet,* he thought with a certain level of disappointment. He knew he was going to be disturbed by this place, but it was unavoidable. There was no way he could have this meeting at The Corporate dock on Mars. Discretion was of utmost importance at this phase. Corporate docking regulation being what they were, it would be impossible to slip this by unnoticed. This was the only way.

"My word," Lucien gasped as they exited the concourse of the docking airlocks and entered the maelstrom of the promenade. "You see, this is what I was talking about. Look at this, this... chaos. This disorder." Lucien spoke as he walked through the crowds of people. A few people caught his words, they were met by a cold stare from Lucien that almost challenged them to address him. "All these dirty monkeys running around here with all their little sad self-interests and greedy little schemes. No structure to guide them." Lucien waved his hands lightly around himself, towards the people. "It's sad really. So intoxicated with the polluted idea of *freedom*, or whatever other bullshit the trade unions are feeding these cattle." That's what these people haphazardly roaming about the expansive commercial space reminded him of. Livestock. Just wandering around and grazing on whatever strikes their fancy. "These people will struggle and toil for the entirety of their lives and accomplish absolutely nothing. They'll be lucky to break a ten percent profit margin by the time their frail little bodies will expire. They'll die with nothing to their name, and no one will remember them." Lucien tilted his head slightly to the back for Brock's benefit. His bodyguard knew better than to walk beside him. Lucien couldn't even imagine the embarrassment of someone thinking Brock was his equal in some regard. "Mark my words," he said. "There's a lesson to be learned here. Goals without a means to achieve them, are just dreams. That's all these people are, *dreamers.*" He said the word like it was a curse. "Endlessly chasing after something that will always be out of their grasp, because some fool told them they had the freedom to do so. Wasted potential," Lucien snorted.

Fifteen minutes later, Lucien and his bodyguard made their way to the commercial docks. While trying not to pay attention to the smell, Lucien eventually made his way spinward until he found the private storage hanger he rented for the foreseeable future. He even paid for the space to have an atmosphere and to be heated to a comfortable temperature.

When they approached the airlock doors into the hanger, Lucien stepped to the side and let Brock pull up the door's log on the touchscreen.

"Four people entered over an hour ago, and they haven't left. No weapons present, sir." Brock droned off while looking dispassionately down at the airlock controls.

Four people? Apparently, there were some loose lips on the Poseidon. *No matter,* Lucien thought quickly and smoothed his jacket.

"Open it," he commanded and entered the airlock as soon as the door would allow him to. Inside the inner airlock, there were a few benches around the space and a collection of ugly Vac suits secured to the wall. They came with the hanger.

Past the inner airlock door, Lucien strode confidently into the cavernous hanger. He tried not to think about how much it was costing him to supply an atmosphere to this giant space. This was a commercial storage hanger, meant to house hundreds of storage containers that were stacked to the roof and lined up into neat little rows. The heels of his designer shoes knocked loudly against the composite alloy of the deck. The sound echoed throughout the vast emptiness of the space as he approached. His hanger housed a single cargo container that was a brief walking distance from the airlock. The container was a large steel box that was larger than the shuttle they used to get here. In front of it, milling around like a bunch of idiots, was Val Biggs and three other people Lucien didn't recognize.

"Gentlemen," Lucien called out from a distance and clapped his hands together loudly. The sound echoed sharply around him. "I can't even tell you what a pleasure it is to finally see you." It had been a long couple of weeks since Lucien learned of the discovery. "Even if there are more of you than I expected to see." Lucien shot Biggs a cold expression that demanded an explanation.

"Ah, yeah." Biggs rubbed his hands in front of him and briefly stared at his boots, like the answers to Lucien's questions were written on the oaf's dirty, leather boots. "This is Trevor Pilson, my chief engineer. Claire McGregor, my geologist. Last but not least, Nigel Ratborn, my pilot."

"Lucien Malum." As corporate doctrine insists, he reluctantly introduced himself to each of them. "Nice to meet you," he added distantly as he offered his hand to each of them. Lucien ground his teeth together as each of them reached out with their disgustingly soiled hands and wiped their filth all over his palm. He tried not to think of all the vile places each of those hands had been. After the tedious formalities were dispensed with Lucien leveled his insincerely friendly gaze on Biggs' scruffy face. "Show me."

"Now?" Lucien sighed as the aged captain just stared at him with those big cow eyes of his.

"Well, I didn't come all this way just to meet your halfwit crew and shake their disgusting fucking hands. Yes, now!" The four of them gawked at him with blank expressions until Lucien used his hands to shoo them into action. "Go."

It was Val who first broke free of the stupefied trance the four of them were in. The large man looked to the tall skinny one, Trevor the engineer, and made a sound like he was clearing his throat while subtly thumbed towards the large container. The engineer broke ranks and hurried towards it. He approached the control panel on the side of it with a sort of awkward shuffling step. *Probably still adjusting to the spin gravity,* Lucien thought. A few beeping sounds could be heard as he touched the screen. After the man cycled the container to open, an alarm klaxon blared loudly throughout the vacant space and warning lights flashed along the container's seams. The tall, unkept man scurried away from the container quickly as a series of loud clicks erupted from the container. The front and back portion of the container then slowly began to lower. The metal clanked noisily against the deck as the two panels came to rest on it. Then came another rapid-fire series of loud clicks before the entire container opened like a blooming flower and the sides came to rest on the deck, revealing the prize inside.

"My god," Lucien uttered quietly.

He couldn't help it. He was swept up in the moment.

"Once we were on the float, Claire and Trevor went to work cutting that thing out of the cube. Did an amazing job too. We were able to salvage the majority of the cube-," Val droned on about the arduous process of getting the strange looking ship out of the giant ice cube and highlighted each point it made on its journey to where it sat right now.

Lucien just let him talk. He stopped listening to whatever nonsense the man was spouting and walked past him to move closer to the ship. The imposing-looking craft was a dull sort of black that seemed to suck up all the light around it into its depths. It looked like a shadowy bird of prey he had seen from the history vids that was tethered to the central platform of the container. It had a long narrow nose that protruded out the front of it like the ancient fighter craft designs of Earth. The nose tapered back to a rather boxy-looking fuselage that probably housed the single-person crew compartment and the weapon bays. The wide wings swept lethally to the rear of the craft and Lucien spotted more weapon bays on the underside. Towards the back of the craft, he spotted two vertical stabilizers poking up past the profile of the ship. Excitedly, Lucien turned back to the others.

"Do you realize what this is?" He regarded each of them with an expectant gaze. Lucien was utterly disappointed when he saw that this rabble didn't truly appreciate the moment. Never before this had anyone, other than a Council member, stood this close to one of these ships.

"It's some sort of fancy ship," the short one with the unfortunate facial features said, Ratborn. Lucien couldn't help but sigh heavily at the man's stupidity.

"It's a Council ship." Lucien snapped his fingers and pointed excitedly towards the engineer.

"Yes! But what else? What else is it?" Lucien challenged the group.

"Ares's ship?" Val shrugged as he offered his weak answer.

Lucien looked at him and smiled while he shook his head slowly. He turned back towards the ship and approached the nose of his treasured discovery. Lucien reached out tentatively and gently ran his hand along its pitch-dark skin. It was impossibly smooth but even so, he felt what he could only describe as scales beneath his fingertips. It was slightly warm to the touch.

"In the old world," Lucien began to say, speaking loudly so the others could hear him. "There was a legend of the Titan God, Prometheus. Mankind, at the time, was nothing more than hunter-scavengers who roamed the lands in small tribes. To spite the other Gods, Prometheus stole fire away from his kind and gave it to man. Man took the fire and built mighty kingdoms until they themselves were able to challenge the Gods." Lucien looked lovingly at the endless blackness of the ship. "*That's* what this is, the holy fire of the gods." Lucien looked back and saw the collection of blank expressions on the four ice miners. Lucien visibly slumped. "It's a metaphor you fucking idiots! The fire represents technology." Lucien turned back to the ship. "I will take this ship, and its occupant, apart piece by piece and I will harvest every little bit of technology I can from this thing. The whole time using all its technological innovations to advance my own standing within the Corporation, of course." Lucien turned back to the nervously shifting group and leveled them with a hard stare. "I will level the playing field, and once again The Corporation will take its proper place in the system." Lucien couldn't help but smile. He felt giddy at what lays ahead of him.

"Ah, yeah." It was Biggs who spoke up first. "That all sounds great and all." He scratched the back of his head absently. "But maybe we can finish up with the rest of the deal, and then we can get out of your hair."

"Of course," Lucien responded and walked back to the group. "About that, there are a few amendments I'd like to make to our arrangement. First off, I'd like to increase your payment by ten percent." At that, Val perked up a bit. "The ship is in amazing condition considering what it has been through and the lengths you had to go through to get it here. Really amazing."

"The ship has some sort of regenerative hull," the engineer spoke up suddenly. "As soon as we got it out of the ice it started stitching itself back together."

"Really?"

"Yeah, the one wing assembly was just barely hanging on when we first got it out, and that canopy was all smashed to shit. A bunch of other things too, but it just sort of *healed* itself on the way here." Val cleared his throat and silenced his engineer. Lucien couldn't blame him, an underling speaking out of turn could not be tolerated.

"Astounding," Lucien replied genuinely impressed. "But also I felt the increase was applicable because the delivery was *sooner* than promised."

"I appreciate that. Thank you," Biggs said and bowed his head humbly.

"However." Lucien held up a finger between him and the group as he moved in front of them. "Secrecy is of the upmost importance to me here. I'm sure you can see that. If word were to get out that I was in possession of such a find, it would make my plans significantly more difficult."

"I assure you Mr. Malum, my crew-." Lucien cut the man off with a look.

"Now, the original compensation was to ensure your silence. Now, I see we have three other bodies here that are privy to my little secret. Which is fine, but if you wish for them to know this secret it will cost you twenty-five percent, per person. The ship you can have. It's yours. You can die in that rusty tub for all I care. No, I'll take the twenty-five percent per person off the remaining credit balance that is owed." Lucien smoothed the front of his suit jacket and gazed on with some amusement while the three crew members looked frantically at there leader.

"Or?" Val asked. Lucien smiled, reached his hand back towards Brock, and snapped his fingers loudly. His bodyguard promptly unholstered his sidearm and placed it into Lucien's expectant hand.

"Jesus Christ!" The geologist cried out. "You're going to kill us?"

"Don't be absurd!" Lucien shouted at her while holding the pistol by the barrel. He was getting tired of all the outbursts from Biggs' underlings. "What kind of person do you take me for?" Lucien snorted at the woman's nonsense as he offered the weapon to Val. "That's not *my* job."

There was a stunned silence that blossomed around Val as he stepped forward and grabbed the gun.

"Val?" The engineer questioned softly as Biggs turned back to his group and shot the man in the face without a word.

The report echoed loudly in the hanger as the large caliber bullet smashed the man's face to bits in an instant. The geologist, Claire, had the whole side of her bookish face splattered with gore a moment before Val put two bullets into her chest. Lucien watched with amusement as her small frame flew back and fell to the metal deck of the hanger in a heap.

"Fucking hell!" The pilot with the oddly rodent-like features yelped before he scrambled away towards the airlock door. He didn't get far. Lucien noted the little man didn't even get a good stride going before his captain shot him in the back. The man leapt forward and fell gracelessly to the deck where he writhed in agony and whimpered like a wounded animal. Lucien watched Val's shoulders slumped, as if part of the man deflated slightly. None-the-less, Val walked solemnly up to his fallen crew member with the gun in his hand. "Jesus! Val! Please, don't-."

The final shot rang out and died away within the cavernous space shortly after. Biggs looked down at his handywork for a moment longer before he walked back and handed the pistol, butt first, to Lucien. He promptly turned up his nose at it. Lucien stepped aside to allow Brock to retrieve the weapon. Behind him, Lucien could hear his bodyguard holstering it.

"So, we're good?" Biggs said with a grim look on his face. Lucien returned the expression with a slight grin and he reached into his designer jacket and pulled out his datapad.

"Transferring the funds now." Lucien used a few swiping and tapping motions on the screen. There was an audible ding that came from the datapad, to signify the transaction was complete. "Congratulations," Lucien said sliding his datapad back into his inside pocket. "You're fucking rich." Lucien gave the man his best fake smile. "Now get out of my hanger. I have work to do."

To his credit, the aging ship captain didn't say a word. He nodded once and made his way to the airlock door without a second look at the bodies he was leaving behind. Lucien waited until the man was through the airlock and the door closed behind him before he turned to his bodyguard.

"Call Corporate Security, and get a detail outside. Tell them, under no condition are they allowed to enter this hanger. I don't care if it's on fire, nobody but me and you enter this place from now on. That'll have to do until I can get a *Golem* up here." Lucien turned back to his prize and waved dismissively towards the corpses. "And clean that up."

While Brock went to work, Lucien walked up to the tethered ship and once again ran his hand against the matte black, scaly texture of it. He walked a full circle around the technological marvel, touching it where he could, leering at the graceful lines of the ship where he couldn't. He paid special attention to the rear planetary thrusters, they almost looked like they had a directional quality to them. Interesting. He noted the strange design of the small drive cone that was nestled between the two thrusters. Lucien wondered if maybe the design was to harness the thrust potential of the engines. He didn't know, but he was excited to find out. As he completed a full loop, Lucien stood underneath the cockpit and yearned to be able to look inside it. To stare down onto the broken god inside. *Because of your hubris,* Lucien thought as he looked upon the nose, *I will make your kind obsolete.*

It was then Lucien thought of the perfect project name for this thing.

He breathed in once sharply and walked up to the cargo container's controls. In the open position, it was located on the side panel on the left hand side, staring innocently up at the roof on the hanger. Lucien bent down and cycled the container to close and keyed his personal code to lock it down. The klaxon sounded off again, warning anyone who might be in the area that the closing procedure was about to begin. The lights started to flash, Lucien slowly backed away from the priceless shadow as the container folded in around the ship once again. He turned back just as the container locked itself down with a series of rapid-fire clicks that erupted from it. Brock was silently approaching from the direction of the recycler. Val Biggs' corpses were nowhere to be found. All that remained of them were three large stains that were quickly drying in the arid air of the hanger, and what was left of the engineer's skull, sprinkled in with the blood.

Lucien led the way towards the door as he pulled out his datapad and queued the hanger's maintenance bots to clean the hanger's floor as soon as they left. Before he reached the airlock Lucien quickly pulled a small container from his pants pocket. He opened it and removed one sanitary napkin, which he used to furiously wipe his hands before he threw the napkin to the ground for the bots to pickup.

"Now, let's get off this spinning garbage dump. I have dinner plans."

***

The Executive Dining Lounge was the best setting Lucien could think of for this meeting. He has been in this room a few times in the past, he even had dinner here once. He had to pull more than a few strings to secure not only a table in this room, but the room itself. Every inch of the expansive walls were covered tastefully with the authentic wood that had been expertly stained a dark shade. Mahogany, Lucien believed it was called. The walls were sectioned off into wide panels that showcased the brilliantly painted portraits of past directors who exemplified what it took to raise above the ranks. And, of course, at the far end of the lounge was the looming portrait of the CEO, looking down on all of them. Along the sides, but spaced away from the wall, were white marble columns that rose up all the way to the painted ceiling of the lounge. Normally, the footfalls of the designer shoes of the executives would be sounding off inside the colossal room like muted gunshots, but tonight the only diners were Lucien and his boss.

"Okay, I have to admit. I'm impressed, Lucien," William Clemente, Director of Special Projects within the R&D branch of The Corporation, and Lucien's boss said as he quietly motioned around the room.

"It's a special occasion." Lucien was momentarily distracted by an image of the expansive chandelier that was reflecting in the high gloss shine of the black marble floor. "I felt it required a certain amount of grandeur." In truth, this dinner was costing Lucien a small fortune, not to mention the favors he had to call in. It was worth it to hear his boss admit to being impressed. And they were just getting started.

"Oh? Do tell."

"Are you sure you wouldn't rather wait until after dinner?" Lucien offered modestly.

"You know me better than that, Lucien." William leveled a playful gaze at Lucien over his neatly folded hands. "Speak."

"I'm going to take over Special Projects," Lucien said quickly and then straightened his tie out of habit. He wore his dark blue Palinelli with a black shirt and matching tie. It was a somber occasion after all, and he wanted to dress for it. Lucien looked at the man with a plain expression and waited.

"Oh?" Clemente said with sudden interest. "Is that so?" The man chuckled slightly while still looking at Lucien with those dark eyes. "Seems to me I have fifty more years until I retire." The man was well over three hundred years old, he only had the slightest hint of grey in his hair, maybe a few thin lines around the eyes when he smiled. The gene therapy can only do so much for a man of William's advanced age. Despite all the money he'd spent, his years were catching up to him. "So, unless there's a promotion coming down the pipe I'm not aware of, I believe I'll continue to manage my sector. You're not foolish enough to just think I'll just step aside, for *you*." William chuckled slightly at that. "I raised you up from a bumpkin researcher in the food services division. I saw promise in you. I saw that same spark of wild ambition in you that I had when I was that young. In a way, I'm proud of you, but no. It's not your time, I'm afraid."

"You're a non-issue," Lucien said coldly and William's chuckling stopped.

"I see." *He understands,* Lucien thought to himself as he saw those dark eyes waiver slightly. He sat and watched William smooth his perfect hair for a moment before he continued. "I hope it's not going to be some ghastly affair like some assassin in the dark slipping a knife between my ribs."

"No." Lucien shook his head slowly. "I would never do something so...undignified, as that to someone of your stature."

The waiter's footfall echoed loudly throughout the room as he approached. He placed the glasses on the table and carefully poured out a serving for each of them. The waiter stood by while Lucien and Bill made polite conversation about the menu options. William was always particular to the beef. The Executive Dining Lounge was one of the few places left in the system that still served beef from actual animals. So, it made sense when he ordered the twelve ounce sirloin. Lucien opted for the fish.

"Well?" William spoke up as soon as the waiter was gone. "You have me at a disadvantage. You know I always liked a good mystery. Just like I know you know there are established procedures for this sort of thing. You're not my only assistant after all."

"Just you're favorite."

"Once I'm gone, that won't matter anymore. So, what's your plan? You do have a plan, right?" William cocked his eyebrow at him.

"Of course." Lucien smiled and sipped his wine. "I'll simply make myself the most favorable option to the board."

"That's a sword that can cut both ways, my boy. You have considerable skeletons of your own."

"Don't worry, I have a trump card." Lucien smiled.

"What could you possibly have that would keep the wolves from your door?"

"I found it." Lucien smoothed the lapels of his suit and took another sip of his wine. It had the loveliest bouquet.

"What did you find?"

"*It.*" Lucien said again with emphasis. He looked as William as he searched his mind for the answer.

"No," he said with disbelief. "Bullshit." William frowned at him playfully as he considered the possibility and the implications of such a find. "Where?"

"The icefields on Europa. In the central region. It was about fifty miles from where I thought it would be, and considerably deeper than I expected. But still." Lucien smiled with a certain amount of pride at the expression on his boss's face. William Clemente then laughed, fully and for an extended amount of time. It echoed off the visages of past Corporate greats.

"I still remember when you came to me with your business plan for this venture. It was ambitious, foolhardy and almost certain to fail," William began to say but Lucien playfully cut him off.

"You still lent me the money I needed to buy the icehauler, and secure the mining rights to the right location. At a crippling interest rate, if memory serves." Lucien tilted his glass towards the man.

"No reason we both couldn't benefit from the venture." William raised his glass to Lucien before he took a quick sip.

The two men paused their conversation as a tight line of servants approached in single-file carrying their meals on golden trays that they held above their heads. Following proper corporate etiquette, the waiters walked up to the table, deposited their dish from their trays before they walked clockwise around the table to form another tight line that headed back to the kitchen. Each remained utterly silent except for the sharp sounds of their heels on the polished marble floor, with their eyes firmly focused on the empty space in front of them. They were the model of professionalism.

"Mmm," William groaned and he placed the first morsel in his mouth and slowly began to chew. He waited until his mouth was empty before he spoke again. "This is simply divine. I assume this is my final meal."

"It is."

"Then you won't fault a man for ordering dessert?" William asked playfully and Lucien managed to look slightly hurt.

"Please," Lucien began as he placed his hand over his heart to show his sincerity. "Order as much as you'd like, my friend."

With that, they paused their conversation so they could focus on the picturesque meal for a time. William cut off small bite-sized portions of his steak and chewed each bit thoughtfully before he finally swallowed it down. Lucien's salmon was perfectly cooked and seasoned masterfully, it practically melted in his mouth. After an appropriate amount of time had passed, William used his linen napkin to dab the corners of his mouth before he resumed the conversation.

"So, you have the ship?"

"Yes," Lucien confirmed after a sip of wine. "In perfect condition. Apparently, the hull has some regenerative quality."

"Really? Fascinating. I wonder how they managed that."

"I intend to find out," Lucien said with a sly smile and another sip of wine.

"The pilot?" William asked promptly as he cut into what remained of his steak.

"Dead and gone," Lucien replied and then finished off the rest of his meal.

"That's a shame." William pointed his fork absently at Lucien. "Might be able to get a DNA profile. Just need a little marrow from the interior of the femur."

"Mmm-mm." Lucien had thought of that as well. Chances are pretty good the massive amounts of radiation coming off Jupiter as probably degraded the DNA to the point of being utterly useless. But it was a consideration.

"You know, you could bring me in on this." William regarded him seriously before he continued. "This would be a lot easier if we worked on it together. I don't have to be an obstacle for you, I could be a stepping stone." Lucien sipped his wine as the man spoke. Honestly, he would have been disappointed if William didn't at least try.

"You'd keep me buried in the lab," Lucien said with a smile as he reached for his glass. "All the while claiming to be giving me freedom, but behind my back you'd be walking the Corporate halls telling everyone who would listen how this was all your doing the whole time. You simply *allowed* me to find it. Then you'll make grand promises to powerful people. It wouldn't matter if you could deliver, you'd have their ear." Lucien never broke eye contact as he sipped his wine. "You'll eventually force me out, and distance me so far from the project, I wouldn't even have authorization to see the ship on a vid screen. You'll take *my* discovery, *my* accomplishment, and you'll use it to launch yourself further up the ladder. When you're done with me, you'll simply cast me aside and forget all about me." William returned Lucien's knowing grin with one of his own.

"This is what happens when you let an assistant get too close," he joked. "They learn all your moves. You would do well to learn from my failure."

"You shouldn't look at it like a failure. If anything, it's a compliment to you. A way to show you I've taken everything you've tried to teach me to heart. After all, when the student surpasses the master, it's not because of the student's abilities, it is because of the master's." Lucien tipped his glass to his soon to be former boss again.

"Your silver tongue won't save you from what's coming. I hope you know that."

"You've prepared me for that, as well."

With that, William finished his meal, and the moment his fork and knife came to rest on the fine china the chorus of perfectly synched footfalls came from the kitchen area. As before, each respective servant came and retrieved the plate in the exact way they had deposited it. With the plate in hand, they once again walked clock-wise around the table and formed a tight line that walked in unison back to the kitchen. Shortly behind them, the waiter approached with the dessert menu. Lucien abstained, the salmon had been quite filling. William ordered the apple pie, with a single scoop of vanilla ice cream. A heartbeat after the waiter excused himself, a servant appeared with a smaller golden tray raised above his head.

"I assume you have your affairs in order," Lucien commented gently after the servant's footfalls disappeared into the kitchen.

"Of course," William said between bites. "You needn't worry about that, my friend. I have secured my family's standing for generations to come. Assuming they are not foolish with it. I do have a son that decided to become a doctor. Not to mention, I have a great-great-great granddaughter that is taking her Arts degree." Lucien winced away from the news like it physically hurt him to hear it. "No matter, they shall fend for themselves from this point on. After a few hundred years, you stop seeing your family as being *your* legacy. Your family tree becomes this grotesque, living thing that you can no longer control."

William returned to his pie. Using his dessert fork to scoop morsels into his mouth, which he seemed to be thoroughly enjoying, given the sounds he insisted on making while he ate. Lucien just sipped his remaining wine and let the man enjoy his dessert.

"How do you plan to do it? Poison?" William motioned down to his dessert. To which Lucien quickly shook his head, before he removed his datapad from the inside pocket of his Palinelli sports jacket and placed it on the table.

"No. I wouldn't ruin your final meal like that. Besides, poison is for women." It was an inside joke between them. Poison wouldn't work on the cunning, old bastard anyway. He had a discriminatory digestive system, which could single out poison, quickly metabolize it and render it utterly useless. "I picked an end befitting a man of your stature."

"Do tell."

"Do you remember that shuttle accident you had four decades ago?"

"My rib cage was crushed by a storage crate that came loose from the rigging. It's hard to forget something like that." William chuckled slightly.

"When they installed your cybernetic heart, I intercepted the organ during delivery and installed a back door into the procedural subroutine of the unit. When I press this button." Lucien used his index finger to point towards the innocent looking button on the screen. "Your heart will simply stop. It won't even raise a medical alarm. You'll simply fall down dead, and that heart of yours will never beat again. The autopsy will conclude it was a coding error in the valve control module. They might even do a product recall because of it. There will be no trace of my involvement." Lucien finished and William just clapped slowly.

"Bravo, my boy." By his prideful expression, Lucien could tell he meant it. "Masterfully done."

William finished his pie and the two of them waited for the servant to appear to remove the soiled dish from their table.

"Honestly, sir, it was the only opening you ever gave me," Lucien humbly offered to spare the man's feelings.

"And you took it! You saw the opportunity and you seized it." William smiled genuinely at him. "You really have taken my lessons to heart." William then breathed in deeply, taking in the fine aroma of the room and looking around to the portraits on the walls. "You know, if I was being sincere with you, Lucien. I would say I was disappointed at your short-sightedness. That ship could take you a lot higher than *my* job." Lucien smiled.

It was William who was being short-sighted, he was still focused on the ship. A technological marvel, to be sure. But even if Lucien could replicate the strange ship with all its advanced and foreign technology, he still needed a pilot. From what Lucien had been able to research on the ship, a normal person wouldn't survive what that ship was capable of. No, the pilot was the key.

"I have no intention of simply settling on *your* job," Lucien said it like the position was suddenly beneath him. "No, I plan to eventually take the Chairmanship of the whole damned division." Lucien thought for a moment before adding, "When I do make it to the Board of Chairs, I will have your portrait hung here for a time."

"I'm sure you will," William said with no real enthusiasm. William took in another deep breath before he ran his hands along the sides of his mostly dark hair. "Well, I think I'm ready to go." William rose from his chair. "How do I look?" He asked, smoothing the lapels of his grey, double-breasted suit jacket which was exquisitely tailor to hide his somewhat rounded midsection.

"You look magnificent, sir." Lucien stepped towards the man and offered his hand. William took it and held it firm before he gave Lucien's hand a firm pump. Unexpectantly, William didn't release immediately. Instead, he reached up with his other hand and placed it on Lucien's shoulder in a surprising display of affection.

"You're my *real* legacy, Lucien," William said solemnly and looked deeply into Lucien's eyes. "Everything I was, you are, and so much more. Give'em hell, my boy."

"I will, sir." Lucien couldn't stop his eyes from stinging slightly as William gave his hand another firm pump before he released his grasp.

He smiled and nodded to Lucien before William turned and started off towards the exit. Lucien gave the man a few proud steps before he reached over and pressed the button on his datapad. He watched closely as his former boss stopped in his tracks, waivered slightly in his stance, and then softly fell to the floor.

Lucien then collected his datapad and returned it to his pocket before he made his way out of the lounge. He paid the staff no attention as he passed, and left them to fuss over the fresh corpse on their black marble floor.

Step one was complete.

Lucien hoped the other steps go as smoothly.

He suspected they wouldn't.

CHAPTER 3

Nikoli Jonlesky

Nikoli woke up to his alarm nosily beeping away at the side of the bed he shared with his wife. He had been sleeping alone for the last year though. A bug in a scheduling program put them on opposing shifts, along with about a thousand other people on the stack. Corporate labor regulations stated family members must spend a minimum of eight hours per day putting in their time at their assigned job. That was the law. Complaints were filed. Applications were made, signed, witnessed, and approved. Yet The Corporate red tape continued. As it was, the only time Nikoli actually saw his wife of ten years was for a few hours at night after his shift ended and before her shift started.

They met in school. They fell in love before they had been placed. They were warned about. *Don't fall in love with someone until you know their career path,* that's what the accepted wisdom was. Sure, have fun and fuck whoever you wanted, but don't let emotions get involved. He couldn't speak for his wife, but

Nikoli didn't have such a luxury. He was hooked on Helena Fouillard the moment he smelled her sweet scent.

When they were placed, Nikoli was destined for maintenance. He was a legacy after all, it was hard to move out from under that shadow, and his grades didn't help matters much. Helena had originally been marked for a general administration career path, but she had been smart and gave the placement officer a handjob under his desk. That got her bumped up to the medical services division, which was more lucrative and offered better initial perks. It was the reason they managed to secure living quarters in the central region of their stack. One level down from the educational level.

A few years in, they had a child. Again, they went against the conventional wisdom and decided to do the conception naturally. *As nature intended,* Helena said to her friends. *It's more fun that way,* Nikoli had said at the time. They had a girl, they named her Bella, after Helena's grandmother. She was perfect. Bella had her mother's eyes, curious little blue gems that looked out into the world with such wonder, and the cutest little smile you could imagine. At age five, their sweet little angel developed bone cancer. A disease the In Vitro genetic screening would have caught, and rectified. Nikoli never said it out loud, but he felt a deep guilt in the pit of his stomach every time he thought about the pain their decision had put their little girl through. So far, Bella had received two marrow transplants, in addition to the three rounds of chemo and targeted radiation treatments for the disease. Yet it still ravaged her small body.

That ends tonight, Nikoli told himself as he sat on the edge of the bed and looked out over the artificially generated landscape that was showcased across the vidscreens of the exterior wall. The wind-swept green meadows of the computer-generated landscape was spread out in front of him. The artificial sun was well above the horizon, indicating it was morning. The picturesque landscape was supposed to be calming for the residents of the Corporate stacks. Far more calming than the inside of the largest dormant volcano in the solar system would be, at least. Nikoli looked at the peaceful scene for a moment longer while he tried not to think about what challenges were ahead of him today. It seemed incredible, like it was beyond what someone like him would normally do, or maybe were capable of. *No,* he told himself, *you can do this. You have to. For Bella.*

Nikoli took a deep breath and pushed himself off the bed. He dressed in his usual coveralls that were the distinct color of the maintenance division, a bland dark grey, with the division logo on the back. He moved to the nightstand, where he retrieved his datapad and stuffed it into his pocket. When he moved out into the kitchen, he noticed there was a message on the info-screen for their apartment. Nikoli walked up to it and quickly opened the message. Instantly the screen changed and showed the long blonde locks and smooth features of Helena. *How did I ever get so lucky?* Nikoli pondered briefly when the image came up. In the image, Helena looked tired.

"Hey Babe, I'm just about to head off to work." Medical techs worked long, strange hours but the work was easy, and the pay was good. Well, better than a maintenance tech anyway. Nikoli checked the clock, Helena should be getting off shift in another hour. "I wanted to let you know I'm going to go in late for my shift tonight, so I can be there when you come home after your meeting. Whenever it is." *His meeting,* that's what they called it, because they didn't dare call it anything else. It was widely believed The Corporation monitored living spaces, as well as open public areas, for deviant behavior that go against Corporate regulations. Nikoli didn't know if he believed that, but for something like this, he wasn't about to take the chance. "Anyways, I guess I'll see you later." On the screen she regarded him earnestly. "I love you. Be safe today." Then she blew him a kiss and the message winked out.

Nikoli thought about the gentle warning as he went to turn the coffee pot on. *Don't think about it. When the time comes, don't think, just act.* He let the pot fill as he moved towards Bella's room.

"Bug," Nikoli called down the short hallway as he approached the airlock door. He quickly activated the vidscreen on the wall with a swipe of his hand. He checked the air quality of her room. Green status bars. When the cancer moved into Bella's lungs, the doctors put her on chems that compromised her immune system. Bella had to wear a Medmask that filtered the air she breathed in, as well as gave her all the chems she needed to get through the day via the nasal injector. To Bella, it smelled like chocolate. The only space in the stacks that Bella could take the mask off for any period of time was her bedroom, because after the scare they had last year they took out a loan and got the airlock installed. "Bug?" Nikoli said again, this time opening a channel into the room. "Mask on?" He was about to activate the room's camera when Bella's little voice rang through the intercom.

"Mask on, Daddy." *Do it for Bella.* Nikoli put on a brave face for his daughter and cycled the airlock. "*Roar!*" Bella roared, like some savage beast, as fiercely as her little body could muster, she crouched down menacingly and shot her clawed hands out in front of her. Bella had painted a jagged set of teeth on the exterior of her medmask, and now every morning she insisted on greeted him with her best *monster-greeting.*

For an eight-year-old, Bella was shorter than she should be. According to The Corporate growth indexes. Her weight wasn't great either. Her small frame used up what energy it had to fight off the cancer, there wasn't any left for her to grow. A couple months ago, because of this latest round of radiation, Bella lost her hair again.

"There she is!" Nikoli exclaimed excitedly. He sank down onto his knee and his daughter trotted happily towards him. The tumor in her hip gave Bella the slightest limp when she walked. As soon as she collided with him, he scooped her up in his arms and spun her around while his little girl giggled merrily. "What's this?" Nikoli asked her with mock concern. "Someone is still in their jammies!" He tickled her belly and Nikoli prayed that this mild bit of play didn't leave any bruises on Bella's skin. Bella nuzzled her mask gently in his cheek. *A monster kiss*, she called it.

"You got up early today, daddy." She complained between giggles.

"No, I think someone got up late." He placed Bella back onto the ground with a kiss to her forehead. "What do you want for breakfast?"

"Pancakes." Bella jumped.

"Pancakes?!" Nikoli asked with mock outrage. "What do you think this is? The Corporate lounge. Go get dressed, little miss. I'll see what I can do." Bella turned and he patted her bottom as she ran back into her room.

Nikoli went into the kitchen and walked up to the food processor. He gave the unit his order before he poured himself a cup of coffee. He drank it down quickly, taking the moment's calm to steady his nerves. When his cup was empty he went back to help Bella with her final preparations for school. Nikoli helped her place her wig onto her scalp and then styled it the way she liked. Today, for a bit of flare, Bella added a hairclip with a bright yellow flower on it.

They ate their pancakes. Bella, as usual, had an extra serving of syrup for hers. Nikoli inquired into her day. Apparently, she had a math test that was scheduled for today, on fractions. When he asked about it, Bella seemed rather confident. Then she went to say that she was really looking forward to art class because their teacher had them working with paints.

"What about you, daddy?" Bella asked after she finished speaking. "Do you have *anything special on the books today?*" She asked, repeating his question back to him. Nikoli just looked at his angel and sighed.

"There's something really important I have to fix today."

After they finished breakfast and the dishes were placed into the recycler, the two of them exited their quarters and headed down the wide corridor to the promenade. The morning rush was in full swing. The promenade housed the commercial and recreational spaces for their level. It was pretty nice compared to others Nikoli had seen. Of course, it was also not as good as some. That was the joy of living mid-stack. Having the knowledge that you had it better than some but knowing full-well you still had a long way to go before you could be *comfortable.*

"Nikki!" They were passing the recreational courts when Nikoli recognized the voice calling out to him from the side. *Fuck sakes,* Nikoli cursed in his head and turned just in time to watch Cole Steiner, wearing the distinctive green coveralls of the agricultural division, weave his way through a throng of people to get to him. "Nikki!" He waved furiously once he had Nikoli's attention.

"Morning, Cole." He greeted the man but he didn't break his stride. Nikoli only slightly slowed for the man. Cole walked up to him and offered his hand as he walked beside him, as was Corporate etiquette, but Nikoli just looked at it. "I'm holding my girl's hand right now," he said to the offered hand and nodded towards Bella who was limping along beside him. "What can I do for you, Cole?"

"You busy today?" The man said excitedly. Nikoli had a strong suspicion he knew what Cole wanted.

"Yeah," he said dismissively. "Just like every other day. What's the problem?"

"That harvester is on the fritz again, I can't even use it. I can't be behind on quota again, Nikki. They'll demote me."

You should be demoted, Nikoli thought bitterly. Jack Carson was the section supervisor before Cole weaseled his way into the position. Nikoli didn't know the hows or whys of it, but one day Jack was simply transferred into food processing. He had to give up the grain fields he had been working for decades, and move into an office. Nikoli wished the man luck, a transition like that can be hard on someone like Jack. Since then, Cole had been slowly running the agricultural level on the stack into the ground.

"Did you put in a work request?" Nikoli asked knowing full well the man didn't. It was part of the man's shtick. Cole was the type of Corporate bumpkin who doesn't have the foggiest clue how to increase profits through productivity. No, Cole made his profit margin by cutting costs. Unpaid overtime, ignoring maintenance schedules, cutting down the fertilizer content of the hydroponic solution. There were many ways a person could cut costs, in the short term. Jack did it on occasion, during the lean years when the yields weren't as high as they should be. Problem with Cole was, that was his entire modius operandi.

"Hey, come on, buddy. Don't bust my balls like that." Nikoli and his association started when he first accepted a job from Cole that was *off the books.* It was another way Cole kept costs down. Normally, Nikoli wouldn't have a problem with that kind of work. Helena did like fresh vegetables, after all. "You know the maintenance roster is usually backlogged a week or so. I need this done today, tomorrow at the latest."

"Put in a request. I'm busy today." Nikoli didn't need this kind of hassle, not today.

"A basket of strawberries? Would that change your mind?" Cole asked managing to sound hurt.

"I like strawberries, daddy." She yanked slightly on his arm as they walked. When he looked down at her, Nikoli could see the area around her eyes were scrunched up and he imagined she had a wide grin on underneath her mask. *God, I miss her smile.* Any other day, this wouldn't be an issue.

"Hush, Bella," Nikoli said sternly and gave her hand the slightest pressure. "I'm sorry Cole, not today. I have a lot of shit to do and not a lot of time to do it in. So, if you'll excuse me, I'm trying to get my kid to school before starting bell."

"Tomorrow then?" Cole asked cautiously as he backed away a step.

"Fine," he said to get the man out of his hair. Tomorrow, if he wasn't dead or in a holding cell, he would be happy to fix whatever that moron needed. "I'll stop by tomorrow morning after shift starts." *Now, fuck off,* Nikoli wanted to add but didn't. Luckily, he didn't have to.

"You're the best, Nikki!" Cole shouted merrily as he scurried away. Probably late for his own shift by now.

"Nikki is a girl's name, daddy." Bella teased him with a slight giggle.

"I know, sweetie." Nikoli smiled down at her. "It's just what people like to call me."

They took the lift up to the educational level. They walked past the numerous colleges and technical institutes as fast as Bella's condition would allow. Nikoli wanted more than anything to just carry his sweet little girl, he couldn't stand to watch her struggle along like that. But Bella was in a stubborn phase, and the doctor's insisted it was the best thing for her. *It's good for her to be a normal child,* the doctor had said in that soothing voice of hers that still managed to sound a tad condescending. The doctor didn't see some of the looks Bella got in public though. Corporate doctrine didn't look favorable upon disabilities. *A burden on one of us, is a burden on all of us.* Nikoli just grit his teeth and returned those gazes with a challenging one of his own. With his eyes, he dared them to say something. Nikoli wasn't a large man, nor did he consider himself a fighter, but these days he just wanted something he could hit.

At the school, he gave Bella a hug and a kiss on the top of her head at the entrance before he sent her off. He was hoping he could sneak away unnoticed but the school's medical officer waved him over for a quick chat. Beverly was an ally, she and the school did the best they could. Nikoli recognized the look on Bev's face as she spoke about the measures they took during the day to reassure that Bella was as comfortable as she could be. He's seen that same look on the doctor's faces as well. The look advised him to *hope for the best, but plan for the worst.*

"Thanks Bev," he said trying to smile. "I know your doing everything you can."

"We just love Bella so much," Beverly said remorsefully. "She's such a joy. Any chance on gene therapy? Maybe a public funding measure?" She asked innocently and Nikoli reflexively clenched his fist.

The Corporation had actually cured cancer. A long time ago. They developed a therapy that reprograms the subject's DNA to identify, target, and eliminate the cancerous cells. Unfortunately, gene therapy was expensive. Far too costly for a child of a maintenance engineer and a medical technician. As an alternative to the costly treatment, the Corporation developed In Vitro screenings to help couples avoid the possibility of such diseases manifesting in their children. At the rate they were going, he and Helena would have to save up for a couple of decades to be able to afford the treatment on their own.

"No," Nikoli said quickly. His application for a Public Funding Measure, which would set up an account people could donate to, was denied six months ago. "She has another round of targeted radiation treatments in a two weeks to try and shrink a couple of the tumors. After that, we'll have to see." He tried to look hopeful when Nikoli spoke of the future. It was exhausting.

Nikoli collected himself after the episode at the school and took a lift down to the maintenance level. As always, the smell of the level struck him. Even with the air recyclers and the purifiers, this place still reeked of machinery. Nikoli waved to a few people he was friendly with as he made his way past the expansive equipment warehouses and the fabrication buildings until he arrived at the maintenance shed. He clocked in a few minutes later than usual but that was okay. Maintenance wasn't so much about maintaining regular hours, it was about the work. Maintenance personnel had to clock in twelve hours of billable time each day and have a general time period in which to do it. Nikoli was on the day shift. In an average shift, not including travel time, Nikoli could usually meet his billable quota around late-afternoon. Just in time to head home for a quick family dinner with Helena before she had to hurry off to her shift.

Today, he would not meet his quota.

Nikoli clocked in and signed out a maintenance cart. As was his habit, he ran a quick diagnostic on the cart. The system check status lights were all green, and the fabricator's mineral stocks were mostly topped up. The nickel stock was a little low, but it would be enough to get him through the day. He took out his datapad and pulled up today's work orders.

The Corporate megastructure was an incredible piece of engineering. Never mind it was built inside a volcano. Nikoli had to admit he didn't understand it. It seemed incredible to him. Maybe that's why The Corporation went to such lengths to distract its citizenry from that fact. He knew what most grade schoolers knew about it. In the beginning, The Corporation was a collection of smaller independent corporate entities from earth who wanted to establish the first viable colony on Mars. It was the single most expensive construction project in human history. While the idealistic governments of the world fought each other over earth's remaining viable resources, the corporations were busy looking towards the future. A future free from governmental tyranny where it could conduct business free from needless intrusions and disruptions.

They picked Olympus Mons because it best suited the complete project, which included allowances for future expansions. They started by capping the incredible eighty kilometer wide caldera on the godly volcano. That alone took over a hundred years. But when that was done, and the corps of engineers had a space the was free of the deadly wind storms that swept across the planet, and someplace they could pressurize, then the real work started. By then, a nation's worth of engineers and construction worker took up permanent residence inside the volcano and went to work. They worked, raised their families, and passed on their vision to the next generation. The next phase was to cap off the expansive magma chamber at the bottom of the caldera with a specially developed cement that utilized the martian soil. Enough to bury a small country, a half mile deep in the stuff. People still joked that the foundation of The Corporate stacks was still drying to this day. On top of that, they placed a giant geo-thermal reactor, the size of which was still a mystery. It was widely understood that the reactor generated enough power for the entire megastructure. Nikoli learned after he started in the maintenance section that the engineers also built a series of magma tubes to vent the pressure from within the depths of the volcano. They build magma dams that also generated massive amounts of energy as it maintained the volcano's internal pressures and kept them within tolerances.

Once that was all in place, they started building the first stack. The Corporate stack, the only one that connected to the top of the caldera. By then, several generations of workers had spent the entirety of their lives building the most impressive structure known to man, and yet most of them didn't have a clear idea who was paying them. Some of them weren't paid at all. A revolt happened, right at the point the numerous corporations on Earth could begin to actually use the settlement as a jumping off point to the mineral-rich moons of Jupiter. The whole place erupted into chaos. The Great Incorporation fixed that. One corporation rose up and swallowed up the others and came to be known as simply, The Corporation. Legend had it that the corporation that came out on top used to be an energy company that had mined all the riches out of Earth, and that's why they were looking towards the stars for the next big business venture. Whoever it was, they had an army at their disposal, and they promptly sent it to Mars to restore order. After that, the history books simply stated that peace was restored to Mars and that the Grand Project resumed. Nikoli assumed a lot of people died before that work continued, but it did.

The atmospheric shield that covered the caldera was turned into a huge shipping port that could handle any atmosphere-ready ship in the system. The business of the Corporation could finally commence in earnest. After that, the expansion was basically on autopilot. With a united populace and a newly devised doctrine to guide them, the Corporation was making the recently tamed volcano a symbol of their power. Technology was invented, innovations were made. After AI-controlled manufacturing robots were developed, the stacks literally built themselves. A whole nation of people had to be reallocated to new positions. The Great Restructuring took a full generation, but as the history vids tell it, it was mostly painless. They told tales of an enthusiastic workforce forming giant queues in anticipation of their new work assignments. After that, the Corporation had nestled itself within its volcano and slowly grew as the denizens of earth fought each other over what profits were left to be found on the overpopulated planet.

Now, there were five stacks in total. The central tower, the Corporate stack, in the middle and the four other stacks formed a half circle around the central stack. Each tethered to each other in numerous locations by wide thoroughfares that were big enough for transport carts and pedestrian trams alike. There were even lanes for pedestrians but as far as Nikoli knew, those lanes only got used during marathons.

Nikoli looked over the work orders and picked his schedule for the day. He would start in his own stack. There were a few official work orders there, easy jobs. But there were also a few people he wanted to check in on. A few favors he wanted to see if he could pay back, just in case he wasn't around tomorrow. After that, he picked an assortment of jobs that would wind his way up the various stacks. His last job was a food processor in a Corporate cantina that was in the shipping and receiving level, at the very top. That's where he would end his day. In all reality, it was a stupid place to end one's day because the trip back down the stacks would be done for free. According to corporate doctrine, *free time was wasted time.* Nikoli didn't mind, he would have his hands full on the trip down today. While he was in the food court of the independent sector, as planned, he would grab a quick bite to eat and sit down at a specific table.

As instructed.

For Bella, Nikoli thought to himself as he started up the cart and pulled out of the maintenance shed.

***

Turns out it wasn't a table at all, it was a bench. Nikoli ordered a chicken curry and went to the instructed location. He even saw the little white cross that was painted onto the leg that signified the spot. Undeterred, Nikoli approached the empty bench and placed his toolbox down by his left foot before he started to quickly nibble at his food.

A few minutes later, within the constantly moving river of people, Nikoli noticed a familiar face walking towards him. He was tall, with skin colored the shade of olive oil and dark locks of hair that were tied back sloppily. After Nikoli recognized the man, he quickly turned his gaze away, afraid some prying eyes might have noticed the look of recognition on his face. Nikoli couldn't help himself, he quickly glanced back to ensure his friend was continuing on his path. To Nikoli's utter delight, and horror, Joe Downing sat down on the bench beside him.

He placed his toolbox down innocently by his right foot, it was identical to the one Nikoli had been instructed to bring.

"I forgot how pale you fuckers are." Joe looked straight ahead as he spoke. "How are you, Nikoli?"

"Good," Nikoli said watching the movements of the crowd as it passed. "How's the leg?"

There had been an explosion on the shipping dock, Nikoli didn't know what caused it. He was there repairing a docking clamp nearby when it happened. He saw Joe underneath a pile of flaming rubble. He didn't think about it. If he had, he probably would have left it to the fire suppression drones and emergency crews, but something inside him spurred him on.

"Not bad." Joe's leg had been severely shattered. "It never worked right after, though. So, I got a new one." Joe subtly reached down and rapped his fist quietly against the inside of his left knee. It sounded almost metallic. "How's your little girl?"

"Not great." Nikoli dropped his facade and allowed himself the truth.

"You know what's in that toolbox?" Joe asked cautiously and nodded down to the ground by his feet.

"I do." The target of his wildest dreams was inside that box. The one thing Bella desperately needed but Nikoli could never give her. The gene therapy for Bella's cancer, custom made to Bella's DNA from the sample he provided Joe months ago. "How does it work?"

"It's a medical injector. Just place it against her skin and pull the trigger, then it's over. She'll get sick though," Joe cautioned gently. "She'll probably run a fever for a couple days but after that." He paused. "After that, my friend, the tumors will shrink and the cancer will clear up. Probably take a month to clear the disease out entirely."

"Just like that?" Nikoli couldn't help the shock in his voice.

"Just like that," Joe confirmed. It was then the first sob broke from Nikoli's body. He couldn't help it. "Hey, hey," Joe said softly but with a firm tone. "Get your shit together, brother. You're not done yet. If I understand your Corporation's bullshit rules, you're not supposed to have that. And you still have to get it by customs. Tears aren't gonna sway those goons at the checkpoints. You better have a plan." Nikoli sniffed loudly and wiped whatever wetness remained on his face. Joe was right. He wasn't at the finish line yet.

"I bribed a guard. He's on shift right now, and will be for the next couple hours. That part is covered."

"Alright then, good. Glad to hear it."

"I can't thank you enough," Nikoli said earnestly. "I have nothing I can give you for this."

"Fuck off," Joe cursed quietly while looking ahead. "You saved my life. I would have been dead if it wasn't for you. And, so you know, this treatment isn't that expensive outside this place. It's pretty common actually. This is just another thing those corporate fucks are holding over your head to keep you focused on getting ahead down there in that place. It's slavery, man. It's fucking sick."

"I know," Nikoli said weakly.

"Listen, Nikoli. I like you, man. You're a good guy. You deserve better than this. If this thing with Bella works out, and after you lay low for a bit, I know a few people who might be able to smuggle you and your girls out of that place. The system is a big place, my friend. With your skills, I could probably set you up anywhere. Any station, any ship."

"I'm just a maintenance worker. I fix things for a living," Nikoli said dismissively while stealing a look at the innocent looking toolbox by Joe's foot.

"Yeah, that's called an engineer where I come from, and they are in high demand, buddy. Shit is always breaking down out in the void."

"It's impossible."

Joe just sighed beside him.

"No, it's really not. But think about it, ok? That's all I ask. But first, go take care of your girl. I'll be in touch." With that said, Joe reached down and picked up Nikoli's toolbox before he quickly rose up off the bench and strode off into the crowd. Seconds later, he disappeared from sight.

Nikoli stood in the customs line with all the other workers looking to return back into the Corporate world. Ahead of him, Dale Cummings, the tall blonde-haired security guard Nikoli met over a year ago, was working the booth. The cart was currently going through the equipment scanner, he would meet up with it on the other side. The toolbox, with its precious cargo, was gripped tightly in his hand. *This is fate,* Nikoli told himself to steady his nerves. *Everything has come together for this exact purpose.* One day, Nikoli had been running the cart fast and loose to get to a job during a particularly unfortunate day. That's when he met Dale, who let him off with a warning and simply sent him on his way. To repay this kindness, Nikoli later *fixed* the man's food processor to allocate larger portions of beef. After that they became friendly, well, as friendly as one could be with the stone faced security guards, anyway. During one casual conversation, Dale mentioned the independent food court on the shipping level and strongly recommended trying a Curry Sampler from a popular cantina. Which Nikoli did, and liked it so much he began taking the odd job from the shipping level, despite the distance, to treat himself to a chicken curry. Nikoli had found after some experimentation that the chicken was his favorite. Then the dock explosion happened, and he foolishly risked his own life for another. Something he didn't even think he was capable of. This new friend that came into the picture that would later speak of an incredible possibility.

This was meant to happen.

Despite that Nikoli couldn't help quietly tapping his foot on the metal deck while the woman in front of him, wearing the blue coveralls of food services, finished her business with Dale. Soon enough, her brief interview concluded, the woman retrieved her bundle on the other side of the scanner and departed.

Nikoli slowly shuffled up to the conveyor belt, deposited the toolbox onto the belt, and forced his hand to release it. He tried not to feel anxious as the small toolbox disappeared into the scanning bay of the apparatus.

"Nikoli," Dale said absently as a way of a casual greeting. The kind gentle acquaintances might exchange.

"Hello, Dale," Nikoli risked a quick glance into the man's face and gave the man the slightest of grins as he handed the man his datapad. "How is your day?"

"Another day, another credit." Dale looked uninterested as he quickly checked Nikoli's work assignments. "You? How did everything go?" He asked and Nikoli's heart jumped in his chest. He couldn't help it, and shot the guard a worried look. *He knows,* Nikoli's mind reeled away from the thought.

"Ah," Nikoli stammered. He couldn't speak suddenly.

"With your work assignments." The tall guard regarded Nikoli with a bemused look and gently wagged his datapad in front of him. Nikoli breathed out quickly as a wave coursed through his body and he nodded quickly.

"Yes, of course. Good. I had to fabricate a new stock dispenser and recalibrate the primary mixture module. It took a while, but I got it done," Nikoli said as he took his datapad back when Dale handed it to him.

"You have a good day," he said with a bit of a grin. Which was unusual for a guard, but Nikoli paid it no mind. The main thing is that he didn't even look towards the scanner's display once, like the contents of Nikoli's toolbox didn't interest him.

Just like he was supposed to.

Nikoli could have kissed him.

"Thank you," he said humbly while keeping his head down, retrieved his toolbox as it exited the scanner's body, and exited the queue as quickly as he could without bringing attention to himself.

Nikoli began his journey back to the apartment he shared with his girls. The toolbox resting comfortably in his lap as he sat in his cart, where he knew it was safe. In the vehicle lift of The Corporate stack, Nikoli allowed himself to dream of Bella running around the play structures with the other kids. With a full head of hair and a healthy weight. At a distance, she would be indistinguishable from the other gleeful, laughing children.

He and Helena could stop paying the fees for all the chems Bella needed. Nor would they have to worried about Bella's room being absolutely sterile, and they could get rid of that stupid airlock.

Nikoli wept again.

With some guilt, Nikoli suddenly realized he would once again be able to feel his baby's little kisses on his cheek. *I missed those so much,* Nikoli thought as he cried quietly into the palm of his hand. But not just that. Her smiles, her laughs, and all the expressions her little face seemed to be able to make. Each different, but still uniquely Bella. In less than an hour, he could erase the mistake he and Helena had made all those years ago that had cost their little girl so much pain. Bella would be whole again. She would be the little girl that nature *truly* intended.

You're not at the finish line yet, Nikoli reminded himself as the wide lift slowly sank deeper into the depths of the stack. Nikoli smoothed the front of his coverall and wiped his face with the palm of his hand. He breathed out forcefully a few times to collect himself before his gaze fell upon the metal box on his lap. A dark suspicion ran through his mind as he looked down at the innocent looking box. He trusted Joe, and yet...

Nikoli flipped the latches on the cheap container, did a quick scan around himself, just to be sure. He took in a deep breath to prepare himself for the next moment and eased the lid back. There, laying inconspicuously on the bottom, was the medical injector. It was shape like a small firearm with a vial of clear fluid nestled on the top of it.

Nikoli quickly closed the box. It made an audible sound as the lid camped shut, and Nikoli noisily flipped the latches closed. It was there, it *was* real. He confirmed it. But he felt a definite sense of danger exposing the treasure to the Corporate air. The next time that he saw that injector would be when he was about place it against Bella's arm.

The lift came to a slow, measured stop on the Corporate level with the thoroughfare that would take him back to his own stack. The lift's clamps engaged loudly around him and the barrier in front of the vehicle queue slowly parted. Three lanes of carts and transports slowly started to ease out of the lift's space. Nikoli was in the center and moved forward with the others. Outside the boundaries of the lift his eyes immediately locked onto a security cart that was parked to the side of the departing vehicle lanes. Two guards stood by it, casually talking while keeping a close eye on the exiting vehicles. They wore powered armor that bore the corporate colors on their sleeve, while the rest of the armor was a dull sort of black. At their side, their firearms stood out menacingly.

Nikoli didn't look at them further. One glance was more than enough. *Stay calm,* he told himself. He was still on The Corporate stack and security was always higher here. *This is normal.* Nikoli kept his eyes forward as he followed the lanes towards the thoroughfare he needed. He drove on and tried not to pay the strangely dressed executives that populated the promenade too much attention. Again, at the exit onto the thoroughfare, Nikoli spotted another security guard parked off to the side of the lanes. More guards in powered armor scanning the scant number of vehicles that were exiting the stack. These guards wore their helmets. They covered the guard's faces entirely and the dark visors made them look even more intimidating. *It's a coincidence,* Nikoli told himself. There could have been an incident within the stack, that would explain the extra security.

He proceeded down the throughfare without a problem. At the entrance to his stack he was relieved to see their wasn't a security cart. But it was short-lived when he spotted a single guard standing by the side of the road up ahead. Nikoli's heart dropped when the guard looked directly at him as he drove by in the maintenance cart. He quickly averted his eyes back to the lane in front of him. Nikoli drove to the stack's vehicle lift. At this time of day, when the day shift still had hours on duty yet, his little maintenance cart was the only vehicle on the lift. Nikoli queued up his level on his datapad and anxiously watched the barrier as it sealed him in the lift. He didn't request the maintenance level, he couldn't wait that long. Instead, he requested his own level. He would take care of Bella's shot first. After, when it's finally over, he would take his cart back up to the level and stow it away.

Bella came first.

The lift stopped on his level. The barrier parted in front of him, and Nikoli pulled out of the lift's space. He drove for about two minutes and he was just about to head around the promenade towards the corridor that headed to the residential block. For a moment, Nikoli allowed himself to relax.

Until he saw the roadblock.

The lane curved around the promenade and Nikoli couldn't help but feel trapped when he saw the two security carts parked across the majority of the lane, blocking any traffic until the guards allowed them to pass. Nikoli spotted a score of guards, all in powered armor. The exact number was irrelevant, it was too many. He felt a cold shiver run through his body. *There!* He spotted a turn off into the commercial sector and Nikoli didn't hesitate. He quickly pulled the cart into a space designated for maintenance personnel and jumped out with the tool box firmly grasped in his hand. He nervously scanned around himself as he made his way towards a bakery he frequents. Nikoli didn't run, he forced himself into a calm-looking stride as he walked away from the cart. His eyes quickly spotted the pair of guards meandering by the edges of the public eating area. That is, until their gaze fell on Nikoli. Then they started moving in his direction, slowly, as if not to scare him by the sudden shift in their direction. It didn't work though. Nikoli was plenty scared.

He shifted his gaze just as he opened the front door of the bakery in a mild panic.

"Hey, Nikoli," the owner called to him as he burst through the door.

"Carol. I need to use your back door. Right now!" Nikoli said sternly as he passed the woman's displays and the serving counter on his way to the back.

Nikoli exploded out the back door and headed down the cluttered alleyway in a full run. He didn't know for a fact the extra guards on his level were here for him, but he couldn't afford to take that chance. He had to assume the gig was up. He didn't know how. Nikoli was sure he had covered all the bases he needed to, but at that moment it didn't matter. All that mattered was getting to his little girl. Everything that happened after that, even his incarceration, was inconsequential. *Get to Bella!* He screamed inside his mind.

He ran down the alley until his eyes caught movement up ahead. He looked just in time to see a guard come into view. Nikoli quickly skirted down the next alleyway that exited out between two buildings.

"Stop!" he heard the electronically filtered call from the guard at the other end. Nikoli ignored it and sprinted between the two buildings. Ahead of him, he could see the basketball court past the eating area of the food court.

Just as he was about to exit from between the buildings, an armored guard stepped into his path and blocked his way. Nikoli didn't even slow down as the guard regarded him and began to raise his hand.

"Hal-," the guard began to say before Nikoli cut him off by collided with the man's armor. *What am I doing?!* Nikoli's brain reeled away. He dipped his shoulder into the guard's chest and bodychecked the man out of the way with every ounce of his momentum.

Nikoli's ears caught the sounds of bystanders' shocked cries as the guard flew to the side and landed awkwardly onto a table, crushing it beneath the weight his armor. Nikoli felt a pop in his shoulder upon impact, and after that his whole right side felt like it was on fire. He stumbled awkwardly, threatening to crash into a recycling unit before he caught himself. Nikoli quickly switched the light weight of the toolbox into his left hand, clenched his teeth and screamed at his body to keep running.

He sprinted up to the basketball court, the players on the court saw him and quickly parted, allowing the sprinting madman to pass. Behind him he heard the loud clanking footfalls of the guards pursuing him, the cries from them telling Nikoli to stop, but ahead of him he saw the corridor for the residential district of his level. *Bella, Bella, Bella,* Nikoli screamed inside his head with each ragged breath as he pushed his body precariously to run even faster.

He ran down the winding corridor, past all the uniquely decorated exterior doors of his neighbors. The whole time feeling the guards gaining on him.

"Priority open!" He screamed down the hall as he approached the living space he shared with the two most precious people in the system. He just prayed the door's voice recognition software wasn't offline. "Nikoli Jonlesky!" *Please!*

Ahead of him, his door hissed open quietly. Nikoli ran for the door as he fumbled with the latches on the toolbox. He launched himself through the door just as a shot rang out behind him. Something punched his calf muscle of his right leg. Nikoli clumsily lurched forward and the toolbox spilled from his hands and clattered across the floor.

"Nikko!" He heard his wife yell as he tumbled into the apartment and crashed to the floor. Pain erupting all over his body. Nikoli watched as the box's lid flew open and the small medical injector flew free from it and came to rest just ahead of him.

Nikoli ignored the heated barbs jabbing the various spots of his body and he scrambled across the floor. *I can still save her,* he foolishly told himself as his ears caught the frantic sounds of the pursuing guards filing into the room.

"Get him!" One of them called out as Nikoli clawed himself towards the injector. He felt their cold armored hands descend upon him, holding him in place. Nikoli fought them off as best he could as he reached for the injector with his uninjured arm. "Hold him, dammit!" It was right there, inches from his grasp.

Then the steel boot came down.

Nikoli's hand didn't stand a chance as the boot stomped down on it. The tiny bones in his hand broke like twigs under the weight, and then the weight just remained there. Digging into his flesh. Nikoli had never screamed like that before. A guttural cry that erupted from his core. There was no place to go to escape the unrelenting agony that was exploding out from his hand. Spittle flew from his mouth and landed on the toe of the boot crushing down on his hand as he cried out.

"Good job, boys," the guard said before he casually lifted his boot off Nikoli's hand to take a step towards the injector. Nikoli looked on for a moment at his disfigured hand that was oozing blood from where the skin was torn apart. His broken fingers were splayed unnaturally at different angles. Though, something else inexplicably caught Nikoli's attention in that moment. A dreadful sort of feeling that he recognized the electronically altered voice that was coming from behind the guard's helmet. He looked up with a frantic expression as the guard reached up and disengaged the helmet's locks before he removed it.

Dale was smiling down at him with a smug face.

"You!" Nikoli shook against the many hands holding him. "We had a deal!" He shouted. "You motherfucker! We had a deal!" Nikoli's pain just fueled his outrage.

"I don't know what you're talking about. I've never met you before this moment." That blonde-haired bastard then smiled down at him and winked. "What I *do* know," he continued arrogantly. "Is that busting the leader of a known smuggling ring is worth a lot more to my bosses than a couple a pissant infractions. And what's this?" He said with obvious cheer in his voice as he reached down and picked up the injector that was directly in front of Nikoli's broken, and bleeding hand.

"Even managed to catch him with said smuggled contraband on his person. You're going away for a long time, buddy." Dale cooed. "And the obvious felonies are just the beginning, don't forget about the other crimes you committed to get to this point. Evading a security officer, assaulting an officer, causing a public disturbance," He said while he ticked the crimes off on his fingers. "And those are just off the top of my head. Yep, a real long time. And me? I'll probably get a promotion for this."

"Dale, please," Nikoli said, switching gears, and looked up to the guard. "You got me, alright? I won't fight it." Like he had a defence for what he had done. "I'll plead guilty to everything, but please, *please*!" Nikoli begged with tears stinging his eyes. "Just give my baby that shot. Please. I beg you!" It was then Nikoli's ears first noticed Bella's cries from her room, and the weak sobs from Helena. They might have been there the whole time. He didn't know, but he heard them now. "Just give her the shot. That's all you have to do." Nikoli pleaded with the man, tried to make it seem like the easiest thing in the world. "Please!"

"This?" Dale regarded the small injector in his hand curiously for a cruel moment before he crushed it in his grasp. "This is evidence." Nikoli watched in horror as the fluid that would have saved his daughter's life ran down the guard's hand.

"NO!" Nikoli fought furiously against his captures again. "I'll fucking kill you, you fucking *fuck*!" Nikoli howled painfully as he wiggled on the ground. "You piece of shit!"

"Shut him up," Dale said dismissively. Nikoli would have continued cursing but then Bella's airlock door hissed open.

Nikoli eyes shot towards the sound just in time to see his little angel rush out into the hall. She was wearing her pajamas, which she liked to wear because they were comfortable and didn't irritate her skin. Her sweet face was twisted up in fear and confusion as she looked upon the terrible scene for the first time.

"Daddy!" She cried and took a single tentative step towards him but the sight of the armored guard caused her to pause. *Good girl, stay there.* Nikola noticed her bottom lip quivered as she cried before something important occurred to him.

"Bella! Put your mask on!" Nikoli cried out quickly to her as he felt the shockstick press into his shoulder blade. It would be the last thing he said to his little girl before the voltage coursed through his body and did its cruel work.

Nikoli stiffened painfully before the world descended into darkness.

CHAPTER 4

Eve

E ve had to admit, when she first saw the rusted, dated freighter, she didn't have high hopes for a lot of creature comforts. The *Cargador* was an independent people -mover, after all. The Corporation transports were more spacious, had better food, and they didn't tolerate the criminal element the same way the independent ones did. But there was no way she would take one of those.

The Cargador was like other people-movers of its kind. These large ships slowly lumbered their way across the system, stopping at the major ports, and some of the smaller ones, continuously moving people around the system. The ship was a simple, boxy design that had the most expensive accommodations at the top near the bridge, and the price index fell the lower on the ship you got. The people near the bridge enjoyed three-piece meals that were prepared by an actual chef. The people in the middle shared strategically-placed food processors and had a shower schedule. The ones near the engine prayed they didn't get radiation poisoning at some point during the trip. Like everything else in the fucking solar system, these ships had a hierarchy to it that just seemed to naturally form over the generations. It was one of the things Oberon had fought against.

And lost.

Eve was enjoying her shower somewhere in the middle of the ship. The people movers maintained a steady 1G thrust, and unlike transport freighter, passengers were allowed to travel about the ship. The transport company though, wasn't responsible for any passenger's well-being if caught outside a thrust chair during a sudden coarse correction, or deceleration burn. If that happened, passengers were given a short warning klaxon before their world tossed them into chaos. Crew were usually given more of a warning. That's why why the joke goes, if you see a crew member running down the halls, get to a thrust chair. Eve didn't expect any problems on this leg of the journey.

She had ditched Nike at Ceres, the large mining and transport station that was the drop-off and pickup point for all the mining organizations in and around Jupiter's orbit. It wasn't easy. The ship took some convincing. Nike could be a bit smothering if allowed. After that, it was a small matter of sneaking onto the largely unregulated station and buying herself a ticket to Russo station, as per Oberon's instructions. From there, she was to find a way down onto Mars and smuggle herself into the Corporate stacks. Not entirely impossible, but she knew there would be...difficulties.

For this part of the mission, Eve took on the form of a middle-aged Caucasian woman with brown hair and an eye color that was slightly lighter than auburn. She chose a height that was just under six feet with a slim, attractive build. Full breasts, but not too big, with an enticing looking bottom. She did this for the same reason a venus flytrap secretes a sugary substance that's similar to syrup across its inconspicuous-looking jaws.

She was trying to attract insects.

These ships were all about costs. Why pay for security when local criminals will pay *you* to hitch a ride and do the job of keeping the passengers in line? All the while extorting them for *insurance*. It was a tidy system where everybody wins, except the poor fucks who couldn't afford the cost of their insurance. They were the ones who paid in other ways. Some offered their bodies willingly to cover the charge. Others did get the choice. Everyone paid though, one way or another.

That's what pissed Eve off.

The semi-warm water ran down her skin from the nozzle above her and into the grate below. The collected water would be recycled, filtered, and sanitized before it was return to the transport's water stores. She stayed in the shower until her allotted time had expired and allowed the water flow to come to an abrupt stop. The shower cabinet remained locked until the system could purge it of the humid air that remained in the space. The sudden blast of sucking air was jarring but not unexpected. Eve then heard the shower's lock disengage. She pulled open the semi-opaque shower door and stepped into the small dressing portion of the stall.

Outside her stall, Eve could hear voices speaking loudly.

"You. Out." One of the voices said. Eve recognized it. After the command was given Eve heard a pattering of footfalls, all silently moving away. She envisioned the other patrons of the shared showers on her deck all quickly exiting the room. Whether they were done using the showers or not.

It's about time, Eve thought bitterly as she slipped on her modest pair of black panties.

Eve agreed with Oberon's vision of uniting humanity again, even if she didn't know what a united species would even look like. She didn't agree with his methods though, not the recent ones anyway. She didn't believe the Council should be skulking around in the shadows, secretly using their talents to manipulate and influence from the sidelines. She couldn't count the number of Oberon's speeches she'd had to endure. They all boiled down to two points. *We're not humanity's police force,* and, *We can't force our own sense of morality on others.* Eve's compromise was simple. She wouldn't look for trouble, but if she found it, she would deal with it.

Her own way.

"Oy! Lovely!" She heard the call come from outside her stall. "Time to come out, love. We all know you're in there. This little cat and mouse game of ours has come to end, my dear." Eve had been avoiding them. Oberon believed in the innate goodness of people, he preached people had to be shown the easiest way wasn't always the best one. Eve didn't know about that. If asked, she would have advised it was best to give people all the rope they needed to hang themselves. And when they did, there was nothing left to do but string them up.

Eve observed this lot. She witnessed how they operated first-hand, and Eve didn't like what she saw one bit. This bunch wasn't the first shake-down artists she has come across. Good ones, the kind Eve can tolerate, see where the disposable income is amongst the passengers and they focus their attentions on that. Gently taking their cut, which was barely noticed by the wealthy, and they generally left the poorer crowd to their misery. Not this lot, they squeezed everyone alike, but they focused their cruelty on the ones who couldn't fight back and wouldn't raise a fuss. They were like wolves, who singled out the weak while the rest of the herd looked on remorsefully from a safe distance while one of their own fell to the wolves' savagery. Each of them quietly thankful it wasn't them the wolves targeted.

Eve collected her neatly-folded pile of clothes from the bench where she left it and placed them back into the clothes bag she brought from her cabin. In her other hand, she collected her toiletries bag she purchased from the ship's commissary along with her clothes, and walked out of the shower stall.

"There she is!" The leader of this pack said gleefully as Eve walked out, in all her semi-naked glory. Eve glanced briefly at the ragtag bunch before she went to the last sink in a long line of stainless sinks that were bolted to the bulkhead. "Not a shy one, are we? *Claire.*"

The leader's name was Deacon Ford. He was a tall man, easily over six feet, but not especially wide. He had a lean, sinewy look to him that went perfectly with his rough-looking face. Ford had a face that bore all the scars of a hard-fought life, with a dozen little marks that highlighted past injuries that didn't heal right. By the look of the crooked, and somewhat flattened nose on the man's face, he had suffered through several breaks in the past. The most menacing mark, in Eve's opinion, was the large scar across the man's throat, right underneath his larynx. Deacon had the look of a survivor, the type of man that fought his way out of the slums through violence and sheer willpower. And by the gleeful expression currently on his face, he would gladly do it again.

"Deacon," Eve said with little interest as placed her clothes bag down beside the sink and casually placed her small toiletry bag on the side, close to the taps. She gave them all a brief glance before she unzipped her bag, pulled out her innocent-looking toothbrush, applied the appropriate amount of toothpaste, and began to brush her teeth. All the while standing in front of them unabashedly, wearing only a pair of panties. Eve endured the titillated leers of the five men and returned it with a bored expression of her own.

Standing closely beside Deacon like a pet, was a short, thin man who had a long sharp nose, and was missing a few of his front teeth. Eve knew the man only as Finch. A step behind and off to the side, was the Ramirez brothers, Greg and Julio. Eve knew they weren't twins, even though they shared similar features and the same stocky build of general laborers. She didn't know which one was older, but only a year separated them. Currently, they stood guard next to the plastic drapes at the entrance to the public shower area. Behind all of them, and standing out in the hall keeping watch, was a true mystery of a man. Eve didn't know the man's name. She only knew what the other passengers told her about him. The giant black man easily towered over the rest of his cohorts, and his wide shoulders made it look like the man would have to turn sideways in order to enter the room. Inexplicably, the man wore a large flowing, velvety robe. Like he was some sort of royalty. From where Eve was standing, she suspected the man wasn't wearing much else underneath. To her utter disappointment, when he noticed her gaze, he took his metal hands and slowly opened the robe, proudly displaying his large swinging member.

Eve just made a face and snorted dismissively at the display.

"So, you guys here for a shower too?" Eve asked innocently after she spat into the sink. "Looks like you could use it. You know, the shower credits are meant to be used every two days, guys. I don't think you can bank them."

"Ah, Claire," Deacon said her name with a certain amount of affection. "Truth be told, I'm going to miss these little *jabby-jabs* of yours. I do like a *spirited* woman." Deacon looked like something suddenly saddened him. Eve couldn't wait to find out what it was. "But alas, the time has come *to pay the piper*, as the saying goes."

"Oh yeah?" Eve perked up. "You guys going to sing for me?"

"No, girlie." Deacon frowned. "It's going to be you who's going to sing a little tune. For all of us," he said menacingly. "A payment for all the little jabby-jabs we've had to endure during this little dance of ours."

"Is this about the *travel insurance*? Because guys, I'm sorry to say I'm still not interested. Honestly, this trip has been pretty relaxing. I mean, my tier has three meals a day, warm showers, and I have my own quarters. When we first met, you kept saying how dangerous space travel is," Eve looked Deacon dead in the eyes as she switched gears. "But as far as I can tell, the only dangers aboard this ship, is you," Eve said and watched as Ford and his crew all smiled wickedly. "And you're not much of a danger at all. So, I think I'm going to be fine." Eve ended it with a smile.

"Think again, puppet." Deacon dipped his head to the small one. "Finch."

The little man fixed his sinister gaze on Eve and took a step forward. The smile on his face widened as he did so.

"Wait," Eve cried out impatiently and held the hand holding the toothbrush out in front of her. The gesture effectively halted the small man in his tracks. "At least hear a girl out first. Fuck!" Eve looked at them with a bitter expression of disappointment. "Okay, I get it. You're serious. Fine. I'll tell you what," Eve began. "You give back every single credit you extorted from the people on this ship. You apologize to them, and me, for all your bullshit. And," Eve held up her finger. "You promise me I won't see any of your ugly faces for the rest of the trip. You do all that, and I might let you leave this room alive." Eve leveled them with a hard glance. It didn't even phase her when they started laughing.

Eve subtly flipped the toothbrush in her hand, exposing the sharpened tip she had filed the hardened plastic end down to. Unknown to any of the cackling men in front of her.

"Enough of this. Finch. Grab her."

The small one looked to his boss and then sneered at Eve as he approached her. He took three quick steps towards her and poised his right hand to strike. *I forgot how slow normal people are,* Eve thought to herself as she patiently waited for Finch to bridge the gap between them. The Motherbot inside her had dumped measured amounts of neurochemicals inside her brain and primed the rest of her body for action the second the small man moved. Eve could see Finch's right-hand coil up into a tight fist. *He's not messing around, this one.*

"Suka!" The small man cursed as he threw the blow. Eve was impressed to hear one of the forgotten languages of Earth. She was less impressed with the word's meaning. *Bitch!*

After what felt like a long wait inside her head, the blow finally came. Eve reached up and easily caught the man's wrist, stopping the attack dead in its tracks. Eve smiled at the shocked man before she used the sharpened end of her toothbrush to stab him five times in a blink of an eye.

Eve dipped down in her stance and punched the sharpened point in the inside of the man's thigh, puncturing the Femoral artery. When she rose up she stabbed the brush into the underside of the man's held arm, all the way to the Brachial artery. Then attacked the man's side, pushing the brush up into the man's liver, where Eve was more than confident she ripped a good size hole into the Hepatic artery. Finch was already dead at that point; it was just a matter of seconds. But Eve still sharply punched the interior Carotid artery on the left side, and then hit the exterior Carotid on the right, for effect. Eve held him a moment longer as his life's fluid sprang from him in gentle spurts like he was a damned fountain. Warm blood splashed across Eve's face, soaked the front of her chest, and sprayed the area around the two of them. It sprayed the mirrors, the sinks, and even the shower stall Eve had just exited.

"Boss?" Finch said as he looked back to the rest of them with a confused expression. He was going into shock. Eve released her grip on the man's wrist. Finch convulsed once while he struggled to maintain his balance, and then he just sank to the ground.

"Whoops." Eve looked at the bloodied end of the toothbrush in her hand with mock surprise. "I totally forgot I was still holding that," she lied dramatically and dropped the pointed brush into the sink next to her.

"You're dead bitch!" Deacon's face twisted up in fury as he bellowed. The Ramirez brothers took this as their cue to enter the fray. "You're going to disappear after this. There won't even be a trace of you left behind for anyone to find." Eve wasn't listening.

She was working.

The first one to reach her was Julio, he was the larger of the two brothers. He rushed her with his arms out in front of him like he wanted to force her to the ground. Eve waited until his meaty hands came down on her shoulders before she clamped her hands around his wrists, pinning them into place. She moved back a step with the man's momentum before she kicked out with her front foot. The kick struck the man's back foot, right below the knee, just as it was stepping forward. The big man lost his balance, teetered forward as if he was going to fall. Eve promptly lifted her other leg and knee him in the face. Julio's body slumped to the ground, momentarily dazed, and Eve pivoted in her stance and threw the man into the shower stall door. The man, and the door, flew into the stall and landed with a large crash.

Eve felt Greg approach her from behind, so when he grabbed her shoulder to yank her around, probably into his fist, Eve was ready. Eve stepped back into the man and gave him a sharp elbow to the face. Greg recoiled away painfully from the blow, and Eve used the stunned second afterwards to grab a fistful of his hair at the back his head. With a loud grunt, Eve smashed the front of the man's face into the stainless-steel sink with every bit of force she could muster. Which was a lot. Under her grasp, she could feel the man's facial bones give way against the hardened edge of the sink. Eve held on tightly to the man's hair even after he sank to his knees. A strange sounding gurgle rose up from the man's throat as Eve yanked his head back. She paid zero attention to the man's collapsed face as she mercilessly chopped down on Greg's exposed throat, crushing it. The blow sent a red gob rocketing up into the air from some spot on his face that Eve couldn't readily identify.

"Julio!" The other brother screamed from the shower stall. Eve looked at him with a shocked expression as she released the still choking corpse from her grasp.

"Wait! I thought you were Julio," Eve said to the recovering man and watched intently as he pulled a small knife from his pocket and unfolded the blade.

"I'm Greg, you fucking cunt!" The man, Greg apparently, howled as he clumsily made his way out of the ruined shower stall and lunged at her with the knife in his hand.

He has some skill with the weapon, Eve had to admit. Greg stabbed low and then high in rapid succession. Each attack she met and easily blocked. He darted in to swipe the blade to the inside across her eyeline, Eve easily leaned out of the way of it. *That was a mistake,* Eve thought to herself as she predicted the next attack. As if on cue, the backhand slash came. She caught the arm, lowered it slightly, and gave the man a savage backhand that smashed into his jaw. Teeth noisily skittered across the hard surface of the deck and the fight left Greg's body. Eve swiveled in her stance and kicked the waning man behind the knee. When Greg dumbly collapsed onto that knee, Eve moved in behind him. With a loud crack, she easily twisted the man's head around until it was looking at Deacon with its lifeless eyes. She let Deacon stare into those eyes for a moment before Eve allowed the body to fall to the deck.

Then Eve turned her gaze towards Deacon, and she slowly started towards him.

"Okay," Deacon said holding up his hands in surrender. "I get it. You're a badass. We'll just leav-," he started to say but Eve shot her fist into the man's chest.

The knuckles of her hand collided with Deacon's sternum, the flat bone that held the ribs together at the front, and smashed right through it. Deacon's pained expression twisted up even further as his body came to the realization it couldn't breathe. Grasping for breath, Deacon sank to his knees in front of her.

"Not interested," Eve said as she reached out and gently pushed against the wheezing man's forehead. Deacon didn't resist, he was having enough problems just breathing. The man just fell backwards and looked up at the ceiling with frantic eyes. Looking for the answer to his dilemma on the bland ceiling tiles. Eve gently shushed the man as she moved in over top of him. She crouched down, regarded the struggling man with an empathetic expression before she spoke. "It will be over soon."

Eve stabbed her thumbs into Deacon's worried eyes and pushed them into the warm goo beyond. Then Eve's fingers clamped down onto the sides of the man's head, and in the next instant, Eve growled fiercely and pulled the man's face apart in a spray of crimson.

Then it was over.

The giant black man stood motionless as Eve lowered Deacon's freshly parted skull back down onto the deck with a mother's grace. She took a slow step forward, feeling the blood of three different men ooze its way down her body. Her nakedness was painted crimson with it, and caked her hair thoroughly. Eve could smell it with every breath, and the coppery taste of it was in her mouth as well. She didn't mind one bit. Unphased by her appearance, as well as the horror show she left in her wake, Eve approached the large, still man.

Her eyes locked with his instantly, and she held his gaze firmly as she confidently strode up to his large form until his limp penis was almost touching her stomach. Eve gave the man a hard look before she spoke slowly.

"What's your name, big man?"

"They call me Anthrax." Eve cocked an eyebrow at him.

"Fuck off. What's the name your mother gave you?"

"Evan," he said slowly. "Evan Williamson."

Eve nodded her head slowly and breathed out.

"Well, Evan, I heard a story recently." She looked into the dark eyes of his. She didn't see fear, just a gentle sort of acceptance. "About a large man who was sent to rape a man's daughter in front of him, because he didn't pay up. He was a poor man, his wife died the year before, and the trip out to the mining colonies was his last chance at a fresh start with his last remaining family member. However," Eve continued and judged the man by what she saw in his eyes. "When this absolute giant of a man showed up at the man's quarters, he didn't rape his daughter, like he was instructed. Incredibly, he served the man and his daughter a quiet meal and spent the night guarding the door while the two slept in their bunks. The next morning the large man said he would pay the man's debt, and left. Never to be seen again." Eve used her tongue to clean the blood off her lips before she spit a red gob onto the deck. "So, I ask you, Evan. Do you *know* this man?"

"Listen," Evan began, it was the first time Eve ever heard his deep voice. "I got family back on the mining colonies. I'm trying to put my brothers through university. I don't mind breaking a few fingers, or twisting a few arms behind some backs. I've sent more than my share of men to the med bays." Evan gave her a challenging look. "I've slapped around plenty of women. Fuck, I even let them parade my black ass around here like I'm some sort of sexual deviant. But I won't force myself on some little girl, that's where I draw the fucking line."

"Well, aren't you a big softy." He was telling the truth, as far as Eve could tell with her limited abilities. His eyes signed the deal for her. They had a tired look to them, like someone who was used to getting ground up in the gears of his life. "That's good to hear, though." Eve pointed sharply in his bare chest. Evan flinched noticeably at that. "Because you work for me from now on, Evan. Do you have a problem with that?"

"Does it pay?"

"Of course."

"Then I don't have a problem with it at all."

"Does Ford have any other colleagues on this ship?" Eve said holding her gaze on him.

"Nope," Evan said and pointed into the shower room with his mechanical arm. Eve noted several buzzing and popping sounds that accompanied the motion that erupted from the shoulder joint. "That was his whole crew."

"What's dickhead's shower code?" Eve thumbed back to Deacon's body. Evan promptly gave it to her. "Thank you. So, here's what's going to happen. I'm going to take another shower, and wash your former co-workers off myself. You're going to get rid of that ridiculous robe, and put on some decent clothes. Assuming you can find some that fit."

"I got clothes."

"Perfect. Put them on, then come back here and clean this mess up. Again, I assume Deacon had a method of disposing of bodies that you yourself are familiar with?" Evan nodded slowly. "Then get to it, and be quick about it. I don't want someone to come stumbling in on this horror show."

"Did you want me to fix the shower stall you broke?"

"I didn't break the stall," Eve replied quickly. "That dumbass's body broke the stall, I just threw him into it." Evan just smiled at Eve's logic. "Besides that, why would I *want* you to fix it?"

"A lot of women use those stalls. They are not exactly comfortable using the public showers. Mothers use them to wash their kids too. There're only three stalls, and one of them is wrecked now." Evan let Eve draw her own conclusions. Eve thought about it and soon nodded her agreement.

"*Can* you fix it?"

"I can fix anything, given amount time and money," Evan smiled briefly before he spoke again. "*And* assuming, of course, you want it done." It was Eve's turn to smile.

"Good answer. Yes, do that. All of it. Then, after all that is done. I want you to go around and return all the money Deacon extorted." Eve thought for a brief moment before she amended her command. "Actually, keep the money you collected from the top tier. Those people won't miss it. Instead, give that money to some people in the lower tiers."

"What do you mean, *give* it to them?" Evan asked with a confusion expression. "Like, on top of the money we already took? Like a gift?" Eve snapped her fingers at him.

"Yes! Exactly."

"Who do you want me to give the extra money to?"

"I don't care," Eve said and turned and walked back into the bloodied shower room. "That's up to you. Oh, and Evan?" Eve turned back to the giant black man. Who looked like he was eager to get to his new duties. "If I ever see that dick of yours again, I'm going to rip it off your body and feed it to you. I'm a lady after all, and I expect you to treat me as such. Do you understand?" Eve asked and regarded him seriously.

"Yes," Evan said with the slightest of grins. "Boss."

***

Eve sat at the four-person table that had two simple benches with no back support. Like most other things on the bustling station, it was bolted to the deck. Space station were similar to ships in that regard. Everything that could be secured, *was* secured. The Russo station's gravity was due to centrifugal force. Even the most optimistic Station Operation Manager would tell you that the gravity on stations was something to be maintained, not a constant. Only planets had constant, unwavering gravity. The station's gravity wasn't fixed either. The spin gravity was noticeably less the closer you got to the center. So, stations were usually sectioned off by rings. The outer most ring, and the part of the station with the most severe gravity, was the docks and Shipping and Receiving. It also included the massive storage warehouses. The next ring inward was the Industrial and Commercial sectors where the majority of the permanent residents of the station went to work and shop. The inner most ring was the Residential sector. It was also the place that Eve would find accommodations for herself and Evan.

But that was for later.

Eve was enjoying her steamed rice that was topped with a fantastic tasting bean curry. With her right hand she nimbly held the chopsticks and took modest bites of her food while she watched the people move by. She held her datapad in her left hand. The nanomachines migrated across the microscopic gap between her fingertip and the device's surface until it made a connection. Externally, she was a woman simply enjoying her food. Which Eve was. But she was also traversing the mind-boggling landscape of the digital universe, using her datapad as a jumping off point to the station's network. From there, if needed, Eve could extend her reach all the way across the system. The motherbot and its vast followers of nanomachines allowed Eve to slice off a piece of her consciousness and use it to search the digital landscape. It was like daydreaming.

The rest of the journey aboard the Cargador was blessedly uneventful. Her new employee, so far, was working out well. As instructed Evan returned the money that was extorted from most of the passengers, as well as dispersed the remaining balance of Ford's account to a few dozen people Evan felt were especially deserving. Eve suspected that Evan secretly enjoyed the work. For Evan, she imagined, this was maybe the first time the large man ever brought an appreciative smile to someone's face. A few of the children gave the large man poorly-drawn pictures which Eve had spied taped up to the bulkhead next to the bunk in the man's quarters. He never said anything about it, he kept that part to himself, but there was no mistaking the look on the man's face.

The bruiser even suggested he should collect *donations* at the farewell gala that the top tier passengers liked to have to celebrate the end of the voyage. Eve was so delighted by the idea that she even sprang for a custom-tailored suit for Evan to wear. It wasn't cheap, considering the sheer amount of fabric that was required the cover Evan's massive frame. Eve went as well, disguised as someone else of course. She managed to secure a ticket to the Gala, and she was seated across from a superbly dressed, older gentleman whom Evan soon approached. Eve watched closely as Evan walked up to their table, his menacing frame loomed over them all as he politely asked for donations for the less fortunate people on the lower decks. Eve appreciated his respectful tone even though the well-dressed man was having none of it.

"I already paid *you people*." He waved off the big man, like he was dismissing him.

"This isn't about that. This is about helping people," Evan said with obvious strain in his voice. Again, the man looked at him with a disgusted look and simply went back to his dinner. Evan simply placed his large metallic hand on the man's shoulder, and a gentle whirring noise could be heard as the long, skeletal-looking fingers of the prosthetic hand began to clamp down on the man's shoulder until he visibly winced in pain. "Don't think of it as helping other people," Evan said darkly. "Think of it as helping yourself."

Eve couldn't help but smile as the pompous man quickly made the transfer on his datapad. As did the rest of the patrons at the table, including her. When the business was concluded, Evan quietly thanked each of them and moved on to the next table. Deacon Ford could have learned a thing or two from Evan.

For the rest of the trip to Russo Station, Evan walked around the lower decks talking to people, hearing their stories, and giving out money where he saw fit. Eve hardly saw the man during the day rotation, Evan returned from the lower decks a few hours before their level's scheduled sleep rotation each day, looking tired but still walking tall. Always with the same little grin on his face.

Eve spotted Evan walking towards the table through the crowd, it wasn't hard, he towered over everyone else in the river of people he weaved through to get to the eating area. Eve ate another bite of her food as the man settled his bulk into the chair across from her. Eve regarded him with her eyes and pushed the other plate on the table towards Evan before she spoke.

"I got you the pad Thai with udon noodles, just like you wanted."

"Thanks, boss." Evan breathed in the aroma of the food appreciatively.

"All that spicy food is going to rot your stomach," Eve declared absently while she completed her tasks in the digital world.

"No way," Evan shot back. "I like it. Tastes like home." Eve noticed Evan pat down the pockets of his coveralls. "Shit!"

"Did you forget your utensils again?" Eve asked with some amusement.

Evan's cybernetic arms, though menacing looking, were an out-dated, basic mining prosthetics. They were designed to be durable, and had the support structure to be able to lift a great deal of weight and easily maneuver it. But the finger and wrist joints weren't designed to handle small instruments with any sort of dexterity. Instead, Evan had a specially-made set of utensils that he could clip into the ends of his metal digits. *Like a swiss-army hand,* Eve joked when she first heard of it. Evan didn't get the joke.

"Shut up," Evan said with quiet frustration as he fumbled with the chopsticks that were provided with the meal.

"It's adorable watching you struggle with that like a baby. Such a big man, only to be brought down by a chopstick." Eve chuckled slightly as Evan finally managed to grasp one of the wooden chopsticks between his forefinger and thumb. Only to snap the small twig in half a second later.

"The polite thing to do would be not to point it out," Evan sneered at her and made a second attempt on the one remaining chopstick.

"No," Eve said and put down her own chopsticks before she reached into her back pocket and pulled out a small metal container. "The polite thing to do is, go down to the engineering deck and convince one of the engineers on duty to let me use one of their fabricators to make you a spare set." Evan wordlessly looked at the container as he took it from her. He flipped open the lid and looked at the contents with wonder. Inside, neatly arranged and labeled with the butt connector ends facing up, were a knife, fork, and spoon attachment for his prosthetic. "The case is titanium, so you don't have to worry about crushing it. Unless you want to, that is."

"I don't know what to say," Evan looked at her briefly with an apologetic expression before he extended his bony, metallic finger and guided it gently into the utensil's socket. He pulled out the brand new fork and looked at it with awe.

"It's not like we're dating," Eve said sarcastically. "Just say *thank you*. After all, I can only stand to watch you eat with your hands so many times. Honestly, I don't know why I can't just buy you a decent pair of arms." Evan just gave her a familiar look. It was an offer she had asked a few times on the journey out here. Each time Evan quietly refused. Eve was beginning to suspect that spicy food wasn't the only thing that reminded Evan of home.

"Thank you." Evan said earnestly, dipping his head towards her. "I have news for you," he said as he reached into the inside pocket of his jacket and retrieved his large steel flask. Evan didn't drink, but glass and other such frail materials didn't last long in his grasp.

"Out with it." Eve waved him on as she returned to her food. The datapad pinged once at her side.

"Well, like you said the Poseidon was here. We missed it by a couple of days."

"I already knew that," Eve said while giving Evan a disappointed look. The datapad pinged in her hand again, this time Evan took notice but said nothing.

"Hold on, let me get to it. So, I talked to a few deck hands I know, and as it turns out, one of them was on duty that day. He said the Poseidon offloaded a massive shipping container from her holds after being on the float in a holding orbit for a day. Thing is, they didn't use any of the shipping crew to off load it," Evan said and held up his finger while he dipped his fork into the noodle bowl and Eve watched with some amusement as the tiny utensil spun on the end of his finger slowly to collect the noodles. It was the first time she witnessed the spinning function. Evan popped the fork in his mouth and chewed quickly before he continued. "The Corporation sent a drone crew up to the station, with their own cargo drones, to move the container into a private hanger on deck twelve." Evan took another appreciative bite and then smiled at her before he continued. "A couple interested parties," Evan began. *Criminals,* Eve immediately thought. "Staked the hanger out for a bit, and saw four spacers with the Poseidon's logo on the back head into the hanger. An hour later some Corporate suit and his muscle enter. After that, three of the spacers are never seen again."

"That's interesting."

"Then there's this." Evan used his free hand to pull out his datapad and slid it across the table towards her. "The local job board. The Poseidon's captain posted, and filled, three positions aboard his ship. A day later, they fucked off back to the belt. Never unloading a single cube of ice." Evan gave her a grim look. "I think three assholes on the Poseidon got themselves killed for whatever is in that container. Question is, what could do so important that three people had to die to keep it a secret?" Evan pondered to himself, as if he was trying to solve some great mystery.

"It's a ship," Eve said absently while her split consciousness worked on her meal and the tasks she still had to complete within the digital landscape. The datapad pinged again when the admissions officer on Ceres Station replied to her message. Eve was composing her response while, at the same time, she was also watching Evan's face drop slightly.

"You already know what's in the container?" Evan asked, slightly deflated.

"Of course. I also know where it went. The Corporate R&D sector, at the bottom of the damned stacks. They want to take that ship apart and reverse engineer it. I can't let that happen."

"Really, well if you're so smart then you probably already know your precious ship is still there in the hanger," Evan said with a bit of a grin because he knew she didn't know that. The expression on her face probably confirmed it.

"What?" Eve looked up from her meal and fully focused on the man. She hadn't expected this. She had expected the Corporation to move such an asset within the safety of the Stacks as soon as possible.

This changes everything, Eve thought as she considered a new path forward. She was delighted by this revelation. The security on Russo station was impressive to be sure, but it was nothing compared to the level of security she would have to negate to enter the R&D section of the Corporation. Here, she could basically just walk into the hanger and take Ares and his ship back with minimal loss of life. It was a fucking gift from the universe, and she wasn't about to let such an opportunity slip away from her.

"Yeah, you didn't know that, did you?" Evan asked smugly and ate another forkful of noodles. "Some sources of mine confirmed it, but boss," Evan cautioned. "It's scheduled to ship out tomorrow."

"Security?"

"There's a Corporate goon on duty outside the door. That's it, as far as my guy can tell." Evan was about to continue when Eve's datapad pinged again in her hand. Her credit transfer went through. "You need to get that?"

"Don't worry about it," Eve said dismissively. "Was there something else?"

"Yeah, we have a problem," Evan started to say and then another ping from her datapad interrupted him. Evan just glared at her curiously for a second before he continued. "Seriously? What the fuck are you even doing with that thing?" Evan used his forked finger to point towards her datapad.

"I'm doing some business."

"Really?" Evan sounded unconvinced. "Your fingers aren't moving on it. You're not even looking at it."

"Don't worry about it. It's a surprise I'm putting together for you. For all your good work."

"I don't like surprises, boss." Evan narrowed his eyes at her suspiciously. Eve misspoke, she had been momentarily distracted and didn't realize how her words might be interpreted. For a gangster like Evan, those words could be construed as a threat.

"Okay, fine." Eve finished her rice bowl and set her bowl to the side. "I'll tell you. But it's not done yet, there's a few people who I need to hear back from. I set your brother, Jerome, up with a scholarship to the geological college on Ceres, for the full four years. I'm also in contact with a university on Earth, you said Bradley was interested in the natural sciences, there's no better place than earth to study it. They are the only ones who actually have *Nature*," Eve joked. Evan just looked at her with his mouth open. Eve took that as a sign she should continue. "I sent up a trust fund for your half-sister, Ruthie."

"I have a sister?" Evan looked at her with shock.

"*And* I also set one up for Jerome's daughter, Talia." Eve gave Evan a empathetic look. "She's one and a half." Evan was speechless, and his facial expressions ran the gamut as well. "You should really go visit them."

"How the fuck do you know that? I barely talked about them? And how are you paying for all this?" At that, Evan regarded her with a strange expression. "Like, who the fuck are you? Really?"

"Shit, man. Calm down," Eve patted the air between them. "What the fuck are you worried about?" Evan pointed at her angrily.

"You're bringing my family into our arrangement. That wasn't part of the deal. I don't know you. I don't know where all this money is coming from, and I don't want my shit getting back to my family."

"It won't"

"How?" Evan raised his voice. Eve looked around and was disappointed to see a few eyes look their direction. "How do you know that? Tell me," Evan demanded.

Eve just returned his angry expression.

"I don't have to tell you *shit*. You don't like our arrangement and the moves I make, you can fuck off. I'm not keeping you here," Eve said angrily and stared the man down for a moment before she continued. "As far as the rest, I did that as a thank you, because I thought you earned it. It was a gift."

"How? How did I *earn* it? I haven't done anything," Evan challenged her. Eve sighed, slightly disappointed at the direction the conversation has taken.

"Okay, you big, stupid asshole. I'll tell you. Because I was keeping an eye on you while we were on the Cargador. I know you didn't pocket any of that money for yourself. I know you gave it all away. Why? Huh? Why not keep it for yourself?" Evan's stubborn silence only frustrated her more. "Come on, out with it!"

"I liked it," Evan whispered his admission.

"What?" Eve barked at him. "What are you, a fucking child now? Speak up!"

"I said I like it goddamnit! Okay? I liked helping them."

"Why?" Eve didn't let up.

"I don't know," Evan said angrily and thought about the question. "I guess I liked being the good guy for a change."

"Okay, great. But why do I get a load of shit when I try to do the same thing for you that you did for those passengers? You don't think I want to feel like the good guy every now and then?" Eve frowned furiously at the man until she saw the gears within his mind start to turn. Then Eve relaxed her expression.

"I guess I didn't think of it like that," The big man said softly. "I thought you were working an angle on me."

"Well, that's a shitty thing to think about someone who's trying to help you. But," Eve softened as well. "I guess it's in your nature to be a tad paranoid. But shit, at least wait until a girl gives you a reason to be paranoid before you freak out."

"Well," Evan said and looked at her. "You *are* keeping secrets from me." He smiled to indicate the previous tension had been released. "Like, where all this money is coming from. And how you can use your datapad simply by holding it." Evan grinned at her slightly. "Or the fact you never go to the bathroom."

Shit, Eve thought as the man eyed her. She didn't realize that the man was watching her *that* closely.

"What? I use the bathroom plenty, trust me," Eve lied to the man's face with ease. Even though the truth of it was that Evan was correct. She didn't use the washroom, because the nanomachines didn't waste anything. So, there was no waste material to dispose of. Eve also didn't have a menstrual cycle, and some part of her hoped humorously that Evan wasn't paying attention to that detail as well. "As far as the datapad," Eve continued and tapped the side of her head a couple of times.

"I had a neuro-link installed a few years back, it lets me use my datapad just by thinking about it. It's not magic."

"And the money?"

Eve sighed.

"*Money*," Eve said bitterly. "It's not money, Evan. It's not even real. Like, have you even seen a credit?" It was a trick question because credits didn't physically exist. "There all just numbers that exist in a database somewhere. Do you have any idea how many millions of credits there are just lying in dormant accounts throughout the system? Never to be claimed by anyone." Evan gave her a confused expression, so Eve tried a different approach. "If I were to reach across this table and snap your neck," Eve began and watched Evan lean back in his chair slightly to move away from her. "What do you think would happen to any accounts that might be in your name?"

"I figure it would go to my mother."

"Do you have a Will filed with the Central Banking Commission that lists her as your beneficiary?" Eve asked suspecting she already knew the answer.

"No."

"Then, when you die, all your accounts will be frozen until someone steps forward with the proper credentials to claim them. People die every day out there in the system. All of them have bank accounts, retirement accounts, investment portfolios, trust funds. Numbers within numbers within more numbers, Evan. When you're as familiar with the digital landscape that's out there in the ether as I am, money isn't an issue."

"So, you're stealing money from dead people. Taking money that should have gone to their families, if it wasn't for some bullshit rule nobody knows about." Eve gave the large man another disappointed look.

"First off, a lot of people know to file a Will with the CBC. Furthermore, I strongly suggest you file one for yourself, as well as tell everyone you meet to do the same. Secondly, I take from accounts of people who have been dead for hundreds of years. *After* I check any genealogical reports that might be available. I don't *steal* from anybody," Eve said with some venom. "Are we good?"

"Yeah, we're good." Evan thought for a moment longer before he added, "Boss"

"Great," Eve replied with little joy. "Let's go then." Eve said rising from her seat.

"What? Where?" Evan asked quickly while he began shoveling his meal in his mouth.

"Deck twelve. We're going to steal that ship."

"Right now?!" Evan looked at her with panicked eyes. He knew it was madness to suggest such a thing. Stealing a ship that was locked down within a hanger in the station was impossible to get away with.

"Right now." Eve wasn't looking to get away with anything. Once she was secured within Hera, there was no force in the system that could stop her from leaving with that ship. The body count was really the only variable that concerned her. She would like to do this quietly, but she also knew that if it came to it, she wouldn't hesitate to end as many lives as she needed to keep Ares and his ship from the Corporation.

The flow of people quickly parted around Evan as he led the way to the docking level of the station. From there, Evan punched up the section's map on his datapad and they worked they way spinward until they were in the part of the section that was allocated for private storage hangers. There were plenty of smaller hangers available, ones that were meant specifically for personal transport spacecraft. *Someone's hiding it in that big storage hanger,* Eve realized as they neared their target. *From the Corporation. But why?* Eve checked the station's manifests. Whoever rented that hanger used a bogus Corporate ID tag that went nowhere. She checked the video logs that were stored in the security system, moments before they were wiped by the station's dated AI. She saw a young-looking executive, small build, average height with blonde hair that was perfectly styled. She didn't recognize his face, but she was quick to notice his cold, reptilian eyes that surveyed everything as he moved through the corridor.

This is a mistake, something inside her warned ominously. Oberon had given her his commands, she wasn't supposed to take the ship now. She was supposed to infiltrate the Corporation and then take it. *But fuck! It's right here.* Only one guard stood between her and her goal. One guard! She had to remind herself that Oberon wasn't perfect. Maybe he simply wasn't aware such an opportunity would present itself when he was making his grand designs for her. It was a possibility.

"Look, when I take this ship, all hell is going to break loose on the station," Eve said to Evan as they made their way down the corridor to the hanger. "There might even be a temporary atmospheric depressurization." Eve stopped him right as the corridor made a sharp turn towards the hangers. "You should get to the hotel and seal yourself in." She eyed him seriously. "Then lay low for awhile until I contact you."

"So, is this it? Between us?" Evan looked remorseful at the prospect.

"I think so," Eve said and gave him a reassuring smile. "Have a good life, Evan." Eve patted the big man on the shoulder.

"You too," Evan said with little commitment. They nodded to each other and parted ways. Evan turned to head back out of the hanger's corridor. While Eve turned and rounded the corner to seize her prize.

She didn't get far.

"Shit!" Eve cursed loudly when she first saw the *guard*.

It stood a little over five feet tall, with an athletic looking build. It wasn't big, nor was it intimidating, which was by design. It's posture resembled that of a regular human being in every way as it stood in the middle of the corridor like a statue. They even dressed it up in a Corporate guard's uniform to help it blend in somewhat. Its featureless grey face stared dispassionately down the corridor at her.

"What's wrong, boss?" Evan turned back to look at her. He only got a few steps himself.

"That's not a guard you idiot," Eve barked at him as she stalked back to where he stood. "That's a *golem*." Eve thumbed angrily back to the corridor.

"It's not?" Evan asked with a certain level of surprise in his voice. "It looked like a guard to me, boss." The large man moved his bulk up to the corner to peer around it to have a look for himself. Eve just let him, she had already disabled the cameras in the area, which would buy them some time before suspicions were raised. And golems weren't capable of recording images or audio. Sure, they could dig inside it's memory core for an image, but she knew that was tedious work, and it would render the expensive cyborg utterly useless afterwards. "Oh yeah!" Evan exclaimed with some wonder when he saw it with his own eyes. "What's a golem?"

"It's a cybernetic soldier The Corporation developed a few centuries ago."

"There's a person inside there?" Evan asked still eyeing it up.

"Kind of, it's just a brain and a spinal column that's hooked up to an advanced, humanoid drone chassis," she said as Eve weighed her options.

"That little thing?" Evan scoffed at the diminutive figure at the other end of the corridor.

"It wasn't a great soldier, they were prone to developing brain lesions from the stresses of the battlefield. The invention of powered armor pretty much rendered them obsolete, But they still made formidable guards." Eve knew that was an understatement. The golem had a vast array of articulating joints that allowed it to move like a human being. It's hardened polycarbonate shell made it very durable, and it hit like a truck because it probably weighed more then Evan did. Inside that small frame was a neuro-linked CPU that was uploaded with an impressive collection of ancient martial arts. Put that all together with the learning and decision-making ability of a human brain and you've created a merciless drone that was probably the most skilled hand-to-hand fighter in the system. It was rivaled only by a Council member, on a good day.

Eve prayed that this was a good day.

"Okay, here's what we're going to do." Eve began to tie her medium length hair behind her head. She didn't want it in her eyes. "I'm going to go over there and keep that thing busy. When you see an opening, I want you to grab it and try to rip its head off." Eve saw the look of surprise on Evan's face. "Or crush its skull with those hands of yours. Whatever, just destroy the brain. That's the only way we're going to stop this thing without shooting it." Eve couldn't help the nagging feeling she had that she was just running towards failure. Like the golem was a dire omen she should be heeding. *I'm so close,* she thought again. It was an intoxicating realization.

"Okay, boss." Evan rolled his shoulders a few times, probably out of habit because his mechanical shoulder joints didn't require loosening up. "No problem." Eve nodded grimly at him and prayed he was right.

The Motherbot inside her, sensing the impending danger, dumped a measured amount of neurochemicals into her system. It felt like lightning coursing through her body, awakening every muscle and priming it for action. She felt like a coiled spring that was waiting to let go of all the tension it was holding on to. Suddenly Eve wasn't so much concerned about the approaching conflict, as she was eager to start it.

Eve exploded around the corner of the corridor in a full run towards the golem. She felt the recycled air blow errant hairs back against her scalp as she sprinted towards her target. Eve kicked off the deck and launched herself towards the golem with her right knee outstretched in front of her.

Once Eve passed a certain threshold, the golem sprang into action with surprising speed.

Its hands came down and blocked her knee, all Eve's momentum instantly halted in one swift motion. She landed nimbly and threw a high hook towards its face. The golem easily blocked it by chopping the inside of her wrist. Eve then went low to strike the thing's ribs, but again, her attacked was blocked by the golem's forearm. Seeing an opening, the golem brought its other elbow forward in a downward arc. The blow probably would have fractured Eve's hardened skull with the speed at which it was coming. Eve ducked under it a moment before it landed and moved behind the cyborg and hooked her arms tightly around the golem's waist as she went. Eve grunted loudly as she pressed her feet against the deck and lifted the golem's body off the deck. Eve guessed it must weigh upwards of three hundred pounds. She lifted its body as high as she could before she arched her back and threw the golem to the ground with a backwards suplex.

The golem's weigh came crashing down on its shoulders and the back of its head. Eve released her grip and scrambled to a standing position. When she looked up the golem was already on top of her. The relentless cyborg was already on its feet throwing punches at her. Eve blocked the first two easily enough but the golem quickly pivoted, which it used to turn and sent a back kick into Eve's gut. It felt like Eve had been hit by a large transport cart as the blow sunk into her stomach, pushed the air from her lungs, and sent her flying back. She collided painfully with the wall and quickly moved her head in time to avoid the golem's next attack. The fist missed her by a fraction of an inch and collided with the metal wall with a loud clang. Eve saw her opportunity and gave the golem two quick uppercuts to its stomach and underneath its jaw respectfully.

Fucking thing, Eve cursed inside her head as she felt the golem's cold hand hook around the back of her head and it pulled her face down into its rising knee. Eve saw it coming. Hell, she would have done the same thing. She let the golem pull her down and brought her elbow down on the top of its armored thigh. The impact rattled up her arm painfully, she managed to block the knee but Eve did little to slow it down. She felt the golem reach down and hook its arms under her armpits. The next instant Eve was in the air. The golem hoisted her up and spun her around until her back slammed into the wall off to the side of where she was. Eve's body fell awkwardly to the ground, where the golem promptly kicked her twice in the ribs before Eve could even look up. When she did, Eve saw its foot raised up and poised to come down. She prepared herself for the worst.

Then a black and silver freight tram crashed into the golem.

Evan pushed the golem onto the ground and crouched over it in a guard position. Eve saw the large metal arm raise up and crash down. The golem brought its arms into its face to cover up and the blow fell uselessly against its forearms. The cyborg wasted no time snapping a quick punch to Evan's face, and when the man was dazed the golem kicked him in the groin.

"Motherfucking cheap asshole!" Evan cried out painfully as he backed away a step. That's all the golem needed. It nimbly flipped itself into a standing position and faced off against Evan again.

Eve feared the worst and struggled to her feet.

Evan shook out his large steel arms and refocused his rage on the golem. He sent his massive fist towards the cyborgs in a comically slow fashion compared to the golem's reaction time. *He doesn't have a chance.* The golem easily blocked the punch and sent a series of targeted punches to Evan's midsection before the big man could bring his other arm to bear on the cyborg. The golem ducked under the wild hook, darted to the side and kicked the back of Evan's knee. The large man's upper body tilted slightly as the leg gave out, and the golem back-fisted Evan's jaw. Blood flew from his mouth as Evan fell away to the side.

Thankfully by then, Eve was on her feet and back in the fray.

The golem was standing over Evan, and Eve moved in behind it. The entire time she felt pain erupt from several spots on her body. Eve just prayed the nanomachines were keeping up with all the damage she was taking. She saw the golem's fist raise up, and Eve hooked her arm around it and threw a few useless uppercuts into its back as she pulled it away from Evan. The golem spun around and they grappled for a moment, each struggling like expert wrestlers looking for an opening in the other's defence. The golem pulled her arms down sharply and lurched forward to headbutt Eve square in the face, breaking her nose with a sharp crack. She already felt the strange tickle of the nanomachines repairing the damage when the golem inexplicably tilted its head to the side. Just in time to avoid Evan's punch. The big man's massive, steel fist struck Eve in almost the same place the golem had. Eve recoiled away from the blow and felt the golem's front kick land solidly in her center of gravity, launching her backwards.

Eve recovered just in time to see Evan's bulk fly through the air and land painfully next to her in the corridor. Eve jumped to her feet, but beside her she saw that Evan was much slower to rise. Unfortunately, Eve wasn't the only one who noticed.

The golem stood down the hall, its cold featureless face regarded her first and then slowly shifted its gaze to Evan, who was teetering on his feet. Eve could almost see it do the cruel math inside its all-too-human brain.

"Evan, get behind me!" She shouted but it was too late. The golem was already in motion. Both the golem and Eve both rushed towards the large man.

Eve was a step behind.

The golem jumped up and solidly punched Evan in the face, but Eve collided with the cyborg before it had a chance to land on its feet. Eve rammed it with her own considerable momentum and sent the golem flying back into the wall beside Evan. She watched with a certain amount of satisfaction as its body solidly struck the metal wall and rebounded to land further down the corridor towards the airlock. Eve saw her opportunity and took it. She darted forward as the golem was recovering off the deck and this time her knee struck it solidly under the chin.

Its body flew back from the blow. Eve landed and reached out with her hand. Her fingers wrapped around the golem's pant leg, and underneath she could feel the shin plate of its leg. She yanked her arm back and the golem awkwardly flopped down to the deck. Eve grabbed on to its leg with both hands, pivoted and swung her body around, throwing the golem against the opposite wall.

It was then that Evan foolishly rushed towards it and grabbed it by the throat, lifting the golem off its feet.

"Got you now, you little asshole," Evan said with a ragged breath as blood dripped freely from his face. Eve could make out the distinct whirring noise as Evan's long metal finger started to squeeze.

Eve wanted to warn him, she wanted to tell him to stay back, but something inside her caused her to pause. *Maybe,* she thought as she saw the golem's neck begin to compress, another second and Evan will crush its spine and it will be over.

The next instant the golem shattered the big man's arm to pieces.

The golem struck out with both hands, simultaneously striking the inside of Evan's wrist and the outside of his elbow joint. There was a loud crack that echoed in the corridor as the elbow joint came apart with a shower of silvery fragments that fell to the floor, along with the golem. Once back on its feet, the golem gave Evan two savage punches to the face before it launched its back leg forward. The kick sunk deep into Evan's midsection and threw him back. The few wires and servomotors that were still connected from the wrist, that still remained clenched around the golem's neck, broke free. Evan flew limply against the wall where his back collided roughly with it and then he gently sank to his knees, and fell face-first onto the deck.

And convulsed once.

"Evan!" Eve looked at the golem with fury in her eyes as she watched the fucking thing pull Evan's severed metallic hand and wrist from its neck and toss it to the side. Eve clenched her fists until the joints of her hands ached. *This was a mistake,* she had to admit to herself as she quickly assessed the situation. "We're leaving!" Eve said sternly to the golem and moved towards Evan, and away from the airlock door. The golem, she knew, would regard her with caution while it slowly moved in behind her and back to its original position. As long as Eve didn't move towards it, or the door, the golem would stand down.

The fight was over. They lost.

Eve turned Evan over and quickly checked his vitals. He was breathing in ragged breaths, and there was a loud gurgling noise that pushed up from his throat with each breath. Blood ran freely down his face and his eyelids fluttered slightly.

"Shit!" Eve struggled to lift the big man up and maneuver him onto her shoulders. She hooked her arms around Evan's knee and grabbed his remaining wrist in a standard carry technique that emergency crews liked to use. Once in place Eve gave the golem, and the airlock door that led to Ares' ship, one last look before she pointed herself down the corridor and ran. "Hold on, Evan." Eve said over and over as she sprinted back to the docks.

Eve reached for her datapad and once she felt it in her grasp she signaled a medical emergency. She quickly picked out a spot where she would meet the medical staff. She listed the nature of emergency as a fall from extreme heights. *Fuck, fuck, fuck.*

"I'm sorry, Evan."

Eve ran as fast as her legs, and the nanomachines, would allow.

CHAPTER 5

Lucien

The board room in the R&D sector fit the grandiose dimensions of other executive rooms. Lucien assumed anyway. This is the only board room he had ever been in. It was rare for executives from different sectors to mingle, rarer still for one to attend a foreign board meeting. It's happened, but when it did it was usually ceremonial. The entire room was a giant rectangle, fifty meters by twenty-five meters exactly. The entire room was covered with panels of polished black volcanic glass that were cut from the interior of the volcano, and then manufactured into panels. They were laid with such precision that it gave the illusion of being seamless. On the left-hand side of the formidable room was a giant illustration of the solar system laser etched into the wall, and then filled with pure gold. It showed the exact planetary alignment the moment The Corporation was formed. It was the R&D sector's corporate logo.

The long table was located in the exact center of the room, and was the same shape as the room, with sharp foreboding edges. The chairman of the board sat at the head of the table, way at the other end of the table. Behind him, a giant portrait of the CEO watched over them all with equal distain. Above them, a giant crystalline chandelier hovered over them all with nothing visible fixing it in place. It was a strange collection of crystals. Each had a sort of angelic glow that emanated from its depths, and they all seemed to arrange themselves into a fascinating construct. The ceiling of the vast room was covered with vidscreens that showed the night sky above them. Whether the image of the stars and nebulas were computer generated or a real image, he didn't know.

Lucien had been to board meetings before. Like the other assistants, when he had been here, he was standing ten feet behind his patron's chair, as was his place. Not today though, and if his plans came to fruition the way he had laid them out, never again. The specially designed leather chair conformed snugly to his body as he sat at his place at the table with the rest of the directors of the R&D sector.

Ten feet behind him, standing at attention, was Doctor Cattivo.

Lucien's announcement would happen at the end of the meeting, which he took as a slight against him and his section. But it wasn't entirely unexpected. The Special Project's chair was revoltingly close to the end of the table. Across from him was the Agricultural section which was currently working on a new soil composition that would boost crop production by five percent. It was so underwhelming it was barely worth mentioning. Beside Lucien, and the only chair further away from the Chairmen, was the Maintenance section's chair. Headed up by Tolliver Hubert, who couldn't even be bothered to wear a suit that was in fashion. The Maintenance section didn't do research. All those trolls did was clean the floors and empty trash bins. They didn't belong here. Lucien couldn't understand how William could stand to sit next to him. Lucien could swear the antiseptic smell coming off the man was burning his nose.

Lucien understood the problem, it was the same problem William had allowed to fester within the Special Projects section. He had a habit of making big promises of grand technologies that he had no idea how to create. His old boss's true talents lay in the subtle, and sometimes fatal, art of corporate maneuvering. At that, the man had no equal. After all, he had headed up a failing section for decades and nobody dared question his many failed projects in all that time. William had a treasure trove of dirt he could use on the other executives at the time. Little tidbits that would ruin each of them. What Lucien wouldn't do to have access to that information now, but sadly it died with his former boss. No, Lucien was on his own from now on. If he wanted to remain in this chair, he would have to fight for it.

Lucien quietly waited for his announcement.

"Now, our next order of business," the amplified voice of the Chairmen began. Lucien sat a little straighter. *This is it.* "Is a bit...unfortunate. Seems one of our esteemed colleagues has succumbed to a regrettable ailment and had to withdraw from the board most unexpectantly. Even though, Special Projects has contributed little as of late," the Chairman said gently. *What?* Lucien sneered in his chair at the slight, but there was little else he could do. The man was right after all. "We can not leave one of our sections rudderless. Because a rudderless ship eventually runs afoul." The Chairman's harsh words echoed loudly throughout the chamber. "Until such time as we can determine a suitable candidate to fill the position of Director of Special Projects, The chair recognizes Lucien Malum as the interim director."

"*The Chair recognizes Lucien Malum as Interim Director of Special Projects.*" A loud electronic voice boomed throughout the room. Just like that, phase two of his plan was complete. He now had all the clearance he needed to move his prize down into the safety of his section without disclosing its contents.

Lucien looked back to Dr. Cattivo and nodded towards the man. Directors weren't allowed to have datapads at the table. So, he signalled the man to start the shipping process. He could have done it personally if he waited until after the meeting, but he trusted Dr. Ernst Cattivo completely. Well, Lucien trusted the man to follow his commands if he knew what was good for him. The man was a genius after all. So, he was smart enough to see that Lucien was going places. Behind him, Cattivo quickly pulled out his datapad and began furiously tapping on it.

"After a six month consultation period, in which we can assess all the potential candidates-," the Chairman began to say but Lucien cut him off when he held up his hand and the AI moderator broke in.

"*The Chair recognizes Lucien Malum.*"

"Mr. Malum," The Chair's said with some venom. "You have something you wish to add? So soon?"

"Yes, sir." Lucien rose from his chair, as was the procedure. "I would like-."

"Speak up, Malum!" The director of Energy Development yelled amusedly from the seat next to the Chairman. "We can't hear you way down here." Lucien pressed his knuckles into the table and sighed deeply.

"As I was about to say," Lucien continued, louder this time. "I would like to amend the consultation period to one full calendar year." The was a gentle murmur that erupted for a moment then died away as quickly as it began.

"Explain yourself."

"I, like many of the other candidates have many ongoing projects. I humbly ask we be given the time to complete the tasks at hand." It was then the director of Special Materials, who sat on the other side of the Chairman, broke into a fit of laughter.

"Not five minutes into your new position, and you're already asking for extensions. I swear it is like William is still with us." Muted guffaws erupted in the space. Lucien silenced them all when he loudly slapped the table.

"I demand the director's previous comments be stricken from the record!" Lucien yelled, sneering wickedly at the offending director. Which he most likely couldn't see from where he sat.

"So ordered," The Chairman said slowly.

"The record has been amended."

"And my esteemed colleague would do well to remember we do not disparage those who have been retired. Perhaps, we should give Mr. Malum another chance to explain why we should grant him an extension." Lucien felt the eyes of the room on him.

"Oh, it's not for me," Lucien said loud and with some merriment. "But what I've heard the other candidates from the other sections would benefit greatly from the extra time. I don't fear the contest, I only wish it be fair. If it was up to me, we would hold the vote right now." It was a bold thing to say, and Lucien did have his trump card burning a hole in his pocket. Almost begging to be used. He'd been waiting for this for too long to waste it on a small gambit like this. He would if he had to, though. "By all means let's parade the other candidates in here and let them tell you of their *accomplishments*." Lucien said the word with obvious disdain. "What would we find, I wonder. I'm sure the candidate from Solar Exploration will tell us all about his amazing finds in all the galaxies we don't have the technology to reach. Oh, maybe we could hear about the new ergonomic level design the candidate from Industrial Sciences is working on. Or maybe the candidate from Food Science has a new breed of tomato for us to gaze upon. If you wished to be underwhelmed by a tired assembly of boring ideas, by all means, bring them in."

"And what would you offer, Lucien?" The director of Technical Innovations asked with genuine curiosity.

"Wouldn't you like to know." Lucien looked around the vast table and eyed each of its occupants. "For decades, William has been trading *my* accomplishments to each of you for his *favors*. You have all benefitted from my work, but no more. Now, my section's accomplishments will be our own, and no one else's. Six months, a year, it makes no real difference to me. Like I said, I don't fear the contest, because I *am* the contest." Lucien eased himself back into his chair while the last of his words echoed off the walls.

There was a deafening silence that followed that filled the space, making it hard to breathe.

"So ordered," the Chairmen's voice finally boomed. "The consultation period shall be extended to one full calendar year from today, and each candidate will be given a chance to put their best proposal to the table. After such time, we shall vote on a new *permanent* director. Is there any other new business we need to address?" Lucien silently breathed a sigh of relief. Another part of his plan fell into place. It was important to him because with more time he had to explore the many wonders within the Council ship, the higher he would rise.

If his bluff had been called, the most he could have done is secured the directorship of Special Projects by using his trump card. If the other jackals on the board ever found out about the ship Lucien was hiding away, they would descend upon it, each taking a piece for themselves for their own benefit, until there was nothing left.

"If there is no further business. The meeting is adjourned."

"Meeting is adjourned. There will be a memorial service for former director William Clemente in the research and development sector's lounge immediately following today's meeting. Attendance is mandatory. Shortly after the service is concluded, a small soiree shall commence in the former director Clemente's honor." The AI

moderator's words went largely unnoticed as the directors and their assistants started filing out.

"Ernst," Lucien called out to his assistant, who was still tapping away on his datapad. Lucien didn't have to say anything else.

"I have a drone crew, and a freighter prepping to make the trip to Russo Station to make the transfer. They will be ready to go within the hour." The bookish man said, never taking his eyes off the screen of his datapad.

"Good," Lucien said grabbing the man by the arm and leading him away from the other exiting executives. "I want you to go with them and see to this, *personally*. I can't afford any mistakes." Cattivo looked up from his datapad.

"I thought my attendance to the memorial service was *mandatory*?"

"I haven't officially named my assistant yet," Lucian said and endured the aggrieved look from the doctor. "Do this, and don't fuck it up, and I'll name you."

"I'm sure I can handle moving a crate from point A to Point B."

"It's not that it's hard, it's *instrumental*. Nobody but our people can lay eyes on it. Nobody. After it's done, make sure to reassign everyone involved and scatter them throughout the stacks. I want a complete blanket over this."

"I understand," the doctor said solemnly. "I'll make sure it's done. Just as you say."

"Good man." Lucien patted the man on the back. "Let's get to it then." He led the way out of the room.

"This must be quite a find to require this much discretion." To that Lucien just smiled.

"It's the future, my friend. And we're going to seize it for ourselves."

***

William's memorial was blessedly short. The attendees all filed into the Corporate lounge where a stage had been set up in front of the extravagantly dressed tables. It had a quaint little podium set up in the center, and off to the side was a medium-sized portrait of William Clemente. His evil little grin regarding them all like he knew something about each of them, which he probably did by the time of his death. Lucien was assigned to a table that was a short distance from where William's body came to settle. He gazed at the spot with affection as the Chairman gave the eulogy. It was brief. William didn't leave this world with many accomplishments to his name. That was Clemente's true legacy. To rise to such a height on the corporate ladder through his little schemes alone. As was procedure, each of the board members of the R&D sector lumbered their way to the podium to say a few words about their former colleague. Some of them were nice, while others were honest. Lucien, when it was his turn, strode confidently up to the podium and spoke from his diaphragm. He said everything he was expected to about his former boss. Honestly, he didn't want to make a big fuss about it, William was dead, and his lack of ambition will be the reason nobody will remember him in a hundred years. Everybody knew it, this was just a formality.

When he was done, Lucien walked loudly back to his seat and continued eating his chicken.

He was here for the soiree.

The lights dimmed throughout the room to an informal level. William's picture had been taken away, and probably thrown into a recycler. The remnants from dinner was taken away with the lavish place settings, and the bar began its evening service. The professionally-dressed wait staff had retired for the evening, and were replaced with physically-appealing servants. As was procedure for the event, the servants wore semi-opaque facial coverings that conformed tightly to their skulls but still managed to conceal their faces. Other than the skin-tight coverings over their genitalia, the servants were completely nude. Their uniforms were painted on. Soft piano music began to play throughout the room, to set the mood, and drinks were served.

The Soiree was in full swing.

Lucien made the rounds, casually sipping his martini as he talked to a few people he was friendly with, the whole time keeping his eye on one person in particular. Bryce Cailleanach, Special Material's candidate for Lucien's job. From a distance he spied the young man of fifty years while the toxins in the air began to take effect. After about an hour, when the man was fidgeting in the corner with a sheen of sweat of his forehead, Lucien made his move. He approached the man, who looked like he was in the depths of a chem withdrawal, with a confident stride and an affable smile.

"Bryce!" Lucien called out to the man loudly and slapped him on the back as he came to his side. Bryce flinched away from the friendly gesture like Lucien had hurt him. "How are you doing, buddy?" Lucien asked with mock concern. "You're looking a little sick." Which to executives is the same as saying, *you look weak.*

"What!?" Bryce looked at him nervously. "No. I'm fine. It's just a little hot in here." He squeezed his eyes shut once and pinched the brim of his nose. *Poor guy,* Lucien thought with some amusement, *he looks like he's ready to tear off his own skin.*

"Really? I find it quite comfortable."

"What do you want, Lucien?" Bryce asked absently and then took a deep breath and tried to steady himself.

"I want to offer you an opportunity," Lucien said with a grin and took a sip of his martini. "Come work for me." Bryce looked at him like he was trying to figure out what Lucien had said. He then briefly chuckled humorlessly.

"Correct me if I'm wrong, but I'm pretty sure I'm already a candidate for your job. Why would I give that up to *work* for you?" He asked like the very idea of beyond comprehension.

"You're wrong," Lucien said quickly. "You're not going to take my job. You're not even really in contention." Lucien looked at him as he wiped the sweat from his forehead and looked at Lucien with a worried expression. "Christ's sake, man! You're still on your first life. Look at you?" Lucien motioned to his slightly round midsection, and then waved his hand around the man's face. "Fucking all grey hairs, and wrinkles. You think you're taking my job." Lucien shook his head as if he was gently teaching a child. "No."

"Mr. Alder seems to think I have a chance," Bryce said with as much pride as the poor fool could muster in his condition. "He recommended me after all. I'm here taking my shot, just like everyone else."

"Are you enjoying the soiree?" Lucien asked suddenly changing the subject. To that Bryce just nodded absently while leering at one of the servants in the distance. "What do you think of the service staff?" Lucien asked innocently with a smile. Bryce's gaze shot to him with a panicked look like Lucien had caught him doing something.

"What?!"

"The servants," Lucien said again and casually pointed to another one by the bar. Bryce's eyes locked onto the servant's perfect female form. Lucien watched in muted disgust as the man licked his lips. "What do you think of them? Do you find them *appealing*? You know, you can fuck them if you want. They won't stop you." Bryce just looked at him with rabid eyes. Lucien couldn't stand to keep the poor boy on the hook any longer. "I'm going to tell you a secret. Just hear me out, and when I'm done, I'm going to make the same offer. But this time, you're going to think about it. You ever wondered why you suddenly feel like you want to rip your clothes off and stick that little cock of yours into whatever hole you can find? You feel it, don't you?" Lucien gave him an empathetic expression. "All these servants around here. They're body paint is laced with a very potent pheromone. I'm not even supposed to be telling you this, but this is a little game we like to play on the junior executives. We bring them here and wait to see which one of them cracks first, and embarrasses themselves in front of the whole room. Look at Thomas over there." Lucien wrapped his arm around the man's shoulder and pointed to Maintenance's candidate, another non-threat. Thomas stood with two other executives. The man was rubbing an olive-skinned male servant's engorged member through the material of his scant covering. To the extreme amusement of the senior executives around him. "Poor bastard looks like he's about ready to drop down and pop that guy's filthy dick in his mouth and start sucking away." Lucien imitated the sound into the man's ear. "You stupid fuck, you thought you were here to position yourself for my job, but you'll be lucky if you leave here without scarring your reputation for a generation. Joseph Adler is not your friend. He didn't put you up because he thought you'd succeed. He put you up because he knew you wouldn't. He wants you to fail so he has an excuse to put you back into a researcher position where he can claim your accomplishments for himself. Because you're *smart*," Lucien cooed into his ear. "He knows he can't keep you under wraps for long, so instead he'll put you under his boot. Hell, Adler bet ten thousand credits that you would be the first to crack."

"Fucker," Bryce said venomously. The pheromones in the air amping up the man's emotions. "You're no better, Lucien. What's your deal? You're going to help me on the condition I agree to drop out of the race?" It was then Lucien discreetly removed the medical injector from his pocket. Lucien quickly stabbed the man's throat and pressed the trigger on the injector." Ow! What the fuck?" Bryce reeled away from Lucien while holding the spot Lucien jabbed with the injector. Immediately Lucien could see the man's clouded expression begin to clear.

"It's the antidote," Lucien said innocently displaying the medical injector in front of him. "I don't care if you stay in contention. I already told you, you're not a threat to my position. Come work for me. I have a project coming up that would be perfect for your talents?"

"Why? So you can do the same thing Adler would? Take my accomplishments and make them your own," Bryce said, breathing a little easier now.

"I have a multi-faceted project coming up, something big. There's enough glory for everyone to fill their resumes. But I need loyal people. People I can trust. I would never be able to trust you if you believed I was working an angle on you. I respect *your* skills. I'd like you, on my team. I could manage without you, but I'd be able to accomplish more *with* you. Will I benefit from your work? Definitely. I'm not going to lie about that, but I've never claimed something that wasn't mine. I will make sure your accomplishments in my service get the attention they deserve. We can climb the ladder together, or I can do it alone." Lucien removed his arm from the man, and backed away a step.

"What's the project?"

"I'm not telling you until you're on my team," Lucien said flatly. The man should have known better. When Bryce finally seemed to have his wits about him again, he regarded Lucien cautiously.

"Why are you helping me?" He asked while looking like a wounded animal.

"Simple. Because helping you, helps me." Lucien didn't see the need to lie to the man. "Like I said, I can do this without you. So, you can take you chances with the man who already bet against you once, or you can take your chances with me." Lucien slid the used medical injector into the man's hands which they accepted almost naturally. "It's your choice. I just hate to see talent go to waste." Lucien winked at the man before he slowly turned away, and left.

Moments later, there was a round of cheers coming from further into the lounge. When Lucien looked to see what the commotion was about he saw poor Gregory Thomas from Maintenance on his knees in front of the male servant he was rubbing before. A little crowd had formed around the man so Lucien didn't see the actual act being done. He inferred all he needed to by the crowd's chants.

"Suck! Suck! Suck!" They older executives around the man cried in unison. All laughing uproariously and pouring what remained of their drinks onto Thomas's balding scalp and down the servant's chest. *It's going to be a hard night for Thomas,* Lucien thought as he looked back to his new recruit and gave him a friendly nod.

Just then his datapad pinged loudly from his designer sport's coat. Lucien slipped behind one of the massive pillars and into its shadow removed the datapad and opened the connection. Cattivo's bored expression came alive.

"The drone crew is currently loading your container onto the freighter. Everything is going as planned."

"So why the fuck are you calling me then?" Lucien barked.

"I thought you'd like to know someone tried to break into your hanger," Cattivo replied with a certain smugness Lucien came to expect from the man.

"Who?" Lucien asked. Cattivo said the culprits had *tried,* so that meant the golem did its job.

"Nobody knows," Cattivo said with the disappointment Lucien felt. "The cameras in the areas went offline during the attempt. There were no bodies left behind, which is a bit of a disappointment. There's a collection of broken metal that has been tossed about, and a few blood splatters." Before Lucien could even ask his next question, Cattivo continued speaking.

"I ran the DNA through the station's database, and this guy came up." A smaller window popped into existence in the corner and displayed a mugshot of a particularly stern-looking black man. "Local gangster. He was arrested a few times in the past on aggravated assault charges. Works with the local criminals." Lucien was quickly scanning over the criminal report Cattivo was summarizing. He quickly noted the prosthetic arms. Lucien thought back to the metal fragments at the scene and morbidly wondered what was left of the man.

"Hospital?"

"Nobody checked in under that name," he said and Lucien cut him off.

"Obviously," he scoffed.

"*Nor,*" Cattivo continued. "Was anyone who fits his *very unique* description been admitted recently into any of the medical facilities on the station. Then there's this," he said and sent the golem's diagnostic report in an information packet.

"Holy fuck!" Lucien exclaimed as he looked over the damage report from the golem. "Looks like our boy was in quite a tussle." The damage was impressive. Lucien imagined there must have been a group of them. *Fucking hooligans!* It's too bad the surveillance cameras were offline. Lucien would have enjoyed watching the golem deal with the threat. "The hanger wasn't compromised?"

"No," Cattivo said firmly. "They never even got to the airlock door from what I've surmised of the situation."

"Okay, finish the job. This is just a distraction. I'll finish up here and meet you in the labs when the freighter docks." Lucien said and ended the connection.

Hours later, as Lucien was heading towards the lift he would need to take down to his section, his datapad pinged. When he checked it, he found a message from Bryce Cailleanach. It only had two words in it.

I'm in.

Lucien smiled as he picked up his pace. The pieces of his plan were falling into place nicely.

***

Days after he finally had the Council ship secured and hidden away within Cattivo's lab, Lucien was forced to muddled his way through the tedium of administrative work. He got rid of the obvious moles of the other directors that William had tolerated and allowed to roam their halls. He dismissed them immediately. The not-so-obvious moles he dealt with in a different manner. He had Brock round them up, and then as Lucien watched on, his bodyguard slowly strangled the life out of three of them. The last two Lucien recruited into his own service. It wasn't hard. By then they were practically eager to join him.

He also dismissed the staff members in his section that had thought were more loyal to the Corporation then they were to him. Lucien had a grand vision for the Corporation's future, and he needed people who believed in that vision. Who believed he was the only person in the system that could see it through. His section would run with little staff in the beginning, but that was fine. Lucien had cancelled most of the other research projects that were ongoing, so his section could focus on his prize. He had been looking over candidates for lab assistants at his desk when his datapad pinged.

"Come to the lab. There's something you need to see," Cattivo said quickly.

Lucien's hurried steps echoed throughout the sterile-looking corridor as he moved. Cattivo, that fucking genius, had figured out an ancient emergency door code that used a certain harmonic signature. The Council ship's airlock opened as if by magic after Cattivo played it a simple tune. Lucien hadn't been there for that. He cursed himself for missing it.

It's the pilot, Lucien thought furiously as he approached the lab door. He placed his thumb onto the receptacle for the Gensig, and once his DNA signature was confirmed, the door opened. Lucien easily found his scientist in the medical room. There were two examination tables in the center of the room. Lucien quickly spied the blackened remains of a partial human skeleton on one table, and the pilot's powered armor on the other. Lucien couldn't tell what state the armor was in, it looked fine to his eyes. Completely intact.

"Doctor," Lucien said almost musically as he leaned in close to the menacing-looking suit as he walked a full circle around it. "What do you have for me?" Lucien noted a distinct pause in which Cattivo sighed heavily.

"A whole lot of bad news, and one small bit of good." Lucien leveled the man with a hard gaze. Ernst simply shrugged. "Your man, Cailleanach used a laser cutter to retrieve a small bit of the hull's skin to analyze this morning and triggered some sort of lockdown protocol we didn't know about. The airlock snapped shut, cutting Jerry's arm off in the process, and now its not responding to any of our harmonic triggers."

"Fuck," Lucien hissed.

"Same for the suit here." Cattivo motioned to the powered armor. "When we first extracted it from the pilot's chair, the helmet was nowhere to be seen. We brought it back to the lab, fished out our friend there," Cattivo said and motioned to the partial skull and spinal column on the table that was surrounded by various bone fragments that Lucien didn't recognize. "And about fifty liters of the finest sand you could imagine. Hell, you're probably breathing some of it in right now."

"What?"

"Relax, it's completely inert. Take a look," Cattivo said and pointed to a screen that was nearby. "It showcased a black hexagonal shape that was completely featureless." Lucien walked closer to the screen and the doctor.

"What is it?"

"I don't know. It's not biological. I know that. It's only seven micrometers at its widest point. It's not water soluble. It's not magnetic. Doesn't respond to any external stimuli. I have a few more tests I can run but…" The good doctor let his reluctance speak for itself. He had run up against a wall with the mysterious sand.

"Theories?"

"It's a bit of a hunch, but I think we're looking at nanomachines."

"That small? How is that even possible?" Lucien marvelled at the tiny speck.

"We're not dealing with the possible. We stopped doing that the second that ship entered my lab."

"Our lab," Lucien looked at the man as he corrected him.

"Of course. Anyhow, after we removed what remained of the pilot, sand included, the suit's helmet folded itself into place from a hidden compartment in the back. So, now the suit's locked up tight as well."

"You're fucking kidding me!" Lucien barked at him. "So, we're back to square one? That's what you're telling me?"

"Not exactly," Cattivo said and motioned further down the counter he was standing at. He moved up to a large clear container that was filled with a clear fluid. "I found *this* inside the pilot's skull." It was the way that the doctor spoke that caused Lucien to step towards the container.

There suspended in the fluid, was a small metallic-looking shard the size of a small seed.

"Before you ask, I don't know for sure what it is. My guess is that it was some central control unit for all the other nanomachines."

"How?"

"You're guess is as good as mine. Ran the usual tests, and it comes up the same as the sand. Completely inert. Except for one thing," Cattivo said almost like he was teasing Lucien. "Look here." Cattivo switched on a monitor that was over the container and a magnified image of the speck came on the screen. Lucien marvelled at how utterly unremarkable it looked. It resembled a tiny grey capsule, with rough-looking ridges along its length. Almost like something had been broken off of it at one point. "Look what happens when I raise the fluid's temperature to match a human's body temperature." Cattivo tapped a few buttons on his datapad. Lucien watched the monitor as it showed the fluid's temperature in the top corner.

The moment the fluid's temperature reached thirty-seven degrees Celsius, the outer skin of the strange capsule started to shift slightly. The tiny ridges smoothed out, and to Lucien's awe, tiny metallic tendrils started to extend out from the capsule's body.

"They come out for exactly ten seconds," Cattivo said from behind him as Lucien watched the monitor intently. As promised, once ten seconds elapsed the tendrils shrank back into the body of the capsule and formed the tiny ridges on the side again. "There's a five-minute cooldown period before it will respond like that again. I *do* have a theory."

"Speak."

"It's looking for a host. We found it in the pilot's skull after all. What if it was implanted into the man's brain?" Cattivo seemed excited about the idea.

"To what end?" Lucien turned back to the man.

"I can't say for certain, it would be irresponsible to guess at this point. But," the doctor said and held up his finger. "I believe there is a way we could find out." The good doctor looked at Lucien with a giddy sort of expression as he too considered the possibilities. *Maybe this is it,* Lucien thought as he looked back to the grey capsule on the screen. *What if this was what made the Council members superhuman?* Legend said, the first member, Oberon had been implanted with alien technology. What if this was it? This inconspicuous, mysterious little grey capsule. What if Lucien had the answer he had been looking for right in front of him.

"Agreed," Lucien said looking back to the monitor and the strange shape. "We're going to need some test subjects."

CHAPTER 6

Nikoli Jonlesky

Nikoli came to already shackled, muzzled, and snuggly strapped upright into the handcart they were using to transport him to his trial. Like luggage. The trial went about as well as Nikoli expected it would. They wheeled him into a small, yet imposing room, that seemed designed to make him seem small. The two superbly dressed lawyers sat across from each other in comfortable-looking chairs behind lavish desks. In the center, and directly in front of the raised platform where the judge sat, was the prisoner's dias. That's where they wheeled him before engaging the caster brakes on the cart.

The lengthy list of charges was read by the prosecution. The overwhelming amount of evidence was presented. Turns out, Dale had ocular implants that allowed him to record every interaction Nikoli ever had with him. Nikoli watched it all on the vidscreen while clenching his teeth. He should have known better. He had been blinded by the possibility of saving his girl.

He knew that. If he had given himself more time, he would have found a better way to smuggle the injector into the stacks.

Nikoli watched as the vidscreen began to show the events of the capture. He saw the moment Dale crushed his hand, reminding Nikoli of his injured hand. He couldn't see it because his head was firmly affixed to the cart, but he didn't feel any pain from it. Only a slight tickle. So, he had to assume a medical sleeve was on it and was slowly repairing the damage. On the vidscreen, the moment that Nikoli was waiting for came. Dale looked down the hallway of the apartment Nikoli shared with his girls, and there in the hallway, was Bella. Her small, frail body shaking with fear. Despite her anguish, Nikoli marvelled at just how perfect she was. He still couldn't believe he was partially responsible for something so incredible. He only wished she had been smiling. That would have been a better image to commit to memory.

The judge quickly pronounced Nikoli as guilty, which didn't surprise anyone in the courtroom. When they asked Nikoli's representative if there was anything he would like to say on Nikoli's behalf, the sharply dressed man politely declined. The judge gave Nikoli forty years medium-duty labor, but because Nikoli was a first offender he was sent to the prison at that at the bottom of the stacks. Somewhere close to the mechanical level. Few people in the stacks knew its exact location. It was better than the mining colony on Deimos, but not by much.

After that, Nikoli was processed with all the efficiency the Corporation could manage. With blurring speed, he was tagged, stripped, deloused and disinfected, scanned, probed, dressed and placed into his prison cell before the beginning of the night shift. Just when Helena should be clocking into her shift. The large, sterile-looking mechanical door of his cell closed behind Nikoli, sealing him into his new home. He was left with the sound of the deep strumming noise that resonated throughout this place, and the constant noise of his thoughts to keep him company. Nikoli promised himself he wouldn't cry that first night.

He broke that promise.

***

The prison at the bottom of the stacks didn't have an official name, of course. Corporate doctrine didn't allow such places to be named. A prison served a purpose nobody wanted to be reminded of. However, Nikoli quickly learned the inmates referred to it as, *Goryashchi Ad*. It was from a dialect that was used in the lower stacks. It meant *The Burning Hell*.

This close to the caldera's floor, heat just seemed to radiate off every surface. The Corporation only allowed the atmospheric controls in the dormitories to lower the temperature to a tolerable level. Out with the work crews, the heat seemed to suck the life out of everyone. Except the guards, of course, they were more than comfortable in their powered armor as they stood guard over them.

Nikoli was assigned to the work crew responsible for cleaning the giant air ducts that criss-crossed around this level of the stacks. Nikoli didn't know where they were in the megastructure. He had worked in Maintenance all his life, and he never imagined that there were air vents this size in the stacks. He didn't know if they were intake, or exhaust vents. The massive ducts were big enough for a transport to drive through, and they went on for miles. The passages had a constant gentle breeze that might have been nice if it wasn't warm humid air that smelled slightly like grease. Some complained about it still, but everyone understood the foul-smelling breeze was still better than no breeze at all.

Their job was simple. They worked in two-man crews. One person, The Scraper, took a long metal pole that had a flat edge at the one end and removed the green lichen that grew on the walls. The other man, The Sprayer, carried a heavy spray tank on his back that was filled with antifungal detergent that could burn your skin. His job was to spray down the walls once the fungus was scraped off. He was also responsible for collecting the loose fungus into a large refuse bag, and emptying it when it was full.

Today was Nikoli's turn to scrape the walls. He worked with a man named Richardo, Nikoli didn't know his last name. He had tanned skin and a slight accent from the lower stacks, but Nikoli didn't know which one. To Nikoli, Richardo's inflections were almost musical. He was a good partner to have because he usually didn't want any trouble. Richardo was a graffiti terrorist. Though, if you were to ask him, he would say he was an *artist* instead of a terrorist. Nikoli couldn't fault him for that. When asked what crime landed him in such a place, Nikoli had a similar answer.

"I was trying to help my daughter," he would say.

Nikoli placed the blade on top of the large rounded vent they were working on, and put some of his weight against the handle of the scraper before he pulled it down the side. The noise of the blade filled the area around them as the lichen was removed and fell into a small pile by Nikoli's feet. Once he was done, he did the other side of the rounded corridor before he inched a step down the vent and started the process all over again. Richardo was further down the vent, spraying down the walls Nikoli had already scrapped.

"Hey, Nikki." *I will never escape that nickname,* Nikoli thought wearily and wiped the sweat from his face before he looked to his work partner. "Tank's empty, bro. I'm going to go get a refill. You want I should take da bag?" From where he was Richardo pointed to the collection bag by Nikoli's feet. He looked down and gave the bag a gentle nudge with the edge of his boot.

"Yeah, might as well." Nikoli dropped his tool and crouched down and filled the bag with what material there was to add to it. He lifted the bag up by its handle and carried it over to Richardo. "You want some help? It's kind of heavy," Nikoli offered, knowing full well the dropoff and refill point was a twenty-minute walk away.

"Naw, brah. I got it." Ricardo lowered the sprayer's nozzle to his leg where a magnetic clamp locked it to his side. He then reached down and hoisted the bag onto his shoulders. "By the time I get back you should be done this sector, yeah?" he motioned down the vent. It was about another hundred yards before the section they were working on butted up against a metal grate, and beyond it was a massive blower fan. The fan took up the entire space and its five giant blades slowly rotated around, pushing the air towards them. "Looks like the stacks are having salad tonight." Richardo said with a weary sort of amusement as he turned away from Nikoli. It was well known that the lichen was put into the recyclers so that whatever nutrients it contained could be added to the Corporation's stock. The lichen growing in this place was just another food source.

"Grab a couple ampoules while your there," Nikoli called to him. The water-filled ampoules were made of an edible starch that was nutrient rich. It didn't taste great, but it kept the hunger pains away and it kept them hydrated.

"You out?" Richardo looked back, his free hand fishing into the pocket of his soiled coveralls.

"Yeah."

"I got two," Richardo said holding them up in his hand. "Here." He tossed one of them to Nikoli. "I'll get more when I'm there." Nikoli quickly thanked the man who simply waved before he turned and walked down the vent back to the dropoff point. Nikoli put the ampoule in his mouth and chewed thoughtfully before he swallowed the mixture down, the whole time watching his companion until he rounded the corner further down.

Nikoli continued to work for a time, slowly making his way towards the giant fan assembly. He thought about his girls as he worked. He tried not to, but in this place there was little else to think about. With good behavior, he may be released by the time Helena was in her sixties. Bella should be...

Bella will probably be long dead, a cruel voice inside his head reminded him. *A cruel, distant memory from Helena's past.*

Nikoli grit his teeth painfully and focused more on his job.

It was then the sound of footfalls came down the corridor and Nikoli paused to see who was approaching. Some part of him expected it to be Richardo. After all, who else would be walking around this section of the vent system. The guards left them alone during the work shift, the inmates didn't need to be watched. There was no place for them to go.

Nikoli turned and saw another inmate he didn't recognize walking towards him. He had a medium build, with dark hair that was cut close to the man's scalp with a severe face that regarded Nikoli coldly.

"This isn't your section," Nikoli called down the corridor to inform the man. The man's pace didn't change one bit at the news.

"Nikoli Jonlesky." His name echoed ominously down the shaft after the man said it. Nikoli gripped the scraper in his hands tighter and turned towards the man. He held it out in front of him like a weapon.

"I don't know you," Nikoli said quickly.

"But I know you," the man said stepping closer. "We have some business to take care of, you and I."

"Stay back!" Nikoli stabbed the space between them with the scraper's blade to keep the man away. It was a futile gesture. Nikoli knew certain forms of sodomy were not uncommon in this place. The long-timers liked to terrorize the new inmates and used it to establish a form of dominance. *Don't fight it,* Richardo had advised him. *It's going to happen, sooner or later. Just let them take their piece, and move on.* Nikoli didn't agree with that when he first heard it, and he didn't agree with it now. "I'm warning you." Nikoli waved the business end of the scrapper towards the approaching man.

"I know you are," the menacing-looking man said as he confidently stepped into striking distance. Like Nikoli wasn't even holding the weapon in his hands. "And for what it's worth, I'm sorry." The man said with a gentle voice. Inexplicably Nikoli even saw a look of muted sadness bloom across his hardened face. It was only for a brief moment, though.

Then he attacked.

Nikoli was momentarily caught off guard by the disarming expression, but there was no mistaking how the man suddenly rushed forward. Nikoli thrusted the scraper forward, intent on cleaving the man's head right off. The man just spun to the side of the attack with shocking speed. Nikoli flinched away from the unexpected move and when he looked again, the man was beside him with his one hand clamp firmly around the shaft of the scraper. His other hand was already in motion.

The man chopped Nikoli hard in the throat. He reeled away from the blow, desperately gagging for breath, when the man's hand came down next on Nikoli's wrist. There was a sharp pain that exploded from it, and Nikoli had no choice but to release his grip on the scraper. Nikoli brought his freshly injured hand into his side. The man viciously tore the weapon from Nikoli's remaining hand and tossed it away. It clanged noisily against the wall of the airshaft somewhere behind the man. Gasping for breath, Nikoli angrily balled his good hand into a fist and threw it at his attacker. The dark-haired man easily ducked under it and immediately responded with a sharp punch to Nikoli's ribs. There was another sharp pain that erupted from his side when the man struck again, and something inside of

Nikoli's body broke. He wanted to move away from the blow, but the man quickly pivoted in behind Nikoli and savagely struck his kidneys.

He cried out and dropped down onto his knee after that one. His body just refused to operate properly as pain radiated out from the places the man had struck him. *You're not beat yet,* Nikoli thought as he willed himself to throw a heavy, frantic backfist at the man. He howled like a wounded animal as he put all his rage into the singular attack.

Which the man caught easily.

He sent a quick uppercut under Nikoli's arm that connected solidly with his jaw. The edges of his vision darkened considerably, and for a moment, Nikoli thought he might just slip into the darkness and leave this all behind him. Then the man stomped down onto the side of Nikoli's shin. The bones in the limb snapped like little twigs, and his leg folded unnaturally.

Nikoli howled loudly.

The cry leapt from his core and rattled his vocal cords on its way out. Suddenly, Nikoli realized that he had a lot more to worry about than someone violating him. But there was little he could do about it now.

The man swept Nikoli's arm to the side like it was made of paper and grabbed the lapels of his coveralls. By this point, his attacker was holding him up. Nikoli would have gladly fallen to the ground. The man quickly turned and tossed Nikoli over his shoulder. There was a blessed feeling of weightlessness before Nikoli's body crashed into the opposite wall of the rounded airshaft and promptly tumbled to the bottom. After that, the man moved in over top of him and the blows started raining down upon Nikoli.

Maybe this is for the best, Nikoli thought inexplicably as the first blow pounded into his face. By then he stopped feeling the pain of the blows, it was there, but it was like it was happening to someone else. He wanted to slip into the darkness, but each jagged blow pulsed through him, keeping him here in this place. He caught glimpses of his attacker's remorseful face. Nikoli wanted to tell him it was okay. That he didn't blame him, and he wouldn't hold the man's actions against him as Nikoli made his way into the next life. *Just finish the job,* Nikoli silently pleaded with the man. He couldn't speak after all, his mouth was filled with a warm fluid that tasted like copper. He was choking on it.

Nikoli thought of Bella when the darkness finally took him.

***

He awoke to a sterile-looking room. His vision was blurred and the lights of the small room sent needles deep into his brain. He tried to look around himself but everywhere he looked his vision swam around his focal point. He couldn't move, not because he was bound. His body felt like it was lost in the ether of his mind. It was there, he could feel its agony but he couldn't find the energy to locate it.

"He should be awake now," a voice in the room said. Nikoli shifted his gaze to try and find it but moving his head proved to be problematic.

"Thank you, doctor," another voice said with a cool confidence. "That will be all. I'll take it from here." Polite farewells were exchanged before Nikoli heard the door to the small room open, and then close.

Then a well-dressed man, with perfect blonde hair and a brilliant smile walked into Nikoli's vision. The young man had a friendly expression, but even in the mist of his consciousness Nikoli could see the cold intellect in his eyes.

"Good evening," the man said regarding Nikoli curiously. "Are you in there? Can you hear me?" To that Nikoli managed to pulled his head down once and grunt his acknowledgement.

"Excellent," the man said. Obviously pleased. "My name is Lucien Malum, I'm the new director of Special Projects in the R&D sector. I would shake your hand, as proper decorum dictates, but you're in no shape to shake anything. *And* if I was being honest, I really don't want to. I'll get straight to the point because I'm a busy man and I find this place...ill-managed," the man said, trying to sound gracious. "I have a project I'm working on. A few drug trials to test the effects of some viral antibodies we're developing. The exact details don't concern you. However, it would benefit you to know that candidates who participate in the trials are given a full pardon afterwards." The man gave him a sympathetic expression, that those eyes of his betrayed, before he continued. "I've read over your file. Believe me when I say just how unfortunate it is when one of the commoners gets caught up in the muck of caring for ones ailing child. Like honestly, what else could they expect from someone of your station. It's your *child*. I would have done the same thing."

A pardon? Nikoli's mind focused on the word. He wanted to say something, there were dozens of questions flying around inside in his mind. Just out of reach. However, when Nikoli tried to speak, he quickly found that his jaw had been wired shut. All that came from his lips was a soft groan.

"Now, I'm sure you have several questions for me. Trust me, we'll get to those, in time. But time *is* money. And you're not exactly in optimal condition right now. So, with your approval, we'll get you transferred to the R&D level, put you in an autodoc, and get you fixed up good as new in a fraction of the time these ingrates would be able to accomplish. Once the trials are completed, your record will be expunged and you will be reinstated back into the stacks with full privileges. It will be like this unfortunate business never even happened." The perfect man smiled widely. "What do you say?"

Nikoli groaned as eagerly as he could.

"Perfect," the man said and produced a datapad from his pocket. "I'm just going to need your gensig to confirm your agreement to enter the trials." The man continued to grin as he held the datapad in front of Nikoli's good hand. He groaned loudly as Nikoli tried to lift his hand to the device. "Here," the man said angrily before he reached down and roughly grabbed Nikoli's finger. "Let me help you." The man jabbed the end of Nikoli's finger into the receptacle on the datapad, which pinged once to confirm the genetic signature was accepted.

Nikoli had a tear spill from the one eye that wasn't bandaged. The man noticed before he turned to leave, the man sighed slightly at the sight.

"Don't worry," he said while wiping his hands with a sterile wipe. "I'll take good care of you."

CHAPTER 7

Eve

Eve was in a sour mood as she ascended from the depths of the corporate megastructure. She rode the grimy-looking lift with the rest of the people looking to escape the stale air of the mechanical level.

She took on the body of a middle-aged man, eastern European decent, medium build, medium height. Again, she wasn't looking to stand out. She went with a short, flat nose, sloping forehead, and a square jaw. With serious eyes that were set deep into her face. For a touch of flare, Eve went with her original eyes color. Ocean blue.

Eve briefly considered reaching out to Oberon and letting him know that she had completed her assignment, but decided against it. *He knows,* she thought to herself bitterly as she rode the lift up into the lower residential section of one of the stacks. Besides that, it probably wasn't a good idea to have him inside her head at the moment.

She was upset with him, and part of her felt like maybe he needed to explain himself a bit. Though, she knew he wouldn't.

Like, who the fuck is Nikoli Jonlesky? Eve asked herself for what seemed like the hundredth time since Oberon informed her what her next task was. She knew he had a plan, just like she knew that she shouldn't question his methods. He earned that, but she had to be honest with herself. Eve didn't see how beating some random prisoner half to death was going to help her retrieve Ares's ship. Surely there were objectives that were more pertinent to accomplishing her goals than that. Oberon had been adamant though.

Eve thought remorsefully about the beating she gave the man. She didn't want to, but it was like her mind was on autopilot as she suffered though the tedium of the long, boring trip up from the belly of the corporation. There was a moment, after he had thrown him against the wall and his body crumpled to the bottom of the air shaft, when he simply quit fighting. She had him in the guard position and after the first few heavy blows landed. He gave up. Eve saw it in his eyes. The fight simply drained out of his body and he looked at her with acceptance. Like he understood what was happening to him, and he was okay with it. Eve would have preferred that he fought her to the bitter end. It would have made doing the job easier.

Eve ran through the list of probable injuries she had left the broken man with. She broke the ulna bone of his forearm, broke at least three ribs, and snapped the tibia and fibia bones of his shin like they were twigs. More than likely fractured his skull when she threw him against the rounded side of the airshaft. As she was beating his head into the bottom of the corridor, the list of broken bones grew. Broken orbital bone on the right side, multiple jaw fractures, and a broken nose. She rolled him onto his side and left him broken and bloodied, with a small pool of blood spreading out slowly underneath him. Oberon had stipulated that she had to be *thorough*.

So, she was.

That didn't mean she felt good about it. What could she do though. *It's all part of the plan,* Eve told herself as she moved with the tight crowd that exited the lift. It was the one part of being a soldier she never liked. Blindly following orders. She hadn't had to do it a lot, even back when she was military personnel she still had the benefit of understanding the larger picture. Though military objectives were pretty straightforward. Go here, kill these people, and blow up these things. Try not to die in the process.

Oberon's plans were more similar to the idea behind the butterfly effect. If you wanted to impact objective C, you affect objective A in such a way that the effect spreads to objective B, which in turns completes objective C for you. It was frustrating because is order for Oberon's schemes to work, you had to give yourself to them without question. Questioning leads to doubting, and doubting gets people hurt. Like Evan.

Like Thomas.

Oberon had warned him. He ordered Thomas not to interfere with the peace summit. *It's their peace, let them work it out.* That's what Oberon had said, and he was right. But Thomas, that proud, stubborn, beautiful fool felt he had worked too hard to get the system to this point. He was determined to see it through. Deep down, Eve didn't see the harm in at least having a presence there. Then the Titania exploded. You'd think Eve would have learned her lesson after the love of her insanely long life was gone in a flash of light. Maybe Thomas wasn't the only overly stubborn member on the Council?

The lower stacks were not as well maintained as the mid-to-upper levels, but that didn't mean they weren't clean. It just meant the residents of these levels had to work harder to keep it up to Corporate standards. Instead of a custodian staff, because the lowers levels didn't have the budget for that, the manager's of the level offer a small compensation for collected trash.

Incentives programs are set up to encourage citizens to form work crews to tackle the ever-increasing job-list for the level. Which had its unintended effects. On the upside, businesses in the commercial district here were allowed more decoration and flair on their storefronts. Some even had the whole side panel on the buildings painted in a mural. The downside was that a lot of the children here spent their days collecting trash and emptying refuse bins instead of going to school.

There were more guards here too. That didn't mean the lower stacks were safer. If anything, the increased number of guards here significantly increased crime because the cold hard truth of it is that the guards were the ones ultimately responsible for most of the crime. It didn't take Eve long to figure that out. Most people already knew the guards were the ones to talk to for illegal chems. They smuggled them down every shift. Hell, most of the guards made more credits on their side hustles than their actual jobs. And those were the studious guards. The lazy ones just shook down the people here for credits whenever the temptation presented itself.

The Corporation promised to be the future of humanity, but it wasn't. It was just more of the same.

Eve made her way to a lift and took it up to a level in the mid-stacks. Once there, she made her way innocently to the recreation center, and dipped into a darkened alleyway by the food court that served the small collections of restaurants here. Away from prying eyes, Eve changed her form to match that of Angela Peters. A fifty-something woman with olive colors skin and long dark hair, that Eve kept in a sensible braided bun at the back. Eve decided to give her a stout build of a woman who works with her hands for long hours. She made her middle a little rounder, and her chest a little flatter. On her face, Eve went with thin lips and spread into a crooked smile. For effect, Eve also included a few small pimples on her face. She wasn't looking to attract anyone's gaze. If you're a woman, that's usually the best way to do it.

Eve walked out on the alleyway, positive her transformation went unnoticed during the brief couple seconds it took place, and turned back towards the recreational center located in the middle of the outdoor courts. She walked through the automated doors and took the quickest route to the ladies change rooms, where Eve had a locker rented out under Angela Peters' gensig. Eve walked up to the locker and touched her thumb to the receptacle. She waited briefly while the nanomachines in her system connected to the door's CPU and relayed the required information.

The door popped open with an audible click.

Eve changed out of the ill-fitting men's clothes she had been wearing and switched into the blue coveralls for the Food Services sector. She stowed the clothes in the locker, locked it, and promptly walked out of the recreational center and found the nearest personnel lift she could find. On the way, she removed her datapad and switched her active ID to that of Angela Peters. She was now a restaurant kitchen manager who worked in a corporate restaurant on the shipping level. Eve doubled-checked her clearances and authorizations while she held the device in her hand at her side. The personnel lift heading further up the stack was the first of many digital checkpoints she would pass on her way up to the top of the megastructure.

So far Eve had created four Corporate personnel profiles. She already used Robert Cortez, that was the profile she used to sneak her way onto the work crew. She already burned that one and scrubbed it from the system. Eve couldn't risk that Jonlesky guy having some sort of ocular recording device, or even a really good memory. Angela Peters was perfect for getting herself in and out of the stacks. Eve also made a profile that Evan could use to pass through customs. When he woke up, that is.

Eve operated in shifts. During the day shift, the one Angela was cleared to spend in the independent sector of the shipping level, she spent with Evan, and getting a feel for the criminal element of the sector. During the night shift, Eve descended into the megastructure to do some reconnaissance on the R&D sector.

That's going to be a touch nut to crack, Eve thought to herself as she waited in the customs queue. First off, no visitors were allowed in the entire sector. The only visitors that were permitted first had to be cleared by the person they were visiting, and then they had to be personally escorted by that person during the visit. So, there was no chance of just walking into the place and strolling the corridors. Secondly, the Special Projects level, the one she was interested in, had even more security. Each person on that level had to be personally cleared by one of two people. Eve immediately recognized Lucien Malum's name, but she didn't know who Doctor Ernst Cattivo was. Either way, she wasn't getting in there with one of her manufactured profiles, no matter how convincing she made it. The only people allowed in that place were people who were supposed to be there.

Breaking in wasn't an easy option. There were way too many detection devices, both passive and active for that to be a possibility. Given enough time, she could figure it out. She didn't want to put that time in though, not yet. Not until Oberon revealed the next part of his plan.

She could always shoot her way in. Security measures only mattered if you didn't want to get caught in the act and you didn't want to kill everyone who might stand in your way. Eve didn't care if the whole universe knew it was her that took Ares's ship back, but she wasn't so inhibited when it came to the loss of life. *You can hate the Corporation all you want, just don't take that hatred out on the people,* Oberon preached. Eve agreed, reluctantly.

The employees of the Corporation are just that, paid employees. The Corporation gives them everything they need, at market price, from birth until their body is unceremoniously recycled back into the food system. Everything these people have ever touched, smelled, seen, and tasted has all been provided by the Corporation. Since the dawn of the Corporation, for a hundred generations, this is the only life these people knew. They didn't have rights, they had obligations.

"Next," the guard said and waved Eve up. She walked slowly, with her head down like she was expected to, and showed the man her datapad the displayed her work schedule and level clearances. "The Corporate diner, eh?" The guard looked at her with a warm smile. "I love the rolls they got there. I don't supposed you could," the man began to say but Eve cut him off with a few soft, but firm words.

"All product inventories are careful monitored," Eve said, shutting the man down. *Nice try,* she thought. "I'm afraid." She gave the man an apologetic look as she pulled her datapad back.

"Well, if you change your mind." He left the rest of the comment open as he waved her along.

"I won't," Eve said sternly and exited the queue.

Fucking corporate bullshit, Eve cursed bitterly as he passed through the customs area. The citizens of the stacks are givens rules that are strictly enforced by the security force. In the early days of the Corporation, they were called Loss Prevention Officers. Some of the high-end executives still do. Problem is, what does the security force do when their residents actually follow the rules? How do they meet their quotas? The Customs officer's clumsy attempt at baiting her was just another example of how the security force in the stacks are actually responsible for most of the crimes they enforce.

It was sick. The whole corporate ethos down there was a perversion.

As Eve made her way to the independent sector, and transitioned from the corporate area to the free area, she couldn't help but be reminded how alike people really were. There was no real difference between the free people of the system and the corporate citizens trapped in the depths of the megastructure. They all wanted to have a stable, safe life where they are free to find love and raise a family. Eve wanted that. She couldn't have children of her own, but she could have a family. And she would want those hypothetical people to grow strong, and prosper. Oberon preached that the problem was when the people who make the rules start corrupting that need to suit their own ends. To Eve, that was human history in a nutshell. On one side, you have the good people who just want to live a good life and raise a family, and on the other you have a comparative handful of individuals who wished for something different. After beating that man half to death, Eve wondered which side she was on.

Eve walked to the public bathrooms in the independent sector, which had a bank of rental lockers along the corridor leading to the washrooms. Instead of taking out her datapad to queue up the unlock code for her locker, Eve simply touched her hand to the door and let the nanomachines make contact. The door quickly popped open and Eve pulled the small nylon satchel out of it and walked towards the ladies' washroom. Once inside, she quickly entered into one of the stalls where she slipped out of the blue corporate coveralls while asking her body to make the necessary adjustments to back to Claire Hughes, the persona she had on the Cargador. Once that was complete, Eve slipped into the comfortable set of clothes she had placed in the satchel. Once she pulled them on with the snug-fitting leather crew jacket, Eve stowed the coveralls in the satchel and walked out of the bathroom. She dropped the satchel back off in the locker she had rented.

Eve was Claire Hughes again, free to run a few errands before he headed to the room she had rented long-term for her and Evan. It wasn't anything fancy, she was trying to keep a low-profile. The independent sector on the Corporate station didn't have the same level of security the stacks had but that didn't mean she didn't have eyes on her.

Eve was maybe through half of her planned stops before she first caught sight of her tail. It didn't surprise her when she first saw them. Evan did say that there was a problem they needed to discuss before she hastily led him away. After she spotted the dark-looking man on her tail that first time, Eve had an idea what it was Evan wanted to tell her. Eve held her datapad in her hand as she went. In her mind, a piece of her was tracking them via the station's security cameras. They stayed well behind and out of sight when they could. When Eve went to an engineer she was on friendly terms with and picked up the packet he had informed her was ready to go. Eve paid the man his fee and thanked him for his service, all the while another side of her watched the two men waiting for her to exit the service docks.

They followed Eve to the accommodation section of the station, Eve quickly ducked into a local cantina and walked swiftly into the bathroom. Eve chose a new face, new nationality, and completely different hair and eye colors and walked out of the bathroom just as quickly she entered it. A few meters outside the cantina, A man with rough hands grabbed her arm from behind and pulled her around to face him.

"Where'd you get those clothes?" The tall scarred man with the greasy locks barked at her. His breath reeked of malt liquor. Eve immediately noticed the man who grabbed her had steel knuckle guard sewn into his gloves, and the man behind him wore personal body armor underneath his long coat. Eve looked at them with shock, which she quickly morphed into her best approximation of fear, as she plotted the quickest way to kill them inside her head.

"This?" She asked quickly and looked down at the arm holding her tightly in place. By his grip, the man meant business. "Some woman in the bathroom paid me a hundred credits to change clothes with her." The large man just growled loudly and looked to his comrade, who just shrugged dumbly.

"Right, fuck off then." The man angrily shoved Eve away from him before he and his companion turned and stalked back to the cantina.

Eve held her face until she got to the hotel room. She touched her hand to the door and waited for the nanomachines to open it. She changed her face back to Claire as she entered the room.

It had been quite the feat getting the large man stabilized and transferred off the station. It cost Eve a fortune in bribes, and she spent the whole trip down from the station with her datapad in her hand so she could scrub any trace of their existence from the station's logs and databases. The medical staff on the transport that took them down to the planet had put Evan into a medically induced coma so he would survive the trip. Once they were docked, Eve paid some of the nurses on the medical staff to wheel the gurney behind her as she made her way to a shady hotel she knew of.

"Don't ask," Eve said firmly to the hotel's receptionist when he glanced at the attended gurney. Her datapad pinged in her hand as Eve transferred an extra thousand credits to the receptionist's personal account. "And don't tell."

The nurses set up the gurney in the room Eve rented. It was a large room, meant mainly to be used as cheap accommodations for small crews who were stationed overnight. It had six bunks arranged around the room, a small kitchenette on the side complete with a food processor, and a door that led to the bathroom. Eve unloaded their bags onto one of the bunks as one of the nurses set up Evan's gurney that came complete with a monitoring station. The other nurse briefed Eve on the care Evan would need over the next couple weeks. She went over all the precautions Eve should take, as well as all the things she should watch out for, and gave her a lengthy list of medications the man might require. Eve thanked them for their work, and paid transferred their hush money into their accounts.

She knew that was a courtesy more than a reality. If pressed, the nurses, the hotel manager, and all the rest she paid for their silence would give them up.

"Hey, big guy," Eve said softly as she looked over to the medical gurney Evan was strapped to. The large unconscious black man just laid still and breathed deeply. She took that as a good sign. She placed the bundle in her hands on the bunk she was using as a workbench and walked over to the gurney and checked the medical display. Vitals were good. Electrolyte levels were within the specifications the nurse gave her. "How are you doing?" Eve asked gently and placed her hand on the man's exposed shoulder joint. The socket for Evan's prosthetic stood out unnaturally against the man's ebony skin and Eve could see the ugly seam of flesh where it was grafted to the metal.

Eve stepped away from him. There was nothing else she could do for him. She walked back to her makeshift workbench and looked down upon Evan's ruined arm. The golem had struck Evan's arm in such a way that it completely snapped the two internal support braces. Which functioned and were shaped similar to the human bones of the forearm. In doing so, the golem also managed to ruin every linear micro-servomotor of his forearm. The servomotors were basically the mechanical muscles of the arm. However, unlike muscle, the servomotors were not overly flexible. They were sturdy enough, but any bend past specifications rendered them utterly useless. Plus, the impact to the joint ruined the rounded hinge joint of the elbow. Every engineer Eve knew would just throw the piece away and refit Evan with a new arm.

But Evan's arms were special to him, and if it wasn't for Eve his right arm would be undamaged. Just like *he* would be.

Eve opened and unpacked the bundle. She careful placed the new forearm braces, hinge joint, and a bundle of undated servomotors for the arm onto the table. As well as a few extra pieces she had made. She had a few ideas for some improvements she could make to the arm. She'd been learning a lot of prosthetic technology as of late, and she was sure she could modify the clumsy mining rig into something that might suit Evan better.

Eve? Oberon's soft voice whispered inside her mind. *Can you talk?*

"I'm pretty sure you know I can," Eve said aloud as she pulled the small personal welding rig she procured closer.

I have your next objective. Oberon then slowly explained what he wanted done. He mentioned a name Eve recognized that caused her to frown.

"I can't help but notice a trend here. I don't suppose I get to know why we're fucking with these people like this?" Eve couldn't help the scorn in her voice.

What I can tell you is, we can't allow his family to be used as leverage against him. We need him on our side, and the only way to do that is to make sure his family is out of the Corporation's grasp.

"And this is connected to us getting Thomas and his ship back?" Eve asked cautiously.

Yes. This man is instrumental to our success.

"That's all I need to know. I'll get it done," Eve said confidently as she grabbed the laser cutter and started making her first cut on the top part of the hinge joint. She would start there and work her way down to the wrist joint. The nanomachines darkened her vision just as the laser touched the metal. "Is there anything else I need to know?" Eve felt she knew the answer, but it didn't hurt to ask.

Yes, Evan is waking up.

Then a cough came from the other end of the room. Eve turned off the laser cutter and dropped it to the bench before she rushed over to Evan's side. The man coughed once more before she made it to his side. She looked down into his dark weary eyes.

"Water," Evan said with a raspy voice.

Eve hurried to the tiny kitchenette's food processor and keyed in cold water. Eve collected the water into a sealed recyclable cup that had a straw protruding out the top. She took the cup and supported the man's head as he leaned forward to drink from it. Evan drank greedily from the cup.

"Easy," Eve warned as the big man's frame coughed once more while drinking. When he was done, Evan breathed deeply, looked at her with his still swollen face, and smiled weakly.

"Did we get the ship?"

"No," Eve said with little amusement. "You fucking idiot, we didn't get the ship. You almost died." Eve looked at the man remorsefully as she remembered that it was her actions that put him here. "I'm sorry, Evan."

"We had to try," Evan said as a consolation. Though, Eve wasn't feeling it. "I would have done the same thing. Don't worry about it. How bad is it?" He asked looking at her earnestly. Eve could see the concern in his eyes.

"You'll be fine," Eve reassured him with a light grin. "A little worse for wear maybe, but ultimately you're make a full recovery in a couple more days," Eve said remembering what the doctor had actually said. *If he wakes up, he should recover normally. If he doesn't wake up...* The doctor had left last open for Eve to interpret for herself.

"Awesome," Evan said with little excitement as he laid back onto his pillow. "So, what now? Where are we?"

"We're in the independent sector on the Corporate shipping level. I rented us a hotel room. We'll be safe here for awhile." Evan breathed in deeply and nodded.

"I have to take a piss," Evan said and looked at her. Eve just shrugged.

"Go ahead. You have a catheter in," Eve informed him with some amusement. "You've been pissing into a bag for almost a week now. One more day can't hurt."

"Great. Good to know," Evan sighed. "I don't feel much like getting up at the moment, anyway. So, I'm guessing my arm's fucked," Evan stated looked over to the empty socket on his shoulder with some remorse.

"I'm fixing it."

"You're fixing it?" Evan asked weakly with some disbelief. "How the fuck are *you* fixing it?" He coughed again. Eve quickly offered him some water, which Evan declined with a shake.

"I'm taking a crash course in cybernetic prosthetics. It's a little outside my wheelhouse but I should be able to muddle my way through." She made it a point to sound as unconvincing as possible when she said it to tease the big man.

"*Muddle your way through?*" Evan repeated her words back to her with some concern. "Boss, am I going to have to learn to wipe my ass with my left hand?"

"Couldn't hurt," Eve said with a smile and the two of them shared a laugh.

"So, what's next?" Evan asked seriously when their laughter died down.

"You know anybody who can smuggle someone out of the stacks?" Eve asked with a cocked eyebrow. Evan was a criminal after all. He just might have some connections in that area.

"A few. Maybe. The Mormons usually are willing to do that kind of work," Evan said pondering the question. Eve already knew about the Mormon's holy mission to rescue the enslaved people of the Corporation, but she also knew their price.

"We need to make contact with someone named Helena Jonlesky, who's somewhere buried in the stacks. Then we have to convince her to leave the Corporation, with her daughter, and smuggle them out of the stacks unnoticed, and get them off planet."

"That's a tall order, boss. Even if she *wanted* to leave."

"It's what our next job is," Eve said with finality.

"Do you know this woman? Is she a friend of yours or something?"

"I almost killed her husband this morning," Eve said flatly. "So, no. I wouldn't say we're friends." Eve then switched gears. "But that's for later. Right now, you need to rest."

"Boss," Evan looked at her with concern. "There's something I forgot to tell you. Something you need to know."

"That Deacon's organization has noticed his sudden absence and they are asking questions?" Eve looked at his bewildered face for a moment before she let him off the hook. "I already caught sight of their goons tailing me in the promenade. Don't worry about them. We'll take care of them if they become too much of a problem." Eve waved it off as she rose and headed back into the kitchenette. "Are you hungry?"

"Hungry enough to gnaw off my own arms, if I still had them," Evan quipped behind her.

"I'll make you some of that spicy gumbo you like." Behind her Eve heard Evan breath in deeply before he spoke with some curiosity.

"Boss, have you been welding in here?"

CHAPTER 8

Lucien

"One minute to threshold," Doctor Cattivo said switching his gaze between the readouts on his datapad and the holographic display on the table in the observation lab.

Through the large, reinforced glass that stood out prominently on the wall, they could peer into the medical room where their subject lay unconscious and strapped to the examination table. Two medical techs scurried about the room and tried to look busy. There was nothing for them to do. The nano-capsule, that's what Cattivo was calling it, was already injected into the man's brain four minutes ago. That's when Cattivo set the clock.

Lucien said nothing and watched the holographic display with great interest. The display showed a real-time, three-dimensional rendering of the man's skull cavity and brain. The nano-capsule was a marvel to observe. The medical techs injected the capsule through a syringe they pressed into the top of the eye socket. Once the syringe was in place, a mechanical solenoid punched the syringe into the prefrontal lobe of the man's brain, and the injector gently deposited the nano-capsule onto its surface. Then the magic happened. For the next four minutes, the nano-capsules utilized the ridges on its side for locomotion and slowly wormed its way into the interior of the brain. When its journey was complete, almost exactly four minutes later, the nano-capsule nestled itself on top of the cerebellum, between the parietal and occipital lobes.

"Thirty seconds," the doctor said as Lucien focused on the brightly colored display. On cue, the metallic ridges smoothed out and formed into the thin tendrils that reached out into the brain if is guided by some form of intelligence. Like it was looking for something. "Electrical activity within the brain is increasing. Fifteen seconds to threshold."

"Come on," Lucien said, quietly encouraging it to fulfill its destiny, and his.

"Three, two, one." The doctor looked up from his pad just in time to watch the display frizzle slightly. Through the viewing-window the body on the table convulsed violently once and then fell still. Cattivo's datapad sounded off with various alarms, and on the side of the holographic display red status bars came into view with their little warning chimes before a large status window opened up to inform the two men the subject had died on the table.

"Fuck!" Lucien cursed and slapped the table. Beside him, Cattivo just sighed.

"It's like the rest. Moments after implantation is complete, the nano-capsule activates and gives the subject a targeted electrical charge that effectively severs the cerebellar peduncles on both sides of the brain stem. Killing the subject instantly," Cattivo said dispassionately.

"Yes," Lucien barked. "But why?" He looked through the observation window and watched the techs rushed about the room to prepare the corpse for disposal. It was the fourth one today. "Did the scans show anything different about this one."

"No," Cattivo said with some disappointment. "I'm afraid we have already learned all we are going to learn from this approach. Of course, there are other, more intrusive methods we could use to study it. However," Cattivo said. Lucien had heard it before.

"*We risk damaging the capsule in the process*," Lucien repeated the man's words back to him. "I know. We've covered every genetic ethnic line?"

"All the ones available to us. There is one ethnic line we haven't tried yet," Cattivo said sheepishly, leaving the comment open. Lucien knew all too well what the man meant, *the Asian bloodline*. That was the only bloodline the Corporation didn't have somewhere within its ranks.

"I'll fucking destroy that thing before I put it inside someone from Earth," Lucien hissed at the man. "Even if it will most likely kill them. No. There's got to be something we're not thinking of here. Something we're missing." Lucien pondered the dilemma while his scratched his chin.

"Well," Cattivo began. "If we had a larger sample size, we could test for more variables. Right now, we're testing genetic variances, which we both agreed was a good place to start, but if it's simpler than that. Could be a specific blood type it's looking for? Or maybe it's age? Maybe it's testing the neural elasticity of the brain? Is it possible to get our hands on a few dozen children? Maybe pre-pubescent?"

"That's not a problem. There are always willing candidates on the lower stacks."

"Yes, about that," Cattivo regarded him cautiously. "I also have a few concerns with how...diluted, our genetic samples have been." Lucien cocked his eye at the man.

"There's not much we can do about that, Ernst. Unless your suggesting we haul a senior executive, or one of their children, in here so we can stroke them out on that table?" Lucien looked at the man with an incredulous expression as he simply shrugged.

"It's an idea." Lucien just looked at him and pinched the bridge of his nose. It was then Lucien's datapad pinged a connection request.

"What?" Lucien snapped angrily. On the other end of the connection he heard is personal assistant's thin voice.

"Ah," Lucas began weakly. "I have a Mr. Dennings from-." Lucien didn't give the man a chance to finish. Nor did he hide his frustration at the intrusion.

"Yeah, I know who he is! What the fuck does he want? I'm busy"

"He's waiting in your office, sir." *What?* Lucien breathed out forcibly. "He insists he has a meeting with you, sir. I didn't schedule anything for today, like you requested, I swear. He just walked into your office and demanded I contact you. Should I call security, sir?" Lucas offered without thinking about the suggestion. John Dennings was the Assistant Director from Human Resources, what was security going to do? Offer the man a cup of coffee?

It's not Lucas' fault, Lucien took a deep breath. He had little patience for fools. Lucien knew that was a failing of his. *This was bound to happen sooner or later, he can't be blamed for the poor timing.*

"Thank you, Lucas," Lucien said graciously. "You did the right thing. I'll take care of it. Offer the man some refreshments while he waits, and then call Brock and tell him to meet me there." Lucien closed the connection and rolled his eyes.

"Something wrong?" Cattivo raised an eyebrow at him.

"No, just more ladder-climbing bullshit from people with too much ambition but no real idea of how to accomplish anything." Lucien gave his Assistant Director a sly grin. "You would do yourself a service to be aware of your own rivals. You're an executive now, you'll be expected to distinguish yourself above the rest."

"I prefer my lab," Cattivo said with a bored look.

"That's my point, my friend. This isn't your lab. You follow *my* direction. If you crave true independence from oversight, you'd better take your head out of your ass and get into the race." Lucien advised the man coldly and turned to walk out of the room.

"You're not worried I may outpace you?" Cattivo asked darkly from behind him. Lucien just snorted and turned back to the man.

"If you know what's good for you, you'll stay in my shadow. That way, no one can see what you're up to." Lucien left the man to think about his words.

He had bigger accounts to close at the moment.

Lucien's designer shoes knocked loudly against the corridor's floor as he made his way past the empty labs on his way to his office. He met Jerry, Cattivo's researcher who lost his arm when the Council ship locked itself up. Lucien offered him a slight smile and the man waved back with his awkward looking prosthetic arm. Lucien paid him little attention as he passed him and soon walked through the entrance to his reception area.

"He's waiting in your office now, sir." Lucas practically jumped up from his desk when Lucien walked into the lavishly decorated waiting area. Brock was there as well, standing silently off to the side. Patiently waiting for his next order.

"Perfect," Lucien replied absently. "Did you serve him a beverage?" Lucien asked when he stopped in front of the man's desk.

"Yes, sir. A whiskey." *Whiskey? The man had expensive tastes,* Lucien thought to himself as he nodded thoughtfully.

"Top shelf?"

"Yes, sir."

"Good man," Lucien smiled and gave the man a reassuring look as he waved Brock over to his side. "No one is to disturb us," Lucien warned. "Do you understand?"

"Yes, sir."

"Good. Brock, Follow me." Lucien opened the wide double doors into his office and confidently walked through the middle with a bit of flair and a joyous look on his face as he regarded his guest. "John! Good to see you, man." Lucien walked up to the man with his right hand out in front of him.

John Dennings was a tall man. He wasn't as tall as Brock, of course, but he was certainly taller than Lucien. Dennings' hand easily enveloped Lucien's as he applied a sharp amount of pressure and pumped his fist once before he released Lucien's hand. John was on his second life, and in Lucien's opinion, too ambitious by half.

"Malum," the man's deep voice said with proper decorum. "Thank you for seeing me on such short notice."

"You left me little choice," Lucien said with a hint of venom. "This must be a matter of great importance for you to haul yourself all the way here. Please, have a seat." Lucien motioned to the chair Dennings just rose from. "What can I help you with?"

"Really," John said with an air of smugness. "I just came here to get the dimensions of my new office. There's a few items I have in my possession that I don't think will work well in such a cramped space. I may have to dispose of them," he said it like it was a real problem he was facing.

Lucien just sighed deeply and smiled. *At least we're passed the pleasantries.*

"I'm a little busy, John. You mind just telling me what the fuck this is all about, so I can get on with my day." Lucien moved around and sat behind his desk and peering at the man with cold eyes.

"Gladly, you arrogant little asshole. I know what you did," Dennings said suddenly and with a hushed voice. "I know you had William killed." Lucien raised his eyebrow. The man definitely had his attention now.

"Do you?"

"I do," Dennings said with a little grin on his face. "I know about the defect you implanted into the software of his cybernetic heart."

"Really?"

"I know about all of it," Dennings said with great satisfaction slowly crossed his legs and leaned back into his chair. Without drawing too much attention to himself, Dennings briefly rubbed his right temple, almost as if he was scratching a itch. Lucien knew better though. "I have all the evidence I need, it will be in the Chairman's hands shortly. So, there's no point denying it any further." Lucien looked at him with mild shock.

"Oh, I don't deny it. I killed William Clemente when we were at dinner together. I installed a remotely activated virus into the CPU of the heart. So, I simply had to pressed a button and he was dead," Lucien said staring at the man with an expressionless face as he confessed to his sin. "I did it to get rid of him. He was in my way, you see, and I don't tolerate things that are in my way. So, I killed him after he finished his dessert. He had an apple pie."

"Ah," Dennings was smiling with a sort of stunned expression on his face. "Well," he stammered slightly to Lucien's amusement. "It is as I said. Soon, the Chairman will have all the proof he'll need to reprimand you, and I will rise into your place. Everything that is yours, will be mine."

"You might find this of interest then," Lucien said and reached down and keyed the bottom drawer of his desk open. "It was something William left for me. So, I suppose I'm handing it down to you now." Lucien withdrew a flat square of authentic wood, a little larger than the size of his palm and held it out in front of himself. Turning it around so Dennings could get a good look at it before he placed it down on his desk in front him. "It's oak. Apparently, it was a highly valued type of wood, back when things were made out of wood." Lucien snorted at the idea. "Why don't you go ahead and place your palm on that for me," It wasn't a question but Lucien was careful with his tone so it didn't sound like a suggestion either. Dennings looked at him with an unimpressed look. "Humor me."

Dennings complied. Just like Lucien knew he would. Dennings was a tall, beautiful man. With the physique of an high-caliber athlete, a full head of thick auburn hair, emerald green eyes, and a smile that could light up a room. He was confident, ambitious, and well-liked. But he was also incredibly stupid. The fool put his palm flat against the wood panel and gently shifted his hand about, like he was caressing it. A smart man would have noticed the numerous tiny gouges in the center of the panel.

"That's does feel nice," The fool cooed numbly.

"I'm glad you like it," Lucien said while sneering at the man. Lucien then snapped his fingers and watched Brock approach quickly from behind. "Because if you take your hand off that panel, Brock will shoot you in the head." Brock then unholstered his sidearm, loudly chambered a round, and pressed the barrel hard into the back of the man's head.

"What is the meaning of this, Lucien?" Dennings complained loudly, but his hand remained in place. The man looked up to Lucien as much as Brock's pistol would allow and Dennings looked at him with a face painted red with outrage.

"There's something else I'd like to show you." Lucien reached down again and retrieved another item. Lucien displayed it so Dennings could see its long narrow blade. "Back when the Corporation had it's first name and was drilling the earth's surface for hydrocarbons of all kinds, people sent messages to each other in these little paper packets that had to be *physically* delivered. There was a whole industry set up to deliver these things." Lucien said with a measure of genuine amazement, which was genuine. Some of the things he had learned about The First World of humanity was simply incredible. "People in our position called these *letter openers*. They would use them to open these *letters*," Lucien said, unsure he was using the word correctly. Lucien absently turned the instrument in his hands, pondering the history of such a thing before he regarded Dennings again. "Although, William had an entirely different purpose for it."

Lucien then stabbed the pointed end of the instrument through the top of Dennings' hand and pushed the dull blade right through his hand until the tip plunged into the wood panel underneath. Then Lucien just held him there as the man writhed in agony.

"What the?" Dennings managed to howl in his agony. To his credit, he didn't attempt to pull his hand away. The barrel of Brock's pistol was still firmly panted into the back of his head after all. Lucien lowered himself down so his face was inches from the man's skewered hand, and he looked Dennings right in his teary, blood-shot eyes.

"Who sent you?" Lucien hissed angrily. Errant strands of spittle flew from between his teeth and landed on his desk. Dennings didn't say a word, but looked at Lucien was a deeply remorseful look. "*Who* sent you?" When the man remained silent Lucien barked at him. Taunting him. "What did you think? You could walk here, to *my* office, and record my confession with your stupid little recording device! You think I would *allow* someone to record *me* in *my own* office! How's your head, you stupid little man?" Lucien jabbed the man's forehead with the index finger of his free hand. "Got a bit of a headache? A little itch behind your eyes, maybe?" Lucien sarcastically asked the man. Dennings looked at him with a panicked expression. "What? You think I didn't know about your ocular implants? Please," Lucien shook his head at the man. "Everybody knows! I'm surprised Hendricks hasn't ripped them out of your stupid head yet." Lucien growled the name of the man's patron. When he did, Dennings looked at him like a wounded animal searching for mercy. Lucien levered the blade of the letter opener forward a bit and watched the man squirm. "You're not smart enough to have figured out anything. So, I ask you one more time, and this time you'd better tell me truth." Lucien levered the blade back again. "Who sent you?"

This time Dennings didn't hesitate.

"Bowers," He squealed loudly. "It was all Bowers' idea! Please! I didn't know anything about it." *Figures!* Bowers was Fred Johnson's candidate for his job. He was trying to position himself for the Chairman's positions. He has for generations. If he were to control Energy Development *and* Special Projects, he might be able to leverage himself into the position in a few decades.

"Call Bowers," Lucien growled.

"Wha?" Dennings looked at him with wide eyes.

"Pull out your damned datapad and call Bowers. Right now!" Lucien barked at the man while he leaned over the desk to keep his weight on the letter opener. Dennings looked at him with those sad, pained eyes and then down to his pierced hand. "With your other hand, you idiot."

Dennings used his free hand to reach awkwardly across his body and pulled the datapad from the waist pocket of his finely tailored suit. He hand shook horribly as he placed the device flat on the desk's surface and made the connection request. It pinged innocently as the request was accepted, audio only though.

"Lucien," Leslie Bowers sugary sweet voice came soon after the connection opened. "I assume it's you."

"Leslie!" Lucien said with merriment. "So, good to hear from you. How *are* you?"

"Good, good. I assume your enjoying my gift?"

"Immensely," Lucien cooed into the datapad.

"You won't mind if we switch to a secure line, do you? I'm sure you'd prefer to speak frankly." Leslie was too smart to say anything even remotely incriminating over an unsecured channel.

"You know me so well," Lucien said with an easy-going flare and waited for the secure connection request to come through. When it did, Lucien pressed his finger delicately down onto the datapad and opened it. He checked the connection status to indeed confirm the connection was secure. "Did you really think I'd just confess to all my crimes like a lower-stacker looking for a lighter sentence, Leslie? I thought we were friends," Lucien said, even managing to sound hurt. He was being somewhat genuine though. He respected Bowers, she was a cool player with a sharp eye and a quick hand. She was the closest thing Lucien had to a friend, except she was better. She was an equal. "So, you could what? Blackmail me? Do you honestly think I couldn't deal with this fool without raising someone's notice?"

"I'd be more surprised if you couldn't. Honestly, Lucien, don't be such a child. This is a gift." It was Leslie's turn to sound hurt. She did a better job of it. "When was the last time an Assistant Director came waltzing into your domain to threaten you? With no security detail, no less. You should be thanking me."

"Should I?" Lucien looked at the searching eyes of Dennings and gave him a wink and a bit of a grin. "Maybe we should have dinner tonight? So, I can thank you personally?"

"I hope that's not a threat because I could really use a bite, and you know I'm partial to the Greek salad the Lounge offers."

"A couple hours then. Say seven o'clock?" Lucien offered while giving Dennings a cold look. "I'm afraid John won't be joining us, though." At that, Leslie laughed.

"I didn't expect him to. Yes, seven sounds wonderful. See you then."

"See you then." Then the connection dropped. Lucien pulled out his datapad just as Dennings began to softly weep into his sleeve. Lucien held the man in place as he opened a channel to the lab Cattivo was working in.

"Yes?" Cattivo sounded frustrated. Lucien was hoping his news would cheer him up.

"Prep for another injection," Lucien said slowly. "I have a less *diluted* sample for you to test your theory on."

***

Lucien and Leslie ate in the Executive Lounge as the dinner service was in full swing. Senior and Junior Executives from all over the R&D sector were enjoying their meals around him, but you'd never know it by the sounds. At their table, the sound dampeners blocked out all other noises, except for the piano music softly playing in the distance. They enjoyed polite conversation, all the while knowing nobody around them were privy to their words. Leslie ordered the Greek salad, as she said she would, with a side order of the calamari, which Lucien enjoyed as well. He had a wonderful chicken stir-fry that was served with steamed vegetables over top a bed of white rice. They sipped white wine with their meals. After the tight line of waiters removed their dinnerware, they were given a drink menu. Leslie ordered a whiskey. Neat. Lucien ordered a dry martini, with two olives.

"So, I'm dying to know. Dennings?" Leslie sipped from her crystal Glencairn glass and looked at him over the rim with a mischievous expression.

Leslie Bowers, like most executives, was a true beauty. Long flowing dark hair. Soft, graceful facial features with a perfect nose and a disarming smile. An ample bosom, and a muscular physique with the dark eyes of an apex predator. As appealing as she looked, the woman was twice as smart, and three times as cunning.

"I can't say for sure, of course, but I imagine his vices will finally get the best of him. I imagine one day, maybe tomorrow, he'll be discovered by some unattractive sex worker in some low-end brothel. Dead. His propensity for illegal chems probably got the best of him." Lucien said speaking like it was all hypothetical. They both knew better.

"I wonder what the cause of death will be?"

"Stroke," Lucien said looking her in the eyes. "If one were to wager on such things, that would be my bet." Lucien took a small sip of his drink while Leslie chuckled softly. "What I can't figure out, is why you'd sent him to me at all? Surely, you could have found a better use for him than that."

"Just another piece off the board," Leslie said and smiled at him. "Everything's not about you, Lucien." She joked.

"So, this wasn't even about my Directorship?"

"It's not yours, yet." Leslie smiled back. "And no, it has nothing to do with it. Though Johnson would benefit from having me in the position, he has other ambitions. And if I'm being frank, I have no real taste for being on opposing sides of you."

"Trust me, I don't revel the opportunity to see you at your worst, either. So, what's Johnson's play?"

"He has a mole on the inside of Human Resources that's going to be promoted into the recently-vacated position," Leslie said as if bored by the prospect. Lucien was intrigued.

"And how do you know your man will be the one Hendricks promotes?"

"Because he's fucking him," Leslie said like it was the obvious answer.

"But Hendricks isn't gay," Lucien stated it as a fact. Because as far as he knew, it was.

"He is now." Leslie popped her eyebrows up once and smiled at him. "You know the pheromones they paint the servants at the soirees with?" Lucien just nodded. "I made a derivative of the compound and made it genetically specific to Hendricks. After a few months parading the man around his section, Hendricks couldn't help himself. The affair has been going on for six months now. Apparently, he's in *love*." They both chuckled at that. Lucien raised his glass to Leslie Bowers, she truly was his equal.

"Jesus Christ, Leslie!" Lucien exclaimed afterwards with humor. "So, you're not making a move on me?"

"Not this time. Johnson is happy to let you have the position, against my better advice, because he feels you'll simply hang yourself if we give you enough rope." Leslie took a sip from her glass and regarded him with a curious look. "Why, what would you have done if we did?" *It's time,* Lucien thought to himself and smiled wickedly.

"I *do* have a proposal for you. If you're interested?"

"Are you going to try and recruit me too?" Leslie smiled widely.

"I know about Jonathan," Lucien said quickly and with some remorse in his voice. He didn't relish this moment, but it had to be done. Leslie's smile disappeared from her face. "I know all about your little family you have stashed away on Ceres." Lucien gently held up his hand when he saw that Leslie was about to object. "Hear me out," he said and waited for her to settle back into her chair. Leslie watched him closely as she took another sip of her drink. "I'm not making a move against you," Lucien said with as much sincerity as he could muster. "I swear. I've known about them for a long time."

"What do you want?" Leslie said sternly, switching gears.

"I want you on *my* side. That's it. You're a great executive. Almost as good as me. I'd be a fool not to have you in my corner. I don't need anything from you. We can go forward the same way we always have. I stay out of your way; you stay out of mine. My hope, is that we could benefit from each other. Johnson isn't fixed into his position. I would see you move into that spot."

"Really?"

"Yes," Lucien said pleading with her softly. "Leslie, there is no other person I'd like by my side as I make my next move."

"Why?" She looked at him like a curious predator. "Why would I help you? Because you have hostages I care about? How long do you think that will last? Hmm?" Leslie pushed back.

"No," Lucien said with a wave of his hand. "I've already ensured nobody else will ever find out about your secret." He gave Leslie a look. "And I'll even go as far as to guarantee their safety indefinitely."

"As long as I'm under your heel?'

"No," Lucien said again displaying his soft frustration at the woman. "As far as I'm concerned, *that* matter is closed. That's my gift to you. Because we're friends, and I treat my friends infinitely better than my enemies." Lucien lowered his eyes towards her. "Which is something you should also keep in mind going forward."

"I'd like to believe you Lucien," Leslie said with a measure of sadness in her eyes. "But this game we play, the things we have to do, it makes it hard to trust someone. Especially if that someone is *you*."

"That's fair," Lucien said with a smile. "Hell, that's almost a compliment."

"How can you guarantee their safety?" Leslie asked, the slight look of concern in her eyes betraying her otherwise cool exterior.

"In all reality, I can't. Not really. Little Jonny could get run over by a tram tomorrow, for all I know. But," Lucien said reassuringly and held up a finger. "I can promise you three things with absolute certainly." As if he was preforming a magic trick, Lucien's one finger turned into three with a wave of his hand. With a cool voice he began ticking off his promises. "I can promise you, if anybody *does* find out, they won't find out from me. I can also promise that *if* somebody finds out, I will know about it before they can act on the information. Lastly, I can promise to treat your secret as if it was my own." Lucien gave the woman across from him a knowing look that promised everything, except mercy for those unfortunate enough to learn *their* secret.

"Aren't you chivalrous?" Leslie asked sarcastically. "My own white knight."

"You don't need a white knight." Lucien quipped. "Nor would I be up for the job. I only wish to be your business partner. All I can do is open my books to you so you can see where my investments lay."

"You didn't open all your books," Bowers said running her fingertip around the crystal rim of the Glencairn. "Like what's in that container you brought down from Russo station the absolute second you had the proper clearances to do so without having to declare what it actually was."

Lucien's datapad pinged a connection request.

"Do you mind?" Lucien asked politely and waited for Leslie's curt nod before he removed his datapad from the inside pocket of his coat. It was Cattivo. "Yes?"

"The medical bay called, that Jonlesky guy is out of the autodoc. He's being transferred to the lab as we speak. He should be ready to implant within a half hour." The doctor informed him dispassionately.

"Okay, I'll be down soon." Lucien dropped the connection. Bowers looked at him with a raised eyebrow.

"What are we implanting, I wonder?" Bowers pondered the question mockingly, but Lucien could see real interest there.

"Not until I know you're on my team," Lucien said and raised his glass to her. "To new partnerships."

"To new partnerships, *and* even better friendships." Bowers touched her crystal glass to his, making the sweetest bell tone that sounded off between them.

They both finished their drinks in one pull.

"Now," Lucien began to say apologetically as he set his glass down. "If you'll excuse me, Leslie, I have research I wish to return to." He rose form his seat, walked to Bowers' side and shook her hand as a farewell. "We'll talk again, soon."

"Have fun, dear."

Thirty minutes later. Lucien watched a miracle happen.

"Threshold *plus* one minute," Cattivo said, utterly stunned as he watched the holographic display along with Lucien. They were the only ones in the room. "What did we just do, Lucien? Did we... did we just make a new council member?" Cattivo turned and looked through the viewing-window into the research bay at the subject laying unconscious on the table.

Lucien just stared at the colorful holographic display of the subject's brain, and his little jewel that nestled itself safely into the center of it. As the seconds ticks away, his success sank deeper into his core. He had done it. Now he was one step closer to leveling the playing field.

"No, Ernst. We didn't," Lucien corrected the man gently. "Whatever we created, works for me." Lucien breathed deeply and tried to calm his racing mind. He felt like the person who first created a drivecore reactor. He just created this incredible power, now he had to harness it. "Ernst, I want you to remove that man's corporate ID tag, and replace it with a blank tag that we can monitor."

"What did you want his name to be?" Cattivo asked with some excitement. "Should we name him after a God as well?"

"Don't be so dramatic," Lucien said with a chuckle and rose to stand beside the man. He looked over the subject's chart that Cattivo had displayed on his datapad. "There's no need to overthink this. Just called him...Nick Jones," Lucien said. He had bigger concerns to attend to then names. "Nice and simple."

"Fine," Cattivo said, obviously disappointed. "What do you what to do with him?"

"We'll keep him sedated for the time being. He doesn't wake up until we have an idea what that nano-capsule is actually doing in there. Also, get a neuroscientist in here. I want to wipe his memories and start fresh. No point having a super-human if we can't control him. Plus, I want to change his face a bit. Nothing drastic, but I don't want someone from his old life recognizing him." Lucien looked back to the man's chart on Cattivo's datapad. "This *Nikoli Jonlesky* person is effectively dead. He died from the injuries he received during the attack while on the work crew. Make sure his wife is paid his full benefits. She deserves that much."

"You're not worried wiping that man's memories will damage the nano-capsule?"

"No. I don't think it will. It's a risk we're going to have to take. Like I said, there's no point to having him awake if he doesn't follow orders."

"But then what? Surely you don't plan to keep the man sedated forever. From what I've heard, Council members can't even be sedated. Sooner or later, we'll have to wake him up. Then what?" Cattivo looked at him like it was a genuine concern. Lucien just smiled at him warmly.

"Then," he said looking into the research bay and his new creation for the first time since his miracle happen. "Then we'll see what he can do."

CHAPTER 9

Nick Jones

He woke up on a table, looking up into the bright glare of an examination light. He didn't know how he knew it was an examination light. To his knowledge, this was the first time he had seen one. And yet, he just knew.

There were three other people in the room. He didn't know who they were. They had never seen them before, nor did he know what they were doing here with him. For reasons he couldn't explain, their presence didn't alarm him. *They should be there,* something small inside him advised.

He looked over his body. He was wearing a white gown, and nothing else. He made a fist when he looked down to his hand. *Yep, those seem to work.* From there he looked down to his toes, and wiggled the clumsy digits. *Everything seems to be in order,* he thought to himself. He briefly considered sitting up, but decided against it. He was comfortable after all, and he didn't see a real need to sit up. Beside which, maybe he wasn't supposed to sit up.

There was a loud click in the distance that was quickly followed by the sound of a door opening. Loud footsteps entered the room and he looked in the direction of the sound. He saw a small well-dressed man with blonde hair neatly arranged into a fashionable hairstyle about his head. He was younger than the other people in the room, but he was quick to notice that the other people avoided the man's eyes. All except one. The older one with the hawkish face walked right up to them and they talked in hushed tones. *That one looks important,* he thought to himself as he admired the young man's grey suit that shimmered in the light like it was wet.

As they talked, he watched them closely. There was an object in the hawkish man's hand. *His datapad,* something inside his head informed him. His datapad shifted in his hands and he briefly saw the screen. He held the picture inside his mind, it was a cranial scan. Again, how he knew this eluded him. *That's me,* he thought. That was his scan. A digital representation of his brain. The scan of from the right side, showed part of his brain that he knew he could identify if he wanted to. But that's not what caught his eye. In the interior, near the brainstem was a brightly colored root-like formation that spread out into the rest of his mind. *What's that I wonder,* he thought to himself as the two men looked over to him a couple of times while they continued to speak. He just numbly returned their looks. When their business was concluded the well-dressed man broke off and walked towards him.

"Do you understand me?" The man said sternly, looking down his nose at him.

He nodded slowly twice.

"Can you speak?" The blonde man snorted. He seemed frustrated.

"Yes."

"Perfect," the man said quickly and rolled his eyes. "Your name is Nick Jones. Repeat it back to me."

"Perfect, Your name is Nick Jones." He repeated the man's words back to him as ordered. The hawkish man snickered in the background, but he was silenced when the blonde-haired man shot him a look.

"Are you trying to be funny?"

"No," he said. *Nick Jones. My name is Nick Jones. Nick Jones. Nick Jones. Nick Jones,* he said the name a few times inside his head. Thinking the name would mean something to him. It was his *name* after all. He, Nick, would have thought the name would have a spark of recognition to it. It didn't.

"No, *sir*!" The man standing over him barked. "I'm an executive after all, and that's how you address executives." Executives *within The Corporation*, he finished the man's sentence. He was part of The Corporation. The Corporation had a megastructure, on Mars, the fourth planet from the sun. It was inside a volcano, a big one, maybe the biggest. People referred to them as *the stacks*. Nick's train of thought was interrupted when the man continued. "You're not stupid, are you?"

"No," Nick said, hoping that was the right answer. "Sir."

"Good," the man said as if it genuinely pleased him. "Because I'm going to be honest with you, and I need you to understand the gravity of your situation." The man regarded him with a questioning look. Nick didn't know how to respond to him so he just nodded. "First off, my name is Lucien Malum, I'm the Director of Special Projects in the Research and Development Sector of the Corporation." He stepped closer and offered his hand to Nick. He briefly looked at it before Nick reached over his body and shook the man's hand. Nick was surprised he just seemed to know how to do the motion. He didn't recall ever shaking anyone's hand before.

"Nice to meet you," Nick said automatically. Even though, he didn't really feel like it was.

"For all intents and purposes, I'm your boss."

"Okay," Nick said, looking up at the man. "Who's that guy?" He asked and nodded his head towards the hawkish man looking on intently in the background.

"That's Doctor Ernst Cattivo, my Assistant Director, and the lead researcher on this project."

"Project?"

"You," Mr. Malum said, and Nick pondered why his brain instinctively chose the formal title.

"I'm a *project*?" Nick looked at him with a curious expression

"You're an experiment," Mr. Malum said with a considerable amount of venom. "And since I'm being honest, I have to tell you, it isn't going great."

"It's not?"

"Not really," Mr. Malum said with an animated disappointment. "No."

"Hey, if this is going to be bad news, you mind if I sit up for it?" Nick asked calmly. Mr. Malum simply nodded. Nick looked over to the other one, Cattivo. He was watching on with great interest.

"Be my guest."

Nick groaned loudly as he levered himself to a seated position. Weak muscles pulling on stiff joints that felt like a collection of rusty hinges. He grabbed the side on the table to help pull himself up. He thought the effort was a lot harder than it should have been. Nick felt the eyes of the two men on him as he moved into position. Nick had to agree with Mr. Malum, if he was an experiment of some kind, it didn't feel like it was going well.

"Weak as a kitten, aren't you?" Mr. Malum said with obvious disapproval. Nick said nothing. He didn't want to draw any more attention to the effort than he already had. "I suppose

it's to be expected though, you *were* sedated for quite awhile."
Nick looked at him with a curious expression. Two questions
immediately popped into Nick's head. *How long was I out for?*
A week? A month? Longer? It was quickly followed by the next
obvious question. To him, anyway. *Why wake me now?* Nick
didn't voice any of these concerns though. By the theatrical
way the man spoke, Nick got the impression Mr. Malum liked
the sound of his own voice. It was probably best to just let
the man speak. Nick also got the distinct impression that the
man didn't like to be interrupted. "It is the consensus of my
research staff that the sedatives are somehow impeding our
progress. My esteemed colleague," Lucien began and quickly
motioned back to the hawkish man. "Even went as far as to
suggest your progress would benefit greater from your *active*
participation." *That was nice of him,* Nick thought skeptically
as he gave the man a small wave.

"Do I get to know the nature of the experiment?" Nick
asked and looked back to the blonde-haired man standing in
front of him. He looked once to Cattivo, Nick followed his
glance just in time to catch the man's curt shake of his head.

"No," Mr. Malum replied sharply. "The nature of the
experiment is immaterial, and your awareness of it might affect
the results. Which we can't have."

"So, what *is it* I'm supposed to do exactly?" Nick asked with
a dull expression. Mr. Malum leaned in closer.

"You're very best, My boy." He was smiling when he said it
but his eyes weren't so jovial. *Don't fuck up,* those eyes warned
Nick. "Absolutely nothing else will do. Everything you do from
this point on, no matter what task we put in front of you, you
must do it to the absolute best of your abilities. If you succeed
in this." Mr. Malum looked at him with a wild expression.
"If this experiment proves to be everything I think it will, if
you become everything I think you will, you'll be the single
most important person within the corporate structure. You,"

he said with some enthusiasm and placed his hand on Nick's shoulder. "Will bring The Corporation into the next era of human evolution." Nick waited until the man was done then he regarded him grimly.

"And if I fail?" He asked gently but with genuine curiosity. Nick watched as Mr. Malum's expression darkened.

"The *recycler*," he said firmly. "Where your body will be broken down into its base components before it is added to the Corporation's nutrition stock. That way," he began to say as a consolation. As if the news should cheer Nick up. "At least the Corporation will gain some benefit from your existence." Nick waited to ensure the man didn't have more that he wanted to add.

He didn't.

So, that was the deal. Nick breathed deeply as he pondered the last five or so minutes. Which, as far as he knew, was his entire existence. He opened his eyes, was quickly informed he was a failing experiment that couldn't fail any more. From this point on, his very existence depended on how well he performed in whatever tasks they had laid out for him. If he did well, he would become some superstar to this Corporation. If not, that would be end of him.

Nick felt like some part of him should be upset with this deal. Like the many questions he had swirling in the ether of his head should take some importance over his current situation. He didn't even know who he was. Sure, his name was Nick Jones. He knew that much, but as he searched the depths of his memory, he couldn't find any other piece of information about himself. Hell, he didn't even know what he looked like. Nick questioned whether or not he would recognize his own face.

The recycler, Nick remembered the man's words. He didn't know what that was, but that wasn't important right now. What he had to do right now was clearly laid out for him. He had to preform. He could figure the rest out later, but right now he had to focus on what was in front of him like his life depending on it. Because as Mr. Malum carefully explained, it did.

"What do I have to do?"

They gave him a new set of clothes and showed him to his accommodations. Nick wasn't expecting much. He was an experiment after all. The Special Projects people didn't disappoint. They assigned him to another lab further down the hall. This lab was smaller than the one he had woken up in. When he first walked in, the room still had an antiseptic smell to it. They had cleared out everything that was in the room and the only furnishings it had were a small cot for him to sleep, a small table with two chairs where he was supposed to eat his meals, and there was also a plain table that was supposed to serve as a desk. On its surface Nick found the datapad they had assigned to him. He looked to the large observation window that stood out prominently on the one wall. Beyond the window were a couple research techs that were still in the process of setting up their work stations. Nick gave them a slight wave when they looked his way. They responded by adjusting the window's settings so his side of the window switched to a mirror. He had no doubt that on the other side, the techs could see him clearly. He wasn't bothered by it though.

Nick was too busy gazing at his reflection.

In the mirror, he saw the dumbfounded expression of a middle-aged white man with a medium build. Well, maybe a little lighter than medium. He was a taller man, but looking in the mirror he would describe himself as lanky, bordering on downright skinny. Nick walked closer to the reflection and was reminded of the effort required to simply lift himself up. He stopped in front of the mirror and looked upon Nick Jones. *Well, I definitely look like a failed experiment,* Nick thought to himself as he looked upon his pale features. He had high cheeks bones, a strong-looking jaw line, and dark blue eyes set deep into his skull. As he looked on, he believed he had quite a few features that would normally be pleasing to look upon, but the fact of the matter was that he looked ghastly ill. *How fucking long did they keep me asleep?* Nick wondered bitterly as he explored the surface of his face. There was a small scar above his left eyebrow, it was barely noticeable. Nick wondered how that mark came to be, he felt he should know. It was his skin after all. He felt he should know the story behind it. Nick wondered if anybody here knew the story behind that mark. And if someone did, would they tell him?

You don't have time for this, Nick thought to himself. The revelation came suddenly and caused a sharp breath. *You don't have the luxury of worrying about what's missing.* The tests start tomorrow. *You need to perform. Jump through whatever hoops these geeks set up for you, and do it well. Once we get to a point we don't have to worry about being quietly euthanized and fed into a recycler, then we can worry about the gaping holes in our memory.*

"Hey," Nick called loudly to the techs behind the mirror and rapped soundly on the window. "Any chance a guy can get something to eat around here?"

A moment later a tech punched in his code and the entrance into the room opened. The tech had his meal in her hands. Apparently Nick was on a strict high-calorie, high-protein diet, and he was thrilled with the portions. The downside of his meal was that it had the consistency of apple sauce. Nick didn't know what he was hoping for. As far as he knew, this was the first meal he had ever eaten.

"Easily digestible, nutrient-rich, food paste," the tech said almost apologetically as she placed his meal on the small table.

Nick didn't care. He was ravenous.

Nick learned his new schedule fairly quickly, and by the end of the third day the routine had become apparent, though each day the task given for him to complete changed, sometimes wildly. The mornings were reserved for the mental testing.

Each day the good doctor and his geek squad came up with a variety of ways to test him. Some days it was as simple as putting a puzzle together. Other days he was to read a report or a fictional story and write a report on the contents of what he had read. On rare occasions, they presented him with an object and he was to sketch or paint that object onto a piece of paper, or canvas. Nick liked those days the best. Each task was timed.

He had his pasty *high-calorie, high-protein* lunch at noon sharp, and he was able to enjoy it in the comforts of his quarters. Nick usually like to eat while reading on his datapad. All the while knowing that the techs behind the observation window were watching his every move.

The afternoons were for the physical education. Every day after lunch, Nick was led to the auditorium. It was a giant square room with stone walls and artificial sunlamps on the ceiling for light, and heat. Each day Cattivo would have some obstacle course for him to complete. On the far wall, was a large digital readout that displayed the time Nick had to complete the course in. Every time Nick went into that room it was different. Some days it was covered with sand. Other days the whole auditorium would be covered in grass of varying lengths. On some occasions, the room was bitterly cold and every surface was covered with white particles of ice inches deep. Nick didn't care for those days. Whatever the terrain, whatever the obstacles, Nick raced against that damned clock to complete the task.

Each day there was a tiny progression. So miniscule it was hard to notice the escalation day to day. At the end of the first two weeks though, Nick looked back on the first tasks he was given and they were almost polite by comparison to what he was doing now.

The mental task became much more complicated. The puzzles became larger and more intricate. There was a particular puzzle the vexed Nick. It had a thousand metal pieces, it was three-dimensional, and each piece was disturbingly similar to the one next to it. When completed, he should have a triangle about three feet tall. Nick had four hours to complete the puzzle. The frustrating part, and the crucial detail Nick didn't realize until it was too late, was that the puzzle had to be assembled in parts. There was a base, the flat part at the bottom, the middle section comprised of three pieces that had to be assembled first, and then put together, and lastly, the tip. Once all three were assembled, Nick imagined that they would all just snap together. He never got to see it completed. His time ran out. Nick worked to the bitter end, and when his failure became a reality, he cursed and swept the puzzle off the workstation, letting it fall to pieces on the ground.

The cute little book reports were replaced with several pages of multiple-choice questions. They were followed by a series of essay questions that had to be answered on whatever subject the textbook he was given was about. That was also when the math started in earnest as well. Nick didn't mind that so much. He thought it would be more cumbersome but once the Corporate Mathematical Doctrine was explained, it became simply a matter of doing the work.

Then, of course, his pasty meal in his room with the geeks, which, by now, Nick greeted every time he entered the room.

"Geeks," Nick would say as a casual greeting and give the observation mirror a curt wave. He had yet to receive a response.

Then came the physical trials of the afternoons. Nick's steady diet of high-calorie, high-protein, low-taste food paste, coupled with the daily bouts of exercise put him back into shape pretty quick. By the end of the first two weeks, he was visibly bigger than he had been when he first woke up on that table. He was stronger, faster, and he moved through the obstacle courses like nimble jungle cats he would read about sometimes.

Nick had about an eighty percent success rate on the physical trials. Some trials, Nick felt, were designed for him to fail.

One that stuck out in his mind, Cattivo's proudly referred to as the Theseus' ship trial. Nick didn't know why, but whatever the reason, the man was quite tickled with the it. Nick was tasked with assembling a giant, wooden ship. The kind which were used on earth to traverse the water during its ancient periods. Nick was given large, heavy, pieces of wood and iron slide pins to lock the pieces into place. Once the ship was created, Nick was to hook up a think length of rope to its bow and drag it across a series of logs over the finish line. The logs were supposed to roll with the ship, making it easier to pull. Nick didn't know about that. He couldn't budge the ship one inch in the hour and a half that remained to complete the task. He grunted, strained, cursed, and howled at the observation booth. But in the end, the ship remained where Nick had assembled it.

By the end of the third week, Nick faced Cattivo's last physical trial. When Nick heard it would be the final trial he grew concerned.

"What do you mean the *final* trial?" Nick asked Cattivo as his little entourage led him down the corridor to the auditorium.

"What part of the statement are you confused about?" Cattivo replied absently as he eyed his datapad.

"Don't fuck around with me, Doc." Nick grabbed the man's arm and halted him. Cattivo was caught off-guard by the move and almost dropped his datapad. Then, of course, one of the guards had to step in.

Nick had little patience for the guards, or their shocksticks.

"You want to touch me again, dipshit?" Nick growled at the guard as he slapped the man's hand off his wrist. Nick stepped up to him. The guards were only wearing personal armor. Nick knew Mr. Malum didn't allow powered armor in his section because someone could easily hack the suit and turn them into a walking surveillance device. Personal armor didn't have visors on the helmets. So, Nick could see the fear in the man's eyes. Nick grinned when he noticed the guard's hand drift down to the stick at his side. "Do it," Nick hissed at the man, daring him to pull the stick free. "See what happens." Both Nick and the security staff were aware that the shocksticks had little effect on him anymore. Nick couldn't explain it. Maybe he developed a tolerance to the voltage, but whatever it was, they didn't stop him like they used to. Now the sudden jolt just pissed him off. Of course, if all four of the guards were to shock him at once, that might do it. It had yet to happen.

"Calm down, everyone." Cattivo pushed Nick and the guard apart. "Seriously," he complained loudly and he looked to Nick first, and then to each of the guards assigned to him. "These infantile displays of dominance really need to come to an end. I grow weary of babysitting grown men who should be capable of fulfilling their duties without conflict, *or* supervision. "And you?" Cattivo turned to Nick. "What has gotten into you? Grabbing me like that." The doctor looked at him with muted shock. Nick could tell by his expression that he was waiting for an answer.

"What do you mean my final trial?" Nick asked again. "Like the last one. If I fail this one, it's off to the recycler?" Nick frowned at the man.

"What?" Cattivo looked at him dumbly before he shook his head. "No," he said firmly and pinched the bridge of his nose. "I meant, it's the last trial that I have *prepared* for you. I supposed, given the circumstances, the miscommunication could be forgiven." Cattivo then turned back down the corridor and continued walking. Nick, like the rest of the entourage, simply kept step with him.

"Well, that's generous of you," Nick said sarcastically falling into step beside the doctor. "I've been jumping through your damned hoops for almost a month now, and I have no idea if I'm even doing well. The whole time, the threat of being recycled is hanging over my head. I'm tired of it, Ernst. When is it going to be enough?" Nick asked the man with some venom.

Ernst just snorted.

"You think you're the only one with some threat over their head? Hmm? Do you really assume that the rest of us don't have to perform as well, in one fashion or another?" Cattivo motioned to the other people in the entourage. Guards and research staff alike. "Because if that's the case, than despite what your test results have been showing, you are not getting any smarter," Cattivo said with a brief smile, obviously pleased with his subtle wit. "Like the rest of us, your continued existence in your position should be sufficient enough to know you are meeting expectations. Besides which, if this was your *final* test," Cattivo said stressing the ominous nature of the word. "Do you really think I'd contaminate the experiment by *telling* you?" *He's got a point there,* Nick thought to himself.

The good doctor led them the rest of the way, without incident, to the auditorium. Cattivo cycled the door to open, and motioned Nick through the entranceway before he followed behind.

"What the fuck is this?"

The wide, cavernous space, for the first time, was utterly empty. Nick quickly noticed that the half of the floor was painted a deep red color, and at the other end of the room, the last half was painted blue. A wide, black line went down the center to separate the two sections. In the distance, standing before the dark line, was a small figure in a guard's uniform. Nick could see that the man was wearing a featureless grey covering over his face that hid everything.

"Who's that guy?" Nick asked nodded towards the figure as the two of them approached it.

"*That,*" Cattivo started to say as he came to a stopped a good distance away from the lone figure. "Is a Golem. A cybernetic being, with the most advanced bipedal drone chassis the Corporation has every produced. It's been uploaded with every fighting method known to the Corporation. All in all, it's quite a formidable foe. Costs a fortune to make," Cattivo said with a shake of his head.

"Cybernetic? You mean there's a person in there?" Nick asked looking at the still figure.

"Hardly, a brain and a spinal column. It was at the beginning of the Corporation attempts into AI soldiers. It has a primitive AI that utilizes the brain and neural tissues for complex problem-solving and motor functions. There is no consciousness present though. None that modern science has been able to discern, anyway."

"So, what? Am I supposed to beat it up?" Nick asked and Cattivo just laughed.

"No," he said still chuckling somewhat. "That would be quite impossible. Your final task Nick is to simply cross that line behind the golem. It has been set to level one conflict resolution. Grappling and body shots mostly, with no real intent to injure."

"Good to know."

"But," Cattivo said and looked at Nick sternly. "It has been instructed not to let you pass that line."

"That's it?" Nick asked looking back to the slim-looking figure. "Just get passed that little guy over there and reach the blue section?"

"Correct," Cattivo confirmed promptly. "By any means necessary. Good luck." The good doctor turned without further word and walked towards the entrance. Which he promptly sealed behind him.

Nick just smiled at the lone figure, who was standing mere feet from the line Nick was supposed to cross. *Fuck it,* Nick thought to himself before he started towards this golem thing at a full run. His battle plan was simplicity in itself. He was just going to barrel towards it and steamroll right into it. Nick wasn't going to try and deke around the thing, it was probably was ready for that, and its fancy cybernetic body was probably much faster than his. Nick was going to run at it at full steam, collide into it and hauled its stupid little body over that line. How much could that thing possibly weigh?

The golem didn't waiver. The only motion it took was to drop into a slight stance and bend its knees a little. Nick lowered his shoulder and collided with the its midsection with all his weight. Nick only had to push the thing back maybe four feet until he was home free.

He maybe got two inches.

Something in Nick's shoulder painfully popped as his momentum abruptly halted. He didn't notice at the time, but the golem somehow managed to hook its arms on the inside of Nick's. Once all the force left his body, Nick felt the golem's hand grab a fistful of the material of his coveralls before it lifted him right off his feet. His legs kicked below him, and Nick uselessly struck the golem's forearms, looking down into its featureless, cold face.

Then it slammed Nick to the ground and darkness quickly folded in from the edges of his vision.

The next day didn't go much better. Like he suspected the previous day, there was no deking around this thing. It was simply too quick. Nick tried starting at one end of the room, and sprinted parallel along the line. The golem effortlessly kept up with him, Nick pushed ahead fractionally and dove for the line. That had been a mistake. The golem threw itself and collided hard with Nick in midair and brought him to the ground. Nick felt something snap in his side as the golem landed on top of him like a large rock. Crushing him. Nick had to be carried out of the auditorium.

The day after that, and against Cattivo's advice, Nick fought with it. He just walked up to it and start throwing punches at it. The golem moved like it knew what was coming, and each time he had a perfect counter for Nick's attacks. Each time it countered one of Nick's attacks, it sent a fist into his midsection, or some times into the meat of his thigh muscle, or maybe the inside of Nick's bicep. This little bastard seemed to know all the places it could hurt a person with a little jab. Undeterred, Nick pressed on. Taking the blows the Golem gave him, all the while slowly positioning himself into place. When Nick was in the spot he had picked out, he sent a heavy hook to the golem's head. It ducked under with ease before punching Nick in the stomach. It was all part of the plan. Nick took the shot and as the Golem weaved away, as was its habit, Nick dove for the line. He was close. Closer than he ever been. Then the golem's hand enviably clamped down around his ankle, effectively stopping all his momentum midair. Nick crashed down to the floor, mere inches from the line. He crawled for the line but the golem simply reached down and grabbed a fistful of his coveralls by his hip and pulled him back. It pivoted quickly, swung Nick around with utter ease, and tossed his flailing body into the air.

Well, that's a dick move, Nick thought as he briefly sailed through the air. He landed hard and his collarbone snapped like a twig. Nick refused the geeks assistance and walked himself to the medbay that day.

In the days that followed, Nick walked swiftly to the auditorium, some days he even led the entourage. He was eager to get to it. Other days that stupid black line was the only thing he could focus on. The mental work in the mornings had become slightly more then tedium, but it wasn't enough to take his mind off that fucking golem. In his mind, the golem became Nick's bitter rival. The one thing standing in the way of his success. Each day he tried, and each day when he failed, the burning frustration he felt inside himself kicked up a level.

After a while, Nick walked to the auditorium in utter focus, like a man going to war. Because he was. Each day he went to war with that damned thing, and each day when he lost, he learned something new. Some new little tidbit he could take back to his room and use to formulate a new approach for the following day. Every night he stared at the ceiling and envisioned himself beating that stupid robot into pieces.

Nick didn't tell anyone, but recently he hadn't had the need to sleep. He couldn't explain it. He fell into his bed each night. It's not like his body didn't need to rest, it did. Nick could lay his head down, close his eyes for as long as he wanted. The whole time his weary body melted into the comfort of the bed. But sleep wouldn't come. Nick didn't even yawn anymore.

Nick looked at the darkened ceiling. It was too dark in the room for the geeks behind the wall to see that he was awake. At least, he thought so. If the geeks behind the mirror knew about his insomnia, they made no show of it. Surely, the good doctor would have mentioned something about it, if he knew. Nick couldn't be bothered with that now. Like most nights his thoughts were consumed with the prospect of beating the golem. On several occasions, Nick had to remind himself that the golem's response level was set fairly low. If that thing wanted it, Nick would be dead ten times over by now. *How do I beat this thing?* Nick angrily thought about the seemingly impossible task of beating the golem. *No,* Nick corrected himself, *I don't have to beat it. I just have to get passed it. But how?* Not for the first time, Nick confused the golem with an actual opponent. The cybernetic marvel wasn't his enemy, it was simply an obstacle he had to figure out how to get around. In that sense, the golem was no different then one of Cattivo math problems. Nick ran over the problem in his head for the thousandth time. *I have to get over the line. The golem won't allow me to get across the line. I can't beat the golem.* It was a hard truth but Nick had to accept it. *I HAVE to get over that line,* Nick agonized in the darkness. But the task was impossible because the golem wouldn't let him over that line. *Wait a minute,* Nick thought as a spark ran through his head suddenly. *What was it Ernst said exactly, "It has been instructed not to let* you *past that line."*

Then it hit him like a lightning bolt, and suddenly the next morning couldn't come fast enough.

"You're in a good mood today," Cattivo said with genuine interest as they made their way to the auditorium. The good doctor, was right. Nick was in a good mood.

Today was the day, Nick could feel it.

"I'm feeling good about today," Nick said with a sly grin as they approached the airlock door for the auditorium. The good doctor stepped forward and punched in his code and cycled the door open.

"That's good," the doctor said absently as he waved Nick through the entranceway, as was his habit for this trial. Nick should have picked up on that sooner, this was the only trial Ernst escorted him personally into the room. As was their way, Nick and Cattivo walked into the room together for a short distance.

"Yep, I think I got your little friend over there all figured out, Doc." Nick stepped closer to the man and slid his arm around the thin man's shoulders. Nick could hear the guards behind them come to attention but Cattivo waved them off quickly.

"What do you think you're doing?" Cattivo looked to Nick with concern in his eyes and gently tried to pull away. Nick held the man fast and forced walked him towards the golem.

"Relax, Doc," Nick said and led the man towards the golem with his arm still firmly around the man's shoulder. Holding him in place. "We're just going for a little walk." The golem turned slightly and regarded the approaching duo. Nick swallowed hard and prayed his hunch was right. "You said the golem wouldn't let *me* past," Nick said to the man casually as they approached the cybernetic guard. "But you never said anything about yourself. So, I'm willing to bet the golem won't lay a fucking finger on me as long as your with me."

Nick felt the man stiffen beneath his arm as they approached the golem. Nick eyed the damned thing, his bitter rival, as he diverted slightly so their new path passed along the golem's right side. Nick didn't slow his pace, and he wouldn't allow the doctor's shuffling steps to slow him either. Nick smiled at the golem as they stepped up beside it, and then they walked slowly past its motionless body.

Nick escorted the doctor across the line, after which, Nick eased his grip on the good doctor and Ernst quickly pulled away from him. Nick noticed the man was breathing hard.

"You reckless fool!" Cattivo shouted. "I didn't program the golem with any such stipulation!"

"You didn't?" Nick questioned the man with genuine surprise.

"No!"

Behind them, they two men heard the echoing sounds of clapping. Nick turned to see Mr. Malum clapping his hands together slowly as he approached them. *Why do I only think of him as Mister Malum? I know his first name.* Nick eyed the man suspiciously as he drew closer. Today, he wore a dark suit, tailored to perfection. As usual. Mr. Malum's matching tie had a tight little knot at the man's throat. Nick didn't like the way the man was smiling. When he neared, Mr. Malum broke down into a brief chuckle.

"The look on your face, Ernst, was priceless."

"I could have been killed!" Cattivo angrily snapped back. The good doctor was still recovering from the tense episode.

"You?" Nick looked the doctor outraged before he pointed towards the motionless cybernetic sentry. "That thing has been kicking my ass all week," Nick frowned at the doctor's display before he turned to the other man. "You have something to do with this?"

"Me?" Mr. Malum said innocently and with some amusement. "I suppose, in a way, I did. A long time ago, I *did* add a parameter to the golem's program that stipulated it was, under no circumstances, to engage with a registered executive of the Corporation. It was more of a self-preservation measure at the time. But I assure you," Mr. Malum said was a hearty chuckle. "Ernst over there had no knowledge of it." He laughed again.

"It's not funny," Cattivo said brushing himself off like he was ridding himself of the anxiety of a moment ago. "What if that *thing* attacked?"

"You don't think I'd keep you safe, Doc?" Nick looked at the man with a wounded expression. "We're friends after all. Right, Ernst?" Nick eyed the man. Cattivo straightened his lab coat and avoided Nick's gaze.

"Yes, well, I don't make it a habit to entrust my safety to the altruistic nature of my *friends*." Cattivo said the word like it was a curse of some kind. Mr. Malum just chuckled again and slapped the man on the back.

"I think the good doctor is just upset that you outsmarted his little test," Mr. Malum looked to Nick was a smile. "Excellent work, Nick. Listen," he said taking on a more serious note. "I understand there's been some frustration about your situation. Trust me, my boy, I understand. But we need you at your very best. Do you know what makes diamonds, Nick? Pressure. That's what we've done here." Mr. Malum motioned around them with pride. "We've created a fucking diamond. You, Nick. Which is why I'm here." Mr. Malum regarded Nick and Cattivo equally. "You're ready for the next phase of your training."

"What?" Cattivo barked suddenly. "Lucien, we've talked about this." The good doctor gave Nick a bit of a side-eye before he continued. "There are certain behavioral anomalies that need to be addressed. There have been *incidents*, Lucien." *Behavior anomalies?* Nick frowned at the man and wondered if this had something to do with the spats he had with the guards in the past. "We have to investigate the root causes of some of these anomalies, and then we need to determine the best courses of action to correct them before we proceed any further." It was clear to Nick that the good doctor wasn't expecting this new turn of events, and he wasn't happy about it.

"I've read the reports, Ernst. Unfortunately, our hands are tied in the matter."

"*Our* hands?"

"Ernst," Mr. Malum shot the man a warning expression. Nick could almost feel the air between the men thicken. "This is neither the time nor place for this discussion. I don't normally entertain discussions about my decisions, but I've allowed you certain concessions based on our relationship," The perfectly dressed blonde-haired man said sternly. "But don't push it."

"What's the *next* phase?" Nick chimed in. Breaking the silence between the men.

"I've arranged for your *tactical* training to begin. I have an associate you're going to meet in about a half hour. A Colonel Soldado, a personal friend, he runs the Special Operations Unit of the Security Sector. In the mornings you will report to him in the Security Sector where he will train you in all manners of combat, as well as familiarize you with the plethora of firearms at their disposal. In the afternoons, you will run through operational drills with his unit. And, if needed, you might assist with some operations I authorize. Any questions?"

Nick couldn't think of any, none that were worth answering. Nick would get the answers to those questions with time. He found it hard to focus on anything right now. *I'm leaving the section,* Nick thought excitedly. Ever since he woke up, Nick had been looking at the same dozen faces for a month. During his downtime, Nick read a lot of articles about The Corporation's megastructure, personal media blogs from various citizens of the stacks, as well as kept up with some of the local new reports.

He found Stack Four's new reports particularly interesting for some reason.

"Nope," Nick replied quickly.

"Perfect. Go wait in your quarters until the Colonel get here and we can make the introductions," Mr. Malum said as a way to dismiss him. Nick looked at him for a moment longer before he turned and walked away.

As soon as he did. Nick heard Cattivo speak up venomously behind him.

"This is a mistake."

CHAPTER 10

Eve

"I think this a bad idea, boss." The big man's anxiety was practically radiating off of him.

Evan walked awkwardly beside her as they made their way through the central promenade of the independent sector. The evening rush was in full swing as hordes of corporate workers, easily identifiable in there differently colored coveralls, made their way to the customs checkpoints.

"So you've said," Eve quipped lightly and looked over to her companion.

Evan's new arm swung naturally, and silently, by his side. Eve admired her work proudly. Despite its more *natural* appearance, she assured Evan that one hundred percent of his old arm was in there. Eve had added an exterior bracing for added support and protection. She painstaking fit custom titanium panels to it for even more protection as well as to give the arm a more natural look. The wrist and hand were the hardest part of the whole build. There were dozens of independently-articulating joints that made creating the exterior superstructure, as well as all the tiny pieces for the shielding for the finger joints, quite a challenge. Eve was now on a first name basis with the fabrication engineer who's been making the parts to her specifications.

Evan liked it so much, he insisted Eve do his left arm as well. That was why Evan was walking with a weird jaunt. His left arm was back on the table back in the room Claire Hughes had rented for the foreseeable future. Eve was about halfway done the refit.

"Yeah, that's because I *really* think it's a bad idea," Evan said stressing the word.

"Is that why you're wearing body armor?" Eve asked giving the man a grin. She watched with amusement as the large black man looked at her as if she caught him with his hand in the cookie jar.

"Well, yeah." Evan sounded slightly hurt. "Because that's the smart thing to do when you walk into a den of thieves with someone they want dead, and you only have one arm. Like, couldn't this have waited until my other arm was done. You haven't even made contact with this chick in the stacks your supposed to smuggle out." Eve cocked her eyebrow at Evan's poor choice of words. Evan immediately caught it. "Sorry, the *woman* in the stacks. Whatever. My point is, we shouldn't rush into this."

"I'm not rushing," Eve said defensively.

"You're literally rushing towards the bar they're at. What the fuck is the hurry?" Evan complained. Eve just snorted at him. "Boss, *what's wrong*?" Eve stopped abruptly and Evan stopped beside her. There was something in the way he asked the question. Like how a friend would. It caught her off guard. Eve allowed herself a shuttered breath before she looked up at Evan with stinging eyes.

"I found out this morning that someone I loved very much is not coming back."

It happened in the early hours of their sleep period. Eve was laying in her bunk scanning over some technical schematics she found while the big man slept. Eve was thinking of incorporating a small retractable blade into Evan's left arm, she was perusing some possible triggering mechanisms. Then she felt it. The tiny spark of intelligence from Thomas' motherbot reaching out into the ether.

Thomas' motherbot had found a new host.

The realization hit Eve like a tonne of bricks because she could immediately feel that it wasn't Thomas reaching out. The Council members were connected...somehow. Whether it was a psychic connection or a simple data connection between their individual motherbots, Eve didn't know. They all felt Ares' loss, internally. Just like she was certain they all felt this new, infantile motherbot reaching out. Only one of them could answer it though. Eve knew Oberon had made contact, and transferred the operational codes for the motherbot to accept its current host. Because, like the rest of them, she felt the transfer being completed. It felt like a bitter betrayal. *Thomas is gone,* Oberon had stressed on more than one occasion. But this was the first time it felt real.

"Oh, Boss," Evan cooed sympathetically. "That's rough. You want a hug or something?" Eve took some delight in looking at the man's questioning expression.

"No," Eve said sharply. "I don't want a *hug.* I want to smash something."

"Okay, yeah. I get that. But that's kind of what I'm talking about. I don't want you running in there half-cocked."

"I'll be fine."

"It's not you I'm worried about, boss. It's *me.*" Evan said with a bit of a light-hearted smile, but the truth of it was there. Eve had rushed into the confrontation with the golem, and Evan had paid the price. There was still some discoloration on the man's cheek.

"You're right," Eve offered as a sort of surrender. "But I'm not rushing because I have some sort of *bloodlust*." She said it like the idea amused her. "We need The Syndicate on board before the Mormons will budge." They had been very clear about that at the meeting Evan arranged. He had warned her that might be a possibly. Nothing illegal gets done on the docks without their approval. Eve was actually impressed with the reach *The Syndicate* had managed. She still thought the name was dumb, though. "I just want to get this done because I think our timeline is about to get bumped up, and suddenly I feel like I'm behind." Eve continued walking, albeit at a more reasonable pace.

They arrived at the back entrance to the shady cantina, *El Infierno Ardiente*. The Burning Hell. The owner, and head of the Syndicate, named it after the prison at the bottom of the stacks where he was sentenced to spent the rest of his days. Renaldo Castille, the head of The Syndicate, was a Shipping director who got caught skimming off the top to fund his growing criminal empire. Castille spent ten years in that prison before Oberon had tasked her with breaking him out. It was a small part of one of his grander plans. Hell, for all Eve knew she broke the man out so that she could walk into his establishment a couple centuries later and ask for a favor. She didn't know, but that's what she was going to do. Only problem was, Athena had rescued the man, not Claire Hughes.

"Hold up," the guard at the door stepped in front of them and held up his hand. "This entrance is for VIPs only." The two of them stopped in front of the man.

"I'm here to see Don Castille." The guard looked at Eve, with her plain face and unassuming coveralls.

"You don't look like one of his usual whores," the guard said with some amusement and reached his hand out towards her. Possibly to inspect the goods. Eve simply remained still. Evan on the other hand...

Evan's new cybernetic hand shot out and his new meaty digits wrapped around the man's wrist as he snatched the man's wrist out of the air in a blink of an eye. The move seemed to surprise both of them. Evan recovered quickly though. He silently applied a painful amount of pressure and the man sank to his knees, looking red-faced for mercy. Evan just burned his gaze into him.

"Apologize," He snarled slowly. "To the *lady*."

"I'm sorry," the man offer immediately, desperately grasping at the metal arm holding him. Evan eased the pressure of the man's arm but still held him tight. "Ma'am."

"That's better," Evan said with a mock sweetness that promised more pain. "Now, go inside and tell your boss *Claire Hughes* is here to see him. He's looking for her, after all. And you make sure to tell him we're unarmed. We just came to talk, maybe do some business. Assuming his dumbass henchmen don't fuck it up." Evan eyed him angrily before he pushed him back towards the door.

"Wait here," the guard said after he straighten himself and disappeared through the door.

"Unarmed?" Eve quipped as she looked at Evan's exposed shoulder joint on his left side.

"Shut up," Evan said with some embarrassment. "It's all I could think to say. I heard it the second it left my mouth." Eve chuckled a bit before Evan spoke again. "This arm is the tits, boss." Evan flexed his fingers out in front of him. "Did you see how fast I grabbed that guy? Like fucking lightning!" Eve just nodded as he admired his new prosthetic. "Hey," Evan later added excitedly. "You think we can play catch later on? Assuming we survive this insane plan of yours."

"Catch? You want to play catch? Like, throw a ball back and forth?" Eve looked at him, mystified by the suggestion.

"Yeah. I haven't been able to catch a ball since I was a kid. Let alone *throw* one. I think I could do it with this arm, though.

I'd like to try." Eve was amused with Evan's enthusiasm over his new arm.

"Sure. Why not?"

They waited a moment longer before the door opened again the and guard silently waved them forward. Eve led the way with Evan close behind as the guard led them through a short hallway, down a metal staircase, and were presented with an open door. Along the wall, leading to the door stood a line of menacing looking tanned men in expensive looking clothes. Each of them openly held a firearm in their arms.

Eve counted three handguns, two recoil-less machine pistols, and one of them even held a mag-gun in his hand. The imposing looking mag-gun worked very much like a shotgun from ancient times, but it used an electromagnetic pulse that fired a solid metal slug along the electromagnetically-charged barrel that accelerated the slug to break neck speeds before it left the barrel. It had a hell of a kick, but that slug destroyed pretty much everything it touched. Eve didn't think the small-framed man knew what exactly he held in his hands, because the weapon usually required a five minute start-up period to charge the weapon's capacitors. And the mag-gun in his hands was currently deactivated. It still looked scary, though.

Eve paid the line of men no mind as she confidently strode into the room. She heard Evan's heavy sigh behind her as they entered a white-tiled space with a metal drain in the center of the floor. It was completely empty except for two metal hooks that hung prominently from the ceiling.

There was a large man standing behind the hooks, wearing yellow plastic coveralls and a large leather apron.

"Fuck sakes," Evan hissed quietly behind her as he entered the room.

Eve walked into the center of the room and looked around the room as if impressed with what she saw. Until that is, her eyes locked onto the tiny surveillance node in the corner. She knew he would be watching, Ron Castillian learned his lesson from the time he spent in the pits of the megastructure. He didn't leave loose ends.

Eve looked right into the node and slowly, but clearly, recited the ten-digit corporate ID number of Ron Castillian. Eve continued to look directly at it with a bored expression while the guard who was at the door touched his ear.

"Yeah, boss." Eve heard the man say quickly. She just waited patiently while Evan fidgeted beside her. "Right away." The guard stepped into the room and waved them back out the door. "Let's go."

Evan didn't take much convincing. Eve looked to the man in the leather apron and blew him a kiss. She walked out of the tiled-room as leisurely as she had entered it, and left the butcher behind her with his disappointed expression.

This time they were led upstairs, into a wide office where the whole one side of the room was a one-sided mirror. Beyond it, the patrons of El Infierno Ardiente were dancing wildly amidst the flashing lights. Eve assumed there was high-intensity dance music playing by the way they moved down there, but no music could be heard within the confines of the office.

The office was an obvious attempt to mimic the corporate splendor of the high executives. The floor looked like black marble that was polished to a high sheen. The other walls of the office had wood paneling colored a warm amber and featured many works of arts that Eve didn't pay any attention to as she strode into the office. She walked past the ivory pillars with golden vines that spiraled around them to the top of the room. Eve scoffed at the numerous nude statues of the Greek gods that The Council Members were named after. All except Oberon, he wasn't named after a god. He was named after a character in some ancient play that was long forgotten. The statue of Athena showed a nude woman with an elaborate golden headdress that flowed down its neck and shoulders.

In its one arm, a golden owl was perched majestically on its forearm. In the statue's other hand was a large golden spear.

In front of them, behind an elaborately carved wooden desk, was an impeccably dressed large man who stared at them suspiciously at they approached. Eve frowned. Ron had gained a considerable amount of weight over the years.

"How do you know this number?" The man asked them quickly. Eve noted some anxiety in his voice, as well as a trace of a Latin accent that he didn't have before. "Tell me."

"She told me," Eve replied and thumbed towards the statue of Athena.

"Oh," Castille said musically, as if he was greatly amused by what he had heard. "Is that a fact? *Her*," he said with some pride as he pointed his chubby digit towards the statue. "I know. You, I do not. Why should I believe you? Because of a number that hasn't been spoken in centuries? I think not."

"You know," Eve said lightly and looked back to the trio of men that filed into the room after them. "This kind of feels like it should be a private conversation. Don't you think?" Castille leveled Eve with a hard stare for a moment before ordering his men to exit the office with a wave of his hand.

"So, now we are alone. So, speak. Convince me I shouldn't have you killed where you stand."

"Your name was Ron Castillian, you were a dirty shipping director for The Corporation when I first saw you. I'm not going to lie, *Ron*, if you looked like this when I busted you out of that hellhole I don't know if I could have carried your fat-ass as far as I did." Castille eyed her suspiciously.

"Boss," Evan gently cautioned from her side.

"Why does this one call you boss? He works for me," Castille challenged lightly.

"He used to. He moved up in the world. He works for me now."

"Really?" Castille hissed slowly before he switched gears. "When I was a young man, There was a particular scent I was-," he started to say but Eve didn't let him finish before she spoke.

"Lavender," she quickly said. "You fucking loved that shit. I swear to god, you used to bath in it."

"*No*," Castille said with amazement, drawing the single word out over a few seconds. "It *can't* be."

"It is," Eve said with a smile.

Ronaldo Castille's shocked faced quickly burst into uproarious laughter. His whole frame shook in his chair and his face turned red from the intensity of his laughter. Eve exchanged a confused look with Evan and followed it up with a quick shrug of her shoulders.

"Something funny?" Evan nervously asked Castille shaking form.

"I don't know," Castille said between bouts of laughter. "What do you think *Claire*?" He asked and burst into another fit. "*Claire? Claire. Claire!*" The frantically laughing man said over and over again, as if he was trying the word out for size. "Claire Hughes?" Castille asked as he settled, teary-eyed and breathless, from his laughter. "How did you ever come up with such a boring, *mundane* name? And this," he said and waved his meaty hand in Eve's direction. "Whatever *this* is. Such a homely look, I don't know how you stand it."

"Yeah, well," Eve started and nodded subtly to Evan. "I'm trying to blend in." She winked.

"Say no more. Please," he said apologetically while placing his hand to his heart. "Sit." He waved to the chairs in front of his desk. Evan waited for her to move towards the chair before he followed. The large man slowly settled himself into his chair, as it might explode any second.

Castille heaved his large frame out of his chair with a audible grunt before his moved over to the wall. With a swipe of his hand, the wooden panel moved to the side and revealed a cabinet filled with expensive looking glasses and brightly colored bottles of all designs. He took one bottle and poured them each a drink into crystal tumblers, which he then brought back to the desk and set in front of each of them.

"Please," he offered with a flourish and a smile before he sat back down behind his desk. "Drink. What's mine, is yours." The three of them took a sip from their glass in unison.

"Oh, man!" Evan coughed. "That's good."

"You sound surprised?"

"I don't think he's ever tasted tequila before," Eve offered with a slight grin before she tilted her glass to Castille. "Which reminds me, what's with the accent? When did *that* start?"

"I'm trying to reclaim my culture. Call it...a hobby. I taught myself Portuguese a century ago, and now all my men on the docks speak it." Castille smiled and winked. "The Corporate linguistic's AI doesn't recognize the language; it confuses it for *Spanish*. Makes operating incognito a little easier. I taught it to my children too, and made them teach it to their children, and so on."

"How *is* your family?" Eve asked conversationally. Castille snorted and took another pull off his drink.

"Oh, my *family*." He rolled his eyes. "It is the weed that continues to grow. I have a few great grandchildren who have migrated to my side. But all my children are dead, all my grandchildren are dead. Most of my family do not even know who I am. Those who do, do not realize we are related. But there are *tens of thousands* of Castilles now, spread throughout all corners of the system like dust." He ended with some measure of pride. "And hopefully, they all speak Portuguese too. I keep track of them, it is another hobby of mine. I had a great-granddaughter born just the other day. Abigail."

"Congratulations," Evan said weakly and raised his glass to him.

"Thank you." Castille touched Evan's glass and drank.

"And the weight?" Eve asked mischievously. The person she knew liked to look a certain way.

"Bah!" Castille waved the question away. "A rival doped my last gene therapy treatment. I have diabetes, of all things."

"They can cure that, you know." Eve smiled at him.

"I think I like it. It *feels* like growing old. Plus, people fear large men more than they do the thin ones. Surely, you know this." Both Evan and Eve nodded.

"You realize that they call you The Butcher?"

"Part of the job, I'm afraid. These days, all I have to do is show people to that room and they start pissing themselves. If need be, maybe I cut off a little piece. It's nothing drastic." Castille chuckled slightly and took another drink. Eve could see the change in the man's eyes even before his next words. "Now, as happy as I am to see you, my friend. I must admit seeing you *here*," Castille slowly brought his meaty index finger down on the top of his desk. "Brings me no pleasure."

"You and me both," Eve snorted before she took another sip of her drink and leveled a hard look at Castille. "I have some business in the stacks."

"So I hear." Castille smiled. "Of course, you have my permission to smuggle these two women out." The man smiled affably and even waved his hand in front of him like he was a King giving a decree. "This will be no small affair, though. The Corporation watches their own closely. I hope you have a good plan in place to get her past customs."

"I do," Eve said lightly, swirling her drink absently in its glass. "I was going to get you to do it." Eve smiled. "Or do you really believe I came all this way just for your *permission*." Eve looked at him, and the two of them exchanged hard looks while poor Evan sipped his drink nervously beside her.

"Of course, I could do this," Castille began. "I have many ways to move merchandise in and out of the volcano. But merchandise is easy to move, if you know how. The Corporation doesn't track goods nearly as well as their cattle. You know they all have trackers implanted in them?"

"So I'll take it out," Eve said with a wave of her hand. She made it sound like the easiest thing in the world.

"Ha! Good luck. They graft it to the radius bone." Castille patted a spot on his inner forearm. "It is no matter, though. I can do it. With enough time and money, I could bring an atmosphere to this barren rock." Ronaldo leaned back in his chair, interlocked his fingers in front of him, and looked up at the ceiling. Eve felt that it was a tad overdramatic. "But to accomplish such a thing, sacrifices will need to be made, bribes will have to be paid, supply chains will be disrupted." He looked at her with a smile. "For you, my friend, I would be happy to do you this favor ."

"How generous of you," Eve commented and waited.

"Ah," Castille smiled remorsefully. "You misunderstand me, I do not *give* favors away. Even to friends such as yourself. I *trade* them." *There it is,* Eve thought to herself.

"Of course you do."

"I have a grand-nephew, I think." Castille's face scrunched up as he thought on it. "Well, I'm not sure of the exact relation. He's one from my sister's tree. He doesn't even work for me, but I've been called upon to assist this poor fool. What can I do?" Castille spread is hand out as if surrendering the point.

"What'd he do?" Eve asked.

"The poor fool killed a corporate man in a drunken fist-fight. In a corporate establishment, no less." Beside her, Evan made a remorseful noise. Castille caught it. "Yes! You are correct. Corporate justice will have him spend then rest of his days in *Goryashchi Ad.* He gets transferred to the stacks in a couple of days. I would do this myself, but I can not be involved. Not *directly.*"

"So, you want me to spring him?" Eve asked as if bored by the request.

"I don't *want* you to," Castille said with some regret. "But if you wish these two women to be smuggled out, *safely,* I believe it is the best course moving forward." Castille smiled smugly. "I already have all the logistics of the transfer. The route, the number of guards, I even have the unlock code for the body restraints. I have everything you'll need to do this for me. And if I don't have it, I shall get for you as quickly as I can. What do you say? Do we have an agreement?" Castille put down his drink and extended his thick hand across the desk.

"We do," Eve said and reached forward to shake it.

Beside her, Evan slowly placed his face into his metal palm and groaned softly.

CHAPTER 11

Lucien

"Okay, I'm here," Lucien loudly declared as he walked into Doctor Cattivo's office. Lucien received the report of the incident and he immediately set up the meeting so the issue could be dealt with. However, it *could* be dealt with. Lucien stopped abruptly and madly looked about the office. Cattivo looked at him with a bored expression that just infuriated Lucien more. "So where is he? Where's the fucking simpleton that might have jeopardized one of the *two* projects we're working on, Ernst?" Lucien howled the question at the man.

"He's on his way," Cattivo said from behind his desk where he was sitting comfortably. He was preoccupied typing absently onto the holographic keyboard displayed brightly on the desk's surface. "Here, come take a look at this."

Lucien swiftly moved around the desk and Cattivo obediently rose out of his chair and turned it to him so he could ease himself into the stylish office chair. Lucien scanned at the screen the good doctor was looking at and saw an enhanced image of a blood sample. The ID label at the corner of the image told Lucien everything he needed to know. Cattivo spoke up anyway.

"This blood sample was taken from Jones one week after implantation of the nano-capsule. You'll note the presence of some trace inorganic material. One part per million, nothing really to worry about."

"You said that's from the nano-capsule shedding inert particles of itself," Lucien stated it like a fact because that's how he understood it, but the looked on Cattivo's face hinted towards something different.

"That's what I believed, yes! I believed it was just the nano-capsule dumping waste material into the bloodstream to be recycled out through the body's natural processes. It was a logical assumption, at the time. For the first three weeks we didn't see a significant increase, the inorganic material stayed around the one to two parts per million. Nothing of concern." Cattivo excitedly leaned in close and deftly pressed a few buttons on the keyboard. The image changed to another enhanced microscopic view of Jones' blood.

"Holy shit," Lucien said with silent shock. Clouding up the spaces between the blood cells were hundreds of tiny black fibers. "Is that?"

"Yes! That's how the nanomachines travel the bloodstream now. In organized groups." Lucien checked the timestamp of the blood sample. "This was taken shortly after Jones's first encounter with the golem."

"When he got knocked out?" Lucien asked innocently.

"*Knocked out*? That *thing* fractured his skull and cracked three of his vertebrae. I thought the whole damned experiment was ruined in one foul swoop."

"You did say his ability to recover from injuries was just short of miraculous." Lucien looked at the good doctor with some pride. "I assume you're going to tell me his newfound healing ability is due to the sudden increase of these *nano-strands*?"

"Oh Lucien," Cattivo said with awe. He looked back to him and saw an expression of child-like wonder on the doctor's face. "It goes much deeper than that." Cattivo punched a few more keys and the screen littered with pictures of anatomical scans. "Three days ago, I had Jones come in for a full body, deep tissue scan." Lucien's surprised expression probably said it all, but he couldn't help himself.

"What? Why? And why wasn't I notified about this?" Lucien asked in rapid succession. To his annoyance, Cattivo just waved off Lucien's concerns. He was too caught up in his excitement.

"Look at this," he said and pulled up the scanned image of what looked like a human femur. Cattivo zoomed the image in so the surface of the bone was visible. As were the delicate black lines that ran down the length of it. "The nanomachines are grafting themselves to the surface of the bones. And look here! There are higher concentrations at the natural stress points of the bone. Do you want to know where the highest concentration is?" In his excitement Ernst quickly tapped a few keys and three small images popped into view. "At all the locations of his recent injuries. The area around his skull fracture has a mathematically perfect lattice mesh around it. And we think it's spreading. The three vertebrae that were cracked?" Cattivo enlarged the image. "Each of them is now surrounded in this lattice mesh. We think it's spreading as well. But that's not all. Here! Look at this scan of the muscle tissue, the nanomachines have interwoven themselves in between the muscle fascicles of a vast majority of his skeleton muscles."

It's working! It was the first thought that popped in his head. The proof of it was right in front of him. The second thought that popped into Lucien's head wasn't nearly as thrilling.

"Why is this the first I'm hearing about this?" He looked at his assistant with contained frustration. For months, Lucien has been hearing about a concerning level of stagnation in the nano-capsules development from the doctor. Only to discover now all those reports had been false, and the nano-capsule has been secretly spreading throughout the subject's body. Albeit slowly, but still.

"I assure you Lucien, I only found out about this new growth three days ago when I did the scan. I wanted to double-check my findings before I came to you with this." Cattivo said gently. "Admittedly, this is because of sloppy lab work on the part of my team. The ones responsible for the error have been found and transferred to another sector. The problem was they didn't check the physical results of the blood work against the reading they were getting from the medical implant. They just took the readings from the implant. They never thought to test it against the blood samples we took." At that Lucien looked at him and showed him his disappointment. Cattivo simply held up his hands. "Trust me, I understand your frustration. These people are lab workers, they're not *scientists*."

"They're *your* people, Ernst. I don't want to hear excuses," Lucien said calmly but with definite venom.

"Of course, I understand, but there's something else you need to see." The doctor pulled up the sensor data from the medical sensor from the time of the subject's first encounter with the golem to now. "You can see that the blood chemistry are all within normal levels, with minor variations in the electrolytes and protein levels. And the glucose and enzyme levels are well within norms as well. Both the medical sensor and the limited data from the corporate ID tag, are completely identical."

"So, the nanomachines are disrupting the sensors?" Lucien complained. The good doctor shook his head quickly.

"No, Lucien, you're missing the point. Both sensor's readings were the same, and showed the normal day-to-day variations we would expect to see from a normal individual. If this was a simple technical error, we would have picked up on it immediately. Instead, we were fed the readings we were expecting to see. Don't you see! That's a clear sign there's an intelligence at work here. Look at what we know up to this point. The nano-capsule grew to a certain point, and created a complex structure of its own inside the brain. Then slowly it began to integrate itself with the brain's tissue."

"Yeah, and the subject's IQ spiked because the nano-capsule was creating new synaptic connections where they didn't exist before."

"Yeah, but then the growth slowed after Jones's encounter with the golem. Because I believe the nano-capsule felt it was necessary, after that point, to focus its efforts more on the host itself."

"As a self-preservation measure?" Lucien shared the doctor's questioning expression.

"What else could it be? What if those synaptic connections weren't just for Jones's benefit? What if the nano-capsule is using his brain for its own processing power. Essentially creating a cybernetic brain that both the nano-capsule, and Jones are able to utilize independently. Which, if true, means the nano-capsule isn't just completing a set number of tasks like a program. We could be looking at an inorganic entity that's capable of sensing its environment and creating a decision-based strategy that's adaptive to external forces. Fuck sakes, the nano-capsule not only detected the foreign elements in Jones's body, but also determined their function, and hijacked the sensors to feed us false information. Because it was *hiding* from us."

"Okay," Lucien said holding his hands up to slow the doctor down. He had heard enough. There's a line between helpful conjecture and wild speculation. "Calm down. Take a breath for fuck's sake. There's a more reasonable explanation for the false readings. Like what if the nanomachines are simply affecting both the sensors in the same way?"

"That would explain similar readings, but these were *exact*."

"Yes, but that proves my point more than yours, because even when the sensors are working perfectly the readings aren't *identical*. The simple fact of the matter is that this *was* just a technical error, and *your* people missed it." Lucien used a calming gesture with his hands. "I'm not saying I don't agree with you, to a point. It is very promising, but I'm not convinced on this whole shared intelligence theory of yours. If it does turn out to be true, I definitely wouldn't look at it as a selling feature, it's more of a defect." Ernst looked at him with a quizzical expression. Lucien continued before the man even had a chance to ask the question. "Because if the nano-capsule begins to spread throughout the man's brain, at what point does the subject cease being Jones and start becoming this *intelligence* of yours. Like, where's the line? And if there is one, when do we know when it's been crossed?"

"Christ, Lucien. What if the entire Council is controlled by an alien AI? What if they have been this whole time?" Cattivo was stunned by the possibility. Lucien just snorted with some amusement.

"If that were true, getting rid of them would be easy. If we could prove that, we could turn the entire system against them. Granted we'd lose our project, but we'd gain an entirely different prize. Honestly, Ernst, I'm not sure which I'd prefer at this point." Cattivo gawked at him in a way Lucien didn't appreciate. "Oh, open your eyes! This whole effort is to level the playing field with The Council once and for all, but this is even better. This way, we could use every other piece on the board to simply wipe them away."

"I just can't believe you'd choose that over scientific advancements."

"I will have both. It is simply a matter of which I shall accomplish first." Lucien smiled smugly.

The two men were interrupted by a weak knock at the doorway. Both Lucien and the doctor looked up in unison, and there, slouching weakly in a poorly fitting lab coat, was Glen Sanders. He was a mid-level neurologist that specialized in behavioral mapping, analysis, and reprogramming. According to Cattivo, the man came highly recommended, but judging how he carried himself, Lucien had his doubts.

"You!" Lucien growled savagely and jumped up from the chair, knocking it back from the desk. He swiftly approached the shivering man, grabbed him by his greasy, sandy brown hair and hauled him into the room. "Sit your ass in that chair!" Lucien pushed the man towards the two chairs in front of the desk that were meant for guests. Sanders collided into one of them with an audible grunt before he scurried around and dropped himself into the seat. "Queue it up," Lucien said to the good doctor as he stalked in front of Sander's chair, put his arm on the seat's armrest and lowered himself down until he was eye level with the fearful scientist. Lucien held his gaze for a moment before he spoke. "I'm going to ask you a question in a few minutes, I'll let you know when I do, because when I ask it, you'd better tell me the truth." Sanders nodded quickly. "Do you have any idea what you've done? Any concept of the damage that may come from this? How badly you've jeopardized *my* project?"

"He does not," Cattivo absently said from behind him. "I did not inform him as to the nature of the meeting."

"Well then," Lucien hissed at the man as he trembled in his seat. "You're in for a real treat then. Show him! Put in on the holo-display."

Cattivo tapped a few of the brightly lit keys displayed on the surface of the desk. The air above the desk stirred slightly before the surveillance feed winked into existence as a large panel that loomed over them. Lucien pushed himself away and stood beside the man as the good doctor played the recording. On the panel, it showed Sanders walking into the medical lab where Jones was laying on the table unconscious.

"I don't understand," Sanders whimpered beside him.

"Shut up." Lucien sternly cuffed the man on the back of his head. "Keep watching."

On the panel, Sanders walked up to his station with a cup of coffee in one hand, and his datapad in the other. He placed his coffee on the workstation's counter with his datapad, then Sanders walked over to the still body. Everyone in the room watched as Sanders first looked up to the medical readout, and then down to the body. Sanders weakly groaned in the chair beside him when they all watched as his hand dropped down and came to rest on the subject's bare chest. A second later the hand moved up to slowly caress the man's cheek.

"Okay, stop!" Lucien barked and leaned into Sanders from the side. "Do you know the subject on the table?" Lucien angrily pointed to the holographic panel that was paused on the gentle touch Sanders was giving Jones.

"No, sir."

"Really?" Lucien gave the man a hard look as he snapped the question before he pointed back to the screen. "Because that looks like a pretty goddamn friendly gesture to me!"

"I concur, Glen. This is most unusual, even if you did know the subject on a personal level. You're a scientist, after all. Maybe you could offer an explanation?" Cattivo offered the man neutrally."

"I understand, s-sir. To be frank, sir, I don't exactly have the best re-recollection of the e-events in question." The man weakly stammered.

Lucien soundly slapped the man with the back of his hand. The sound of it resonated about the small office. Sanders yelped like a wounded animal and retreated away from Lucien as much as the chair he was sitting in would allow.

"Does that jog your memory, you ingrate!" Lucien looked back to Cattivo. "Play it," he commanded and turned his fury back onto Sanders. "Look at it!" Lucien growled loudly and pointed to the panel.

Sanders was visibly sweating by this point as he looked up weakly at the panel. Still holding the side of his face where Lucien struck him. The surveillance recording played on. On the panel, Sanders now moved back to the workstation and picked up his datapad to initiate the upload of the behavior template. In the chair, Sanders swallowed hard as he watched the recording on the screen.

"And what are you doing here?" Lucien turned to Sanders.

"I'm initiating the upload, sir."

"So you admit that's you?" Lucien motioned to the holographic panel above the doctor's desk.

"It looks like it's me."

Lucien slapped him again.

By this point the neurologist was folded up into the chair like he was trying to hide from the other two men. He had his hands in front of his face and, to Lucien's utter disgust, the man appeared to be weeping. Lucien reached down and struggled to pull his hands away before he slapped him solidly across the face again.

"You think I'm playing games here, you little turd. Ernst! Show him." Behind him Ernst did as commanded and the panel behind him changed.

"Do you recognize this behavioral profile, Glen?" Cattivo asked calmly. Lucien kept a hard gaze on Sanders' face as he looked up to the panel and studied the profile.

"No," Sanders finally said, looking to Cattivo for mercy.

"Interesting," Ernst said, scratching his chin.

"Why?" Sanders asked quietly and looked quickly between the two men. It was Lucien who answered the man.

"Because that's the profile you uploaded, you *STUPID FUCK!*" He screamed into the man's face. Sanders yelped again at the intensity of Lucien's voice and recoiled away from it.

Lucien just leaned in closer to the sniveling neurologist. "You remember that question I told you about? The one you better answer truthfully or I *will take you apart*." Lucien smiled wicked at the prospect. "Here it comes. You ready? Who the *fuck* do you work for?" Lucien slithered in even closer to the man.

"You, sir." Sanders squeaked so quietly Lucien barely heard it. Lucien pulled back his arm and balled up his hand into a tight fist. He may not know who this asshole works for. But Lucien knew one thing for sure, it wasn't him. He was going to find out the truth.

"Lucien! Wait," Cattivo said a moment before Lucien was about to strike. Both he and Sanders looked to the good doctor. "Glen, what do you remember of the events in question?" Sanders looked to Lucien quickly and then back to the doctor.

"I remember walking into the lab. They were serving hazelnut coffee in the break room that day, and I was pretty excited about that. I remember putting the coffee down, and the next thing I remember I was drinking from it."

"Do you remember doing the upload?" Cattivo continued.

"Not specifically, to be honest. But I know I did it." Sanders looked fearfully at Lucien after the admission. He had his arms folded menacingly in front of him but he took a step back from the man and allowed him to continue. "I was happy about it, proud even. I remember thinking I didn't have to worry about it anymore. I *swear* to you, sirs. I did not upload *that* profile." Sanders pointed erratically at the profile on the panel. "I would never do that to you, sir." He looked to Lucien when he said the words.

"But you did," Lucien hissed. "And you're going to pay for it"

"Lucien," Cattivo interrupted him again. He looked to the doctor quickly and with obvious frustration painted across his face. Cattivo regarded Sanders with cold eyes. "Glen, this is a major problem for us. And it appears like you are exclusively at fault. I think it's time for you to start focusing on the solution instead of trying to explain away what you can't remember doing." Lucien gave Ernst a look which he recognized and replied by gently holding up his finger. "Can we wipe his personal memory again and start fresh?"

"No, sir. The inorganic matrix has spread to the entirety of the brain. I can't promise an attempt now wouldn't negatively affect the matrix. Nor can I promise the procedure would even work."

"Fucking great!" Lucien threw up his hands. Sanders flinched away from the unexpected movement. Cattivo just nodded.

"Well, if that's the case. I suggest you go back to your office and start researching a strategy to counteract this *malignant* profile," Cattivo offered gently. Like he was coddling the man. Lucien found it infuriating.

"You had one job!" Lucien cut in angrily, shaking his finger at Sanders. "I signed you on for a five-year contract for *one* job. And you fucked it up."

"Well, now he has two." Cattivo said, obviously trying to calm Lucien. Which just added to Lucien's annoyance. "Glen, from this point on, the only thing that will save your career, is solutions. So, I suggest you get to work on them immediately. You are dismissed." Ernst said with a bored wave of his hand.

Sanders didn't move. He simply pivoted his gaze towards Lucien.

"Get the fuck out!" Lucien roared at the man and lunged towards him with his hand held high, as if to strike.

Sanders practically fell out of the chair as he scrambled away from the desk and ran out the door. Lucien looked to Ernst and threw his hands out.

"What the fuck? *You are dismissed,*" Lucien imitated the doctor mockingly to his face.

"I think there's another possibility we *both* might be overlooking here."

"Do tell," Lucien said with some suspicion.

"He might be telling us the truth." Cattivo went back to his keyboard. "I'm going to play the clip again for you. Tell me if anything strikes you as odd."

On the panel the clip played again. Like before, Lucien watched Sanders enter with his cup of coffee and his datapad. Which he promptly puts on the workstation before going over to the subject to check the readout and grab a quick feel. Then Sanders walks back to the workstation, and picked up his datapad again to initiate the transfer.

And something did indeed strike Lucien as odd.

"Play it again," Lucien said, calmer now. He watched closely as the clip played again. "He's blinking weird," Lucien stated and pointed to the image.

"What? Really?" Ernst pressed a few more keys and zoomed in on the image. They both clearly could see the slow rhythmic blinking of Sanders. Almost every ten seconds the man blinked once slowly. "Oh yeah, that *is* weird." Lucien turned to him with a quizzical expression.

"What were you talking about?"

"I was going to mention the fact that Sanders picked up his datapad with his left hand, and started typing with his right to begin the upload," Cattivo said sounding slightly amused. Lucien just shrugged.

"So?"

"Sanders is left-handed."

"Okay," Lucien looked at him confused. "But we know for a fact that *is* Sanders on the screen. He would've had to provide a gensig just to get into that room. *That's* Sanders." He pointed to the screen.

"Undoubtably."

"So, what are we saying here? Mind control? You're suggesting someone remotely took control of the man's body through telepathy?" Lucien slowly spelled it out so Cattivo could hear just how ridiculous it sounded.

Cattivo just raised his eyebrow.

"We are dealing with a Council artifact. One which I imagine they would go to great lengths in order to get it back under their control." Lucien looked at him with wild eyes. He hadn't considered that. But now that it was out in the open, it was all he could think about.

"Shit!" he cursed. "Can they do that?" Cattivo simply shrugged.

"No idea. But if anyone in the system *could* do it, it would be them. Think about it. Jones has had the nano-capsule inside him for two months now-."

"Three," Lucien corrected.

"I'm not counting the month you insisted on keeping him sedated." Cattivo said and Lucien was mildly amused by his annoyance. "During that time, we've already seen some astounding improvements the nanomachines have made to the man's physiology. He's smarter, faster, and my tests even suggest he's ambidextrous now." Cattivo then took on a grim expression. "Rumor has it The Council's founding member has had the nano-capsule inside him for almost a *thousand* years. I can't even imagine what a truly symbiotic relationship with a fully formed nano-capsule would even look like. It's not a stretch of the imagination for them to have unlocked some deeper secrets of the mind."

"Well shit," Lucien complained. "How are we supposed to defend ourselves against that?"

"I don't know," The doctor confessed quietly. Obviously stuck inside his own head, figuring out the problem for himself. "But we should probably be hyper-vigilant going forward."

"Agreed. I'll have an extra detail of guards assigned to the entrances. We should also establish a buddy program with the lab techs. Nobody who works on sensitive material does so alone. Plus, we can brief the techs on what to watch out for." Lucien saw the unimpressed look Cattivo was giving him.

He simply shrugged. "I am fully cognisant that won't help against mind control, but it may discourage the attempt if the individual doing it was aware we know he's doing it. Plus, it might help mitigate the damage done."

"That's true."

"Honestly, Ernst?" Lucien looked at the doctor with concerned eyes. "How bad is this behavior profile going to fuck us?"

"It's hard to say," Cattivo began after scratching his chin for a moment. "He does have a disturbing tendency to use familiar terms when talking to his superiors. Calls me by my first name on a regular basis, even after I discouraged it. His programing with relation to you seems to be intact." Lucien hadn't noticed that, but he didn't let Cattivo know. The subject always used Lucien's formal name when addressing him, like he was supposed to. "And in some instances I would even go as far as to say the malignant profile was beneficial at times. With the golem, Jones wasn't bothered by his continued failure, quite the opposite. He seemed to be enthralled by it. Which was unexpected."

"But?" Lucien asked cautiously.

"But, he's overly aggressive at times. Especially with the guards. He almost beat a guard into unconsciousness when the man inadvertently referred to him as *Nikki*. That's a concern, for sure."

"Do you really believe that this twit will be able to come up with a way to counteract the programming?"

"That's the old nature-vs-nurture argument, isn't it? If anyone can, it's Glen. That *twit,* is probably the best in his field. I don't want to speculate, but I honestly don't see why not. One thing is for sure, we're going to have to confine Jones to the section again. We can't risk him being out in the stacks and having him triggered by something else. How soon can we get him back here?"

"Another week," Lucien said knowing the doctor wouldn't be happy with that answer. "If I pull him out any sooner than that, it might raise questions. The colonel has a special assignment for our boy, as well as some internal affair issues Soldado is dealing with."

"How's Jones doing with the Colonel's training? If memory serves the man is a bit of a legend in the military circles."

"More like a living god," Lucien snorted. "The man's a legacy. His family has been in charge of training the Corporate Militia since its inception."

"How is it he's only a colonel then?" Cattivo asked with genuine interest. Lucien just laughed at the man's naivete.

"Because a vast majority of the Board of Chairs believe if he ever had operational control of the military, he'd take over the Corporation. Soldado is an extremely dangerous man in every sense of the word. So, the CEO gives the man enough power to placate his ego but not enough to remove himself from underneath The Corporation's thumb."

"And how exactly did you convince him to train Jones?" Lucien laughed again.

"Oh, *that* was easy. I simply told the man I had a someone he couldn't break that was destined to be the next generation of super-soldier, and that he would out perform every man in his squad. Including Soldado."

"Clever," Cattivo said absently. Lucien could see something behind him had caught the man's eye. "What *is* he doing?" Ernst asked to no one in particular with a hint of annoyance. Lucien traced the man's gaze behind him.

Outside Cattivo's office, back in the body of the main lab, was the tech who lost his arm when the Council ship suddenly locked up. Lucien was pretty sure the man's name was Jerry-something. He was slouched over and lurching stiffly towards the office door. His wooden steps slowed even more when he noticed Lucien and the doctor gawking at his display. Lucien could see the sleeve of the man's lab coat had been torn clean away, exposing the frail-looking poly-carbonate prosthetic.

"Grr, pleez." He sputtered and stammered stupidly trying to speak. "On! Ron!" Lucien was about to call out to the man to find out what this nonsense was all about. However, when Jerry's arm shot out explicably and with an unnatural sort of jagged speed, Lucien's words caught in his throat. His prosthetic arm stretched to the side and a series of tiny little pops rattled off along its length and bits of the arm's shielding flew off in all directions. Then a fine mist erupted from the prosthetic.

That's when the alarms went off.

Behind him, Lucien heard Cattivo's frantic voice screaming at the top of his lungs.

"LUCIEN, GET DOWN!"

Lucien watched transfixed as the mist enveloped Jerry-something a second before it ignited. For a wonderful moment Lucien saw the brilliant light engulf the tiny man and simply erase him from existence, as if by heavenly force. *This is it,* Lucien thought. *This is where I die.*

Something struck his side and forced Lucien to the ground. Then the rapidly expanding fireball overtook them like a super-heated invisible wall of force and flung their bodies into the chaos. Lucien felt his skin burn. When he breathed in, he smelled his own flesh cooking for a fraction of a second before the super-heated air scorched his lungs.

Then darkness blessedly took him.

CHAPTER 12

Nick Jones

Nick thought of the blonde woman again last night while he laid in his bunk. He was perfectly aware the geeks behind the glass were monitoring him closely. After all this time, Nick didn't even mind anymore. He missed sleep though. He was almost at the point where the gentle process of sleep was beginning to elude him. Like, he still knew what sleep was, but Nick was starting to forget what it felt like, or even what the whole point of sleep even was. He remembered waking up and feeling a little like a newborn each morning. Stiff and groggy, with heavy eyelids. He still remembered the heavy-sort of weariness that came before sleeping, and how it was vaguely similar to how one felt immediately after. Like, the body needed a period after sleep in which it could boot up.

It seemed ridiculous to Nick now. Now, he was always awake. Always alert. He still pretended to sleep, even though, he was fairly sure the geeks knew he didn't sleep anymore. They still hadn't mentioned it to him, though. These *sleep* shifts were the only time when he wasn't being tested, trained, or scanned in some manner. It was the only time when he could just be *him*, even if it was spent motionless in the dark.

Lately, Nick had been spending this time thinking of the woman he saw in Stack Four.

Colonel Soldado wasn't thrilled to have an untested *experiment* attempt to pass through his Special Operations training regiment. The Special Operations personnel were genetically modified soldiers who were considered the best-of-the-best within the Corporate Militia. They were selected at birth, raised according to the *Soldado Method*, and when they reached a certain age, they received the gene therapy that made them superhuman. Well, superhuman compared to other people. To Nick, they were pretty stiff competition right up until the point they were no longer any competition at all. There was a steep learning curve when Nick first began, but once he got ahead of the curve, there was no slowing him down. He worried at first that the men of the Special Operations would look down on him. He was an *experiment*, after all. Maybe even be a little sore when the experiment started to show them up a little. Soldado's men weren't about egos though. They were about a strong unified team, and if a member could strengthen that team, then he was welcomed with open arms. Some days, Nick wished he didn't have to go back down to the Research and Development level at the end of his shift. He felt like he belonged with Soldado's men. The Colonel said he would try to pull some strings to get Nick permanently assigned but he didn't like his chances of pulling that off. Mr. Malum would never allow it.

The Special Operations had an oversight responsibility for the Security Service. Soldado had Nick doing shadow-shifts with guards from different stacks that Soldado had complaints about.

"It'll be good for you," the colonel said at the time. "The Militia is about the people, Nick. Everyone else in the corporation has to worry about deadlines and work quotas. *We* worry about the people. That's our job."

Nick was assigned to Stack Four. He was to shadow some asshole named Dale Cummins, and newly promoted shift supervisor who was roaming Stack Four with a heavy hand. Nick was assigned to the man as a new recruit, and Cummins didn't waste a minute making sure Nick *knew how things worked*. Before lunch, Nick recorded a dozen major infractions. Any one of those would be severe enough to warrant a demotion. Nick said nothing all day, just followed behind the man nodding obediently as he harassed and bullied the people of the stack, noting all of it for his report he would make to the Colonel later.

Until he accosted that woman.

By this point, Nick had witnessed this man, wearing body armor and carrying a sidearm, terrorize people all day. On more than one occasion, Nick had to take a deep breath and walk away. Then this woman came along. Nick spotted her first. It was like his eyes was drawn to her form as she passed in front of him with the countless other people making their way through the level's promenade. She was dressed in a medical technician's uniform. She had a small frame, but something about how she carried herself stood out to him. She had golden blonde hair that fell down past her shoulders. She had it tied in the back in a simple ponytail. Nick gazed upon the soft features of her face with a strange feeling of familiarity.

Then Cummins moved in on her.

Nick stood a safe distance back as Cummins started talking her like the two of them had a past together. From what Nick could ascertain the woman's husband had died some time ago and it sounded like Cummins was pushing himself on her, making lewd comments to her as she tried to move away from him. Then he reached out and grabbed her shoulder, and she turned with a look of horror painted across her smooth features.

That's when Nick couldn't stand it anymore.

He stepped in, interrupting Cummins mid-comment and dismissed the woman. Nick then took up a position between Cummins and the rapidly retreating woman. He looked at Nick with abject rage and reached out and grabbed a fistful of Nick's uniform before Cummins hauled him into a nearby alley and pushed him up against a wall. The whole time, Nick relented to the movement while secretly fantasizing about putting the man in the medical unit. Cummins wildly threatened Nick. He just stood and listened with a bored expression while strands of spittle flew from his mouth as he shouted in Nick's face. He struck Nick, as well. He was fine with that, just another infraction to add to the list as far as Nick was concerned. But then he said something in his rage that triggered something deep inside of Nick. Something unexpected.

"...And if I want, I'll go down to that bitch's apartment and fuck her in front of that crippled up little girl of hers..." It was part of his tirade, a meaningless little snippet of verbal diarrhea. Nick didn't know the woman, and only found out she had a daughter when Cummins mentioned it. However, when he said the words, *her crippled up little girl,* Nick saw red at the edges of his vision. A burning heat erupted inside of him. A sort of hatred sparked up that threatened to consume him entirely. He didn't think about it. Nick just acted.

He grabbed Cummins by the throat, and easily lifted the man off his feet. Nick looked up at him with burning hatred in his eyes.

"No, you won't," he growled hoarsely.

Nick put Cummins in the medical unit. He didn't wake up for three days. When he finally did, Dale Cummins was promptly informed that Nick was a member of the Special Operations. Then the list of his infractions were read off to him before he was stripped of his position. After which, Dale Cummins was read the list of charges filed against him for assaulting a member of the Special Operations. Nick imagined after that point, that everything happened rather fast for Cummins. It was the last time Nick ever saw or thought about the man.

But the woman.

The woman from the encounter stuck with him like no other person he had met. Nick didn't even know her name. He didn't know anything about her, and yet...She invaded his thoughts in a way her image had no right to. Worse yet, some nights Nick started thinking about the woman's daughter. He couldn't explain it. He started thinking about who this woman's daughter was, what this little unknown person might look like. Nick didn't know why, but he imagined this little girl would have her mother's petite nose. Maybe this little girl and her mother would have similar smiles.

Nick, one night, thought about the mother and her child when something inexplicable came to him. It was like a flash of recognition that he couldn't explain. Two words. Individually, the words meant nothing to him. But when he thought of them together and tried to discern their meaning, his eyes would begin to leak.

Monster kisses.

Nick promised himself he would find out why.

***

Nick was happy to get the prisoner transfer assignment. The upper level of the megastructure was normally off limits to Nick. It was one of the stipulations Mr. Malum put onto his contract, one of the many Soldado overlooked when it suited him. The Colonel knew the score. He knew Mr. Malum wanted the grisly old soldier to train Nick personally, because he was the best. To Soldado, it meant that he could take liberties when he felt like it. The worst thing Mr. Malum could do was rescind the contract, which to Soldado, wasn't much of a threat at all.

Nick could see that he was quickly becoming an asset in certain people's eyes. Definitely Mr. Malum and the good doctor back in the Special Projects section. But now the Colonel was also starting to look at Nick with those envious eyes. Like Nick was a power source that he was trying to harness for his own purposes. Nick didn't mind, he enjoyed the training. Whether it was firearms training, hand-to-hand combat, or the tactical exercises and drills, no matter how good Nick did, Soldado knew a way that Nick could improve. Plus, the assignments let him roam amongst the other citizens of the stacks.

And there were also the independent eateries in the shipping and receiving section. Nick would sample different kinds of dishes in the market here each time he was assigned to the level. It was a nice treat he allowed himself. He found the chicken curry particularly enjoyable.

Nick promised himself he would stop in at one of his favorite eateries for lunch after the prisoner transfer was complete.

The job was easy enough. Transport a prisoner handcart from the independent level's Port Authority through the heavily populated promenade, clear the prisoner through the customs checkpoint, and finally load the handcart onto the security lift. That was their job. It was a cake run. The Colonel had mentioned during his briefing that he suspected one of the other guards was on the books with the local organized crime ring. The Syndicate. Soldado explained that the criminal organization had been around for hundreds of years, and probably would be for hundreds more. The Syndicate wasn't the problem, not really. The problem was the guards. As Soldado explained, guards on the take weren't guards at all. They were mercenaries at that point. Just people selling themselves out to the highest bidder. *That* Soldado could not abide.

During the briefing, Soldado expressed concerns because intelligence reports suggest the prisoner, a lowly scientist who got carried away with his fists, shared a familial tie to the head of The Syndicate. A man known only as *The Butcher*. Soldado wasn't taking chances. Nick was to tag along with the guards and ensure everything went smoothly.

Nick reported to the corporate guard station on the independent section. As always, the guards were less than thrilled to have Special Operations looking over their shoulder. Nick was quickly informed that the guard station's remaining powered armor was being serviced, and Nick would have to make due with a simple set of personal body armor that was sized too small for his frame.

Typical, Nick thought sourly as he took the armor and made the necessary adjustments.

The standard deployment for a low-level prisoner transfer was three guards, each in powered armor. One man operated the cart while the other two walked in front and behind. With Nick, they switched to the four-man deployment pattern. The two guards in the powered armor took the lead, with the cart and its operator in the middle, and Nick taking up the rear position.

The two front guards were issued heavy pulse rifles. Nick was trained on those rifles, and he liked them. They electromagnetically fired a somewhat brittle tungsten-copper alloy bullet, which was important when firing in an atmospherically controlled environment. Nobody wanted to inadvertently trigger an explosive decompression event by piercing an exterior wall. The rifle fired in three round bursts, and sounded like arcing electricity. Personally, Nick preferred the single-fire setting. The guard controlling the prisoner cart also had a pulse rifle. It was holstered to the guard's left-hand rear mount, which would allow him to easily access the weapon by simply reaching over his left shoulder, if needed.

Nick had the standard-issue Special Operation sidearm. The RPC1020. Like most Corporate names, everything you needed to know about the weapon was in the name. It was a recoilless-propellant-cartridge pistol that fired a 10mm bullet with a twenty-round capacity in the magazine. It wasn't his. Unlike the other members of the unit, he didn't get to keep his sidearm. It was a shame because Nick had a few ideas for some modifications he'd like to try. Modifications could only be made to permanently issued weapons, though. It was another rule in the seemingly endless list of rules The Corporation had. His sidearm was a basic automatic pistol that fired 10mm cartridges loaded with a gasless propellant. Honestly, it was considered a relic. But they were still readily available and fairly cheap to fire, so the Corporation kept plenty of them around. Nick liked them because they were reliable.

They started out shortly after the beginning of the day shift. The promenade and the corridors were sparsely populated because just about everyone was already on-shift, and the morning rush had yet to begin in earnest.

It was ten minutes of procedure to sign the prisoner out from the Port Authority, then a twenty-minute walk to the checkpoint where they would offload their cargo.

About ten minutes into their walk to the checkpoint, all hell broke loose.

They held a tight formation as they walked through the restaurant district of the promenade. The wide lane they were on ran straight through it. Restaurants, bakeries, and various other eateries of all kinds could be found here. The outdoor eating area lined the sides of the lane as they walked through. Nick noted only a few patrons seated at the tables, quietly eating their breakfast. A few of them looked up from their meals to watch the guarded convoy past but none of them paid them any real attention.

Then the explosion happened.

Light and sound erupted all around Nick with such an incredible intensity it crushed him in one blow. *Flashbang,* his brain informed him as his eyed flared painfully from the flash

-burn, and Nick was forced down to his knees from the ringing in his ears that caused him to momentarily lose his balance.

Then something struck his chest.

Nick didn't have time to register the minor impact, which knocked him off his feet, before the electricity came. He was completely cut off from the world around him as burning lightning coursed through his body. All his skeletal muscles spasmed painfully, paralyzing him as Nick grunted to just breathe. His ears continued to ring but his vision cleared. Through clenched teeth Nick forced himself to look down at the point of impact on his chest, all the while feeling electricity burn through him mercilessly.

There on his chest, was a node of some kind that had attached itself to the breastplate of Nick's personal armor. With his sore, teary eyes, Nick could see the electricity arcing out from the contact points. He fought against his spasming muscles to make a fist, and growled painfully as he forcibly swept his forearm down his chest. He felt his forearm strike something solid, and pushed through.

Immediately the pain and spasming muscles came to an abrupt end as the node skittered away from Nick's body. He took one full breath while he collected himself before Nick was up on his feet scanning his immediate surroundings. He awkwardly stumbled a few steps to the prisoner cart. Behind it, Nick saw the guard who was tending it frozen in place.

"Com check," Nick panted into his throat mic as he approached the cart. The guard had one of those nodes attached to the outer casing of the battery pack. *Perfect,* Nick thought sourly as he saw gentle wisps of smoke wafting upwards from the armor's joints. The weird object must have overloaded the armor's servo-motor CPU. It would be a full minute before the back-up system booted up. Until then, the guard was trapped inside the armor. "Com check," Nick said again as he approached the front of the prisoner cart.

It was empty.

The two guards in front stood motionless like statues. Nick saw the same nodes on the battery packs as well. *Fuck,* Nick cursed as he blinked hard a few times and gave his head a little knock on the side to try and end the incessant ringing before he quickly scanned the area around him.

The morning patrons of the food court were all on the ground clutching their ears, and blindly searching for a safe spot underneath their tables. *There!* Nick spied a woman entering the alley between two eateries. It was only a second before the woman disappeared from sight, but that was all Nick needed to know she was his target.

The woman was caucasian, easily six-feet-tall with a medium build. She had long blonde hair that was woven into a thick braid at the back of her head. Her clothes were what partially gave it away. The woman wore black military-style pants, and a black shirt with full sleeves. Nick didn't see a visible weapon on her person, but that meant little. What really gave the woman away, was the look on her face when she glanced back at him for the brief instant before she disappeared into the alleyway. Nick didn't see fear on her face, and her expression bore a certain recognition that caught his eye.

It was like she knew him.

With no other leads, Nick chased after her as fast as his recovering body could muster. All the while panting into the throat mic.

"This is Delta Guard of the prisoner convoy! We have been compromised! I repeat, we have been compromised. The asset is on foot with an accomplice. Female, blonde hair in braid at the back, black combat fatigues. Unit is in pursuit, heading southeast through the alleyway. Request immediate assistance pinged to my location. Over?" Nick stumbled a few steps, still feeling the effects of the flashbang. Through the ringing in his ears, Nick heard the faintest sounds of white noise coming through the comms channel. "Acknowledge!" Nick barked before he audibly cursed. *Radio's out,* Nick added it to the list of fuck-ups that went wrong so far on this operation.

This woman, whoever she was, single-handedly took down their whole squad, *and* escaped with their prisoner, in less than thirty seconds. Using those power nodes to disrupt the powered armor internal computers were impressive work, Nick had to admit. But he tempered that with the fact that the voltage required to do such a thing should have probably killed him.

Nick's body recovered as he ran awkwardly for the alley. He could feel it. The knots in his tight muscles loosened, the ringing in his ears settled, and his vision cleared completely before he reached the mouth of the alley. Nick was comforted by the fact that his prisoner would be suffering from the same effects of the flashbang, but more so than Nick, and the man would take much longer to recover than he did.

Nick was in a full run before he hit the T-intersection up ahead and came to a skidding stop. He quickly checked his sides. Down the left-hand alley, maybe about fifty feet, he saw them. The woman was ushering his prisoner down the alley, towards the corner that led down another alleyway.

"Stop! Corporate Security!" Nick shouted as his hand reached down for his sidearm.

The woman pushed the man forward and looked back once, but neither of them stopped.

So, Nick fired.

Fifty-feet was a long distance for a side-arm, but Nick was a crack shot. He fired three quick shots in a tight group. He watched two of bullets collide uselessly with the building's corner, but the third shot caught the woman in the side just before she disappeared with the prisoner around the corner. Nick watched with some pride as the bullet threw the woman to the side before she too disappeared. *Must be wearing armor,* Nick thought. If she wasn't, then that bullet would have torn right through her abdomen and left a spray pattern on the wall of the building behind her.

Nick sprinted forward towards the next intersection with his weapon in front of him in a two-handed grip. He slowed slightly and moved close to the building as he approached the corner. Nick would move around the corner, using it for cover, and pick off his targets before they could even reach the next intersection. Nick didn't have the benefit of knowing the exact layout of the commercial district of the promenade but he knew enough to know these alleyways were for trash collection and deliveries, and could be a little like a maze if you didn't know them. Luckily, he didn't have to know them. This chase was all but over. Once he rounded the corner, there would be no place for them to go. Because nobody could outrun a bullet.

Nick pushed his back up against the building by the corner, took a breath, and moved around it with the gun in front of him.

The hand holding the pistol was snatched up in a vice-like grip the second it peeked out past the corner of the building. Nick was pulled off his stance and into a knee that sunk deeply into his midsection, forcing all the air from his lungs in an audible grunt of pain. Nick had been hit like that before, back when he was fighting with the doctor's damned golem. Before Nick could recover, the woman slapped his sidearm out of his hand with ease and then, for good measure, she chopped him in the throat. The woman in the braid wasted no time as she circled around Nick's stunned body and delivered a sharp kick to the back of his knee. He didn't have a choice. Nick fell onto his one knee, giving the woman the perfect opportunity to move in behind him and slip her arms around his head in a rear-naked chokehold. Nick felt the woman's forearms clamp into place, instantly cutting off the blood supply to his brain.

Ten seconds, Nick's brain informed him and started a timer that counted down his remaining seconds of consciousness.

"You're out of your league here, kid." The woman said into his ear as she clamped down on the hold, and Nick felt like she was trying to squeeze his head right off.

Five seconds.

Nick uselessly slapped the forearm around his neck, while his other hand drifted down to his leg. He pulled the shockstick free from its magnetic sheath and stabbed it backwards by his ear, right where the woman's head should be.

Behind him, Nick heard the woman yelp in pain and felt her hold on him lessen as she instinctively moved away. *Let's go for a ride,* Nick thought to himself and pushed off the ground with all his might.

That's when he noticed this woman's disproportionate weight.

Undeterred, Nick threw himself, and the woman still hanging on around his neck, flew backwards. Nick even felt his boots momentarily leave the ground as he hurled them backward. They struck the side of the building, close to the corner Nick had just come around. Nick felt the impact rattle his bones. He could only imagine what it must have felt like for the woman on his back.

He didn't wait to ask her.

Nick threw his head back and headbutted her with the back of his skull. It honestly, didn't feel great. It felt like he had just bashed his head into a concrete pillar. But he was rewarded with the feeling of the woman's nose breaking against his skull, though.

Nick pulled down the locking arm of the choke hold, sent a sharp elbow into the woman's ribs, and pulled the arm over his shoulder to throw his attacker to the ground. At least, that was the plan.

Instead, the woman used the momentum to gracefully execute a forward flip, and landed in front of Nick. *What the fuck!* He was sure the surprise he felt inside was echoed by the expression on his face. That's also when Nick noticed that he was no longer holding her arm.

She was holding onto his now.

He didn't know when it happened, and this bitch wasn't about to give him a chance to figure out how she did it. The blonde-haired woman pulled his arm down as she spun around. Nick barely had time to register the kick before her boot collided with the side of his face. Nick felt the world spin around him. Even though, he was painfully aware he was the one actually doing the spinning.

When he landed, the shockstick was nowhere to be found, but the pistol was inexplicably in front of him. Nick glanced down the alleyway, and his prisoner was just about to stumble around the corner of the next intersection and out of sight. If he lost him now, he might not have the chance to recover the asset later.

Nick lunged for the pistol.

"No!" He heard the woman scream as Nick came up into a shooter's stance. A fraction of a second before he was about to put a slug in his prisoner's brainpan, the woman's boot collided with the side of the pistol.

BAM!

The shot went wide, and Nick missed his chance. On the plus side, he had the woman right where he wanted her. In her zeal to reach the pistol, the woman overshot her kick, and Nick didn't hesitate to move in behind her. With the pistol still in his one hand, Nick wrapped his arms around the blonde-haired woman's waist. If felt like Nick was wrapping his hands around a tree trunk, weighed about the same too. Regardless, Nick grit his teeth and heaved the woman up and backwards as he arched his back in a backward suplex. From his experience with the golem, this really hurts. And judging by how much this bitch weighed, it would hurt her even more.

The woman's body collided with the ground with a solid impact that felt like a boulder crashing to the floor. Nick released his grip after the impact and rolled away with the pistol still in his hand. He came up ready to put a couple of slugs into the body on the ground.

But she wasn't on the ground.

His blonde-haired attacker was already on her feet and reaching for the pistol in his hands. Nick took a quick step back and moved his free hand forward to shield himself as he brought the pistol back to his hip.

BAM!

Nick fired blind at the approaching figure, knowing he would hit something. The bullet caught the woman in her forward leg. Nick didn't see the impact. He was locked onto her burning expression as she rushed towards him. When the bullet struck the meat of the woman's thigh, the leg was forced back and she pitched forward.

Right into Nick's free arm.

His forearm caught her across the chest. He kept her away from the pistol by his hip while he breathed through his teeth and pushed her back, firing his weapon as he did.

BAM-BAM-BAM!

The shots echoed around them as he pushed against the opposite building's back wall. The bullets tore into her midsection, and droplets of blood sprayed the space between them as she staggered back. Nick saw the white-hot rage of her expression flinch slightly with each shot that tore into her gut. He pushed her all the way back to the wall, and it was his full intent to empty his magazine into her.

However, when Nick went to squeeze the trigger on the pistol a fourth time, nothing happened. He quickly looked down at his sidearm by his hip, and he saw the woman's vice-like grip on top of the slide. His heart dropped slightly when the pinky finger of her hand shot out and pressed the magazine release button on the side, close by the trigger. Nick watched with muted shock as the magazine tumbled to the ground between them, which she promptly kicked away.

"I think we've had enough of *that*," she growled with droplets of her own blood running down the smooth features of her face. *She should be dead,* Nick thought to himself as he looked at her dumbly.

Then she headbutted him, and broke his nose.

"That was for earlier," She hissed with venom in her voice. Nick barely registered it before her leg snapped out and struck him solidly in his midsection.

Her boot thankfully impacted with the molded Kevlar breastplate of his personal armor, it took the brunt of the blow. However, the sheer power of the kick sent him backwards. The next instant Nick collided with the wall across from where he was standing. His back struck the wall first with a bone-jarring impact, and he was sure he must have cracked or broken something, then the back of his skull rebounded off the wall with enough force to cause his vision to dim slightly at the edges.

When Nick looked up next, the woman was holding the empty pistol out in front of her, like it was a prize.

"You know," She started to say waving the pistol at him. "I wasn't looking to get in to it with you." Nick just looked at her, biding his time. "I was actually hoping to avoid it. But here we are. You may not know this, but I have a score to settle with you." Nick frowned at her. He had never met this woman before in his life. If he did, he was pretty sure he would have remembered it. "And I think it's time to pay the bill, junior." The blonde-haired woman tossed the pistol away. Nick caught a look at her midsection as she did. He saw the blood on her shirt, as well as the number of large bullet holes in it. Beyond it though, he just saw pink flesh. *That's not good,* Nick thought to himself as he looked upon the woman's visage that was practically radiating with fury.

"I don't even know you," Nick said, scrambling for more time. The woman just smiled.

"Oh, but I know you," she said as if amused. Nick's heart dropped as she sunk down into a fighter's stance. "You have something that doesn't belong to you. It belonged to a friend of mine." Nick frowned at her.

"I don't know what the fuck you're talking about," he growled slowly. "How do you know me?" Nick asked. At this point he wasn't just stalling for time anymore.

"I've never met you before today, actually." Then she shrugged absently. "Not this version of you, anyway." With that said, the woman relaxed her stance and let her hands fall to her sides. She took a step forward. "Did you pick this face?" She asked, motioned towards him with her hand. "Or did someone choose this for you?"

"Are you calling me ugly?" Nick sneered at the woman as she took another small step towards him, fully aware of the blood leaking down his face. Nick straightened up slightly and was pleased that he had fewer aches than he did a moment ago. *Keep her talking,* Nick thought to himself as he held her gaze, while his right hand slowly drifted towards the double-edged knife sheathed behind his back.

The woman just laughed softly as she took another step.

"I *do* appreciate a man with a sense of humor." The blonde-haired woman used her knuckles to push up on her chin, cracking her neck joints.

"Glad you find it so funny," Nick hissed and grabbed the knife. He pulled it free in a reverse grip, lunged forward and slashed across the woman's throat. He could have sworn she had a grin on her face as she easily leaned away from the attack, and responded with a quick shot to his ribs that stole his breath away. Undeterred, Nick came back and stabbed at her chest. He knew she would be there to block it. He counted on it, in fact. Nick used the knife's blade to hook the woman's arm and leveraged them down and away from her body. Nick leaned back and thrust his knee into the woman's newly exposed gut and felt it sink in with great pleasure. He pulled it back and used his heel to mercilessly kick her on the inside of her thigh. The braided woman dropped down expectantly and Nick automatically raised the knife up and stabbed it down on the back of her shoulder.

The woman audibly grunted and dropped down, only to surge forward to wrap her arms around his lead leg. After that, she simply lifted Nick off the ground and heaved his body over her shoulder. Nick wasn't in the air long enough to be disorientated by it. He landed hard on his back, again letting the armor take the brunt of the impact before he rolled away and scrambled to his feet. The woman just turned to him with a wicked smile on her face as she reached over her shoulder and pulled the knife free.

"You dropped this," she said sweetly and then with a flash of her arm, threw the knife at Nick.

His knife sunk deeply into the meat of his right thigh. It was like a magic trick she had just performed for him. One second the knife was in her hand, and with a wave of her hand, the knife's tip was punching into his leg. Nick howled and waivered slightly in his stance. He wanted to drop, but his attacker was moving fast towards him with a savage sneer on her face.

The two straight punches to his face were easy enough to block, and when the woman dropped her retreating hand, Nick saw his opening. He sent a hard hook to the woman's face, fully intending to separate her head from her body with the massive blow. She simply ducked under the attack like it was the easiest thing in the world and promptly punched the knife currently sticking out of his leg. She struck the back of the knife's hilt and drove it deeper into Nick's thigh.

This time he did drop.

Nick couldn't help it, he just folded slightly over top the woman's frame. She just rolled her shoulder and sharply elbowed Nick in the face. The blow caught him off guard and Nick stumbled back painfully. Pain flared from all over his body and his vision dimmed dangerously. Luckily, the spinning back kick the woman hit him with woke Nick up a bit. The blow also took him right off his feet and planted him on his ass again. A good ten feet back from where he was standing. Nick grunted painfully as his body finally settled onto the ground.

It's over, Nick thought to himself. The way his muscles flared painfully as he struggled to rise up again told him he didn't have much left to give this bitch. When he looked down, Nick saw the knife was still planted solidly into his leg. *Oh yeah, I forgot about that.* Nick stared dumbly at the knife as he lifted himself to a kneeling position. He was breathing heavy. Blood ran freely down his face and dripped on the ground in front of him. He counted two cracked ribs, possibly broken. Multiple contusions all over his body, too many to count. Nick was pretty sure his jaw had fractured on that last elbow. On several spots of his face, he felt the swelling begin to take hold.

"Jesus! Look at you," the woman said with obvious disappointment. "You're still bleeding." Nick looked at her with utter disdain. Nick had done enough damage to that woman to put a normal person in an autodoc for a week, if not the morgue. By his count, he had shot her four times, and stabbed her once. Yet, she still looked fresh. If it wasn't for the bullet holes and the blood stains on her exposed skin, you'd never know the woman had been in a fight. "I have half a mind to rip the Motherbot right out of your skull," she said with a dangerous look on her face.

Nick didn't know what she was talking about, and he didn't feel up to asking. *Just keep stalling,* he thought as he watched the blonde-haired woman gracefully stalk towards him. There was no winning this fight for him, that much was clear. He could still, however, keep this woman busy long enough for his back-up to arrive. Surely the flashbang explosion and the number of shots Nick had fired must have alerted someone. Even with the radios down, there had to be someone closing in on his location.

The prisoner had escaped. He had to accept that. He had failed that objective. But if he could keep this bitch busy long enough, maybe they could take her alive and interrogate her. Maybe he could still recover from this failure.

"Bitch," Nick began to say with a hoarse voice. "You want something from me." Nick reached down and pulled his knife free from his own leg. He yelped when he did it, he couldn't help that. "Come get it!"

"*That* is the last time you are going to call me that," she said with utter confidence and moved forward.

Nick was worried about just how accurate that statement might be.

He weakly limped himself away from the menacing woman as she walked towards him with a playful sway of her hips. Nick positioned himself in the middle of the alleyway. He wanted as much room as possible around him to maneuver away from this beast of a woman, if that was even possible. He held the knife in front of himself and he just waited for the next round of injuries to come.

The woman didn't disappoint.

She darted in quickly and covered the distance between them in an instant. Before Nick could prepare himself, he was defending his life against the woman's attacks. Unlike before, Nick had no interest in attacking the woman, he concentrated his efforts on blocking the blows he could and trying to mitigate the damage on the blows he couldn't. He was fighting a losing battle. It was only a matter of time. *She could end this whenever she wanted,* Nick thought to himself drunkenly as he recoiled away from another quick jab to the front of his face. Nick didn't even know exactly where the blows were landing anymore, everything hurt.

In the fog of his concussed brain, Nick picked out the tell-tale ping of the woman's datapad sound off from her pocket just as he thrust the knife forward. It was a mistake. He knew that the second after he did it, but by then it was too late.

The woman caught his knife hand by the wrist, stretched out his arm in front of her chest and just held him there. Nick swayed dangerously in her grip.

"My guy reached the rendezvous," the woman with the thick blonde braid and specks of blood painted on her perfect face said. To Nick, she almost sounded apologetic, which couldn't be good for him. "Time to go."

Then she promptly broke his arm holding the knife.

She winked at him before she thrusted her knee up and struck his out-stretched arm past the elbow. Nick didn't scream, he didn't have it him anymore for such grand gestures. The best he could manage was a tired, pained groan as he looked in disbelief as his arm bent sharply, and unnaturally around her knee. The knife must have fallen from his hand. Nick honestly didn't know and he wouldn't be given the opportunity to find out. The woman struck Nick in the mouth, and he watched bloody gobs of spittle fly from his mouth. *That's it,* Nick said to himself as he felt his weight sink to the ground.

The woman was having none of that though.

Nick felt an open-handed uppercut connect underneath his jaw and put him right back onto his feet. He couldn't explain what was keeping him up. He looked to the woman, who had moved back away from him. He watched her sink down dangerously into her stance. She looked like a coiled spring for that brief moment before she launched herself at Nick.

There was nothing he could do.

The woman raised up her elbow and stuck Nick in the center of his armor, and all her weight and momentum was instantly transferred into his body. Nick couldn't describe it, there was pain, a strange sensation like gravity had violently shifted for him and he was sent flying through the air. There was a blessed feeling of weightlessness, but it all came crashing down when he finally landed. He was still hanging onto consciousness at this point, somehow. He felt his body flopping against the ground before it rolled to a stop.

"You mind if I keep this?" Nick slowly, and with some effort, rolled his head towards the sound. He blinked hard to clear his vision, but he managed to see the woman disappear casually around the corner of the building. His knife held delicately in her one hand.

A few hours later, Soldado roused him from the autodoc to inform him there had been an explosion at Special Projects. Apparently, it was some kind of attack. They were still assessing the casualties.

At least I'm not the only one having a bad day, Nick thought to himself.

It was a cold comfort.

CHAPTER 13

Eve

By the time Eve turned the corner of the building, the nanomachines had already re-absorbed the blood on her face and extremities through her skin, and healed all the visible signs of damage. The dark clothing she was wearing would hide the other blood stains enough that most people passing her would just think her shirt and pants were soaked through with something.

Eve limped slightly as she walked, trying to look casual and nonchalant as she matched the pace of the other morning patrons rushing about as the security alarms continued to blare around them. She quickly stowed the bloodied knife she took from *that man* carefully into the side pocket of her pants.

She clenched her jaw as Eve forced herself to ignore the pain she felt as she made her way to the drop-off point.

Fuck! Eve cursed inside her head as she struggled along. *I forgot how much getting shot hurts.* The Motherbot gave her a detailed list of the damage it was currently dealing with. The first bullet she took in the side, blew her liver pretty much in half. The second tore through the muscle of her thigh before the bullet bounced off her reinforced femur and fragmented, sending tiny shards of metal ripping through the surrounding muscle tissue. She felt the injury flare painfully with every step. Bullets three through five tore a bloody path into her gut, blowing a chunk out of her stomach and perforating her bowel in several spots before the bullets left out her back. Except for the last one. It impacted her spine and the resulting shrapnel shredded her kidneys. Not to mention the knife in the back that punctured her lung.

And those were just the intrusive injuries.

She had a list of the fractures she incurred from the fight. Eve had to admit, she wasn't expecting the back suplex after she kicked the gun and ruined his shot. *That was a good move.* Eve couldn't help but notice that his technique was similar to how she took down the golem weeks ago. Though, she didn't really appreciate the feeling of all of her weigh come crashing down onto the back of her shoulder. That kid fractured one of her vertebrae and damn near broke her left collarbone on that one.

Eve walked away from the scene for about five minutes before she spotted the family-friendly pub that Ronaldo owned that was setup as her drop-off point. She altered her course slightly and walked casually towards it. It was too early in the morning for the establishments that served alcohol to be open. The Corporation had some rules the Port Authority of the independent zone had to abide by. That was one of them. Eve spotted a chubby balding man peering nervously out the front window. Eve gave the man a slight wave when he looked in her direction.

"Puta Merde!" The man cursed in Portuguese when he unlocked and opened the front door for her and stepped aside to allow her to enter. "What's going on out there?" He asked quickly as he shut the door behind her, somewhat muting the

blaring alarms. "They said there was an explosion in one of the food courts on the newsfeed," the smallish man said and looked at her expectantly.

Eve just chuckled on her way by him.

"Probably best if you didn't know," she said with some amusement as she made her way to the bathrooms in the back. Castille must have had a reason to keep the man in the dark about the specifics of her mission. It wasn't a surprise. It was how the man operated. He organized his operation like a terrorist organization. Individual cells working independent of each other, and with members that had no knowledge of the other operations outside their own individual cell.

Eve walked through the empty, unlit restaurant and pushed open the door to the ladies' room. She locked the door behind her.

She felt Oberon's presence in her mind a second before his actual voice popped into her thoughts.

How's Ares? He asked with genuine interest.

Eve was alone. She felt she could risk verbalizing her thoughts.

"Don't call him that," she said with venom as she moved to the end of the counter with its numerous metal sinks built into it. Eve knelt down to the access panel that was below the last sink in the line to remove it.

Eve? Oberon started to ask. Eve could tell he was amused by something. *Are you in pain?*

Eve sighed.

"He shot me a few times," she said defensively. "It's not a big deal."

He shot you? A few times? As in, more than once? Eve was happy Oberon was only in her head, and not standing in front of her at the moment. She was pretty sure she wouldn't appreciate the look on his face by the giddy way his thoughts sounded.

245

Eve reached into the cramped space for the bundle she put there herself the day before.

So? Oberon asked, pushing the issue. *How is he?*

He's more like Thomas than I'd like to admit, Eve thought to herself absently and then immediately caught her mistake.

I heard that. Oberon responded quickly. Probably to remind her he was still inside her head.

"You weren't supposed to," she said bitterly, unpacking the clothes she had stowed in the nylon bag. "But yeah, he does remind me of *Ares.*" She said the word like it was a strike against the kid. "He's brash, stubborn, and entirely too confident in his abilities."

But the other side of that coin, is a man who is willing to sacrifice himself for his ideals. One who believes in himself, and won't quit until the mission is accomplished.

"I guess that's one way to candy-coat it." Eve grimaced slightly as she lifted her stained shirt over her head. "So far, I'm not impressed."

He did *manage to shoot you. A few times.*

"Yeah, well, he paid for it." Eve removed the bloodied pants and stood in front of the mirror in her underwear while she perused a few places of concern on her body. The bullet holes were all sealed but the flesh covering the hole wasn't overly pretty to look at. It looked like scar tissue. In another hour, the repair would be complete and the flesh would be unblemished again. Her back was even worse. The two bullets that did manage to exit her body left holes the size of golf balls in her lower back. They had scarred over already, like the knife wound in her shoulder.

You didn't hurt him too bad, did you? We are *trying to recruit this person, after all.*

"He's fine," Eve snorted, "-ish." She was forced to pause when a sharp pain coursed through her. She still had a good deal of digestive enzymes eating away at her insides. Fortunately,

Oberon didn't comment on it. Even though, Eve was pretty sure he felt what she felt when he was connected like this. "It's nothing he won't recover from. Besides, it's good for him." That's how the Motherbot worked in the beginning. It responded to external stimuli. Like, if you break a bone, the nanomachine will make that bone five times more resistant to breaking. If you tear a ligament, the Motherbot will reinforce it. Any little damage you receive would be repaired and then that area would be strengthened, hardened, or shielded in some way. "He should thank me," Eve said, she wet the towel that was also in the nylon bag and quickly wiped herself down.

I doubt he'll see it that way.

"So, you're not connected to his Motherbot yet." Eve made it sound more like a fact than a question, which, she was pretty sure it was, or else Oberon would know exactly what the new guy thought of their little dustup.

Not as yet. It made contact, but it's still in the early stages of development. Plus, it's still reconfiguring itself to the new host. So, that might lengthen the process.

"Uh-huh," Eve said absently as she started to ease herself into Angela Peters' fresh blue coveralls. "As much as I love these chitchats of ours, Oberon, if there's some bad news I need to know about, I'd like you to get to it. I have to smuggle myself back into the stacks in about five minutes before they lockdown the area completely, if they haven't already. How's my timeline?" She asked knowing it was really the only thing that could go wrong. Everything else was on-track and proceeding as planned. The timeline was really the only thing out of her hands, so, of course it would be the thing that caused her the most grief.

Not good I'm afraid. Something out of my control popped up.

"Yeah, there's a lot of that going around," Eve quipped as she zipped up the coveralls and checked herself in the mirror before she changed herself to Angela Peters. One of the two remaining corporate profiles left at her disposal. Eve watched as her thick braid unwrapped into a long tangle of hair spilling down her shoulders. A moment later her hair shortened to shoulder length and the tint slowly darkened to a solid brown color. "Anything I need to worry about?"

I stumbled across a rather ingenious plot to kill Lucien Malum. I can't stop it; I can only slow it down. It will happen within the hour. I don't know exactly how it will affect our timeline until after it happens, but it's not going to help us. I know that much. How are things on your end? Have you made contact with the wife?

"No," Eve said supervising her transformation in the mirror. "I have Evan keeping an eye on her in the stacks. I'm on my way there now. I have Castille on board, but he needs time to get all the pieces in order. I'm still a week away from the bare minimum," Eve confessed. Oberon was silent for a moment. Eve imagined he was mulling over all the variables in that impressive brain of his.

Proceed as planned, for now. If anything changes, I'll let you know. Then, like a wisp of smoke in a breeze, Oberon was gone from her mind.

Eve packed up the bloodied clothes into the zippered nylon sack, she deposited it back into the cramped space underneath the sink then replaced the panel that was covering it. She put her datapad back into her pocket. Eve checked her face in the mirror and she collected her new auburn hair into a ponytail at the back. With that done, the transformation was complete.

Eve walked out of the bathroom moments later as Angela Peters, to the utter shock of the proprietor who was tidying up behind the bar.

"Don't worry about it," Eve said in Angela Peters' voice as she walked past the man with her eyes on the front door. "*If you know what's good for you, you'll forget everything you saw the second I walk out that door,*" Eve said in perfect Portuguese.

"*Sim, Senhora.*" *Yes, Ma'am,* the man replied and went back to his tasks. He knew the score. He was on *The Butcher*'s payroll after all.

Five minutes later, on the way to the custom's checkpoint, Eve no longer felt any of the ill effects from the fight. In the checkpoint's queue, while she was waiting in line, the Motherbot informed her that all the damage had been repaired.

"This is a weird time for you to be entering back into the stacks," the guard looked up from the work schedule on her datapad and gave her a disapproving look. "Says here you should still be on shift." Eve asked the Motherbot to raise her body temperature a few degrees before she sliced off a bit of herself to complete some tasks in the digital landscape.

"I don't feel well," Eve said with a bit of a hoarse-sounding voice. For effect, she even barked out a gentle cough. "I think I'm coming down with something." She watched as the guard initiated a quick thermographic scan of her body. "My shift supervisor should have put a notation on my permit file," Eve said absently. Partly, because this was supposed to be a minor annoyance to Angela Peters. But also, because the guard really wasn't listening to her.

"Yep, you are running a little hot." The guard pushed a few more keys on his console. "Your supervisor did indeed put a notation on your file. Looks like everything is in order," the guard said like he was disappointed by the news. Eve longed for the days when she could get past a guard simply by saying she had bad menstrual cramps, as her splice returned from the digital landscape. "You know what happened in the food court?" He suddenly asked sternly. Eve looked at him with a bored expression and shrugged.

"Some kid set off a firecracker? I heard it. So what?"

"Do you know anything about it?"

"Do *I* know anything about a kid setting off a firecracker?" Eve gave the man an incredulous expression, but still kept her tone somehow submissive.

"It wasn't a goddamn firecracker," the guard snapped back with a hint of anger in his voice. "It was a prisoner's escape. Somebody attacked the guards. Do you know anything about *that*?" Eve made a show of flinching away from the guard slightly, like she was afraid of him.

"No," Eve said calmly, maybe even sounding a bit taken aback by the inference. "I bake bread all day. What would I know about *that*?" Eve then let out a loud series of barking coughs. It amused her to see the guard lean away from her with a disgusted expression.

"Fuck sakes! Put a damned medical mask on before you infect your whole stack." The guard reached under his console and pulled out a cloth medical mask which he quickly handed to her. Eve smiled inwardly as he obediently took the offered mask and put it on. She didn't have a problem with covering her face one bit. "I'm putting you on a forty-eight-hour medical watch until you get yourself checked out at a medical clinic. Your privileges will be restricted until you are cleared."

Eve scoffed at the man.

"You're kidding me? For a cough?" Eve complained slightly and looked at the man with a look of disbelief. It was expected. If she didn't take at least a little offense to the restriction, the guard would have probably noted it. It was part of blending in.

"Don't argue with me," the guard said sharply. "Just get yourself checked out." He said and waved her through.

Eve smiled contently at the guard as she walked past, which he couldn't see because of the mask.

***

"How's stack life?" Eve asked quietly after she reached over and knocked loudly on Evan's metal shoulder. She smiled as the large man slightly jumped and flinched away from her voice. He was sitting on a wide prefab bench to the side of the pedestrian lane across from the recreational fields. Eve had switched back to Claire Hughes a few blocks back.

"Jesus! Fuck!" The large man cursed loudly, drawing the attention of some passing pedestrians. Eve shushed him as she moved around and took a seat next to Evan's massive frame. "Don't fucking scare me like that."

"You're such a baby," Eve teased him quietly. "What are you so worked up about?" She asked even though she had a pretty good idea what was eating at him.

"Fuck you. You don't know what it's like living in this place."

"I do, actually." She interjected. Evan was unphased by the comment and continued on.

"I can't even take a piss without something pinging my datapad for a recognition code. Even when I'm just walking down the lane, something is pinging it," Evan snorted.

"Just don't loose that datapad I gave you. You'll be fine."

Eve set Evan up as a student within the stacks. It would give her assistant the freedom he needed to traverse the mid-stack range. As a joke, Eve set him up in the culinary program in the university. To her surprise, the man actually started to attend some classes.

He had the time.

Evan had learned Jonlesky's wife and daughter's routine very quickly. He found out Jonlesky's wife, Helena, was authorized for an emergency shift change. Now, Helena took Bella to school in the mornings before she clocked into her shift. After Bella was finished school, Helena was allowed to clock out to pick up her daughter, prepare a meal for her, and was even allowed to spend a couple hours in the evening with her before she had to return to the medical facility to finish the rest of her shift.

Evan was there with them in the mornings, unseen in the background. He followed Helena to the school drop-off, and secretly escorted the woman to her work. Evan then attended morning and afternoon classes, incredibly, and was there for the school pick-up. Evan usually ended his day by following Helena to work.

"I can't imagine what it would be like to be here without a datapad."

"You're basically a non-person," Eve quipped. "Doors won't even open for you at that point. How's our girl?" Eve asked, scanning the casual flow of people as they passed by.

"Good," Evan responded quickly. "She should be by in a couple minutes with the little girl."

"Bella."

"Yeah," Evan said absently as he looked up at the artificial sky, as if mesmerized by it. "Little cutey, that one." There was a pause before Evan spoke again. With a deeper voice. "What's wrong with her?"

"Who says anything is wrong with her?" Eve asked innocently. Evan just glared at her with a knowing look.

"I'm not stupid, boss. In the afternoons, the woman practically has to carry the girl home. A few times, the little girl's wig came off. Not to mention all the times I've caught Helena crying."

"She has cancer. She's dying." Eve watched as the large man just nodded solemnly. "Have there been any problems?"

"Naw," Evan said with a wave of his hand. "It's been pretty quiet." Evan then perked up as if something suddenly came to mind. "A couple days ago there was a guard that kind of got in her face. I think he knew her. I couldn't hear what he was saying but whatever it was, the woman didn't like it. I thought I was going to have to step in and test out *lefty* here," Evan said and brought up his new prosthetic with flare.

"Did you?"

"That's the best part, boss." Evan looked at her with an amused expression as he continued. "His partner stepped in, shooed Helena away, and then took the guard to the alley over there. Some words were said, and then his partner beat the *living* shit out of him." Evan chuckled as he recalled the events. "Like, it was *bad*. There was a medical evac and everything."

"What happened to the guard who did the beating?" Evan chuckled again.

"Fucking nothing," he said it like he was impressed. "He said a few words to the responding security guards and then just walked away from it. Big guy, too."

"What did he look like?" Eve asked and listened intently at Evan's description. "Yeah, that's probably our guy."

"Like, *your* guy?"

"Yeah," Eve said, thinking of the altercation Jones had with the offending guard. She wondered about something. "Did Helena recognize him?"

"No. Why would she?" Evan asked, confused by the question.

"Because *that* was her husband. At least, it was."

"Fuck off," Evan exclaimed suddenly. "I thought you said that Jonlesky guy was a runt. That dude was no *runt*."

"I never said he was *a runt*," Eve said dismissively. Evan just made a suspicious noise.

"I'm pretty sure you did, boss." Evan chuckled slightly. "So what? These corporate fucks changed his face and turned him into some sort of *super-guard* or something?"

"Oh," Eve said quietly. "They did a lot more than that." *Or did me and Oberon?* It was hard to say who was ultimately responsible for the new player on the board. Lucien Malum and his cohorts for wanting to implant the Motherbot, Oberon for finding quite possibly the only candidate in the solar system who could serve as a host, or Eve for delivering the man to them on a platter. Truth was, they all had a hand in the birth of Nick Jones.

"Why?" Evan asked naturally.

Because he's a long-lost descendant of Thomas Ferguson, Eve answered inside her mind. She didn't know how. She could guess though. Thomas was a popular guy before *and* after he became a member of the Council. She made a note to herself to check the genealogical records, even though she was pretty sure she wouldn't find the answers she was looking for. Oberon knew though, and one day she would make him tell her.

But that was for later.

"Ours is not to reason why, Evan." She looked at him gravely. "Ours is but to do and die." She looked at his confused expression for a moment before she let him off the hook. "Don't worry about it."

"Figures." Evan snorted and the two of them watched the people drift by. Well, Eve did. She noticed Evan was keeping a watchful eye on the artificial sky.

"How's class?" Eve asked lightly. "Are you learning anything?" Evan snorted.

"I found out why all their food is bland as shit. Did you know they have a list of *banned* spices? Like, what the fuck did paprika ever do to these assholes? Not to mention everything even remotely spicy is strictly forbidden, for some reason I haven't been able to figure out yet. Nobody at the school will even talk about it."

"You're not attracting too much attention, are you?" Eve reached up and loudly knocked on his metal arm through the sleeve of his coveralls again. "Because that would be bad for us. I already had to break one dipshit out of prison, I don't want to make it two." Evan chuckled a bit at that. Even though he wasn't supposed to.

"Don't worry about it," Evan mockingly repeated her words back to her. Eve frowned, and briefly considered the possibility that their relationship was becoming too familiar. "I tell people I used to work in Maintenance until my arms got ripped off in some gory way and I got reassigned. Last person who asked,

I said my arms got caught in a recycler and was dissembled right before my eyes."

"That's not how recyclers work," Eve scoffed. "There about a dozen safety systems that prevent that exact thing from happening."

"They don't know that shit," Evan laughed. "Like, for being the most advanced civilization in the system, these people are really dumb." He motioned to the slow moving crowd on the pedestrian lane.

"Specialized knowledge set, buddy. They learn what the Corporation wants them to learn. What's appropriate for their work assignments. Each of these people are masterfully trained to do their job and only their job. Like the pastry chefs here, for instance, are the best pastry chefs you'll find in the entire system. Bar none. Same goes for each of them. The Maintenance workers here," Eve went on with another example. "Are the best engineers anywhere. They can *literally* fix anything. Their knowledge base and skill set make them the smartest people in the stacks by far. And yet, here they are seen as little more then janitors." Eve then shook her head. "Wasted potential."

"Yeah," Evan said, quietly conceding the point. "They're pretty nice though. Polite. Friendly. Not like some of the roughneck assholes back in the mining colonies."

"Yeah, they're good people. What exactly are you looking at?" Eve asked the big man who was still watching the giant vidscreens of artificial sky.

"About every five minutes, a flock of birds crosses the sky and disappears behind that building." Evan traced a path that ended at a taller building off in the distance. "In the exact same way." Something to the left of them caught Evan's eye. "Heads up," he said quietly to her looking back to the sky. "Helena is walking towards us." Evan then gave Eve a quick description of the woman before he added, "And she's carrying Bella today."

Eve spotted their target easy enough.

Helena Jonlesky walked quickly while holding her child close to her midsection. Bella's little face was tucked into her mother's bosom and her small arms were wrapped weakly around Helena's neck. Bella's little legs swung freely as the two made their way towards them. Helena poise's struck Eve when she first saw the woman. She carried herself with a strength and dignity that made her stand out in the crowd of people coming towards them. She walked a little taller than the rest, and had focused eyes that went well with the determined expression on her face.

As they passed by Eve saw the medical mask on the child's face. Someone had painted little jagged teeth on the front of it.

"Do you have Castille's package?" Eve turned back to the large man as the pair walked by.

"You mean *The Butcher?*" Evan said with an annoyed tone that reminded Eve of a nagging housewife. "You know, when you said you were going to talk to the man in charge, I assumed you meant the man in charge of the extortion operation on the docks. Not the head of the whole goddamn organization," Evan complained as he reached to his side, pulled out a small plastic container and handed it to Eve. "I almost shit myself when I saw that room with the hooks. Next thing I know, I'm having drinks with the most wanted man in the whole system."

"What can I say? I have friends in high places," Eve quipped as she open the container to check the contents. Everything looked in order so Eve closed it again and set it to the side.

"So, what's the plan, boss?" Evan looked at her with an expectant face. Eve just shrugged.

"I'm going to let her get settled a bit, and then I'm going to have a chat with her. You are going back to your apartment and you're going to make dinner for us. Show off some of your new culinary skills." Evan just snorted.

"If you want bland, bullshit food, I'm sure I can whip something up for us. You planning on sleeping in the stacks tonight? My apartment's kind of small, boss. There's only one bed." Eve grinned while reaching into the breast pocket of her coveralls and pulling out a small bottle of tabasco sauce.

"That's okay, I'm sure you won't mind sleeping on the floor," Eve said and slyly presented him with the bottle.

"Holy shit," he said quickly. He snatched the bottle out of her hand and held it like a prize. "I'll sleep in the goddamn hallway for a bottle of this stuff. Okay, yes! Tonight, I'm making us something special. You mind if I show this to my friends at school, boss? They'll fucking lose their minds when they taste this stuff."

"Your *friends at school*?" Eve asked incredulously while pinching the bridge of her nose. "Whatever." She waved it off. "Just don't get caught with it. I'll take it from here. Head back to the room and get started on dinner." Evan nodded once and rose off the bench.

"Righto, boss. Good luck with Helena. I'll see you later." Eve said her goodbyes and watched the man make his way towards the residential district on the other end of the promenade. The big man crossed the recreational courts and made his way past the food courts. After that, Eve lost sight of him.

Eve waited another five minutes before she scooped up Castille's container, rose off the bench, and entered the loose crowd of people making their way along the pedestrian lane. Eve entered Helena's residential district, and walked the corridor up to the Jonlesky residence. She stood outside the door for a moment and took a deep breath before she pressed the call button.

She waited.

"Hello?" A woman's voice came softly over the intercom.

"Mrs. Jonlesky?" Eve asked gently before she introduced herself.

"I'm sorry, I don't know a *Claire Hughes*." The voice said her name with suspicion.

"No, ma'am. We've never met. I'm a friend of Nikoli's. I was hoping I could come in to discuss something important with you." There was a silence that stretched out for seconds before the door finally opened.

Helena stood in the doorway, blocking the entrance with her small, but fierce frame. She had an unimpressed look on her face as she quickly looked Eve over.

"And how *exactly* did you know my husband?"

"Like I said, we're friends." It felt like a bit of an exaggeration. So far, every time she has been in his presence, she had beaten Nikoli half to death.

"*Were* friends," Helena corrected with some venom. "Nikoli died." Helena's voice caught in her throat when she said it, like she was still getting used to the idea. "And I can't imagine what kind of friend you could have been to him if you didn't know this already."

"That's partially what I wanted to talk to you about," Eve said and then nodded towards the interior of the apartment. "Can I come in and talk for a bit?"

Helena looked at her disapprovingly for a moment longer before she slowly stepped to the side and allowed Eve to enter the apartment. Eve also noted that Helena quickly scanned the hallway before she closed the door.

Helena led Eve to a small dining room table and offered her a drink. They sat across from each other with a hot cup of tea in front of them as Eve laid it out for the poor woman. Castille's container lay ominously to the side. Eve wasn't exactly a people person. If she was being honest, she usually just strong-armed people into doing what she wanted. Here, she wanted to be honest...to a point.

Eve told Helena that Nikoli was still alive. There was no point dancing around that fact. Instead Eve led with it, and then explained that Nikoli volunteered for an experiment. She told Helena that The Corporation spared no expense in erasing

Nikoli Jonlesky from The Corporate registrar. Eve ticked off all the ways using her fingers. They erased his memory, changed his physical appearance and his vocal tone, and implanted him with a new corporate ID tag. Eve felt that it was important to stress the fact that for all intents and purposes Nikoli Jonlesky *is* dead. But also, that The Corporation would use Helena and her daughter to control Nick Jones. The person Helena's husband had now become. This meant that Helena and Bella were no longer safe within The Corporate megastructure. Eve told Helena all about the new life that was waiting for her and Bella on Ceres station.

The lies Eve told came out of her mouth just as naturally as the truth did. She didn't tell Helena her true identity, and didn't even mention The Council or Ares. She left out the Motherbot that was implanted into her husband's brain, nor did Eve explain what it would turn her husband into. Eve simply said she didn't know the nature of the experiment. She only knew that the Nikoli they all knew and loved was gone. She told Helena that she met Nikoli in the lab before the experiment. Eve told a brief story of their friendship, which was all lies, and then told Helena about the fictitious promise she gave to Nikoli to get his family out.

Then, as her big finisher, Eve opened Castille's container and showed Helena the medical injector that would cure her daughter's cancer.

"It's what Nikoli wanted," Eve finished with that, and then took a sip of her tea and gave Helena a moment to let it all sink in.

Helena narrowed her eyes when she leaned forward and look at the injector with a muted curiosity. Eve had to admit her reaction was a little underwhelming, which was concerning. Helena sat back and she also took a long sip of her tea, the entire time regarding Eve with a cold expression.

"Get out of my house," Helena hissed at Eve as soon as she placed her cup on the table. Eve just sighed.

"Helena, I understand your apprehension, but if you'll just listen to me-," Eve said gently, hoping she could still sway the woman with the furious eyes in front of her.

"Oh, I think I've heard quite enough." Helena held her composure but her eyes told Eve everything she needed to know. "You people are sick, you know that. My husband was a good man. He followed the rules every day of his life. That is, until *you people* tempted him, *us*, with the one thing, *the one opportunity*, we couldn't resist." Helena pointed an angry finger at Eve and shook it furiously as she spoke. "It is bad enough you took my husband from me, now you return and try to use the same bait to trap me as well. No! Get out of my house! Now!" Helena shot up from her chair and angrily motioned to the front door of the apartment. "And take your *gift* back to your masters!" Helena nodded to Castille's container and the injector within it. The woman refused to even touch it.

"Okay," Eve held up her hands in surrender. "I'll go. But I'll leave the injector. Get it tested, if you don't believe me."

"Oh no! The second I touch that thing, you'll arrest me. You take it with you, I'll have no part of it," Helena said firmly.

Shit, Eve cursed inside her head. She didn't blame Helena. Honestly, the story Eve told her was a bit far-fetched. Most reasonable people probably wouldn't believe it either. Even if ninety-percent of it was true. Plus, she had to consider Helena's mindset as well. The poor woman lost her husband, and it was obvious that the loss with still fresh with her. Plus, she had Bella to think about too.

Whereas Eve just had her rapidly shortening timeline to think about.

"Okay, fine." Eve rose from her seat, reached into the container and pulled out the injector. She slowly started towards the hallway that led to the bedrooms. "We'll do this the hard way."

"No!" Helena shrieked and darted in front of her, blocking Eve's path. "You will *not-*," she started to shout, but Eve balled up her fist and gently sent it a sharp jab into the woman's solar plexus. Helena folded immediately to the ground clutching her stomach and grasping for breath. Eve stepped past her. "No... *please,*" Helena weakly whispered from the ground.

"I'm helping her, *and* you," Eve said with a disappointed look on her face before she keyed the intercom system, and commanded the Motherbot to augment her voice to replicate Helena's. "Bella? Sweetie?" Eve said clearly to the Helena's horrified expression. "I need you to put your mask on, baby. There's a nurse who's going to come in and give you a vitamin shot." Eve looked back to Helena who was still recovering on the floor. She was looking at Eve with tears in her eyes and a pleading expression that begged Eve to stop what she was doing. *I'm helping them,* Eve reminded herself. Even though, at the moment, it very much felt like Eve was the bad guy here.

"Mask on, mommy!" The little girl's voice came.

Eve closed the intercom channel and looked back to Bella's mother who was struggling to stand.

"You stay there," Eve said sharply. "I don't want to scare her." Eve saw the tears in Helena's eyes drain down her face before she added, "I'm *helping* you," Eve said again. *Whether you like it or not,* Eve finished inside her head.

Eve cycled the airlock door to open and entered the girl's room, leaving Helena at the mouth of the hallway.

"RAWR!" Bella roared loudly and jumped out from behind her bed into a fierce stance with her little digits poised out in front of her like claws. Eve took on a look of shock and jumped back from the kid's display in mock fright.

"Oh my God!" Eve exclaimed and held her free hand to her heart. "You scared me so much. Look at you. Such a scary little monster. Oh, and what big teeth you have Miss Monster," Eve lowered herself down in front of the little girl and smiled warmly at her. "I have a shot here I'm supposed to give you," Eve said cautiously with a sly look on her face. "You won't bite me if I try to give it to you, will you?" Bella giggled slightly at that, the electronic augmented sounds of her laughter darkened them slightly through the mask.

"No," Bella chirped gently. "I'm a *good* monster."

"Well then," Eve moved closer to the small frail-looking child and rolled up her sleeve a bit. "I don't have anything to worry about, do I?" Eve smiled at her and held the injector to the girl's tiny arm and pressed the trigger.

There was a small metallic clicking sound as the syringe struck home and then a barely audible hiss could be heard as the plunger pushed the gene therapy treatment into Bella's bloodstream. A few moments later, the syringe retracted with the same clicking noise, and it was over. Bella was cured.

"That didn't hurt at all," Bella said looking at the spot on her arm where the injector pierced.

"No? What a strong monster you are. I've got to go talk to your mommy for a bit now. I'll see you later, Bella."

"Bye-bye." Bella waved quickly before she walked back to her drawing table. Something on the child's wall caught Eve's eye. Seems Bella was quite the artist. The walls had little pieces of paper with her artwork scribbled all over them. One in particular caught her eye.

"Hey, Bella?" Eve called back to the child while eyeing a poorly drawn picture of Bella and her parents walking hand-in-hand down a forest path. "You mind if I take this?" Eve looked back to Bella and pointed to the drawing. "I have a friend who would really like it," Eve said and watched as the tiny child just shrugged innocently to the question.

"Sure."

"Thanks," Eve said, pulling the picture down from the wall and folded it into a neat square she could slip into her pocket. She exited the room and cycled the airlock door closed.

Immediately a program started the decontamination routine for the small room. Eve slowly walked up to Helena. Nikoli's wife backed away from her weakly. Eve couldn't blame her for that. "She going to get pretty sick in the next couple days," Eve said and offered the woman her hand. "That's normal. It's all part of the process. But I need you to understand that under no condition can you take Bella to a medical facility." Helena looked up at her, listened to her words, nodded her head slowly. She reached up and took Eve's offered hand. Eve effortlessly helped the woman to her feet. "As far as anyone else is concerned, Bella still has cancer." At that Helena shook as a gentle sob escaped her lips.

"Is she...is she really cured?" Eve could see in Helena's desperate eyes that she truly wanted to believe it.

"Not yet," Eve said gently, almost apologetically. "But she will be. Soon." Helena leapt forward, wrapped her arms around Eve and cried uncontrollably. Eve was taken back by it but soon returned the embrace and quietly reassured the sobbing woman that everything would be okay.

Suddenly, retrieving Hera and Ares' flight suit, while also recruiting Jones to their cause weren't Eve's only priorities.

"Thank you," Helena breathed weakly over and over again into Eve's ear. Eve gave her some time to get it out before she gently pulled the woman away.

"Don't thank me yet, we still have a ways to go before you and Bella are truly safe." Eve reached into her pocket and pulled out her datapad. Once the nanomachines made contact Eve sliced off a bit of herself and darted through the digital landscape. Shortly after, Eve's datapad pinged several times, signalling the completion of the tasks. "You and Bella have just been authorized for a week's medical leave. Stay here, take care of your daughter, and don't talk to anyone. I have someone watching you," Eve said quietly and watched the sudden concern bloom over the woman's face. "A friend. His name is Evan.

After tonight, you need anything, anything at all, you call his name." Eve said looking at her with a reassuring expression. In her head, Eve was already figuring out the shifts she and Evan would have to take to ensure one of them was watching the pair at all times. Eve also had her digital-self hack into Helena's datapad and upload a tracer program that basically turned the woman's datapad into a fancy surveillance device for Eve. "I'll be back in a couple of days. After the fever has passed, we can start talking about getting you out of here. Because I'm sorry to say this, but you *are* leaving the Corporation. You and Bella both." Eve looked to the woman apologetically before she continued to strong-arm the woman.

Thankfully Helena said something that made Eve feel better about herself and the plan she made for the pair.

"You promise?"

CHAPTER 14

Lucien

He opened his eyes to bright lights and blurred images he couldn't discern. Lucien groaned weakly and tried to shield his eyes, and found he couldn't move his body. He felt it. Well, he felt the pain from it. So, that had to be a good sign.

"Lucien?" A sweet voice came from somewhere in the room. He tried to turn his head towards it but even that part of his body wasn't working right. "Lucien?" The voice came again. This time he weakly groaned his reply, and moved his tongue around the arid environment of his mouth. Lucien felt a presence move in beside him.

"Water," Lucien painfully breathed out. His voice was nothing more than a weak rasp. There was motion by his side, and a plastic straw was gently placed to his lips. Lucien wrapped his cracked lips around it and sucked greedily. The cool fluid was glorious as it washed down his throat, cleansing the foul taste from his mouth. Lucien coughed slightly.

"Easy," the voice cautioned. Lucien didn't listen to it, he just kept drinking until the cup was empty. He released the straw from his mouth and eased his head back onto the pillow.

"Who?" He asked simply before he cleared his throat.

"It's Leslie. Leslie Bowers." Lucien looked towards the blurred shape and tried to focus his eyes, but to no avail.

"Leslie?" *What's she doing here?* It was the first thought that came to his weary, clouded mind. Lucien tried to look for a reason for her visit in the depths of his mind, but then soon realized he had bigger problems.

"I can't move," Lucien confessed weakly. "I can't see." His throat hurt terribly with every word. Again, Lucien coughed.

"You just got out of the autodoc, dear. It's going to take some time for the sedatives to wear off. Your eyes probably hurt because your retinas are new. I imagine that too will pass with time. Lucien?" Leslie had a hint of concern in her voice that cause Lucien to dread what she had to say next. "Do you remember what happened?"

What happened? The question flared through the fog of his mind as Lucien tried to think back. He could recall Cattivo's office. He and Ernst were interrogating that incompetent scientist. *What was his name?* Lucien asked himself the question over and over again inside his brain but no matter how hard he tried, Lucien couldn't remember that fool's name. He remembered watching the man scurry out of the doctor's office. Him and Ernst shared a few words and then...Something happen. *Was it an accident? Something from one of the labs? No,* Lucien thought suddenly. *It wasn't an accident!* Then a dark expression bloomed across Lucien's face as his mind conjured up the final moments before the explosion.

"Who was it?" Lucien growled darkly.

"Snell from Technical Development, and Trup from Industrial Science." Leslie coldly listed off the names and paused for it to sink in. *Motherfuckers!* Lucien screamed inside his head, externally it came out sounding like a low growl. *A bomb?!* Lucien couldn't believe the recklessness of such an act. "They fitted one of your lab techs with a prosthetic that was rigged with a firebomb. The tech's name was-," Leslie was about to say the name, but Lucien beat her to it.

"Jerry!" Lucien hissed the name between his teeth. "I know the man."

"That's him. Anyways, the good news is it *was* a firebomb, so the physical damage was kept to a minimum. Your research supervisors have checked in and there have been no major adverse effects to your ongoing *projects*." Leslie said the word with a hint of intrigue that concerned Lucien. "A few of your staff had to be treated for varying degrees of burns, but nothing serious. All in all, for an attempt to kill you and disrupt your work, those two did a pretty piss-poor job."

"Lucien! Get down!" Ernst had said. Lucien remembered the man jumped towards him and forced him to the ground just before the fireball overtook the office. With a hint of sadness, he also remembered how the good doctor had hugged Lucien's body close to his. Ernst had sacrificed his own body to save him from the worst of it.

"Cattivo?" He asked, and suffered through the awkward pause before Bowers finally spoke.

"He's...stable, for now. There are some decisions that will need to be made there. But technically, he *is* alive."

Technically? What the fuck does that mean? Lucien groaned weakly as the questions flared up inside his head again. Ernst Cattivo was probably the only person Lucien would call a friend. Like Leslie, he was more than a simple colleague and intellectual equal. They also knew each other's sins, and they both accepted each other despite them. He was also one of the two people Lucien actually enjoyed being in the company of.

He growled again.

"Hey now," Leslie cooed with a maternal tone, and stroked his stubbled head. "Calm yourself, darling. You need to rest, you're in no shape for retribution." Lucien shuttered slightly with frustration. Leslie was right. He was too weak. "I've already traced the chemical composition of the accelerant they used back to Trup's lab, and I have an informant inside Snell's section that's digging up some evidence for me." Leslie stroked his head again and spoke softly into his ear. "Leave this to me, dear. You rest. Let me serve these little piglets to you on a platter. Legs bound, with nice juicy apples in their mouths. We are *partners*, after all. What is done to you, is done to me."

"Thank you, Leslie." He looked to Bowers' blurred image. Lucien direly wished he could see the woman's face so he could judge her intent. A person like Leslie Bowers conveyed her true motives on her face, and in her eyes. Leslie's sweet words were often times like the stripes on a tiger. Just camouflage that allowed her to get closer to her prey.

"Rest up, dear." Leslie gently patted his cheek and turned to move away, presumably out of the room. "You can thank me later by telling me all about that *fascinating* ship in your lab, and by introducing me to whoever this Nick Jones person is. Ta-ta for now, love."

Lucien heard the door into the room he was in open and close again. After that, the only sounds were the hum and clicks of the machines he was hooked up to.

Shit, Lucien cursed inside his head. The nature of his research was supposed to be the carrot that he could use to string Leslie on, if needed. Now that she knew, they were true equals. Trusting each other not to slit the throat of the other. Lucien didn't foresee a problem with Leslie knowing about the Council ship in his possession, or the fact that he implanted a corporate citizen with the one piece of technology that could make him a god. He calmed down by reminding himself she was going to learn the truth at some point along the way.

What is done to you, is done to me. That's what Leslie had said. Lucien smiled, because if that was the case, he was eager to find out what the future held for Snell and Trup.

***

"We're almost there, sir." Brock drove the transport slowly down the vehicle lane that circled the independent sector from Shipping and Receiving. He knew that the slight jostling of the transport caused Lucien some discomfort.

The nano-restorative process Lucien had to undergo to remove the burn scars left behind from the explosion left his skin feeling raw and exposed. Every slight movement caused the expensive fibers of his tailored suit to feel more like broken glass being scraped across his skin. It was a small price to pay to remove the ugly, deformed flesh from his body. Lucien sat tall in the back with both of his palms resting on the large metal ball on his new cane. Leslie had gotten it for him when she learned about the fused ligaments in his right knee joint. That, too, shall be fixed in time.

But time was a precious commodity these days. Snell and Trup had their respective Directors propose moving up the vote for the Special Projects Directorship. A vote was taken, and the proposal passed. The original six-month period was re-established. That meant the vote for his job was now in one short week. It was an annoyance, but he would be ready for it.

Before the explosion he had already removed the biggest threats from contention. Hell, Lucien even managed to turn two of them to his side. The candidate from Maintenance already disqualified himself at the soiree, and two more candidates were removed from the running this morning. Lucien was currently on his way to inform them. That left only two more candidates who were still in contention for his job. But honestly, the candidates from Solar Exploration, and Agriculture weren't really candidates at all. Not when they were compared to him. He could probably have them *removed* as well, but honestly, he had other things to worry about.

Like what to do about Ernst. The poor doctor had put himself between the blast and Lucien, and he paid the price for it. Three of Cattivo's limbs were so badly burned they had to be amputated. The fourth one was rendered useless as the heat fused the joints of the limbs and damaged the nerves beyond repair. Cattivo was kept in a coma, which was a kindness. The doctors said that if he was conscious, he would be in constant pain. The machines connected to him controlled the major functions of his body. Honestly, the doctor should be dead. Science and technology were the only things keeping Ernst alive. The people in his care advised Lucien to simply let the man die, but Lucien couldn't accept that. He couldn't accept the monumental loss of potential accomplishments if he were to let Ernst's genius fade from existence.

No, Lucien had other plans for the good doctor.

"We're here, sir." Brock pulled the cart in front of the lavish, independently-owned restaurant. It was styled to have a dark chic, which to some extent, Lucien found pleasing to his eye. But he couldn't see himself trudging up to this cesspool just for poorly-cooked food and watered-down alcohol.

Bowers had set up the meet. For weeks she had been feeding the other executives tales of Lucien's declining health. To the point that Lucien's eventual death was all but certain. Then, after she had the evidence she needed to close their books permanently, Leslie set up the meet to simply extort them for some favors. She had set it up in the independent sector, claiming it was neutral territory where they didn't have to worry about prying eyes. The utmost discretion was needed for such a sensitive situation, after all.

"Thank you, Brock," Lucien said as he exited the cart. To the sides of the establishment, out of sight of the patrons, was a contingent of corporate guards in powered armor. Lucien craned his neck to the side to loosen the tight muscles in his neck before he slowly made his way towards the door. The reinforced tip of his cane tapped loudly against the ground as he went.

Tap-tap-tap.

With a snap of his fingers the guards on both sides quickly fell in behind him.

Lucien waited as they kicked in the front doors of the establishment, quickly filed into the restaurant and took up positions on both sides of the entrance. Lucien waited a moment longer before he entered through the ruined entrance, past the broken pieces of the door that still hung on its hinges, and walked into the restaurant.

Tap-tap-tap-tap.

Lucien stabbed the cane down hard with each step as he walked into the collection of stunned expressions and fearful faces that watched him move into the center of the room.

"Everybody out," Lucien said, almost conversationally after he leveled a hard gaze at the two men at Leslie's table.

Behind him, a series of high-pitched whines came as the guards powered up their shocksticks.

"You heard the man!" One of them shouted. "Fucking out! Now!" The guards tore into the restaurant with brutal efficiency. Tables were overturned, and shouts of protest erupted, which were soon followed by screams. Glasses and dinnerware crashed and broke against the ground as the guards forcibly removed every patron from the restaurant and collected the staff into a tight circle kneeling on the ground with their hands behind their heads. Lucien simply stood in the center of the commotion and locked his steely gaze upon the two nervous men at Leslie's table.

When it was done, Leslie's table was the only one that stood unmolested amongst the chaos.

At the table, Leslie smiled and slowly reached down beside her chair for her posh leather handbag. She pulled it up to the table and then slowly stood from her chair. Bowers looked to her stunned comrades at the table as she reached into her bag and slowly pulled out two apples, which she placed in front of both of them. Lucien smiled smugly as Leslie casually strolled away from the table and walked to his side.

"As promised, darling." Leslie's bright red lipstick shined like blood on her lips when she smiled.

"Thank you, Leslie." Lucien peered at the two men. "You two have been busy, haven't you? Busy-busy-busy," Lucien said in rapid succession as he approached the table. *Tap-tap-tap.* He moved to Leslie's seat and eased himself into the cushioned chair. Lucien glared at each of them and watched with predatory amusement as they squirmed in their seats.

"Lucien, whatever it is that Bowers told you is pure fabrication, I assure you." Trup spoke up first after he quickly straighten his darkly-striped tie. He would have continued but Lucien silenced him with a wave of his hand. Snell jumped in his seat at the slight movement.

"You needn't say anything more," Lucien said in a reassuring tone. He then awkwardly reached over the table and plucked Trup's wine glass up and cradled it lovingly in his hand as he sat back down. "We're past that now." Out of habit, he checked the wine's clarity in the restaurant's lights before he brought it to his nose so he could smell the bouquet. His sense of smell had yet to return. Lucien frowned when he sipped the wine; it was too bitter for his liking. "I'm not here to ask you your involvement. Nor am I here to assign blame to anyone. Believe me, guys, I've done my fair share of dirty deeds in the past. I get it. Only so many people can fit onto the corporate ladder, some executives are bound to fall off." Lucien paused to eye each of them for a second. "Or be thrown off. It's important to me that you understand I don't fault you one bit for the attempt you made on my life." Lucien then chuckled lightheartedly. "I would have done the same thing." Then Lucien stopped laughing. "What I can fault you for, is damaging my labs, delaying my work, injuring my staff, *and damn near killing my best friend*!" Lucien screamed the last part. He hadn't planned on saying *best friend,* it slipped out. But it felt right to him.

"You can't prove anything," Trup said definitively.

"*You're* here, aren't you?" Lucien motioned around to the chaos around them. "In this *shitty* little restaurant, eating their *shitty* food and drinking their *shitty* wine. So, obviously you believe Leslie has something on your dumb asses. And I have what Leslie has. And as of eight o'clock this morning, so does the Chairman. He seems to think what we had was enough to prove quite a bit," Lucien said with an amused cadence in his voice as he pulled his datapad from the inside pocket of his blazer. He hummed a merry tune during the time it took to send the packets to the men's datapads. "Which is why you've been fired." Lucien watched with great satisfaction as the two men read their termination slips with horrified expressions. "If you'll look down near the bottom," Lucien said smugly taking another sip of the man's bitter wine. "You'll see I've been named adjudicator of your estates." He let the piece of information sink in for a moment.

Their lives were already forfeit. The termination letter stated they were no longer members of the Corporation. They were free agents now. Their possessions, their wives, as well as any children that they may be responsible for, were now under Lucien's jurisdiction. If he wanted, Lucien could terminate their contracts as well.

"Jesus Christ!" Snell exclaimed reading over the last bit of the letter. "You can't do this, we're executives!" He looked incredulously at Trup, like the man had all the answers. Trup was a *real* executive. He still sat tall in his fashionable dark suit, even though the worried look on his face betrayed the sense of calm the man liked to exude. John Snell was just a pudgy lab assistant with too much ambition and not enough good sense. "He can't do this, right? We're goddamn *executives*!"

"No, you're *terrorists*. *Executives* follow rules. *Executives* understand there is a certain unspoken decorum to these things. And you, gentlemen, have crossed the line in a most grievous manner. A knife in the back is one thing, but blowing up a whole section using an unknowing lab assistant as a suicide bomber? Could you even imagine the chaos that would happen if every executive could simply blow up their competition? Use your head, man!" Lucien reached over and tapped Snell on his shiny, oversized forehead. Lucien looked at the man with a disgusted expression for a second longer before he let the expression drop. He then gazed at Mark Trup with a bored expression. "You, I understand. Setting this poor-fucking-idiot up to take the fall if anything were to go wrong." Lucien wagged his finger at him playfully. "Your mistake was not subletting the custom-made accelerant to another division *outside* Research and Development. You only compounded the mistake by not immediately killing the lab tech who developed it." Lucien gave Trup a brief, mocking laugh. "Do you realize how quickly the man gave you up? I only had to cut off *two* of his fingers." Lucien held up the pinkie and ring fingers of his left hand to show which ones he took from the man.

"I was getting around to it," Trup said as a disappointed sigh. "We were led to believe you were on your deathbed."

"'*Getting around to it*', '*Led to believe*'," Lucien mockingly repeated the man's words back to him. "Words of a failure," Lucien said loudly so the entire room could hear him before he turned back to Trup. "Your laziness was your undoing."

"Lucien! Jesus!" Snell turned to him red-faced with tears forming in his eyes. "I'm sorry. Please. I didn't mean for any of this to happen." Snell furiously pointed at Trup. "It was all *his* idea!"

"I believe you," Lucien said in a soothing voice to calm the man.

"I'm sorry," Snell said again, more pathetic this time. If that was even possible. Lucien regarded him with a cold stare.

"Let me teach you a quick lesson about the problem with *I'm sorry*." Lucien leveraged himself on his cane to lift himself out of his chair. "Put your head on your plate," Lucien said, calmly pointed to the mostly empty plate in front of Snell.

"What?" Snell squeaked.

"Put your *fucking* head on your *fucking* plate!" Lucien awkwardly lunged towards Snell and grabbed the man by the back of his neck and savagely forced the man's head down. The entire time, the man beneath his grasp whimpered weakly. "Good," Lucien said once his head was down. He released his grip and moved back. "Now turn your head and look at Trup." When he did, Lucien took the large metal lion's head on his cane and placed it against the side of Snell's head. So, he could get a feel for the weight of it. "Are you looking at him?"

"Yes," Snell sobbed obediently.

"Tell me again how sorry you are," Lucien growled.

"Lucien, I am-," he started to say but Lucien cut him off. He raised the cane up with both hands and smashed it down on the man's head four times in rapid succession.

On the first blow, Snell yelped weirdly and his whole body convulsed once violently. The second blow cracked the man's skull open and sprayed the immediate area with the man's blood. The third broke it apart completely and spilled grey matter onto the table, in front of Trup's horrified expression. The fourth blow broke the plate Snell's head was resting on and sent gore flying. When he was done, Lucien looked down at his broken skull with a sneer on his face.

"I'm sorry too, John, but *sorry* doesn't put your fucking skull back together, does it?" Lucien asked the leaking corpse on the table. Lucien took a napkin from the table and wiped down the head of his cane. He then removed a sanitary tissue from the packet in his pocket and wiped down his face and hands. Lucien breathed deeply and just looked at Trup.

"Are you going to bash my head in, too?" Trup asked with a certain amount of fear in his voice that Lucien found very satisfying.

"No," Lucien said calmly as he made his way around the table to Trup's side. *Tap-tap-tap.* "I wouldn't want to waste good materials." Lucien reached into the front pocket of his blazer and removed a medical injector. He quickly placed it to the side of Trup's neck and pulled the trigger. By the time Trup reacted to the attack, it was too late.

"What was that?!" Trup looked back to him and groped the spot on his neck.

Tap-tap-tap. Lucien walked back and planted himself back into his seat. He was somewhat out of breath.

"Relax," he said with a wave of his hand as he reached for his wine glass. Lucien noticed a small piece of Snell's grey matter had attached itself to the side of his wineglass. He used the salad fork to promptly remove it. "It's a mild sedative. It will take effect in a minute or so. I didn't want to rob you of the opportunity to enjoy the last couple minutes of your life."

"You said it was a sedative?" Trup looked at him confused.

"Oh, it is. But you'll never be conscious again after you close your eyes. You see," Lucien said with some excitement as he leaned forward. "I'm going to take you back down to my lab and I'm going to harvest your brain and spinal column, as well as any other bits of you I might need to save my friend. Whatever is left, I'll throw into a recycler. I thought I'd flay enough of your skin off to make a fashionable purse for your wife, as a way of condolence. But instead, I think I'll marry off your daughters to Snell's sons." Lucien thumbed over to Snell's gaping skull that had its contents strewn across the table like a welcome mat. "I'll make sure Daisy and Dehlia enjoy a wonderful life of mediocrity in the mid-stacks, pumping out children for Snell's idiot offspring until the end of their days." Lucien watched as the man's eyes grew heavy. "Sure, the age difference might make the match a tad unsightly for your girls, but I'm sure they'll find their way. After all, from what I've heard, the Snell boys have a bit of a mean streak to them." Lucien smiled. Trup had several offspring, but Lucien knew the two youngest daughters were his favorite.

"You're a bastard," Trup sighed as his head dropped. The man drunkenly caught it just to limply raise it up to look Lucien in the eyes once more. Even through the haze of the sedative, Lucien could see the fury in the man's waning eyes.

It tickled Lucien, because it was the look of a man who knew he had been beaten.

"And then some," Lucien whispered after the man's face fell forward into what remained of his pasta dish.

CHAPTER 15

Nick Jones

After the bombing of the Special Projects section, Nick enjoyed a full week of relative freedom. Nobody from the section contacted him after it was closed for the investigation. Nick found out both Mr. Malum and Ernst had been hospitalized. It was Soldado that told him that someone tried to assassinate Mr. Malum for his job, in some corporate powerplay that Nick didn't really understand or even care about. Someone had tried to kill Mr. Malum and failed. That's all he needed to know. It didn't surprise Nick when he heard the news. The only real surprise was that nobody had tried sooner.

Nick's routine didn't change that much. He still trained in the morning with Soldado, and then ran training operations in the afternoon with the Special Operation members. In the evenings, Nick would do a shadow-shift with a troublesome guard for the last half of the day shift. *To set them straight,* Soldado had said. After what happened to Cummins, Nick was gaining a certain fearful reputation amongst the guards responsible for the stacks. Some even went as far as to plan retaliatory action against him.

It was a simple setup. Childish almost. The guard he was shadowing led him to an empty warehouse on the Maintenance level where a dozen of his disgruntled comrades were waiting with large pipes in their hands, and menacing looks on their faces. Nick left their broken bodies in that warehouse. He was sure some of them would probably die before the medics got there. He left one conscious enough to hear his parting words.

"Next time," Nick said, looking down at the man. "Bring more guys."

After that, Nick was supposed to go back to Special Projects, to be poked and probed by the geeks, have a bland calorie and nutrient-rich meal that was strictly portioned to his meal plan, before he retired for the evening and lay in his bunk in the dark, pretending to sleep.

But Special Projects was closed.

For the first time since he woke up, Nick had free time at his disposal. He didn't know how long it would last. Mr. Malum and Ernst weren't going to be in the hospital forever. So, Nick took advantage of it to scratch two itches that had been clawing away at the inside of his brain.

Nick started with the woman in his dreams. Back when he still dreamt.

It was the woman Cummins had been harassing before Nick stepped in. He knew that. But he had been dreaming of her face before then. When he first saw her face, she was walking along the pedestrian lane. To Nick's muted shame, it was probably his gawking that prompted Cummins into action. Since then, Nick had thought of that woman in the darkness of the night in the safe space behind his eyelids. He thought of her face, of her flowing blonde hair framing the delicate lines while she smiled. Her sweet eyes that looked up at him and twinkled like gems. He thought about a lot of things. Soon, his mind conjured up little pretend scenes that would play for a mere instant inside the depths of his mind before disappearing like smoke. Little snippets of her life that he imagined she had. Nick pictured her in the mornings, brushing her hair as she got ready for her shift. He couldn't explain it, but he felt that she was the kind of woman who liked to be early for her shift, and liked to present herself in a certain way to the world. She was a mother in some of the conjured scenes, a good one. Nick didn't even know what it meant to be *a good mother*, but he just knew that she was.

Nick, on some occasions, tried to imagine what the woman's child would look like. When he did, he always pictured a small framed child that looked somewhat frail. When he tried to imagine her face. Because, for some reason, he always pictured the woman having a little girl. The same two words flashed inside his head that made his eyes water like some Pavlovian reaction.

Monster kisses.

Finding out the woman's identity had been fairly simple. As was covering his tracks. Nick felt a definite sense of foreboding when he thought about Mr. Malum finding out about this woman. He was pretty sure they were watching him at all times, which meant it wasn't much of a jump to imagine they would be monitoring his digital tracks as well.

Soon after he stopped sleeping, Nick developed a *ghost protocol* for his datapad. It was a program that erased any digital trace of his datapad when he was on the network. The hardest part had been figuring out the coding language. He spent a full night writing the code for the program inside his head. There wasn't a trial-and-error process, it either worked and the ghost protocol was created, or it wouldn't, and his attempts would probably alert his handlers.

Thankfully, it worked.

Using the protocol, Nick first uploaded a hand-drawn sketch of the woman he made on his datapad a while ago. The facial recognition program quickly came back with her corporate file. Helena Jonlesky. *Jonlesky?* That was an unusual name to find in the middle stack region. *Ethnic* names like that usually resided lower down. Maiden name was Fouillard. She was thirty-two years old, about to turn thirty-three in a couple of months. She had a husband, deceased, named *Nikoli*. *I know that name,* Nick thought inexplicably for a moment. The file stated the husband died in prison. Nick wondered if he had sent him there. He checked the dates of the arrest and it didn't match up. It was before Nick was...Created? Awoken? Born? He didn't know what it was, but it was before his *time*. He paused for a moment when he saw that a young female was listed as Jonlesky's dependant. *She does have a little girl,* Nick thought to himself and was oddly concerned by how unsurprised he was. Like, of course she did.

The little girl's name is Isabella.

Helena, Nikoli, and Isabella. Nick played with the names in his head. *Nikoli, Helena, and Isabella.* It felt natural, and foreign at the same time, as he replayed the names in his head. As if he was trying them out for size. Like, the words were a puzzle of some kind, and if he just said them in the right order, he would unlock...something.

Soon after, Nick came to the inevitable conclusion that he had to see this woman. This *Helena Jonlesky*.

Nobody even questioned him when he walked out of the Special Operations section. He reported in after his shadow-shift, and instead of retiring to his quarters, Nick headed to the reception area of the section and then just walked right out the door. Like it was the most normal thing he could ever do. Like he enjoyed this kind of freedom every day.

Nick wasted no time and headed up to the Shipping and Receiving level. The nice thing about the Special Operations recruit uniform, is that it meant you could pretty much go anywhere in the corporate megastructure and no one would look twice at you. Hell, most people who recognized the uniform crossed the pedestrian lane to avoid him. The customs guard just idly waved him through the checkpoint.

Nick walked straight to the food court.

The chicken curry was amazing. Nick was pretty sure it was his favorite. While trying a trio of different dishes, Nick used the ghost program to hack into the Human Resources database for Stack Four. The Jonlesky woman should be on-shift at the moment. He had plenty of time. He planned to do a little reconnaissance of the medical facility she worked at, and then follow her home. He didn't want to confront her. Nick couldn't even fathom what he would say to her, but something inside him just wanted to see her. Somehow, he felt that would be enough. *What the fuck?* Nick was surprised to find the database listed the woman as being on a medical leave. He didn't know why, but he feared for the woman's dependant. The little girl, Isabella. Nick shoveled the food quickly into his mouth, suddenly feeling a sense of urgency that wasn't there before. He dug deeper into the mystery before him, and found the little girl has bone cancer. Nick stared dispassionately at the datapad while he thought of the implications of what he had learned.

Nick left his remaining food on the table, stood up and walked back towards the customs checkpoint. Nick stormed past the citizens of The Corporation who were obediently waiting in the queue and gave the guard working the checkpoint a look that almost dared him to try and stop him. Nick tried to calm his nerves on his way to the central lift. He had a long way to go yet. He had plotted the quickest, most efficient way in his mind well ahead of time, but it didn't stop the anxiety that was strangely boiling up inside him. *Not fast enough,* something inside harassed him as he rode the pedestrian tram to Stack Four. Something inside Nick pleaded with him to run, just *fucking* run as fast as his body could move him, towards Helena and her sick child. *This is the fastest way,* Nick told himself, over and over again as he tapped his foot on the tram's floor.

At Jonlesky's level, Nick could barely contain himself to a walk as he crossed towards her residential district. He broke pedestrian protocol and pushed past people on the lane, and when that wasn't enough, Nick abandoned the pedestrian lane altogether and stormed across the manicured sports fields. He paid no attention to the players from the game he was interrupting, or their protests. One even made the mistake of standing in Nick's path.

"Hey man! What the hell?" The player didn't say anything else, he didn't get a chance. Nick shoved the man hard with his open palm.

"Get out of my way!" Nick growled angrily at the idiot who either didn't recognize the uniform, or the *don't-fuck-with-me* expression on his face. Either way, Nick sent the man flying backwards to a skidding halt in the grass where he left him, wheezing on the ground, and continued on his way.

Nick saw the entrance to Jonlesky's district, and also caught the movement of the two guards in personal armor approaching him swiftly from the side. Nick recognized one of them, he had done a shadow-shift with the man a few days back. Nick watched as the guard grabbed his comrade's arm and quickly nodded his head at the man. *Not this guy,* that gesture said. The two quickly changed their path and walked in the opposite direction.

Nick was in a haze as he entered into the district. Before he knew it, he was standing in front of the entrance to the Jonlesky residence without a real clear understanding of how he knew which door was hers. Regardless, Nick stared at Ms. Jonlesky's door for what seemed like a long time. Motionless. The emerald green call button was practically glowing beside the door it stood out so much in his mind. *All I have to do is press that button,* Nick thought as he looked at it. He would press it, and the woman would come to the door. *All I have to do is press* that *button, and Helena Jonlesky will be standing in front of me.* Something inside him, some tired whisper of a presence, begged him to press that button.

Nick reached for it.

And stopped. He looked down at his hand as it shook, inches away from the button. He felt dread start to well up inside him at the prospect of seeing what was on the other side of that door. Like whatever it was, or whoever it might be, would break him apart inside. The dread screamed at him to immediately stop what he was doing, and walk away. *What would I even say to her?* Nick wondered as he looked down at his trembling hand.

Movement from the corner of his eye brought Nick back to the here and now. He quickly turned to face a large black man who came to a shuttered stop when he recognized the Special Operations uniform.

"Oop," the large man said dumbly and quickly held out his hands to steady himself. Nick noticed the man had metal hands, that looked to be expertly fashioned to resemble a human hand.

"You live here?" Nick asked the stunned man sharply.

"Umm," the man stammered slightly. "Yep. I live just down the hall, around the corner." The man used a shiny digit to point down to the next intersection.

"You know this woman?" Nick asked and pointed to the door he was in front of. "Miss Jonlesky?"

"Yes. I do. She's a good woman," he said quickly still keeping his hands in plain view. "I don't know what a guard would want with her, though."

"I'm not a guard," Nick hissed and looked at the door. "I just," Nick started to say and paused. Unsure of how he would word it. "I heard about the medical leave, and I got...concerned, I guess. I wanted to check in on her." Nick looked back to the emerald green button. "Make sure she was okay." Nick looked back to the man, leveled him with a hard stare. "So? How is she doing?" He asked sternly. Not so much asking for information, as demanding the large man give him what he *needed* to know.

"Ah," the man stammered nervously. Nick blamed the uniform. There was absolutely no reason for a Special Operation recruit to be in front of Ms. Jonlesky's door like he was. He wasn't surprised the man was taken back, but it was frustrating watching the man search for his words. "Good," he finally said. "She's doing good. Real good, in fact."

"And the medical leave?"

"That? Her little girl came down with a bug of some kind. Not a big deal. You know how kids are," the black man smiled and said it like he actually expected Nick to know what he was talking about. "Probably just picked something up at school. Anyways, Helena's been working a lot lately so she probably just took a few days personal time to hang out with her kid." Nick nodded at what the man said. "I'm sure everything is fine. That little cutey will probably be out playing with the other kids in no time." Nick frowned at the man. He didn't know why, but something about that last statement didn't *feel* right.

"What's your name?" Nick asked, out of habit.

"Evan. Evan Thompson." The man's expression shifted to one of sudden concern. "Am I in trouble for something?"

"No," Nick replied quickly and shook his head at the man. "Thank you for your time. You can go," Nick dismissed the man. The large-framed black man, Evan, slowly lowered his metal hands and dropped his head a bit as he hustled by Nick and disappeared around the next corner.

Nick looked to the door again.

Everything is fine, Nick repeated Evan's words in his mind. *Everything is fine.* He didn't need to press the green button. He didn't need to confront whatever was behind the door. *Everything is fine.* Ms. Jonlesky is fine, and so is her daughter. *Walk away. Before it's too late.*

Nick breathed deeply once and then turned away from the door and walked out of the residential district. He didn't know what brought him here with such blinding urgency, or why he jumped down this rabbit-hole so quickly. But now, it felt dangerous. Like pursuing it uncovered some defect in his programming. A defect he should be hiding away from his handlers. Nick walked back to the closest lift he could access and thought of how he would explain away this little venture if it ever came back to him.

Nick slowly made his way up the megastructure and concocted his story. If asked by whoever, but Nick had a strong suspicion it would be Mr. Malum, he would simply say he was following up with the woman to make sure she wasn't being harassed by other guards. It was a razor-thin excuse and, if pressed, Nick would fall back and claim the woman was simply an excuse to venture out into the stacks. A silly reason to enjoy a bit of freedom. That was more believable, especially if he didn't lead with it.

With that curiosity sated, Nick focused on his other itch the next night. The bitch that kicked his ass during the prison break.

With a smile and a wave at the receptionist, Nick ended his shift the next day and walked out the front in such a carefree manner he almost had a skip in his step. Again, he made his way up to the independent sector of the Shipping and Receiving level and found himself a quiet table at the food court. This time Nick drank a beer with his plates of chicken curry while he used his Ghost program to quietly hack into the Port Authority's mainframe.

Annoyingly, the Port Authority had jurisdiction over the investigation into the prison break. Nick looked over the lead investigator's notes, watched the surveillance videos, and read over the reports of the physical evidence at the scene. They had absolutely nothing on the mysterious woman who weighed twice as much as she should, was stronger than could be believed, and moved with the speed and grace of a dancer. The sketch Nick provided was fed into the system-wide database and came back with no results. *Probably had reconstructive surgery,* Nick thought to himself. That would explain the negative result from the facial recognition search. It didn't explain the negative result for the DNA search. The explanation for that was in the blood samples they collected at the scene. Which were marked as *Confidential,* with an *eyes-only* protocol that was specific to Mr. Malum or Dr. Cattivo. That was a minor obstacle. He saw his blood sample first, and immediately noticed the notation.

Inorganic material: 20%

Should I be worried about that? Nick thought to himself as he scanned over the rest of the blood work. That seemed normal to his untrained eye. He looked at the *unknown* sample that was collected at the scene of his beating. Immediately he saw it.

Inorganic material: 92%

He looked, but there was no further analysis as to what exactly the *inorganic* material was. Nick also noticed something else peculiar about the unknown sample, no DNA was recovered from the scene. *How's that possible? I shot that bitch five times.* Even with the high levels of inorganic material that was present, surely they must of found some usable DNA to extract.

Nick poured over the surveillance video after ordering another plate of chicken and another two beers. He grew frustrated as the video feed blinked out on every camera a second before the woman was about to enter the frame, and didn't come back on until after she was gone. It was like a rolling surveillance blackout followed the woman everywhere she went.

Nick looked over the whole file numerous times. Searching for anything that would steer him towards the mysterious woman. The whole investigation was an effort in futility as the investigators just uncovered more questions than leads. Nick only found one piece of information that he would consider *actionable*. It was one line near the bottom. A tiny snippet that was probably meant to be forgotten.

The Syndicate may have some involvement.

Well, if that's the case, Nick thought to himself as he closed out of the screen on his datapad, *then let's go ask The Syndicate.*

***

El Infierno Ardiente, that was the name of the bar. The Syndicate had people everywhere. It wasn't hard to find one that would answer his questions. Nick just started at the bottom and slowly worked his way until he found someone high enough on the food chain to actually know where The Butcher could be found.

Nick approached the three men stationed at the bar's rear door, with his hands out in front of him in plain view. He unabashedly wore his uniform, even though a part of him thought it might have been smarter to dress a little more inconspicuously. It was getting late in the night, or early in the morning, depending on how you looked at it. He would be due back soon, and Nick didn't want to stretch this out into a second night. Besides that, he just came for some answers.

He didn't want any trouble.

"Stop," the bigger of the three men stepped forward. All three of them were large men, but this one stood a good deal taller than the rest. This meaty-looking gorilla extended his hand towards Nick. "State the nature of-," he started to say but lost the words when Nick's fist collided with his jaw. The man's head spun to the left and he simply dropped to the ground like someone had disconnected his power supply.

The one to Nick's left moved in first, Nick swatted his punch to the side and gave him a sharp uppercut underneath the his chin. While he was still recovering, Nick reached up and wrapped his hand around the back of his neck and pulled him down into his rising knee. The blow landed with a soft crunching noise and Nick pushed the limp man's body away from him a moment before the last guard grabbed him from behind.

A meaty arm reached over his right shoulder to grab him in a headlock, Nick latched onto the intruding arm before he locked it in, and swiveled sharply to the left and elbowed the man behind him in the face. Then Nick lowered himself down, pulled the man over his shoulder and threw him hard to the ground. He wasted no time and punched the man hard in the throat. He left him gagging for his last breaths as Nick knelt down and started to search the man. Nick removed a large automatic pistol from a shoulder holster inside this man's jacket. Nick pulled the slide back, and ejected the loaded round. He quickly checked the weapon's condition before he reloaded the round and tucked the weapon into his pocket.

"Hey! Hey *you*!" An electronically augmented voice boomed throughout the alleyway. Nick looked around himself quickly for the camera he obviously missed. "Yeah! *You*!" The voice called to him. Nick didn't see the camera, so he just stood and faced the door. "What the fuck do you think you're doing?"

"I want to talk to *The Butcher*," Nick said slowly as he reached into his pocket for his datapad. He pulled up the sketch he made of the woman from the prisoner escape and held it out in front of him. "About her."

"Is that guy by your feet *dead*?" The voice asked with a certain amount of indignation. Nick looked down and saw the man's lifeless eyes staring up to the artificial night sky.

"Looks like it."

"Goddamn it!" the voice curse loudly. "I think I was related to that one," the voice complained quietly, as if he was talking to someone else. "So, you wish to talk to *The Butcher*," The voice said in a menacing inflection. "And this is how you go about it? By killing one of his...*my*...grand-nephews? Or whatever he was. *Filho da puta!* I would have let you in! Did you honestly believe I didn't know you were coming? Is this how the Special Operation boys do things these days? Deplorable. Disgraceful. What? You think you're just going to shoot your way in with that pistol in your hands." Nick patted the barrel of the pistol against the side of his thigh impatiently.

"I'm *still* thinking about it, if I'm being honest. Are you going to open that door? Or am I?" Nick asked the reinforced door coldly.

"*Eu deveria apenas matar você, e acabar com isso!*" The voice said angrily over the intercom. Nick didn't know what he was saying, but his accent made the words sound almost musical. "Fine! Yes! I will open the door, and have one of my associates escort you directly to me. But first, you will drop that pistol. And when my man cuffs you, you will not resist." Nick didn't like the sound of that one bit.

"Nope," he said clearly as he dropped the pistol onto the abdomen of the dead body by his feet. "You can have the gun, but any man of yours that touches me is going to end up like your *grand-nephew* here." Nick pointed to the dead body on the ground.

"Deal! But if you injure one more person, I will cut pieces off you until you beg me for mercy! And then I will keep cutting. I will spend a small fortune keeping you alive just so I can cut off more pieces off your body." Nick looked at the door with a bored expression.

"Seems fair."

There was a loud metallic click that erupted from somewhere inside the heavy door, and a second later another sturdy-looking goon with olive skin opened the door and waved Nick through with his meaty hand.

Nick followed the man down a hallway that was lined with angry looking men in black suits. Each of them had a weapon of some kind in his hands. Machine pistols were popular amongst the goon squad that was on display for him. But Nick also spied a few menacing-looking pulse rifles, a few cartridge-fire assault rifles, and one guy even had a Mag-gun in his hands. Nick smirked at the small man with the large gun in his hands when he noticed it wasn't turned on. He was led to a large extravagant room lined with expensive-looking marble statues of naked people with golden adornments. Through a large window on the side, Nick could see a sea of people gyrating amongst a collection of flashing colored lights. At the end of the room, was a large ornate wooden desk, with a large leather chair behind it was currently facing the other direction. All Nick could see was the tall back of it, it's occupant was completely concealed behind it.

"What the fuck are you doing here?" Nick immediately recognized the voice that asked the question. The sound of it kicked Nick's heart rate up, and he balled his fists up at his sides.

"You!" Nick growled as the chair spun around and the tall, blonde woman from the prisoner escape looked at him with a concerned expression on her face. Anger flared within his body as Nick breathed in and took a step towards the woman behind the desk.

"Ah!" The woman held out her hand and halted Nick with the gesture. "We're not fighting in here," she said definitively.

"I think we are, actually." Nick took another step.

"No, we're not." She looked at him with a calm scorn. "You didn't come here to fight, after all. You came to talk. So? Let's talk."

"I came to talk to *The Butcher*, about *you*."

"Okay," she said unphased by what Nick said. "So, here I am. What do you want to know?"

"Are *you* The Butcher?" Nick nodded to her.

"No," the woman chuckled softly. "I was just in the neighborhood when you started your little rampage at the docks. It was pretty obvious what you were doing. So, I came here and waited for you to show up."

"So?" Nick asked spreading his arms a bit. "Where is he?"

"You just killed one of his nephews," the woman said with mild shock. "You think he honestly wants to talk to you? You're lucky you're not dead right now. I can't even imagine why you'd kill that guy like that." Nick just frowned at her.

"He was a criminal," Nick said simply. The woman scoffed at him.

"We're all criminals to someone, kid." The woman leveled him was a knowing look. "Just because you can, doesn't mean you should." The woman raised her eyebrow at him and let the quiet between them grow.

"Who are you?" Nick asked, narrowing his eyes at her. It was time to get to the brass tacks of this meeting. Nick didn't come here to be preached to by a holier-than-thou fugitive.

"My name is Eve Carter," she said the name clearly and paused. Nick watched as she studied him closely. As if he might have some reaction to the name. "I'm better known as Athena," the woman with the thick braid at the back of her head said. Again, she seemed to be waiting for some response from him. Nick just shrugged. "Of *The Council*?" She gave him an incredulous look as she asked the question with some frustration. Again, Nick shrugged. "Jesus! You don't know anything, do you?" She looked at him as if waiting for a reply. Nick didn't feel like he had to justify the remark with one. He didn't come here to answer her questions, after all. *Just keep her talking,* he thought to himself. "I need a drink," The blonde woman said and rose from the desk. She motioned to the chairs in front of the desk. "Sit," he commanded lightly. "You're making me nervous standing there like that. You want a drink?"

"No," Nick said slowly moving towards the offered chair. He quickly scanned the woman's body as she moved. "Thank you." She didn't appear to be armed, but that meant little.

"No," the woman said light-heartedly as she approached a panel on the wall and touched it gently. A brief moment passed before the panel slid open and revealed an impressive drinking cabinet. Mr. Malum had a similar one in his office. "You're having a drink. This is the only chance you're going to get to taste *real* tequila. Trust me, it's worth it." She said absently as she poured them both a glass from a crystal container that had writing on it that Nick couldn't understand. "It might even wash that murderous look off your face." She set the tumbler in front of him and smiled warmly at him.

"You tried to kill me," Nick growled slightly as he took the glass and gave the contents a quick whiff.

"Pfft! That was a light beating, at best. Don't be dramatic." The Carter woman sat down behind the desk and took a sip from her glass.

"I was in the autodoc for a full day!"

"Yeah," Carter sharply replied. "And you *should* have been in there for a week. Besides that, you shot me five times, you don't hear me bitching about it." Carter took another drink, and then motioned for Nick to do the same. "Drink. It's good stuff."

Nick did. The foul-smelling, amber liquid burned a path down his throat. Nick couldn't help the bitter look that bloomed across his face.

"That's fucking gross." Carter looked at him amused.

"Keep drinking, it gets better."

"And how is it you're sitting there offering me drinks, and not in the morgue?" Nick looked at her seriously. "I shot you. I saw those bullets rip into your belly. I got sprayed by your blood. You should have died, and you didn't even slow down. Not to mention the fact that you're freakishly strong, and weigh a goddamn ton."

"Wow, that's rude." Carter responded with mocking outrage. "And I could ask you the same things. How is it you walked off that stun charge? There were enough volts in that thing to

drop an elephant. It was meant for powered armor, after all."
What the hell is an elephant? Nick asked himself with increasing frustration. "Not to mention the flashbang had little-to-no-effect on you. Plus, you may not realize this, but you're freakishly strong yourself. You're still pretty light though, but that'll change when the nanomachines spread."

Nanomachines?!

"What?" Nick asked quickly. Cutting her off.

"It's the answer to all of your questions, Nick. Nanomachines. Tiny little robots that-."

"I know what nanomachines are," Nick snapped back.

"Do you?" Carter replied with some disbelief. "I don't think you do. You may *think* you do but you've never run across nanomachines like these. The Motherbot," She started to say and tapped the side of her head. "Manufactures, and regulates, and ever-increasing army of specialized nanomachines that integrate themselves to every part of your body, making you better in every way a human being could be better. That's what's inside every member of The Council. It's what makes us who we are. And it's what's growing inside you now."

"Growing?" Nick asked not even trying to hide his concern.

"Yes, Nick," she said looking at him with a challenging expression. "Growing. You're still in the first stage. You're Motherbot is still young. You have a long way to go before you're on my level." Nick raised an eyebrow at her comment. Carter just sat there with a content smirk on her face. "Have you stopped sleeping yet?" That got Nick's attention. He obviously did a poor job of hiding his surprise because the woman continued before he could answer. "It's one of the side-effects. With the Motherbot in control of your brain's autonomic functions, there's no need for it anymore. What about the washroom? Do you still piss and shit?"

"Are you saying you don't?" Nick asked astounded.

"There's no need for it," Carter simply said with a shrug. "There's a lot you don't know, and a lot you need to prepare for."

"Really?" Nick asked skeptically while looking at her.

"Yes," She replied exasperated.

"Let's assume the fantastic amount of bullshit you're feeding me is actually true, why tell me at all?" Nick posed the question to the woman behind the desk and studied her carefully.

"The long answer is, we're trying to recruit you," she said with deadly seriousness.

It didn't stop Nick from chuckling.

"Well, you're doing a terrible job," he quipped. "I fucking want to kill you, not join your stupid little club." Nick added *The Council* to the long list of things he had to research if he survived this little parlay. The fact that she knew about the sleeping issue was a cause for concern. Nick couldn't figure out how she would know that.

"The short answer is," Carter continued undeterred by what Nick said. "I need you to stay out of my way. I have a few operations on the go, and I don't need you fucking them up more than you already have."

"Oh yeah?" Nick said with sudden amused interest. "And what *operations* would those be?" Nick challenged her.

"You know that ship Malum has locked up in that lab of his?" Carter asked like she already knew that answer. Nick just nodded slowly. "I'm going to steal it?" At that Nick laughed loudly.

"The fuck you are," he said mockingly to Carter's unimpressed face. "Now, I *know* you're crazy. You'll need an army to fight your way down to the Research and Development level. Even if, by some miracle, you even make it to the hanger where the ship is, they'll lock down all the lifts by then. You'll be trapped down there." Nick took a generous sip of his drink. "You might be a super-soldier, but sooner or later, a stray bullet would clip you in the wrong way, or a grenade, or maybe you just run out of bullets. You'll lose, and you will die down there."

"I'm touched that you're so concerned with my well-being, but don't worry. I'll be fine. The only problem I would have, is you." Carter used the index of the hand holding her glass to point in his direction before she sipped her drink. "And the only problem you'll give me is fucking up my timeline, which is fine for me, but I'm trying to do this cleanly. With as few casualties as possible. You won't die," she said with an absolute certainty. "But a lot of other *innocent* people will die trying to stop me. This." Carter waved the hand holding her glass in a slow circle in front of her. Indicating the little parley they were sharing. "Is an effort to prevent that from happening. You can't stop me." The blonde-haired woman leveled him with a cold stare that chilled Nick's blood. "I'm taking that ship back. The only question is how many people have to die along the way." She gave Nick a challenging look.

"When?" He asked curiously.

"Four days," Carter said with a dispassionate look. Nick just returned the stare. "Which brings me to the second mission I've been tasked with completing."

"I'm all ears," Nick said thoroughly amused. He couldn't wait to hear what the next impossible feat was going to be. Was she going to kidnap the CEO?

"Helena Jonlesky," she said. *What?!*

"What do *you* have to do with *her*?" He hissed the question out. "I'm not going to let you hurt her," Nick instinctively threatened the woman.

"Who said anything about hurting her? How do *you* know her?" She challenged. Nick almost physically flinched away from the question. "Why did you go to her apartment? You know your dirty little tracks were all over the corporate network. Your little program may stop people from knowing *who* was doing the searching, but it doesn't stop anybody from clearly seeing that *someone* was looking into Helena. You think Malum's stupid. He'll connect the dots. He'll figure out it was you,"

Carter scorned him like he was a child who got caught with his hand in the cookie jar. "Once she's on his radar, again, it will make my job much more difficult."

"What's your mission?" Nick asked her slowly. Weighing his options.

"I'm going to smuggle her out of the megastructure. I've got a nice life set up for her and her daughter on Ceres. She'll be safe there."

"She's safe here," Nick countered.

"No, she's not. Sooner or later, Malum will use her and her daughter to try and control you."

Nick didn't dispute the statement. From what he knew of Mr. Malum, that seemed like exactly the kind of thing he would do. There was only one mystery here, and Nick was about to get to the bottom of it.

"Why? Who is she?" Nick heard the small amount of desperation in his voice. He couldn't help that. Carter just looked at him coldly.

"Do you really want to know?" She asked. Immediately a dark part of him spoke up inside his head. *NO!* Suddenly, Nick was in front of the Jonlesky door again, looking at the same green button that would open up something terrible inside him if he pressed it. "You doing okay there, chief?" The woman asked lightly. Nick looked at her and then to his shaking hand that was still holding the crystal tumbler. *Walk away,* a smooth sinister voice inside him called out for the darkness.

"No," Nick said and immediately his hands stop shaking. "It doesn't matter who she is. If you try to take her out of the megastructure, you'll just get her, the child, *and* yourself killed in the process." He looked at her with a renewed confidence. "You might be some badass super-soldier, and you might be able to walk around up here with impunity, but all that will end once you step into the megastructure. A couple guards with powered armor would rip you to shreds, and there are hundreds of them down there. And what do you have? A plucky attitude, an enhanced body, and some two-bit gangster in your corner. It's not enough, lady." Nick smugly finished off his drink and gave her a cool look. Athena, Carter, whoever this crazy bitch was, pulled out a neatly folded piece of paper from her pocket and slid it across the desktop to him. Nick stared for a moment and then looked at the woman's daring smile.

Nick picked up the paper and carefully unfolded it.

"She's your wife," Carter said.

Monster kisses!

There was a flash of white lightning the painfully coursed through his body. Nick flinched away from the paper's image and the tumbler in his glass shattered as his hand instinctively clamped shut into a hard fist. Shards from the crystal tumbler embedded themselves into his flesh and blood leaked out between his fingers.

"What is this?" Nick shot up from his chair. "What are you doing?" He frowned at the woman and looked at her with murderous intent. From behind the desk, Carter held her composure and slowly shook her head.

"I'm not doing anything, except telling you the truth."

"The fuck you are," Nick hissed at her and pointed at her accusingly with a bloodied finger. "I don't know what your angle is, but I'm not going to sit here and listen to your bullshit mind-games. I don't know Helena or Isabella Jonlesky. And they certainly don't know me."

"She actually goes by Bel-," the bitch kept pushing her lies. Nick had enough.

"Shut up!" Nick growled and slammed his fist down on the desk. "I've had enough of your shit," he started to say while he carefully folded the piece of paper in his hands again. "You want to go try to break into the stacks for some suicide mission, go ahead. Do either one, it doesn't matter to me. You'll die just the same and you'll accomplish nothing." Nick stowed the folded paper into the pocket of his pants before he turned and stormed towards the exit.

"Whatever, kid," The woman said from behind him. "Four days. Just stay out of my way."

Nick angrily turned back before he reached the door.

"If I ever see you again, I'm going to twist that pretty head of yours right off your fucking body." Nick turned back to the door and flung it open.

"Oh, it's a date!" He heard her say before he exited the office.

CHAPTER 16

Eve

Aww, Eve smiled to herself, *that's sweet. He thinks I'm pretty.* She had only revealed the rugged looks of her real face in some vain hopes that she would connect with some part of Thomas that was inside him. And maybe she had. He did call her pretty, after all.

Eve changed back to Claire Hughes when she heard the Castille's secret door open. A second later Ron's bloated frame waddled through.

"And just like that," Ron complained. "I'm supposed to let this man just walk out of my place. After he insults me! *Two-bit gangster!*"

"Relax, *Ron.* Have a seat," Eve gestured to the guest's chair in front of the desk. "I'll pour you a drink. You'll feel better." She got up and refreshed her own drink and poured two fingers of Ron's prized tequila into another crystal tumbler. "You can try to kill him, but you'll just end up losing more relatives," Eve said sounding bored as she placed the tumbler in front of Castille.

"Why? Do you not believe I could kill him?" He meant it as a joke, Eve was sure. But she wasn't taking chances.

"No, because I won't *allow* it." Eve gave the man a hard stare as she raised her glass to him. Castille snorted dismissively and leaned forward to touch her glass.

"Saude," he said automatically and took a small sip. "I heard what you said. Four days is difficult, yes, but it is doable." Castille smiled and winked at her. Eve returned the smile.

"Good, because you have *two* days to secure the lift out of the stacks, and get my people to the docks."

Castille choked on his drink.

"No. This is not possible," he snorted angrily. "You ask too much." Eve sighed.

She had reached her limit with him.

Eve shot up from the chair and grabbed the corner of the large ornate desk Castille loved so much. In one motion that was so swift it caused the air within the room to shift, Eve threw the desk to the side with one hand. The beautifully carved wooden desk crashed into the opposite wall with a loud series of cracks. It didn't break apart, like she was hoping, but it was visibly disfigured when it settled back to the ground.

Nobody noticed though.

Eve lunged at Castille and wrapped the lapels of his expensive suit up in her fists, and she easily lifted his bulk right off the ground. He looked over fearfully with his wide, panicked eyes towards the door into the office as it burst open, and a score of heavily-armed men rushed into the room. The high-pitched sound of weapon capacitors charging filled the room.

"*Sair! Sair! Saia Agora!*" Castille shouted and wildly waved his men back.

"I ask too much?!" Eve said the heated words loudly, because there was a lot going on. She wanted to make sure that she had his attention. She did. "You listen to me, *you piece of shit!*" Castille was still madly waving his men back. Eve eyed them as they slowly filed back out the way they came, watching her closely. What could they do? Castille's massive frame shielded her perfectly. If they fired Castille would be the first one hit, she would make sure of it. "Your sole purpose in this pathetic, self-serving, centuries-long life of yours, is to do this *one* thing. *This* is why I broke you out of prison. *This* is why I've allowed your filth to fester, and spread to the nine corners of the goddamn solar system. So, you can do this *one-fucking-thing* for me. This! Right here, is why I've turned a blind eye to your organization's bullshit all this time. But no more. '*I ask too much*'!" Eve shook the man as she repeated his words back to him. "You got a number, you greedy sonofabitch? Give it to me, and I'll pay it. But you don't get to say *no* to me. Ever! You're going to do this one thing for me, and if you do it right, maybe I'll forget you exist. And as long as you don't remind me, you might never see me again. If you *don't*, I'm going to take a *hard* look at your organization." Eve growled the word. "And if I don't like what I find, I'm going to *burn* your entire operation to the ground. And when I'm done with that, I'm going to work on your family tree. I'll cut off any branch I don't like."

"No! Please! I misspoke! I swear to you!" Castille squealed overhead.

"Two days!" Eve growled loudly at him. "You have two days to ensure your continued existence in this life." Eve shook the man once more before she let his bulk fall to the ground. Castille wasn't ready for the sudden drop and he crashed awkwardly to the ground where he looked up at her with a trembling fear. "I would get to it, if I were you. Because you *do not* want to see me again. If you do this right, you won't."

Eve left the calamity and chaos she had created within the large office and strolled out into the hall. She coolly exchanged hard looks with Castille's men as she slowly made her way out of the building and walked out into the same alley Jones had minutes before.

Eve made her way to the bank of lockers where she had her coveralls stashed away. Once she was changed back into Angela Peters, Eve suffered through the tedium of descending the stacks. Jones had put her in a foul mood, and Castille just compounded it. Or maybe it was the old feelings of the walls closing in around her as she neared the completion of a long mission? This one wasn't even especially long, but it had been difficult in other ways.

Meeting Thomas' successor might have been part of Oberon's plan all along, but it was never part of hers. *He was handsome,* she allowed herself to think. Not as handsome as Thomas had been. Eve knew she shouldn't compare the two because they were two totally different people, but she couldn't help herself. This Jones character is a shadow of the man Thomas was. Plus, Thomas wasn't a pre-programmed drone like Nick Jones was. *We have to get him out of here,* Eve thought to herself as she waited quietly in the sterile-white personnel lift with the other citizens. Jones would outgrow the Corporation, and exceed their ability to hold him. That much was a certainty. But a lot could happen between then and now, and the longer Nick stayed under the Corporation's influence, the harder it would be to bring him back to the Council's side. But that wasn't part of Eve's mission.

She just hoped Oberon had a plan for that.

Two days, Eve thought to herself as she walked onto Stack Four and made her way to the lift that would take her down to Helena's level. *I'm going to pull off probably the most ambitious mission of my career.* It wasn't the most dangerous. Eve had done things that were far more dangerous to her own personal safety than this. That didn't mean she didn't worry constantly about the people involved who weren't super-soldiers. It wasn't the deadliest, or at least, if everything went according to her plan. It shouldn't be. If everything went according to her plan, she should be able to pull this off in less than an hour, and with single digit casualties.

If everything went according to plan.

She would say this was her most ambitious mission because it had her relying a lot on other people to come through for her. That is why she felt it was necessary to twist Castille's arm a bit, and remind him that failure will have consequences. Apparently the absolute fortune she was paying him wasn't enough of a motivation for the man. *If they don't respond to the carrot, show them the stick.* It was one of Thomas' favorite sayings. Eve didn't have such doubts with Evan. He would die to get Helena and her girl to the transport. She didn't doubt that, but she prayed it would never come to it. The other sticky point to her plan was that Evan and the girls had to get free and clear before she could steal the ship. Timing was important. Evan could use the chaos and confusion she would create breaking into Special Projects as cover to slip up to the Shipping and Receiving level using Castille's forgotten cargo lift. Eve thought about going with them, but it was a one-way trip up Castille's lift. Once Helena and Bella were out of the megastructure, their ID chips would ping the central computer and the Corporation would be alerted of their absence. If Malum found out, he might lock down his sector in response. Then more people would have to die. How many more? Eve wouldn't know that number until the job was done.

That was the unacceptable part to that approach.

At Helena's level, Eve briskly walked along the empty pedestrian lane to her district. The vidscreens were showing the first hints of sunrise, and the dim light of the artificial sunrise only partially lit the level. The gentle light of the tall lamps lining the lane provided most of the light for her to see by. Eve walked into Helena's district and straight for her door.

She pressed the green call button.

"Helena?" Eve said quietly. "It's Claire."

The door opened quickly, and Helena's smiling face stood in the doorway.

"Claire!" She exclaimed. Helena was wearing a light blue robe loosely tied over her modest sleeping wear. "Good morning! Come in. Come in." Helena waved Eve into the apartment and quickly closed the door as soon as she was through the entrance. The moment the door clicked closed, Helena threw her arms around Eve's shoulders and squeezed her tightly. "It is a miracle! I didn't think it was possible. I don't know how... how I can ever..." Helena stammered as the sobs broke through.

"What!?" Eve asked slightly concerned as the woman shook in her arms. "What is it? What's wrong?" Then down the hall came the joyous call that answered Eve's question perfectly.

Nothing was wrong.

"Claire!" Bella's voice called from her room and tiny footsteps came running from down the hall. Eve hadn't visited for a couple days. Last she saw, Bella was in bed with a fever that left her shivering with a sheen of sweat covering her body. Apparently, a lot had changed in a couple of days. "Claire!" The call came again a moment before Bella's tiny frame burst out from the hallway.

Bella wasn't wearing a mask. Her bright smile was on full display as she trotted towards Eve. The color had returned to her cheeks, there was a definite bounce in the kid's step, and incredibly, even a slight shadow of dark stubble covered her scalp.

"Monster girl!?" Eve called out playfully and with some surprise. "Look at you!" Eve bent down and the small girl collided with her in a big hug. "How do you feel?"

"Good," Bella said. Eve looked up to Helena who was wiping happy tears from her face.

"It is a miracle," she said again.

"Oh, we're just getting started," Eve quipped lightly. She scanned around the apartment before she released Bella and looked at Helena again. "Where's Evan?"

"I sent him home."

"You what?"

"Come," Helena motioned to a seat at the kitchen table. "Sit. I'll make us some coffee." Helena practically skipped to the kitchen. "You work him too hard, Claire." Helena keyed in their drink order and waved absently at her.

"I do?" Eve asked with intrigue.

"Yes. He cooks for us, runs errands for us, and even insists on bringing us fresh strawberries every morning. It is too much. It was late, we don't need to be watched every hour of every day. So, I sent him home. I gave him the night off," Helena joked and then chuckled slightly. "Can you imagine it, *me*, giving someone a day off? Like an executive."

"Yeah, that's pretty unbelievable." Eve replied with some strain in her voice just as her datapad pinged. It was Evan messaging her.

Don't listen to her, boss. I'm wandering around the promenade. That intrusion program is still running on Helena's datapad. I can hear everything you guys are saying.

Good boy, Eve smiled inwardly. She shouldn't have doubted him.

"Are you staying?" Helena asked when she returned to the table and placed the warm cup in front of Eve. "I could make some pancakes."

"Yay! Pancakes!" Bella cheered and hopped in place.

"That's actually what I came to talk to you about," Eve said and tilted her head towards Bella. Helena nodded and turned to her daughter.

"Bella? Go play in your room for awhile. I have to talk to Claire, *woman-to-woman*." Helena made it seem like the two of them were in some exclusive club.

"Aww," Bella whined slightly. "When do I get to be a *woman*?"

"Not for a long time, little missy," Helena said and patted her on the romp slightly, prompting her to leave. "And you should be thankful for that." When her child was out of earshot, Helena looked back to Eve with a look of concern. "Is there a problem? With the *plan*? Because I was thinking, maybe we could stay here for a couple-," She started to say, but Eve stopped her with her hand.

"There's no problem. We're all set. In two days, we leave."

"Two days!?" Helena blurted out suddenly. "That's so soon." Eve could see the inner turmoil in the woman's eyes. It was to be expected. Helena was having doubts. Eve watched the woman slowly trace the rim of her cup with her finger. "Listen, Claire. I don't want to sound unappreciative for what you've done. I am. But I have been thinking," Helena started to say with a sheepish look on her face.

"Don't," Eve cut in sharply. "If you don't realize it, let me explain the choices you have in front of you when we first met. You could live out the rest of your days within the megastructure, safe and secure, and watch your little girl slowly die in front of you. *Or,* you could start a new life somewhere else, and watch your little girl grow up." Eve looked at her apologetically. "I'm sorry, Helena, I made that choice for you when I cured your daughter. You can't stay here now. If you do, you'll go to prison and Bella will grow up with a new family." Eve looked at her earnestly. "Did I make the wrong choice for you?" Helena stopped tracing her finger along the rim of her cup and looked gravely at Eve.

"No," she said firmly. "You made the right choice." Helena dipped her head and looked into her coffee. "I'm afraid, Claire. I'm so afraid. I just got my little girl back, and I'm so afraid of losing her again. I'm sorry. I'm not strong like you are." Eve snorted at that. Before her was a woman on her first life, who had only known the life The Corporation had provided her with. And now, she with willing to throw it away for the opportunity of seeing her girl grow up. Helena Jonlesky wasn't an augmented super-soldier. She wasn't named after some ancient God. She wasn't a feared member of The Council. She was just a woman. A mother fighting against the odds to raise her little girl.

"Maybe not," Eve said looking deeply into the woman's eyes. "But you have an entirely different kind of strength, Helena. It carried you this far, didn't it? Your daughter's illness, the loss of your husband. You survive all of that. You're plenty strong. And you're going to need it going forward. We're not out of the woods yet. You want to watch your girl grow up?" Eve gave her a challenging look. "You're going to have to fight for it." Helena returned Eve's challenging look with one of fiery intent.

"Yes," she said quietly but resolutely. "You're right. I'm sorry, Claire."

"Don't be sorry," Eve said lightly. "And don't be afraid. I'll make sure everything will go fine."

"Two days," Helena said with a deep breath. "What do we need to do?"

"Well, for one. You're going to have two new roommates for those two days. I hope that's okay?" Eve sipped her coffee and watched as Helena waved it off lightly.

"Please," she snorted. "You are family now. What is mine, is yours." Eve just nodded.

"We should get Evan in here. There are a few details we need to hammer out." Helena nodded and rose from the table.

"I'll get dressed," she said and took another sip of her coffee before she lifted herself from the table. "Ask Evan if he would like some pancakes, as well." Just before Helena entered the hallway, she turned back to Eve. "And ask him if he could pick up some strawberries, as well. Our little monster has developed quite an appetite," she said with a smile that probably couldn't be removed from her face even if she wanted to.

Helena disappeared into the hallway just as Eve's datapad pinged.

Already got them in my hand, boss. I'll be there in 5.

***

Eve took the central lift down to the Research and Development level, near the bottom of the megastructure, with all the other research staff and lab techs who were heading towards their shifts. These people travelled to the depths of the megastructure every day with the same people. They congregated close to the coffee bar built into the side of the lift, huddled in groups and conversed about their lives outside of the R&D level.

Nobody even looked at Eve.

The reason she was the best at infiltration missions was because Eve did her homework. It was a point of pride. Ever since that day she first stepped into the interior of the megastructure, Eve uploaded a virus that gave her access to the extensive surveillance network within the stacks. Once that was done, she simply had to figure out which cameras she needed to monitor. Eve found her target after the first week. Melissa Linson was a short woman. There was no other word for it. At five-feet, she stood like a sapling in a forest next to her colleagues. She had short, unassuming brown hair that hung limply about her ears. She had a pretty face, soft features, and a few unsightly pimples dotting her forehead. Melissa also had a crooked smile that showcased a number of mismatched teeth, though, she rarely smiled. When she did, it was usually to the same person.

Once Eve had her target, she had the surveillance system relentlessly follow the woman. Eve needed to know how she presented herself on a daily basis. What clothes she wore the most. Did she accessorize her white lab coat in any way? Did she wear jewelry? Was she right-handed, or left? Who was she friendly with? All these details Eve learned during the weeks-long period she had been studying the woman.

Two days after Eve and Evan had strawberry pancakes with the Jonlesky's, Melissa Linson opened her apartment door to find Eve standing there in the hallway, with a shockstick in her hand. After the initial jolt, Eve sedated her with something that would keep her sleeping for most of the day. She quickly took the woman's appearance while she stood over Melissa's sleeping form. It wasn't easy. Melissa Linson's frame was at the absolute minimum Eve could squeeze her volume of nanomachines into. As it was, Eve's version of her was fractionally thicker to compensate for the difference. Thankfully, the security checkpoints didn't check a person's weight, Eve would never be able to get anywhere inside the megastructure if they did.

Eve had the nanomachines absorb her datapad into her forearm, from this point on she would need to be constantly connected to the digital landscape. Just in case. Eve stripped the woman of her clothes and lab coat. She placed her unconscious form on the bed, took her datapad, and placed her apartment on a priority lockdown, so, only security and medical staff would be able to access the apartment. After that was done, Eve exited her apartment as Melissa and briskly made her way to the central lift.

In the exact same way Melissa Linson did everyday.

The checkpoints inside the Research and Development level were designed to process people quickly through the queue. The guards here worked the same shift everyday, checking in the same people, at the same time of day. As long as nothing disrupted their tedium, the guards hardly noticed the faces of the people they were clearing. Eve just held up Melissa's datapad that had the algorithmic keycode that was unique to her. The system instantly recognized the code and cleared her.

The guards waved her through at each checkpoint without even looking at her.

The checkpoint at the entrance into Special Projects wasn't going to be as easy to get through. In fact, it was impossible. One problem was that the genetic sample for the advanced gensig had to be fresh. So, no cutting off someone's finger and using it to bypass the sensor. Nor, could she extract a blood sample and store it under a false flap of skin at her finger's tip. But the biggest problem, was how goddamn quick it tested for the presence of DNA, which was unfortunately quicker than the time it took for the nanomachines to make contact and manipulate the system. Eve would fail that test almost the same moment she placed her finger on the receptacle.

Eve mimicked Melissa Linson's shy little walk perfectly on her way to the Special Projects entrance. Where Jessie Collins and his partner were working the checkpoint. Eve looked up and saw the man rise excitedly from his chair and give her a slight wave. Eve noticed that these two had a budding little romance going. It was cute. Eve hoped she wasn't about to ruin that for the woman.

"There she is," Jessie said enthusiastically as Eve approached his booth. The gensig receptacle was sticking out ominously in front of her. Jessie checked the clock on his station. "Wow, someone's in a hurry to get to it today. How are you doing, Mel?" This was the only person Melissa Linson allowed to use the shortened version of her name.

Eve placed her hand down gently on the side of the gensig's console, as if she was trying to appear leisurely.

"Good," Eve said quietly and offered a small grin. As was Melissa's way. "Did you get a chance to read that book I told you about?" Eve asked with as much interest as she could muster and brushed her hair out of her eyes. The whole time nanomachines spread out from her finger that she placed by the console's seam. They traced a microscopic trail into the gensig's interior. *Come on!* Eve urged the nanomachines on while she stalled. *Come on!* "The one with the zombie's?" Eve asked hopefully. She knew Melissa had recommended the book a while back. The two hadn't spoken about it since.

"Umm," the guard started to say sheepishly. Eve just looked at him with hopeful eyes. "I started to read it, but I couldn't get into it." Jessie scratched the back of his head nervously. "Plus, I had my quarterly review. So, that kind of sidetracked me." Eve let her expression sink with obvious disappointment. Inside the console, the nanomachines made contact and Eve sliced off a bit of herself and sent it to work hacking into the secure network of the Special Projects section. "But I plan to get back to it here, real soon."

"How far did you get?" Eve perked up. Behind Jessie, Eve could see his partner rolling his eyes.

"I finished chapter four," Jessie said as a consolation.

"Oh," Eve said. "Those are just the introductory chapters. It is a little slow in the beginning," Eve said with an apologetical tone. "But once you get to the double-digit chapters, it really starts to pick up."

"Oh sure, I have no doubt. It's really well written." *Got it!* Eve shifted her focus to her digital self and just left Jessie to stew for a moment as she frantically scoured the Special Projects system. "You know," Jessie blessedly continued without prompting. "Maybe we could grab a cup of coffee and," Jessie leaned in and started to say.

He was cut off by the radiation alarm.

"What the fuck!" Jessie's partner yelped as he almost fell out of his chair in surprise as the klaxon blared loudly. Jessie himself flinched away from the noise and looked around himself like shots had been fired. Eve looked down at Melissa's datapad suddenly, and feigned abject horror.

"Oh God," Eve said grimly. "No!" She looked to the guard she had been flirting with as Melissa. "The contamination field has been breached!" She yelled at him and waved her datapad in his face. "It's leaking radiation into the section! We have to evacuate!"

The two guards exchanged terrified looks.

"We should notify our-," Jessie partner was about to say. Eve just screamed at him.

"There's no time! We have to get everyone out!" Eve bolted past the checkpoint without even looking at the gensig. "Get your radiation suits on, and start clearing the labs!" Eve swiftly commanded and ran in to the section. She left the two guards scrambling towards their emergency lockers where the protective suits were stored.

Eve knew where she was going. She knew the lay out of the section. She moved forward, fighting against the throng of labs techs who were rushing to exit. "Get out!" Eve screamed to the retreating staff. "Everybody needs to evacuate the section now!" Eve waved her arms and pushed people gently towards the exit.

Eve turned a corner into an empty corridor that had one uniformed guard forcefully approaching her.

"Where do you think you're going?" The guard sneered at her. "There's a radiation leak, all personnel are supposed-," the older guard began to say gruffly and reached out for her. Eve swept his hand aside and jammed the same medical injector she had used on the real Melissa Linson into the man's neck.

Eve caught the man in her arms as his limp body started to sink to the ground. She quickly relieved him of his sidearm and slipped the weapon into her pocket just before a trio of lab techs hurried out of one of the labs further down.

"Help me," Eve called out to them and make it look like she was struggling with the body. "He has radiation poisoning!" All three of them rushed to her side and took up the unconscious man into their arms. "Is there anyone left down there?" Eve asked quickly and pointed down the corridor she had to go. The lab tech she was speaking to quickly shook his head as he helped with the guard's bulk. "Okay," Eve said and motioned to the unconscious guard in their arms. "Get him out of here! Now!" Eve commanded them. The fearful lab techs nodded obediently and rushed the man in their arms towards the entrance.

It was then that Eve was alerted by her own datapad that an Apprehension Order had been issued for Helena and Isabella Jonlesky. *Shit!* Eve couldn't explain it. There was absolutely no reason for that order to be issued. *There's no time to figure it out,* Eve shook the thought out of her head. She had to adapt to this new problem. Eve paused in the corridor and focused on her digital self. She quickly messaged Evan.

Get out! Get out now! They are coming for the girls! I can turn off the tracking chips, but they'll know what level she's on. Move!

Eve quickly moved her digital self over to Human Resources database, looked up the girls ID numbers, and then took those numbers back to The Central Monitoring system and turned off the girl's positioning sensors. That would only hide them for so long. Any lift they entered, any checkpoint they crossed, would ping their ID chips. Then the gig would be up. She brought herself back to the here-and-now enough to continue towards Cattivo's lab. With each step she anxiously awaited Evan's reply. Praying they still had time.

We're gone, boss. We're on our way.

That would have to do, Eve admitted to herself as the dread started to bloom within herself. She was locked in down here. Evan would have to take care of the girls. Eve told herself they didn't have to go far. The access to Castille's secret lift was in the central pillar of the megastructure. Hopefully, Evan and the girls could get across the causeway before they locked the level down.

Hopefully, Eve said the word again inside her head. It felt woefully inadequate. The Corporate machine was about to descend on Helena and Bella, and Eve was at the bottom of the megastructure. Eve might as well have been on another planet for how easily she could get back to the girls. *Shit!* Escorting the girls to the lifts was supposed to be the easy part. Now it would be a life or death struggle she wasn't exactly sure Evan was prepared for. He was smart, capable. She trusted him, but he had his limits.

He was only human, after all.

Eve felt the best way she could help Evan and the girls now, was to get to Ares' ship and create a bigger problem for The Corporation than the Jonlesky's.

Eve walked up to the airlock door that led into Cattivo's lab and quickly cycled the large door to open. Eve's focus was split between the here-and-now and the digital landscape, or else she would have reacted to the guard in the black suit of powered armor that stood in the doorway, with his mag-gun.

BOOM!

The mag-gun sounded like thunder as it fired the metal slug into Eve's midsection. The nanomachines absorbed the bulk of the kinetic energy from the blast and probably prevented the slug from ripping her in half, however, Eve's body was violently launched backward. She was lifted right off the ground as her body spun awkwardly in the air, crashed to the ground painfully, and rolled a few more feet before her body settled to the ground. The Motherbot inside her head screamed various warnings as Eve's breath was caught in her throat. Eve tried to move, but the nanomachines inside her quickly informed her of the extensive damage to her midsection. The impact of the slug basically reduced her abdomen to jelly. Eve slowly rolled herself onto her knees while she used her one hand to keep her organs from spilling through the gaping hole in her belly long enough for the nanomachines to patch it.

Back down the corridor, the black armored guard noisily racked another slug into the mag-gun's chamber.

"You know," an electronic voice started to say. Eve instantly recognized it. *Shit!* Eve's overly ambitious plan was falling apart around her. "There's only one bitch I know who could take a shot like that, and not be killed instantly." Nick pointed the barrel of the mag-gun at her. "Though, she doesn't look like you do."

Just then, inside her body, Eve's datapad received another message from Evan.

We got a problem here, boss.

"You got me, kid." Eve smiled at the blackened visor of Jones's power armor and she changed back into her original body. Complete with Eve Carter's real face. "Do you remember what I said to you last time?" Eve feigned weakness. It wasn't hard, she was still leaking from the rapidly decreasing hole in her gut. Eve pretended to winced in pain and doubled over as she tried to rise, only to subtly retrieve the pistol from her pocket.

Bam!

The small pistol barked out a single shot from her hip. Jones didn't even move when she produced the pistol. Probably felt perfectly secure locked away safely inside the powered armor. Jones knew small arms fire wouldn't penetrate the armor of the suit.

Eve wasn't aiming at the armor though.

The tiny bullet struck the mag-gun's capacitor that was built into the stock of the weapon. There was a loud crack that erupted with an intense flash of light as the bullet violently shorted out the high-voltage capacitor of the weapon and sent sparks flying everywhere. When it was over, Jones looked down at the weapon in his hands that had just been rendered useless by Eve's bullet. She could sense his frustration as Jones tossed the weapon away.

"You want to do this, kid?" Eve challenged him as she saw him reach for his sidearm. "Let's fucking *do* it!"

CHAPTER 17

Lucien

"So, you're sure this will work?" Lucien asked, coldly eying the visibly-shaken neurologist. Lucien didn't blame him. This was Glen Sanders' last chance, after all. A fact Lucien wasn't shy about reminding the man.

"Oh yes!" The man replied excitedly and looked to the large fluid-filled container that had Trup's brain and spinal column suspended within it. Lucien spied the numerous wires and micro-tubes that were hooked up to it, essentially keeping the organ alive until it was implanted into the cybernetic host being created in a different lab. "Once the carapace is complete, and the brain is hooked up to the internal support system, the rest should be fairly rudimentary. Me and my team should be able to splice in the numerous neuro-connections within a day or two. Then after we link up the external sensory inputs to the brain, then we should be able to do functionality tests." The man proudly motioned to the two other lab techs assigned to him.

Lucien just smirked at him, because the truth of it was that he couldn't be trusted to work alone anymore. The idiot thought he was being rewarded for his obedience. He was an unfortunate necessity for Lucien's plan to transfer the good doctor's mind into a cybernetic carapace. One that was fit for Cattivo's genius. Lucien was working on it himself. Cybernetics were his speciality when he had been a budding researcher.

And if what Ernst had said, before he was burnt to a crisp, had any truth to it, none of his staff could be trusted to work alone.

The Council *are* involved. The blood samples at Jones's assassination-attempt proved that. Nobody could account for the utter lack of DNA in the unknown sample that was collected at the scene., but Lucien had his suspicions. They were only confirmed when he finally got access to the forensic file.

92% inorganic material.

Who else but a full-fledged Council member would have that many nanomachines in their system? Or any? That is, assuming the inorganic material in the *unknown* sample was the same as the inorganic material found in Jones' blood. But Lucien was sure of it. He fought tooth-and-nail for the physical evidence so he could study the unknown sample more closely. Goddamn bureaucrats at the Port Authority must have been giddy to deny him his request. It came back later that same day. *Jurisdictional prudence,* they wrote in the denial letter.

Lucien was tempted to write them a strongly-worded letter, and have it hand-delivered by a squad of armored guards.

He took a deep breath and brought himself back to the present.

"No, you idiot!" He barked at the already cowering scientist. "Can you transfer Ernst's mind into that...that *thing*?" Lucien pointed to the floating brain and spinal column in the tank beside him.

"Oh! That?" Sanders visibly relaxed and waved off Lucien's concern. "That's a simple copy-and-paste procedure."

"How long until it's ready for the carapace?" Lucien asked absently as he peered into the cloudy fluid in the tank. Sanders quickly checked his datapad for the answer.

"We're still mapping Doctor Cattivo's brain. Unfortunately, that will take probably another day to complete. After that, maybe another full day to rebuild the neural network inside the blank." *The Blank,* that's what the research staff referred to Trup's brain and spinal column now. Lucien enjoyed the term. He liked the idea that he had erased the man entirely. "Sir?" Sanders squeaked. "I feel I should, once again, remind you of the dangers involved with what we're doing. Though, technically Doctor Cattivo will be able to see and hear, it will be a completely digital interface. Studies have shown the long-term effects of a golem's brain suffers psychological trauma akin to acute sensory deprivation. That is why we use an AI as the operating system, and not an actual person. Sir, he'll go mad." Sanders looked at him with an expression that begged him to reconsider.

"You don't think I know the risks?" Lucien shot Sanders a disgusted look and snorted dismissively. "I was making golems before you were born. Studies have shown? I *wrote* some of those so-called studies. The key word you're overlooking here is, *long-term.* This is a temporary solution. Gestating a new body for Ernst will take time. A year, at least. I can't afford to be side-tracked that long. He was so close. So close to cracking the secrets of that damned ship." Lucien straightened up at smoothed the front of his custom-made, sapphire blue, suit jacket. "Besides, it's what Ernst would want."

"But the deprivation?"

"Jesus Christ, Sanders. Give it a rest. Those test subjects were below the corporate baseline for intelligence. They were criminals, mental deviants, and chem abusers. Doctor Cattivo is a certified genius, in the top one percentile of the entire megastructure. I'm sure someone like him could handle some *mental stresses.*" Lucien scoffed at the idea. "Hell, he might even enjoy it. He may not want to go back," Lucien quipped lightly but Sanders didn't seem to appreciate the joke.

"That's the other thing, sir. We can't transfer the Doctor's mind from the golem. Or else we will be copying over the mental trauma as well. Maybe even exacerbating it during the process. When you're done with…umm…I mean, when it has *served its purpose*," Sanders said carefully. "We'll have to deactivate it and wipe its brain completely. Then we can upload the standard golem AI. No sense wasting a perfectly good carapace."

"Of course," Lucien said, slightly annoyed that Sanders made a point of mentioning it to him. "Okay," Lucien said checking the clock on the wall. "I have to go," he quickly informed Sanders. "Inform the day shift that I want hourly reports. I have a meeting to go to," Lucien said absently while he ran through the mental checklist he made for today. It was a big day, after all.

"Oh yes!" Sanders perked up. "It's being made official today, isn't it? Good for you, sir!"

"It's not official yet," Lucien said modestly. "There's still going to be a vote." It was technically true, but in all reality, Lucien was the clear choice out of the *remaining* candidates. The actual vote was simply a formality he had to endure.

"Seems a little early for a board meeting," Sanders said innocently. Probably muttering to himself more than asking a real question. The comment still dragged a rake across an already sore nerve within Lucien.

It was part of the tedious gauntlet he was being made to run in order to reach the finish line since the attempt on his life. He spent three days in an autodoc, and another two recovering in his bed. After that, the first couple of days were spent accessing the damage, gathering intel, and exacting his revenge on Snell and Trup. Only then could he focus on repairing the disarray within his section. There were still some minor repairs to be made, staff that had to be replaced. And, of course, he had to care for Ernst. That carapace wasn't going to build itself, and Lucien couldn't trust anyone else with the task.

It didn't leave a lot of time for sleep.

Thankfully, the neurocaine patches helped with that. The tiny trans-dermal patches supplied him with a twelve-hour metered supply of the potent stimulant. Lucien had been wearing the patches for the last week. They kept the constant ache from his ruined knee at bay, as well as removed any fatigue from his body while keeping his mind sharp. That was important. Lucien felt like he had the eyes of the Corporation on him this last week.

"There are a few members of the board that enjoy watching me struggle," Lucien said dispassionately. "No matter. Once I give my speech today, they'll all fall in line behind me."

"You've got a big speech planned?" Sanders dumbly asked. Lucien rolled his eyes at the obvious attempt at brown-nosing.

"Of course, I have a speech planned," Lucien sneered at him. "What kind of idiot accepts a directorship without having a speech prepared?" Sanders just looked at him like Lucien was scolding him. *Why am I even talking to this person?* Lucien asked himself before he continued. Sanders was a member of the team, after all. And Lucien was excited to tell someone. "I have a big reveal planned for the meeting. A discovery that will change everything."

"Is it the ship?"

Lucien looked at him coldly.

"How do *you* know about that?" Lucien asked with sinister curiosity. Sanders shouldn't know about that. Lucien's paranoia kicked up as he considered the possibility of a leak within his section. Sanders suddenly looked worried.

"People talk around the break room. Nobody said anything to me about it. I just heard things now-and-then, and figured it had to be some sort of ship you were working on. I didn't mean to overstep my bounds, sir." Sanders took a cautionary step back. Lucien waved it off.

"I suppose, after today, it won't be a secret anymore. You *are* a member of my section. I shouldn't fault you for figuring something out on your own, for a change. Yes, Sanders. It is about a ship. A very special ship." Lucien looked up at the clock again. "Now, if you'll excuse me." Lucien turned to leave, but was stopped when Sanders spoke up quickly.

"Have you talked to Bryce yet?"

"Cailleanach?"

"Yeah, he was looking for you last night. I think it was important."

"I'll see him at the meeting." Lucien walked out of the man's lab without another word.

Lucien walked the corridors through his section towards the entrance and tried not to be too badly discouraged by the bitter reminder that Ernst wouldn't be there for his big moment. He *should* be there. He would have been there if it wasn't for Snell's empty-headed ambition. Lucien breathed hotly as he walked. His only regret was that he could only kill Snell the one time.

Move dammit! Lucien cursed at his crippled knee joint as he hobbled as fast as he could. He exited his section without even a look towards the receptionist. *Tap-tap-tap-tap.* Lucien allowed a slight slouch because it eased the pain in his back and allowed him to move fractionally faster. *Tap-tap-tap-tap.* Lucien shot challenging looks at the people in the corridors who dared shoot him a puzzled look at his slight dishevelment as he moved along like some frantic hobbling cripple. In a tailored suit that cost more than most of those people made in a year.

Lucien finally arrived at the entrance to the Research and Development's corporate offices. He stopped before the wide ornate doors of the entrance to catch his breath and straighten his suit. Out of habit, Lucien went to smooth his hair only to be reminded that his beautiful mane of honey-blonde hair had been reduced to a pale growth of stubble. *No matter,* Lucien told himself, *this is your day. You don't need to be pretty to be successful.*

It certainly doesn't hurt, another voice said.

"It'll grow back," Lucien whispered to himself before he straightened up and strode confidently through the doors. Behind the wide reception desk shaped from black volcanic rock with the golden Research and Development emblem stamped on the front of it, was the dark-haired receptionist with the bluest eyes imaginable. Those eyes almost seemed to glow as they peered lovingly towards him. To say that the woman was beautiful was an understatement. The woman behind that desk was genetically modified to fit exact specifications. In a real sense, she was built to look like the most beautiful woman you could imagine.

"They're waiting for you in the boardroom, Mr. Malum," the raven-haired receptionist said affably and obediently pointed down the corridor towards the boardroom.

Shit! Lucien looked to the large ornate clock that was ticking loudly behind the massive desk. Lucien only had two minutes before the meeting actually started. Executives and their assistants were to be present ten minutes before the start of any meeting. It was a rule.

Tap-tap-tap-tap.

"Jesus! Lucien!" Cailleanach exclaimed in a subdued manner when he saw Lucien tapping his way down the corridor. "Where have you been? I've been trying to call you for ages. They're about to start the meeting," he said anxiously as he rushed to Lucien's side. Bryce was wearing a nice salmon colored suit. Obviously from the tailor Lucien had sent him to.

Since Ernst was still recovering from his numerous injuries, Lucien was forced to name an Interim Assistant Director. He chose Cailleanach because it would draw the man closer to him. It was a gesture of goodwill to reward the man for moving over to his side. Lucien wanted to make sure Cailleanach knew he appreciated the leap of faith the man took. He took a step down on the corporate ladder, after all. Such blind loyalty needed to be rewarded.

"I got distracted," Lucien hissed as he moved towards the door. The truth was, he didn't consider how much longer it would take him to make the relatively short journey to the level's corporate offices in his newly debilitated condition. Cailleanach reached for Lucien's arm, as if he was going to aid him into the room. "Get your hands off me," Lucien quietly barked at him and glared at the man as he flinched away.

"I was only trying to help."

"Don't," Lucien replied promptly. "How do I look?" He asked as he smoothed out the lapels of his suit jacket and fought against the ache in his back to stand straighter.

"Good," he answered immediately. Lucien frowned at him slightly. *Only good?* He scoffed inside his mind. Lucien was about to successfully take the directorship of the Special Projects section for himself. He didn't want to look good. Lucien wanted to look amazing.

"Okay," Lucien said. He couldn't let good be the enemy of perfect. He was blown up, after all. It's hard to look amazing after something like that. "Let's go."

"After the meeting, Lucien, there's something I need to talk to you about."

"I heard you wanted to talk to me. There will be plenty of time for idle chatter after the meeting is over and my announcement celebration begins." Lucien patted the man reassuringly on the man. "We'll talk then, I promise."

"Okay," Cailleanach said and nodded excitedly. "We should get going." He stepped forward and quickly opened the large door to the boardroom and held it open so Lucien could enter. "*Director* Malum."

I like the sound of that, Lucien thought to himself as he smiled widely and entered the room with a slow confident stride.

"Interim Director of Special Projects, Lucien Malum." The moderating AI calmly announced their arrival. *"Interim Assistant Director, Bryce Cailleanach."*

"Why does everything from Special Projects always sound temporary?" Johnson quipped from his seat at the Chairman's side. Muted guffaws erupted around the board's table. Lucien clenched his teeth and forced a grin while he moved towards his seat. Now was not the time for petty remarks. He would have to suffer through it.

"My dearest apologies for not making the early assembly." Lucien nodded towards Leslie who was standing behind her director. "There were matters beyond my control I had to attend to," Lucien said lightly, but loud enough his voice would carry to the others at the long table, as he took his seat.

"Yes," Adler called back. "I imagine there would be a lot to *attend* to after Technical Development's clumsy attempt on your life." There was tension around the table as the director of Special Materials looked venomously to his side. Nathanial Eggleton tried to look offended as he scoffed at the very notion.

"Don't presume you can lay my assistant's bumbling at my feet. I had no knowledge of the scheme. If I had, I would have fired the man myself!" Eggleton said defiantly. "If anything, it's Industrial Sciences who should be at fault here." He waved noncommittally across the table at the Director of Industrial Sciences, Davin Swartz.

"Please," Swartz shot back loudly. "The only thing Trup did wrong was, he didn't patent the accelerant. As I understand it, it was quite...*effective.*" Swartz then waved affluently. "Well, *that*, and he got caught. I, too, would have immediately interjected if I knew such a plan was afoot. Even though, I would have found it hard to believe *any* director's assistant would be so gullible as to fall for such an obvious trap. But, I guess, that's the kind of people Technical is rising up these days."

"You can't fault them for that," Johnson quipped. "They have such a shallow pool of talent to draw from. Honestly, it's a bit of a surprise the bomb went off at all."

Lucien even chuckled softly at that one.

"Gentlemen!" The Chairman's voice boomed throughout the room over the intercom. "The past is just that, *the past*. We have assembled here to move forward. We are the guiding light of Research and Development. Don't let *common* squabbles tear us asunder. Mr. Malum? Is there any issue you wish to raise with one of your colleagues, concerning recent events, before we begin the meeting?"

Lucien stood up. The reinforced tip of his cane tapped the ground loudly as he rose.

"No, sir. It is simply the game we play. I harbor no ill-will towards those who play it." *As long as they follow the rules,* he wanted to add, but second-guessed himself because he thought it would make him look weak.

"Indeed. Well said. With that behind us, let us not mention, *or repeat*, the unfortunate events that have befallen the Special Projects section. Mr. Malum, you have our sympathies. Also, you have the board's apologies. If we had been fully appraised of your *condition*, we would have sent a transport for you."

"I appreciate that, sir. But I assure you, my condition is both a minor inconvenience and blessedly temporary."

"This is welcome news," the Chairman said over the intercom as Lucien took his seat.

With that, the meeting commenced.

Lucien tried to find a comfortable spot in his chair as the moderator ran aloud the minutes from the last meeting. Today's meeting would run on for hours. His chair, as well as the other executive's chairs, were scientifically designed, and made with the finest materials, to ensure comfort. Yet

Lucien was having a hard time finding a place where his lower back didn't bitterly ache.

After the minutes were finally completed, the board began with the old business from the last meeting that got carried over to this one. The maintenance budget for the wastewater refinements was a hot button topic. The Director of the Maintenance section brought forward his newly revised budget proposal and presented it to the board. When he noticed the unimpressed expressions around the table, the Director again stressed his point that these refinements represented what had to be done right now, but it also made a significant investment into the future. He also slyly mentioned that if the previous director had made similar investments during his tenure, the cost wouldn't be as high as it was projected to be now.

It was a good proposal. So, Lucien voted for it.

The new budget passed with a seven-three vote. The rest of the old business was brought forward to be discussed, and in some cases, debated. Regardless, objections were addressed and resolved in due course before the motions were either voted on, or shelved for further discussion.

Then the new business was proposed.

Lucien adjusted and then readjusted himself in his seat. At certain points his back spasmed painfully. He suspected that the Neurocaine patches were wearing out. He had two on at the moment but Lucien couldn't remember clearly when he had applied them. It might have been as long ago as a few days. He considered leaving the after-party early. Even though his absence from the event would be noticed, and probably talked about, he didn't care. Lucien just wanted to lay down and sleep as long as his body needed. Lucien thought bitterly of Ernst, laying in his autodoc capsule, in the medically-induced coma. He had so much to do yet. *I can't help Ernst if I'm a strung-out junkie, who's too crippled to walk across his own section.* Lucien frowned secretly at his own thoughts. There was some truth there, though. Lucien had been stretching himself too thin, trying to put out all the figurative fires in his sections.

After I've accomplished my goal, Lucien thought to himself, *then I'll rest. Not before.* He was precious minutes away from the last order of new business on the agenda for today's meeting. The Directorship vote, which would be followed by Lucien's prepared speech. *Then,* it would be over. He would have access to the full Special Projects budget, he could hire additional staff, implement the increased security measures for the future, and focus on the things that really mattered. Lucien had a list of things he could do that would make his life easier. Top of the list was getting his ruined knee replaced as-soon-as-possible, and getting the cosmetic skin therapy to erase the few scars that still remained from the fire that were covered by his expensive suit. Then there was Ernst.

After, Lucien scolded himself. The vote was the next item on the agenda. While the others were bickering over the new colors proposed for the Executive Lounge's quarterly renovation, Lucien went over his speech in his head. He timed his presentation. Five minutes, and fourteen seconds. Lengthy, but not so much so that it would take away from the content. The structure was fairly simple. A brief introduction where Lucien would point towards his humble beginnings, without actually disclosing any real information about himself. He would punctuate it with an anecdote from his childhood. When he first learned of The Council. Lucien would use aggressive tones when he talked about how this *Council*, that nobody elected, appointed, or commissioned, took it upon themselves to regulate human expansion. Lucien would switch to outright anger when he talked about how The Corporation was forced to capitulate to. *"But NO MORE!"* That was the point in the speech he would really have to sell. This wasn't just a speech, after all.

This was a rallying cry.

Once he had them roused and angered, Lucien would drop his big reveal on them. The Council ship. He would start the next part by ensuring that they all knew the lengths he went to find it, and the faith he had in himself against insurmountable odds. After that was established, Lucien would dive into all the technological accomplishments that could be gleaned from it. All leading to the crescendo of his speech, *"No more will we have to bow down to a militarist group of super-soldiers that have run unchecked throughout the system for TOO LONG!"* Passionate words that perfectly outlined his agenda. To find a way to oppose their oppressors.

When the vote came, it was unanimous. As Lucien knew it would be. After all, the viable candidates have been removed. Lucien would win. Each person at the table knew that before they even entered the room. He was the clear choice. Any executive who voted against him now would be throwing away their vote, and exposing themselves as another threat Lucien needed to deal with.

They all clapped uproariously for him. Lucien humbly rose, it was harder than he liked to admit, and it surprised him how much he actually needed his cane in that moment. He bowed graciously to each of the other directors, even Maintenance.

"Mr. Malum, a few words." The Chairman's words echoed throughout the chambers.

This is it, Lucien smiled to himself. He did it. A lowly cybernetic engineer who worked his way out of the prosthetic lab, and in two short lifetimes, rose himself up to be a Director of his own section. Lucien breathed in the sweet scent of the room and tried to commit this moment to memory. He wanted to remember this day for a long time.

It was time for his victory lap.

Lucien breathed in deeply, smiled, and began *his* victory speech.

"Gentlemen," Lucien started to say.

Before he even got the next syllable out, he was interrupted by a muted alarm that came from behind him. All eyes of the room shifted to it. Lucien had to lean on his cane in order to shift his gaze behind him. There a befuddled, and horrified Cailleanach madly fumbled inside the many pockets of his new suit in search of his datapad. If looks could kill, Lucien's expression would have reduced the man to a fine red mist where he stood. When the fool finally did pull out his datapad, it slipped through his twitchy, nervous fingers and clattered to the ground. Blaring that stupid alarm the entire time.

"Sorry," Cailleanach said as he scrambled for it.

"Take your time," Lucien heard one of the other directors quip with great amusement.

This can't be happening, Lucien thought to himself as he helplessly watched the scene play out. Cailleanach finally silenced the alarm and looked briefly to the datapad's screen. Bryce shot Lucien a look that was pleading with him to tell him what to do. Lucien glared at the man and slowly dragged his thumb across his throat. Cailleanach fell back into his place with the datapad gripped tightly in his hand.

"As I was saying," Lucien chuckled nervously, took a calming breath to center himself. He could recover from this embarrassment. Once he gets going with his speech, the others will forget about Cailleanach's bumbling antics. Lucien cleared his throat, and began again. "Gentlemen, I-."

A loud klaxon exploded into the room. Lucien flinched away from the offensive noise. Luckily it didn't last too long, the Chairman soon silenced the alarm while leveling Lucien with a hard stare from across the expansive room.

"Perhaps, Mr. Malum, you would like to convene with your subordinate." *What?* Lucien said and shot a look towards the others at the table, who were all looking at him.

"But...my speech?" Lucien said dumbly, looking towards the Chairman.

"It appears we will have to forego that particular formality. You have business to attend to." The Chairman's words echoed throughout the room with a finality that was crushing. It was the AI moderator that added salt to the wound.

"The Director of Special Projects, Lucien Malum, is excused."

"Of course!" Lucien shouted his compliance while, at the same time, voicing his outrage. Lucien turned sharply and viciously pushed his chair away from himself like it suddenly disgusted him.

Tap-tap-tap-tap!

Lucien made his way for the boardroom door and Cailleanach quickly fell in behind him.

"Lucien," He started to say.

"Shut up!" Lucien hissed. "Not until we're out of the room." He couldn't believe he even had to tell the man about basic boardroom decorum. *Fucking excused! On my first goddamn day! Right after the vote!* Lucien couldn't imagine what misstep he had taken along the way that would lead to this humiliation. Once they were outside the room, Lucien waited for the door to close before he lunged for Cailleanach. "What is it!? What is so *goddamn* important I had to be excused?" Lucien screamed at the man. He was thankful the large, boardroom door was soundproof.

"There's a radiation leak in our section," Cailleanach yelped as Lucien let his cane fall to the ground and he wrapped up the man's lapels into his angry fists. "Communication has been cut off with the interior and no one can get inside." He looked at Lucien with pleading eyes, which only enraged Lucien even more.

"What?!" Lucien shook the man, ignoring the heated barbs that flared up in his back.

"The blast doors came down. To contain the leak!" Lucien shook him again.

"WHAT THE FUCK IS GOING ON OVER THERE?!"

CHAPTER 18

Nick Jones

Nick didn't tell anyone about his meeting with Athena. He didn't want to expose himself to the scrutiny that would follow. Part of him just knew that if he did warn someone, it would somehow get back to Helena Jonlesky and her child. As far as anyone knew, when Nick returned to the section, he had just been reassigned to Soldado's unit for some extra training, which, technically, he was. No one knew about his *free time* though, and he didn't feel like he should offer the information.

When he reported back, the section was still in disarray. Ernst was no where to be seen, and Mr. Malum was too busy, doing whatever it was that he did around here not to bother with Nick except to inform him that he was confined to the section. Which was just fine with him.

He was waiting for Athena.

Nick wasn't taking chances. He moved his little cot into Ernst's deserted lab, walked it through the lab with the menacing-looking suit of powered armor that was laying motionless on an examination table, and into the hanger where the Council ship was parked. The strange ship was propped up on three industrial lifts. One under the pointed nose of the craft, and one under each of the forward-sweeping wings. He set the cot up near the door, and spent his time in the sparsely lit hanger with the strange fighter-craft looming in the distance.

The first day Nick spent organizing the transfer of his own powered armor he had been requisitioned while stationed in the Special Operations unit. He was getting some flack from the property manager because Nick was no longer stationed in Soldado's unit. Soldado cleared up that red-tape real fast. Shortly after Nick messaged the man, his requisition request was approved. After that, Nick walked down to the guard station in the section and checked out a mag-gun. The weapon came loaded with five shots. There would be no reloading, because after those five shots, the capacitor for the magnetic pulse driver would be depleted.

"If you can't kill whatever you're shooting at after five shots with this motherfucker," Soldado growled during his training session with the weapon. *"You picked the wrong opponent."* Nick was familiar with the weapon. He saw what one shot did to a ballistic dummy.

He wouldn't need more than five shots.

When the armor arrived in its transport cart, Nick was pleased to see that Soldado sent a sidearm with it. Nobody even looked at him twice as he wheeled the bulky handcart, with the armor on full display, through the section and into Ernst's lab. Apparently, the geeks were too busy with other things to be bothered, and the guards simply knew better. After his time with Soldado, Nick technically outranked every guard stationed in the section. Nick moved the handcart in close to his cot, and placed the large mag-gun under it where he slept.

Then he waited.

Nick thought about Helena Jonlesky, he couldn't help it. At some points, he actively tried not to think about the woman, and her little girl. *She's your wife,* Athena's words tormented him every time he did. *No!* Nick forced himself to say within his mind. She couldn't be. He had met Helena. Nick stood so close to her, he could have reached out and touched the smooth skin on her cheek, and she didn't look at him twice. During the entire interaction, she regarded him as coldly as she did Cummins. *No!* Athena was playing mind games. Nick couldn't deny that he had some strange infatuation with the Jonlesky woman that he couldn't explain. He was drawn to her; he was mature enough to admit it. But even so, he wasn't so blind as to think that the feeling was reciprocated in any way. She didn't know him, she never did. The fact that he felt something for her at all just pointed towards a defect in his programming. A defect he didn't want exposed to the light of day.

On the beginning of the second day, Nick was convinced that Athena had discovered his interest in the Jonlesky woman using the scant digital footprints he left behind during his search of the woman. After that, it wasn't hard to see how she planned to use the Jonlesky woman, and her daughter, against him. That's why Athena was so upfront about all her plans. She wanted to play on Nick's emotions so he would guard the Jonlesky woman and try to thwart the attempt to smuggle the duo out. Which would ultimately just lead to both of their deaths. Nick knew that, and he suspected that Athena did as well.

That bitch was probably relying on it.

She was counting on Nick's little mental defect towards the Jonlesky woman to cloud his judgement. She was hoping to shift his focus somewhere else, away from her true target. The ship. Eve Carter didn't give a shit about the Jonleskys, she was just using them. Nick didn't know for sure if the attempt

to smuggle them out was real or not, but he couldn't afford
to find out. He prayed it was a ploy, because if it wasn't, then
Helena and her daughter were in dire danger.

At the start of the third day, about a half hour before the
start of the morning shift, the radiation klaxon blared loudly
throughout the lab's hanger where Nick was sitting. *So, that's
how she's going to do it,* Nick smiled to himself as he stood and
walked towards the powered suit of armor. *That's pretty smart,
actually.* Nick hadn't considered that possibility. For a moment
Nick considered that there might actually be a radiation leak
somewhere on the section. Nick shook his head slowly. *No,
it's her.* It's Athena. He was sure of it. And if not, the powered
armor would protect him against any radiation leak.

Her little plan was coming together inside his head. Nick
still had no clue how the woman was able to get this far down
in the megastructure, it was one of the many mysteries about
her. Nick couldn't be distracted by that thought. He knew the
radiation alarm would trigger a section-wide evacuation. All
personnel had five minutes to evacuate before the blast doors
would descend from the ceiling at all entrances into the section.
A collection of inch-thick steel doors would effectively cut off
the Special Projects section from the rest of the megastructure.
Locking the two of them in.

Perfect.

Nick keyed the powered armor's entrance protocol and the
chest and abdominal plates separated down the front with a hiss
of pressurized air. Nick used the hand-holds of the transport rig
to climb up and ease himself into the legs of the suit. He lowered
himself until his feet slipped into the molded boots. Then he
slipped his arms into the sleeves until his fingers slid into the
reinforced gloves. Using a series of hand gestures, Nick initiated
the lockdown procedure. The chest and abdominal plates closed
in around him. With a loud hiss, the neuro-muscular skin-suit
sealed around him and evacuated the air to form a tight seal

against his skin. Nick kept his head still and looking forward as the transport rig lowered the reinforced helmet onto the suit. He was looking through the viewscreen of the visor as the suit booted up the heads-up display. The status lights were green across the board, and he had a good seal.

He was *good-to-go*.

Nick nimbly stepped down off the transport rig. He reached underneath his cot to retrieve the mag-gun, and began charging up the capacitor as he made his way towards the entrance into the lab.

She shouldn't be here, Nick thought to himself as he watched Melissa approach the lab's door on the airlock's viewscreen. Melissa Linson worked at the other end of the section. According to evacuation protocols, that woman should be at the muster point at the section's entrance for the head count. The only people responsible for clearing the labs were the guards. *It's her!* Nick didn't know why he suspected the diminutive lab assistant, maybe it was because of how incredibly unassuming the woman was. Or maybe it was the definite purpose to her walk. Melissa wasn't checking labs as she went down the corridor. She walked straight towards Cattivo's door. Whatever it was, he convinced himself it was Athena. He just felt it. Like a growing sense of...something inside him. It was her. Nick believed it enough to lower himself into a solid stance and leveled the mag-gun with the airlock door.

He just prayed he was right about this.

BOOM!

The mag-gun didn't have a rapport like most firearms, it sounded like a lightning strike. A deep resonating sound reminiscent of crashing thunder exploded out from the gun. The gun's massive recoil inched Nick back fractionally. The slug hit the small woman in the belly. *It's her!* Nick screamed inside his head as *Melissa* flew back into the corridor and flopped across the ground like a cheaply-made doll. Nick knew what damage to expect. If that slug hit a normal person at that range, that person would be separated into two pieces.

"You know," Nick said confidently as he took a step out of the lab. "There's only one bitch I know who could take a shot like that, and not be killed instantly." Nick pointed the barrel of the mag-gun at her. "Though, she doesn't look like you do."

"You got me, kid." *I know that voice!* Nick looked at the small woman as she struggled to raise herself. Then inexplicably Nick watched as the fake Melissa Linson changed her entire form. On her hands and knees, Nick saw her body grew larger. He figured the injured woman grew almost two extra feet and filled out her frame in less than ten seconds. *What the fuck?!* Nick couldn't believe his eyes as he looked into Eve Carter's face. "Do you remember what I said to you last time?" Athena went to stand, while holding her hand over the giant hole in her abdomen, and Nick watched her falter somewhat.

Or at least that's what he thought. Admittedly, Nick never even saw the pistol.

Bam!

Nick didn't hear the shot. The mag-gun in his hands let out a loud crackling sound that over powered any sound that the tiny pistol would have made. The bright flash that erupted around him triggered the visor's dampening effect, and the HUD informed him that the weapon in his hand had been rendered inoperative. *Great,* Nick thought bitterly as he tossed the large weapon to the side and reached for his sidearm.

"You want to do this, kid?" The hoarse question came from down the corridor. "Let's fucking do it!" The dampening effect cleared just in time for Nick to see the woman rushing towards him with the pistol in her hand, aimed at him.

Things went downhill from there.

Nick remembered thinking Athena was crazy, like legitimately mentally unbalanced, when he saw her rushing towards him with nothing more than a small handgun and a fierce expression on her face. In his experience, people ran away from powered armor. Not towards it. And they sure as hell didn't attack someone wearing it.

Bam!

The sidearm didn't last. Nick drew the large .50 caliber cartridge-fired, automatic pistol from the magnetic holster on his right hip only to have the weapon go clattering to the ground when Athena shot his hand. The hands were lightly armored, the bullet didn't puncture the suit, but it fractured two of his fingers. And just like that, Nick was unarmed.

When Athena got into range Nick swung his big arm in a wide arc, but she just dropped down onto her knees and used her momentum to slide right by him.

Bam!

She spun and shot him behind the knee, where the armor was lightest to allow for increased flexibility in the joint. The bulk of the knee joint's armor was on the front. Again, the bullet didn't puncture the neuro-muscular skin suit but it felt like someone had just kicked his leg. Nick's knee faltered and he stumbled. In his mind, he pictured where she was and came back with a powerful backfist to strike her. But she solidly chopped his arm and blocked the attack.

Bam!

The bullet impacted Nick's armpit and pain reverberated throughout his body. The kevlar and carbon fiber-laced skin suit would protect him from the bullets puncturing the suit or his body, but it did little to lessen the actual impact of the tiny bullet. Again, it felt like someone struck his armpit with a heavy pipe. Then Athena grabbed a hold of the armored collar of the breastplate and yanked him down so she could jam the gun into the neck joint.

Bam!

Nick gagged loudly as the bullet punched him in the throat, but Athena didn't slow down one bit. She pulled him to the ground and shot Nick in the face one time. The inertia dampeners in his neck joint absorbed as much of the shock of the bullet as they could, but Nick's head was still thrown back. When he looked up again though, he saw Athena's boot come crashing down on him. Nick's head rattled slightly inside the helmet as an incredible force slammed into the front of it and sent it crashing down into the floor. The HUD winked out for a brief moment but Nick wasn't paying any attention to that.

Athena was raising her boot up again.

Nick timed it perfectly and caught her leg before she was able to bring it down again. Nick squeezed her leg hard, hoping to crush the bones of her ankle, before he threw her to the side. Athena's unusual weight wasn't a problem for the muscle suit, which amplified his strength considerably. Nick tossed her body to the side like she was a pest he was dealing with. Nick heard the loud crash of her bulk strike the corridor's wall, but he was too busy getting to his feet to enjoy watching the impact. The slight yelp from the woman would have to do.

Nick was on his feet and charged towards Athena just as she was recovering. With a savage grunt, Nick launched himself at Athena and collided into her with all his weight. He bodychecked her into the wall of the corridor, and was pleased when he compressed her body enough to forcibly drive the wind from Athena's body in a loud yelp. The prefab alloy wall section behind her noticeably dented inward. He didn't give her time to recover, he couldn't. Nick reached out and clamped his hand down onto her shoulder. The bands of servo-motors in the skin-suit's forearm flexed as his fingers dug into the meat of the joint. Athena cried aloud, and Nick smiled within the suit.

Then he hit her in the stomach.

Nick balled up his other fist and drove it into her midsection, around the area he shot her a moment ago with the mag-gun. He felt his fist sink deeply into her gut and Athena once again cried out before her body folded around the blow. Nick's fist was bloody when he pulled it back. He yanked Athena's form back against the wall and reared his bloodied hand back. This time he was going for the face.

Bam!

The shot hit him square in the visor. *She still has the fucking gun!* The thought madly flashed threw his mind as it was thrown back. The HUD winked out as Nick felt Athena plant her foot onto his front thigh and launch her impressive weight upwards. Her knee struck him under the chin and sent him flailing backwards Athena landed gracefully, pushed off the ground, spun once while in midair, and kicked him right in the chest plate of the armor.

The blow didn't hurt, not exactly. The sheer force of the impact winded Nick and send him backwards. He was sure he was going to fall onto his back. Luckily the opposite wall stopped his momentum with a bone-jarring abruptness. Nick awkwardly fell to his knees as he struggled to keep his feet beneath him, and failed. He braced himself for the blow that never came. When he looked over Athena had sunk down to one knee and appeared to be breathing heavy. She looked at him with pleading eyes.

"Stop," she said with labored breaths. "We don't have to do this. I have to tell you something." She looked at him with a concerned expression. "It's about your family."

No!

"Shut up!" Nick growled loudly as he rose to his feet to face the woman once again.

"It's important!"

"I don't want to hear it!" Nick screamed at her and advanced suddenly to stop her from saying anything else. Nick was tired of her head games. She was losing, and Athena knew it. That's why she was resorting to this bullshit. Nick didn't think. His anger caught the best of him as he moved forward and led with a hard front kick.

Athena was ready for it.

She caught the kick with a sweeping motion of her arms and raised his leg up slightly as she moved to the outside of his leg. Athena then brutally kicked the inside of his other leg. It was Nick's turn to cry out as a sharp pain exploded in his leg. He probably would have fallen of his own accord, but Athena had other ideas. She pivoted sharply and used her weight to pull Nick off his feet before she spun him around by his foot and sent him crashing into the wall

The HUD flashed a series of warnings that caught his attention as he fell awkwardly to the ground. The knee joint Athena just hit was giving off a fault code for the position sensor, which wasn't great because it meant the suit's CPU would only allow the joint to bend or straighten so much without the sensor's input. *Get up!* A voice screamed inside his head as Nick scrambled up to a kneeling position and turned to see where Athena was at.

That's when her knee collided with the chest plates of his armor. A compression warning flashed across his vision and Nick felt something give in the armor's front as the air was pushed from his lungs. Nick spied the barrel of Athena's gun as she thrust it towards his neck again.

Bam!

The shot went wide as Nick's hand flashed up and caught the barrel of the pistol and forced it up and away from him. With a twist of his wrist, Nick wrenched the gun out of Athena's grip and she growled in pain as the finger caught in the trigger guard was bent back until it snapped by the middle knuckle. Nick balled up his other fist and hit the first target he saw. He struck her squarely in the sternum and felt something inside the woman break.

Athena made a sound reminiscent of a weak hiccup as she stumbled back a few steps, obviously struggling to breathe. Nick saw red as he rushed forward, wrapped his hands around Athena's throat and lifted her body right off the ground as he forced her back against the opposite wall. It felt like he was trying to squeeze the life out of a metal pipe as he gripped her throat. Nick growled and squeezed so hard his fingers hurt. Athena reached up and grabbed a hold of his thumb on his left hand and wrenched it to the side. Nick didn't cry out when his thumb broke, he just growled and lunged forward to headbutt the woman in the face. When she still held onto his thumb, Nick did it again. Blood splattered on the visor of the helmet when Athena's nose broke and it started to pour down her face. She released her grip on his thumb. Nick slammed her body against the wall and felt her legs kick weakly against the powered armor as he looked into her dimming eyes.

"I don't know Helena, or Isabella," Nick growled angrily as he watched the life fade from her eyes. Nick wanted it to be the last words she ever heard. "They're *not* my family."

Then his arm exploded with a white-hot pain that caused Nick to release his grip on Athena before his legs failed him, and he dropped to his knees. He looked to his arm and saw the bloodied tip of a knife poking up through the top of it. Nick recognized that knife point. He didn't have to look down to know Athena had pulled the knife from its tactical sheath on the front of his armor. Nick just knew.

"Her *name*," Athena wheezed and then coughed weakly. "Is Bel-."

Monster kisses!

"SHUT UP!" Nick howled like a wild animal. He used his hand with the broken thumb to slap Athena's hand that was holding the knife away. Nick prepared himself for the agony of the knife being torn out of his arm. He used that pain, coupled with the white-hot rage inside him, to backfist Athena with an animalistic cry that filled the corridor.

Athena made a strange sort of yelp when the blow landed and the force behind it threw her from his field of view. Nick turned to watch her crash to the ground gracelessly, rolled once, and then settled face-down on the floor. He cradled his injured arm close to his chest and scanned the numerous alerts that flashed across the HUD.

The vibro-knife severed a good deal of the neuro-muscular servo-motors of his skin-suit, not to mention the fact that the knife damn near cut Nick's arm right off. He felt the blade glance off his humerus bone and slice through his bicep. Blood flowed freely down his side and pooled on the ground beside him. He focused on his breathing, like Soldado taught him, and took the pain he felt and tried to contain it. Nick tried to place it into a box in the back of his mind. He didn't know how much longer he would stay conscious, but it didn't matter. *Focus on the mission,* he told himself as he looked over to Athena.

She wasn't doing too great either.

Nick didn't know how the woman did it. Any one of those blows he landed would have killed or severely crippled a normal person. Hell, a person wearing powered armor would be dead by now. The mag-gun shot alone would have ended it. Even now, Athena had managed to raise herself up to her hands and knees. Nick witnessed the blood leaking down from her face and pooling underneath her. She looked to him with a mangled face that hinted towards a broken orbital bone, a shattered nose that was pushed into her face, and a broken jaw that hung open limply.

Nick's heart sank when he looked into her eyes though.

He recognized that look. She wasn't beat, not yet. Not by a long shot. Athena's blue eyes look at him with an intensity that filled the space between them. She breathed deeply, just like he was, and she just glared at him with eyes that promised more pain was yet to come. Athena let her gaze fall back down to the floor. Nick watched as she brought her uninjured hand up to her jaw. Athena began massaging her jaw, and then with one sharp motion and a weary groan, pushed it back into place.

"There's a," Athena wheezed painfully before she loudly cleared her throat. When she spoke again her voice was noticeably clearer. "There's an apprehension order out for Helena and her daughter." Nick could see her move her tongue around the inside of her mouth. Athena spit out a tooth and glared at him before she continued. "I can't hide them forever."

"Then they'll be apprehended," Nick said with a heated tone as he rose to his feet, still cradling his bleeding arm. "Helena will go to jail, and the kid will go to another family. And it will be *your* fault. *You* did this!" Nick tore his *good* arm away and pointed at her. His HUD informed him that the skin-suit was pumping a clotting agent over the affected area. Nick just hoped it would be enough. Though, it wouldn't stop if it wasn't.

"You can still get to them," Athena said with an annoyed tone. "I've pinged their locations on your datapad, as well as the lift in the central stack you need to get them to."

"Fuck you. I'm not going anywhere."

"You can't stop me." Athena also lifted herself up to her feet. When she looked at him again, Nick could see the ugly, torn flesh on her cheek from where the blow had landed, and was disheartened to see that it was no longer bleeding. *Fuck, she heals quick!*

Nick took a step towards her in a fighting stance.

"I'm *going* to stop you. And when I do, I'm going to find Helena and her kid and make sure they stay where they belong. Right here, *with me!*" *Wait? What?* Nick questioned what he had just said. He didn't mean to say the last part. *It doesn't matter,* he told himself, *focus on the mission!* Nick raised his left hand, with its thumb that was pointing off in an odd direction.

He looked at Athena and growled as he forced his thumb to fold in around his fist. A popping sound followed by a sharp series of stabbing pains emanated from the area as the injured thumb popped back into place. Nick displayed his clenched fist in front of him, like a challenge.

"Jesus, listen to yourself. Why are you even fighting it?" Athena asked absently with a hoarse voice. She held the knife out in front of her in a forward grip. "What did you do with the picture?" She asked sinking into a stance of her own with a pained wince. Nick didn't even know how the woman was still standing right now.

"I burned it," Nick lied. The folded piece of paper Athena gave him was in his pocket. It was the only place he knew it would be safe. It was...special. Though, he didn't want Athena to know that. She would use it to keep pressing in on the defect in his programming to try and get an advantage on him. He couldn't allow that.

"You're such an asshole," Athena said disappointedly and rushed towards him with the knife in her hand, leading the charge.

Takes one to know one, Nick wanted to say, but there wasn't time. In an instant, Athena was on him, pressing the attack. Nick stood his ground and just let her come. Like two lone warriors on a bloodied battlefield, the two of them faced off against each other and attacked with lethal intent.

Athena slashed down on both sides of Nick's centerline, and with each attack he managed to get his hand up and take the strike on the forearm plate of his armor. The Vibro-knife was a weapon where the knife's edge was laser sharpened, and the blade vibrated at a high frequency to further add in its ability to cut and pierce. Nick knew the knife was cutting into the armor, that fact was highlighted by the tiny sparks that followed each strike. He had time though, the armor was thick. It would take her awhile to completely compromise the suit slashing at it the way that she was. It was the stabs he had to watch out for.

Nick knew what she was doing, she was testing his ability to defend himself. Looking for openings she could exploit. He didn't press his attack as he did before. The power balance had radically shifted in this fight. The knife in Athena's hands, and Nick's severely injured arm, changed everything.

There!

Nick turned his arm to shield his face, and then he saw her pull the blade back to her hip. Nick shifted his one remaining arm, readying himself for the strike. When it came, he didn't waste it. Nick used his forearm to block Athena on the inside of her forearm and guided the knife harmlessly to the side. Nick reversed his direction when he had a good angle on the strike and sent a swift blow into the woman's ribs with enough force to lift her up onto her toes. Athena grunted painfully and folded around his fist. Nick pulled it back sharply and punched her in the face with enough force to spin her away from him and send blood splaying through the air. He reached out with his good arm and clamped his hand around his shoulder. Nick clenched his teeth and growled as he yanked Athena off her feet and used his weight to throw her against the opposite wall.

Nick tracked her as she loudly collided with the prefab wall section. He didn't wait for her to recover before he launched himself at her with a heavy front kick that was meant to collapse her ribcage. Incredibly, Eve pushed off the wall and rushed to meet him head on. Nick saw her flip the knife over in her hand into a reverse grip, right before she spun away from the kick and disappeared behind him. Nick wasn't too worried about his back, there was a lot of armor covering his shoulders, spine, and lower back. Especially around the shoulder where the...

Shit!

Nick felt the impact, heard the sound of tearing metal, and saw the HUD blare a list of disturbing warnings. One stuck out above the others.

Power supply compromised

Then the electricity came.

Nick painfully clenched his teeth as it coursed through his body and caused his muscles to spasm. Like his body was trying to rip itself to pieces.

Power levels falling.

There was a loud pop from behind him and the voltage raging through his body abruptly ended. Nick fell to one knee, suddenly exhausted, and when he peered through the visor, he no longer saw the heads-up display. In the corner of his view, was a timer that was slowly working its way down.

9:49...9:48...9:47

Athena had rammed the knife through the back armor and into the suit's power supply, she used the blade to short it out. Nick had ten minutes before the suit turned into dead weight. He knew there was a slight caveat with that. Strenuous activity would wear down the auxiliary battery faster. The back-up battery was meant primarily so the operator could escape, and possibly aid in his survival until help arrived. Suddenly, this fight had a time limit.

And Athena probably knew that as well.

Nick turned to face her and was pleasantly surprised to see she was picking herself, rather slowly, up off the ground. Nick couldn't help but smile when he noticed she was smoking and the knife was nowhere to be seen. He was fairly confident the knife was probably sticking out of the battery pack casing on his back. Athena's hands were shaking but when she looked towards him, he could see that she wasn't done yet.

Nick prepared himself.

Without a word, the two of them moved towards each other with cautious steps. It was Athena who bridged the gap between them first and she stepped in with a flurry of blows. Nick blocked what he could with his good arm and let the armor do its job on the ones he couldn't. The strike rattled his core when Athena's fist connected with his midsection, and the ones that connected with the helmet blurred his vision dangerously. Athena reared back and brought her leg forward in a menacingly round kick to his midsection, on instinct, Nick raised his leg and checked the kick with the shin plate. Athena visibly winced and sharply yanked her leg back after her shin bone struck the metal shin plate of his armor. Athena teetered on her freshly injured leg, and Nick didn't waste it.

He punched her solidly in the face.

Athena stumbled back onto the ground and Nick saw his chance to end this once and for all. He couldn't waste it. He couldn't let this woman get away with what she did. What she was *trying* to do. He wouldn't let her take them away.

Nick stepped towards Athena's dazed form on the ground. When he was within the perfect range, Nick quickly raised up his boot and savagely stomped it down on the inside of Athena's knee as she lay there on the ground, recovering.

Crunch!

Nick didn't know what exactly broke in the joint, but something shattered under the weight of his boot. Blood splashed out from underneath it. Athena promptly bolted up into a sitting position and locked her frantic gaze on Nick's boot. He reared his left hand back and viciously backhanded the woman across the face, promptly ending her screams. More blood sprayed through the air, and Athena was sent back to the ground.

Make it count, he told himself.

Nick stepped back and reached down for Athena's other leg. He growled like a wild animal with a bloodlust as he hauled her body up over his head, and then he turned and savagely pulled her down over his shoulder. He slammed Athena's limp body onto the floor with a wet slap. Again, he watched as blood splashed across the floor. Undeterred by the gruesome scene, Nick turned while still holding onto Athena's limp leg and tossed her body down the corridor towards the lab before he lost his footing and fell to one knee. He watched Athena's slack body ricochet off the corridor wall in the distance before her body landed in a heap in front of the lab door. Athena's body painted every surface it touched with the woman's life's blood.

It's over.

Nick breathed heavily as he looked to the timer in the corner of his view.

1:29

More than a minute to spare, Nick quipped inside his head and groaned aloud. *No one could survive that,* Nick said to himself as he replayed the gruesome scene in his mind. He saw her skull fracture and damn near split open on the floor. He recalled with some guilt how her eyes bulged from her head upon impact. And that was before he tossed her down the hall and bounced her body off the wall. *No could survive that,* he told himself again.

And yet.

Go make sure, A voice told him. *Finish the job.* Nick placed his good hand on his knee and grunted loudly as he pushed himself up. As promised, Nick would go over to the body and twist the woman's head off. He told himself it was a soldier's death. Athena deserved it. Before today, Nick wouldn't have believed a human, enhanced or not, would be able to stand toe-to-toe with someone wearing powered armor. But Athena did, and she almost won. *She had to know the odds were against her,* Nick reasoned with himself as he breathed deeply and steadied himself on his feet. He had a little over a minute left on the timer. *I better get to it.* Nick focused on slow, even steps as he approached the still body at the other end of the corridor stained with droplets and smears of Athena's blood.

Then a thought occurred to him.

Didn't I drop my sidearm somewhere over there? It came to him because Nick reasoned it would be more humane to just put a bullet in her head. However, when he looked up and scanned the area ahead of him the large pistol was nowhere to be found.

Then Nick noticed Athena's body was laying in a different position from a moment ago.

Shit!

The puzzle pieces came together in his mind pretty quickly after that. Nick sprinted towards the body with a sickening feeling of dread blooming inside him. Nick could only watch as Athena's still form suddenly rolled over.

With his pistol gripped in her two hands.

BAM!

Nick was three steps into a full sprint when the slug struck the front of the helmet. It was a blessing that the bullet didn't penetrate the hardened quartz visor. The bullet *did* effectively halt his momentum in a cruel instant. The impact struck the visor, Nick's head immediately stopped, but his lower body didn't. It felt like Nick had been clotheslined by a giant. His legs kicked up until his was practically horizontal before gravity pulled him down to the floor.

He spent a few moments verifying that he wasn't dead or dying. Nick watched the timer in the corner of the freshly cracked visor count down to zero and he waited for the ringing in his ears to clear. Suddenly, instead of wearing a physically-enhancing suit of powered armor, Nick was wearing three hundred extra pounds of weight over top of a rubber suit that fought against every move he made. Nick groaned as he struggled to make the Emergency Ejection sign with his *good* hand. His injured thumb didn't appreciate the movement at all and wasn't afraid to voice its objection.

Ejection was a strong term for the system. It was simply a residual charge the suit held onto so the operator could exit the suit. With a hiss of air, the front chest and abdominal plates separated and spread open. The skin-suit loosened around his body, and Nick felt a wave of nausea overtake him as he pulled his injured arm out. Nick wiggled himself out enough so he could pull his legs out. Nick pulled off the ruined helmet and tossed it to the side just it time to watch Cattivo's lab door closing.

Athena was standing beyond the door, hunched over and covered in her own blood, with her one hand on the interior door controls. He could see she was in obvious pain. She teetered in place as she stood there. Like at any moment she could topple over.

The last thing Nick saw before the door sealed shut, was Athena's smug smile and a cute little wave.

Goddamnit!

Nick picked himself up. He swayed on his feet slightly as a fresh wave of nausea overtook him. He wanted to sprint towards the door as fast as he could, but his left knee sent a sharp pain up his leg that threatened to topple him. The best he could managed was an awkward, limping trot as he held his still-leaking arm against his body.

When he approached the door controls, Nick saw the panel was completely dead. He cursed inside his head as he ran through his options for getting into the room. As quick as he could move his tired and injured body, he move to the opposite side of the lab entrance and ripped open the Emergency Door Control panel located to the side of the wide door. Nick knew the doors were hydraulically operated, and in times of power loss the door would seal shut. What Nick couldn't figure out was how the woman cut the power so damned easily. *Focus on the mission!* Nick pulled down the heavy lever that disengaged the door from the hydraulic mechanism before he pulled out the cranking rod until it locked into place. Using the small button on the side, Nick folded the rod into a crank arm, he grunted as he used his *good* hand to start turning the crank clockwise.

It was hard work. Definitely not something he enjoyed doing with the condition his body was in. Each full rotation caused several spots on his body to flare up painfully, and Nick focused on his breathing as the edges of his vision dimmed slightly from the exertion. He grunted painfully each time he turned that crank, and was disheartened to see the door only move fractionally with each turn of the heavy crank. He built up a rhythm, and growled hotly as he turned the crank, the entire time watching the door inch open. *Come on! Come on!* He screamed inside his head as he cranked.

I don't have time for this bullshit, Nick thought as he kept madly turning the heavy crank. He had to get to the Jonlesky's. *I have to make sure they're safe.* He wasn't exactly sure how he was going to do that. If Athena was right, and there was an apprehension order out for the pair, there was little he could do to protect them from The Corporation's bureaucracy. He couldn't worry about that now, he just had to get to them. He'd worry about the rest after. Surely, there was some way he could clear this up.

Maybe Mr. Malum could help.

But he couldn't even begin to help them until Athena was stopped, once and for all. Even if it killed him. *Do you, though?* A voice whispered inside his mind as he cranked. *You don't have to be here. Athena wants to steal some ship we don't care about? Let her.* This *doesn't matter. Helena and Isabella matter.*

"*Focus* on the mission," Nick hissed through his teeth as he worked. The thought seemed like a betrayal of everything that he was. Nick couldn't just let this woman steal Corporate property from the megastructure. What kind of an example would that set for the rest of the system. If Nick allowed this woman to just waltz out of here with that ship, the rest of the system would see it as a weakness.

And The Corporation wasn't weak.

Nick wiped all other thoughts from his mind when he saw the slowly-increasing gap into the lab widen enough for his body to slip through. Nick abandoned the crank and rushed for the opening. Nick blindly squeezed himself through the gap and scanned the interior of the lab for his target. Athena was there. She was hunched over the strange-looking armored suit on the examination table. Laying on its chest by the armor's helmet. Athena looked at him with a weary expression.

"You're fucking dead," Nick said harshly as he stalked towards her. Athena made no attempt to move from where she was. She didn't prepare herself in any way. She just looked at him with a bloody expression of someone who had accepted their fate. Nick was bruised and battered, but Athena could barely stand. He had to finish this, quickly.

For Helena and her daughter.

Nick scrunched up his face in anger as he moved around the table with the armor on it to approach the woman. He reached for her.

And an armored hand painfully clamped down on Nick's wrist, effectively halting all motion.

"What the fuck?" Nick cried out as he tried to pull his hand away from the supposedly inert armor, but to no avail.

"Sorry, kid." Athena peered up at him with an expression that betrayed what she said. Nick looked at her with abject horror when she eased herself off the armor's chest and slowly leaned in close to the helmet and whispered a single word to it. "Subdue."

CHAPTER 19

Eve

Eve steadied herself on the lab's sterile-looking counter as she let her body slowly sink to the ground. Once she was settled, Eve grunted as she reached down and arranged her legs so they were flat against the floor and pointing forward. that would help when it came time for the nanomachines to repair the numerous fractures in her legs. Right now, Eve hissed with each ragged breath and suffered through the tiny pricks and barbs of her skull putting itself back together...again.

She picked out a spot on the examination table and focused on it as she tried to control her breathing. All the little pieces of herself that she sent out into the digital landscape inside the megastructure were all whispering in the background. She was too scattered to pay attention to them right now. Eve was struggling to just stay in the here-and-now and not give in to the sweet embrace of darkness that was creeping in from the edge of her vision. The Motherbot was also trying to inform her of the various problems that were going on inside her bruised and broken body. *Just fix it,* she said inside her mind. *Whatever it is, just fix it.*

Eve was reminded of the scuffle that was going on beside her when Jones crashed into the counter to her left. She weakly turned her head to see what the commotion was about, and Nick Jones's wounded, angry form was wrestling with Ares' powered suit of armor.

It had almost killed her to charge the armor a measly five percent.

The Motherbot vehemently objected against halting the large-scale repair effort that was going on inside her body to charge the armor, but Eve was in charge. She got to make the decisions. The Motherbot complied and focused its efforts on inducing a voltage to charge the suit to the lowest operational level. She managed to do a slight tick better. All the while her brain was swelling dangerously inside her head.

It had to be done, though. She was beat.

Jones had taken away all other options available to her. All that was left was to blow Jones's head off with the heavy handgun. That would probably kill him at this early stage of development. Eve was mature enough to admit that she wasn't sure how she felt about that, but Oberon had been clear in his instructions. *Jones* must *survive.* Another unacceptable option was trying to go toe-to-toe with him again. Eve didn't like her chances in her current condition. She could hold him off for a time, but the injuries would eventually get the best of her. Eve wasn't sure what would happen to her after the point she lost consciousness, but she knew Ares' ship would remain in The Corporation's custody, and the poor Jonleskys would be apprehended. Not to mention, Evan would probably be killed trying to protect the Jonleskys, or he would be executed if he was caught as well. Complete failure on all fronts. *This* was the only way Eve could still accomplish all her goals.

The rest was up to Jones.

Eve watched dumbly as Ares' armor slapped Jones around a bit before it moved underneath a weak punch from Jones and swept the kid's legs out from under him. Jones crashed on the floor to the side of Eve. He cursed loudly as the armor moved in over top of him, snatched up his flailing hand in its clawed gauntlet. The armor pulled Jones into an armbar, and stretched the arm back until it almost broke in two. Nick had zero leverage in the position he was in, he wasn't going anywhere. That didn't stop him from wiggling uselessly on the ground, and cursing wildly. Eve just looked at him dumbly as he struggled, she tried to focus on his face, she eventually gave up and went back to looking at her spot on the examination table.

Jones soon quieted down.

"Long day, huh?" Eve asked drunkenly while looking at her spot. Then she remembered it was still early in the morning. The day had technically just begun. The mental slip made Eve chuckle.

"Fuck you," Nick spat from the ground. Eve nodded weakly. Nick was right. Fuck her. She was the one that had moved all the pieces in place for this moment to occur. Eve wondered absently if this was part of Oberon's plan all along. Even if it was, he couldn't be blamed. She was one who did it. She was the one who was gambling three *good* lives on a one man's ability to fight The Corporation's programming. It isn't a small feat. They'd been doing it for centuries. They're pretty good at it.

So yeah, maybe fuck her.

"You," Eve began to say only to be interrupted by a bone-jarring series of coughs that racked her body with a fresh wave of pain. "You have to save them. You're the only one who can do it now," Eve said slowly and forced herself to enunciate the words properly. Inside her mind, a slice of herself was desperately trying to get her attention.

"Go to hell! You put the Jonleskys in this position," Nick accused her venomously. "*You* save them!" His last words sounded like a plea to Eve's ringing ears.

"I have to fly...the ship."

"Why?"

"*Because*," Eve said with drunken annoyance. Like Nick should know the answer already. He was a soldier after all. "The ship is more important than the Jonleskys, and I'm the only one who can fly it out of here." Eve then slowly shook her head. "No. You're the only one who can save them."

"I can't!" Nick shouted angrily. Eve looked in his direction, tried to focus in on his face, and spoke slowly.

"Is that honestly what you believe? That you *can't* do it?" Eve weakly challenged him.

"No! That's not what I meant!" Nick spat and struggled some more against the armor's steel grip.

"Then what?" Eve tried to raise her voice but it just hurt her bruised throat, causing her to cough again. "What's stopping you from getting them to that lift? You do that, those two will live happily ever after. I promise you that." Eve paused to catch her breath. "I have it all set up. You just have to get them to the lift."

"I can't," Nick said with a hint of remorse.

"You can."

"I can't! I can't do it, you fucking bitch! I just can't! I can't do anything for either of them. Helena *or* Isabella! Can't you see that?!" Nick punctuated his words with more useless struggling. Eve shook her head again.

"Her name is *Bella*," Eve said absently.

"No!" Nick howled and thrashed like a wild animal beside her. "No! You can't! You fucking bitch! Whore! I'll kill you! I'll rip you apart for what you've done! No!" Nick continued to thrash about uselessly in the suit's grasp like a caught animal still figuring out what part of itself it had to gnaw off in order to escape. "I can't... I mean, I'm not...but they're...I don't..." Eve's vision started to clear just as Nick's thrashing ebbed and she could see the questioning look on his face. Like he was searching inside himself for the answers. Eve knew that look. She had worn it herself more than a few times. Shortly after, Nick breathed in deeply and looked at her with focused, albeit angry, eyes. "I'm not him," he said and shook his head, like Eve should have known. "You can't just say a few words and expect me to suddenly become a completely different person. This *Jonlesky* guy. Maybe, I *was* him. Once. But, I'm me now. I'm not Nikoli Jonlesky." Eve could see it was a painful admission for him. She could see some part of the man really wanted to be Nikoli Jonlesky again. But Eve understood what he meant, because some things simply can't be put back together after they've been broken apart.

"That's good," Eve said softly while nodding her head, trying to console the man. "Because let's be honest, Helena and Bella don't need Nikoli right now. They need you, *Nick Jones*, because you're the only person in the megastructure that can get them to that lift." That much was true.

Eve's digital self was monitoring the situation carefully. Checkpoints had been setup at all access points in and out of stack four, and search parties were combing through the level. There's only so much Evan could do. Currently, Evan was sticking to the commercial district. Probably staying out of sight until something came along that could get them to the central stack undetected.

"Where does the lift go?"

"Shipping and Receiving. I have people standing by on the other end that will smuggle them onto a freighter heading to Ceres."

"Just like that?" Nick looked at her skeptically.

"Just like that," Eve breathed and nodded again.

"Let me up," Nick said sternly. Like he wasn't asking. Eve simply snorted.

"And what'll happen if I do?" They shared a look that lasted a few seconds before Nick spoke again.

"I'm going to clean up your mess," Nick growled. "I'm not going to let anything happen to my...*Nikoli's* family." Nick looked at her with a burning expression. "I'll get them to that lift."

"What about the ship?" Eve weakly thumbed back in the direction of the hanger.

"Fuck that ship. If you want to take Lucien's precious ship and try to fly it out of here, go ahead. Like I said, you'll just die trying. But those two can't stay here, you made sure of that. I'll get them to that lift. I swear." Nick glared at her for a moment longer before he added, "Let me up." Eve didn't know if was the steely look in the man's eyes, or the numerous head injuries she was recovering from, but she believed him. Eve believed him enough to take a chance.

But still.

"Just so we're clear, if you try to attack me again, our friend here will be forced to step in. I don't think you'll like what happens after that point," she warned with some amusement.

"Yeah, I kind of figured that part out on my own." He looked up at her with impatience. "Let me up."

"Release him," Eve said slowly. The powered armor reacted immediately and released its hold on Jones, stood up, and took a small step away.

Jones picked himself up off the floor. Eve quickly noticed that he was still cradling his right arm close to his body, and blood covered his uniform all down his right side. Luckily, the black material of his uniform hid the color quite nicely. He shifted uncomfortably on his feet and Eve suspected that he may still have an injured leg from when she kicked the inside of his knee.

"Where's my pistol?" He looked down at her and asked. Eve raised her hand and weakly pointed to the spot on the floor where she dropped it.

"Pick it up by the barrel," Eve cautioned when she saw him move towards it. "Or the armor will *relieve* you of it. You're still considered a threat." Nick moved over the to spot and slowly bent down and picked the pistol up by the barrel like she had instructed. The entire time, Nick kept a watchful eye on the tall suit of armor that loomed over both of them. "Try not to kill anybody."

"What?" Nick looked at her, confused. "Why?"

"It's a rule," Eve said, not especially willing to get into the finer points of Oberon's philosophy of non-violence at the moment. Nick looked at her for a moment longer before he responded.

"That's a dumb rule," he said simply. "Listen, this doesn't make us friends. As far as I'm concerned, you're still my enemy." He leveled her with a cold look.

"I'm really not," Eve said softly while giving him a bored expression. She wanted to sound genuine and reassuring, but it was the best she could manage. She was exhausted.

"Kinda feels like you are. Next time I see you," Nick began but Eve cut him off. *What is it with this guy?*

"*Next time*, I won't have my consciousness split five ways from Sunday. Keep that in mind while you're dishing out the threats." Eve gave him a slight grin. "Kid. Get going, you're wasting time we don't have. I'm going to hold off my launch for as long as possible. But I don't think we have more than an hour to get them to safety before the shit is going to hit the fan around here."

It wasn't a lot of time.

"Fuck sakes!" Nick hissed and turned to storm off towards the opening in the airlock. Eve watched him disappear through the small gap and heard his uneven foot falls echo down the corridor as he hurried away.

"Guard," Eve said to the towering powered armor and let herself slip completely into her digital self. It felt glorious to shed the aching, throbbing shroud of pain.

She badly needed to heal, but that didn't mean Eve had to be in her body for it. She didn't have to feel her torn flesh pulling itself back together, or feel her bones pop themselves back into position before the nanomachines started to painfully knit them back together. People in the system believed that Council members were invincible. The truth is that they were immortal. Eve, like other Council members, knew there was a huge difference between the two. There was a running debate amongst them over which hurt more, the injury, or the healing.

Instantly the fog of her mind evaporated as Eve stepped into the digital landscape. She tracked Jones on the surveillance cameras as he made his way to the entrance into the section. At the same time, Eve checked the firewall into the section's mainframe. It was solid still but there were a lot of people who were lazily trying to get in. Sooner or later, those attempts would be a lot more forceful.

At five percent, probably four now, the powered armor would probably be operative for another twenty minutes. Eve figured she needed a solid ten minutes before she would be able to stand on her own two feet, and probably another ten minutes to be able to pilot the ship. She briefly wondered what shape Hera would be in, not the operational part of the ship, Eve had no doubts the craft was flight-ready. Eve was worried about the ship's AI.

What condition would Hera be in after all this time?

Eve separated the massive blast doors that blocked the entrance into the section, to the amazement of the staff stationed in a huddled group further down the corridor. She allowed the huge door to part just enough for Nick to trot past easily before she closed them again. *Okay, I have ten minutes,* Eve said to herself and set up a timer for herself and jumped into the landscape of the megastructure in earnest.

She had a lot to do , after all.

CHAPTER 20

Nick Jones

What the fuck am I doing? A part of Nick screamed inside his head. Admittedly, it was a mess in there right now. Suddenly he was filled with the realization that he was not who he was ten minutes ago. He was still Nick Jones, he was at the controls. But there was someone else there too, weeping in the background, as if grievously injured. Nick suddenly had intimate knowledge of the man. Not everything, not even close. Nick just had pieces of the man's life. Things that gave what he already knew context. Nick knew they were *his* memories, he *knew* that, but they didn't feel like his. Nikoli Jonlesky had a rich, full life with his wife and daughter. But Nick Jones woke up on a table, and was given an ultimatum. He was both of those people. At the same time.

Nick couldn't focus on any of that right now, though.

Nick trotted up to the lose crowd of staff members that had equal amounts of disbelief and curiosity on their expressions. Like some believed he should be dead, while others wanted to know what was going on inside the section. Nick gave them all a cold stare that warned them to stay away from him. Only one didn't have the sense to recognize it.

"What the hell is going on in there, Jones?" It had been Dietrich, the new guard shift commander. Luckily, the man stepped up towards Nick on his left side with a look of indignation. It just made things easier.

"Out of my way!" Nick snarled as he strong-armed the man and shoved him to the side like he was a rag doll. He wasn't in the mood for half measures. The shift commander scrambled to get his footing as he sailed backwards, and bounced off another guard before they both tumbled to the ground. No one else from the group dared to try and stop him as he trotted by.

Faster, goddamn it! Nick screamed inside his head as he fought against the heated barbs in his leg that flared up whenever he put weight on his wounded knee. *Faster!* Nick clenched his jaw and put more weight on the leg and pushed past the sickening stitch in his knee. For better balance, Nick risked moving his right arm in time with his steps. A firestorm of white-hot lightning coursed through his arm with every little bit of movement. But it was moving. That's all that mattered. Nick's stride evened out and he picked up speed and he raced down the corridor towards the center of the level, where the lifts were.

Then his datapad pinged in his pocket.

I'm watching you on the cameras. Take a maintenance lift up. It's faster. Crossover in the lower stacks. You'll draw less attention to yourself.

Nick didn't question it. Nor did he need to be told who it was directing him. He knew. He couldn't explain how Athena was able to do the things she did, but right now, it didn't matter. He was glad for the help. He hated that woman, but he couldn't deny that she seemed to care about Helena and

Bella...the Jonleskys. In this one instance, he supposed that made them allies. But he wasn't happy about it.

Nick sprinted for the maintenance lift.

The door opened, as if by magic, as he sprinted towards it. He banged against the back wall of the lift to halt his momentum. An instant later his datapad pinged again.

Hold on. I'm overriding the safeties.

He had just enough time to reach out for the grab bar before the lift's door closed and it rocketed up the central stack like a rocket ship. Nick's body was being pulled to the floor under what felt like a full 2G's of thrust. His knees ached wildly and threatened to completely buckle, but thankfully they didn't. Almost as soon as the lift shot upwards, it started to decelerate so rapidly that Nick's feet were almost lifted off the ground. The jarring stop yanked him up briefly and he fell back down onto one knee when his weight settled.

Then the lift door opened.

Nick was in the perfect sprinter's stance when it happened, and he didn't waste it. He pushed off his good leg with all his might, bolted out the lift door and sprinted down the corridor.

"Make a hole!" Nick shouted as he moved through the corridors and pushed people out of his path. His mistake was using a military term. "Get the fuck out of the way!" That got a better response. All the finely dressed executives jumped to the side as he came barreling through.

At the open-air promenade, Nick ran straight for the causeway to Stack Four. By the time he made it to the causeway over to the other stack, the stabbing pain in his knee evaporated. His arm still throbbed and flared painfully with each wild swing of his arm but it was tolerable. Nick grunted and growled as he pushed himself down the vehicle lane of the causeway. He approached, and passed maintenance carts and cargo transports alike. Much to the absolute amazement of the vehicle's operators.

Nick didn't pay attention to any of them as he passed. In his mind he saw an image of Bella laughing with all her might. In the vision, she wore a mask that covered her smile but her joy was painted across her whole face. A medical mask couldn't hide it. She was both the most precious thing in the world to him, and a complete stranger. *She's, our daughter!* The whimpering voice inside him screamed. *Move your ass!*

Nick cruised into the promenade of the level he was on. He wasn't exactly sure where, somewhere in the lower stacks. The businesses here had colorful storefronts, some of the walls showcased expertly drawn graffiti. The vidscreens of the artificial sky had a few panels that were inoperative and it betrayed the intended effect. Small pieces of trash kicked up by the breeze of Nick's wake.

Then the datapad in his hand pinged again.

Head to security lift 5 in the southeast corner of the promenade.

Two minutes later, Nick barreled into the lift. Athena sent another message shortly after the lift started to ascend.

Three guards in personal armor are going to get on at the next level. One of them should be your size. Remember, no killing.

Nick just snorted dismissively as he stood tall and waited for the lift to come to a stop.

"Boys," Nick said as a greeting when the lift's door open and, as promised, three guards in personal armor filed into the lift.

"Looks like we're all going to the same place," the taller guard said casually when he looked over and saw Helena's level was already selected.

The lift's door quietly closed and ascended the stack.

"Is that blood?" The guard to Nick's right asked with a hint of concern when he looked down and saw Nick's blood-stained hands. He absently looked down at his hands, as did everyone else in the lift, before Nick turned and looked at the guard remorsefully.

Then he leaned in and headbutted the guard, right on the nose.

The guard let out a high-pitched yelp, he fell back against the lift's side holding his face, blood leaking out between his fingers. Nick turned and used his left hand to backfist the taller of the three guards. Nick wasn't holding back. Blood sprayed against the wall as the stunned guard spun around by the force of the blow. Nick lunged forward for the shockstick on the guard's hip. He wrapped his fingers around it and pulled it free from its magnetic holster right before the other one behind him wrapped his meaty arms around Nick's throat. The guard behind him pulled his upper body backwards just as the one with the broken nose pushed himself off the opposite wall. His bloody face twisted up into a snarl as the man held his clenched fists out in front of himself. Nick raised up his boot and kicked the man solidly in the chest, sending him back against the wall.

"What the fuck are you doing?" The one behind him frantically cried out before Nick sent an elbow back into his ribs. The man behind him grunted and fractionally lessened his grip. It was all Nick needed to drop down, pull the man over his shoulder and throw him into the one with the broken nose. The two guards collided awkwardly before they both clattered to the ground.

Then Nick promptly jabbed the shockstick into their necks and pressed the button on the handle. Each of the guards grunted painfully and spasmed violently before their bodies fell still. When it was done, the one Nick back fisted was slowly rising himself up on shaky legs. He was still facing the lift's door and was breathing heavily. Nick gently touched the stick to his neck and put him to sleep as well.

It was the guard who tried to choke Nick who was closest to his size. Nick quickly stripped out of his soiled uniform and replace it with the guard's. Nick also took the man's personal armor and his holster. He tossed the guard's pistol aside and jammed the .50 caliber pistol into the holster.

When the doors opened again, Nick exited looking like a regular on-duty guard.

He didn't run. He walked out into the promenade area with the datapad in his hand.

"Are you there, Athena?"

Yes.

"I need you to find me a security cart," Nick said and pulled up the level's map. Nick could see Athena had already uploaded the positions of the level's guard population into the map. Nick assumed these locations were live because he could see the little red dots slowly moving about the map. In the commercial district of the promenade, not far from Helena's residential district, were three blue dots that were huddled close together. The blue dots were currently stationary inside a clothing store. They had five dots moving around in their proximity. Three were roaming around the vicinity, but two were moving from building to building. Those two were a block away from the three blue dots.

Suddenly a yellow dot pinged into existence on the map. The security cart. It was two blocks further to the east. Nick ran for it.

The cart had a pair of guards that were keeping watch by the vehicle. Nick walked up to them and led them to a quiet alley where he quickly, and quietly, dispatched them. He hustled out of the alley and hopped into the cart. Nick powered up the cart and shot down the lane towards the commercial district.

Faster! The broken voice inside him pleaded with Nick to move faster, but Nick fought against the urge. *No!* He needed to be smart about this. There were two dozen guards searching the entire level. He couldn't attract too much attention to himself or they'd all descend upon him like wolves to the scent of blood. He couldn't fight them all off. At least one or two of them would probably be wearing powered armor, and running into one of them would be disastrous.

Nick growled as he forced himself to follow traffic regulations on his way to the commercial district. When he spotted the shop where the blue dots were located, Nick pulled off the lane and hit the emergency flashers before he exited the cart and sternly walked towards the shop. Ahead of him, Nick spied the two searching guards enter the front door of the clothing store where his dots were hiding.

Nick quickened his pace.

He quickly scanned the area around the store before he entered through the glass doors.

"-if you've seen this person?" The lead guard was asking the woman behind the counter who had a worried expression on her face. He was holding up his datapad for the woman to see.

Neither of the guards turned to look at whoever it was that just walked into the store.

Typical guard hubris, Nick thought as he took the shockstick and jammed it into the kidneys of the lead guard's partner, who convulsed violently before dropping to the ground.

"What's the-," the other guard started to say before Nick grabbed a fistful of the his hair in his tired and weary right hand. *You should've worn your helmet,* Nick thought cruelly as he rammed the guard's face into the counter's flat surface twice. Nick's injured bicep painfully protested the motion and sent white-hot needles up his arm.

"Where are they?" Nick growled at the woman behind the counter. *Megan. Her name's Megan. She's a friend of Helena's.* Nick didn't pay any attention to the new information and just stared at the woman expectantly. Neither of them paid any attention to the bright red stain on the sterile-white countertop. The woman raised her shaking hand and slowly pointed towards the back storeroom. Nick grabbed the guards by the back collars of their personal armor and hauled the two limp men to the back of the store.

The door opened a few steps before Nick reached it, and a large black man with metal arms stood in the doorway.

"You," Nick said with some surprise as he recognized the man's face from the encounter outside of their...the *Jonlesky's* apartment. "Evan."

"Holy shit!" The man grinned widely. "I never thought I'd be happy to see *you*."

"Where are they?" Nick asked sternly while holding the guards in his hands.

Evan stepped aside and allowed the girls to exit.

Nick's breath caught in his throat when his saw them. Helena was standing defiant, and strong with their little girl nestled into her arms. Nick's eyes watered inexplicably at the sight of them.

"*Lena*." Nikoli's pet-name for Helena slipped softly from his lips. He didn't mean to say it, and he didn't know why he did, but it just felt natural. Helena frowned slightly at the name.

"What did you call me?" Helena flinched away when she heard it, like it caused her pain. But after she looked at Nick with fresh, searching eyes. Eyes that he now avoided.

"Let's go," Nick said sternly and motioned for Helena to exit the store.

Nick deposited the unconscious guards inside the storeroom. And like the other guards he had run into today, tied them up using whatever he could, and disabled their communication gear. Nick tried not to pay any attention to the mounting list of crimes he'd committed. So far, he'd earned himself at least a life's imprisonment. He was seriously hoping to avoid the death penalty, if possible. *It will be worth it,* the weak voice inside him stupidly said.

Get to the lift!

Nick led the trio past the horrified woman, Megan, and scouted the area outside the store before Nick waved the others out of the doors. He led them to the security cart and opened the back doors. Inside were two prisoner carts, one adult and one child sized.

"You're not going to-," Evan started to say and looked at him with a worried expression before he looked back to the two carts.

"What?" Nick just looked at him in disbelief before he shook his head. "No. Pull that shit out of there and just leave it on the side of the lane." Nick left the large man to work before he turned back to the girls. "I'm going to need you two to load up into the back of the-," Nick started to say impassionately before Helena interrupted him.

"You are him, yes?" Her bottom lip quivered slightly as Helena reached up and slowly caressed Nick's cheek. "I did not recognize it when I first saw you. Nor did I believe it when Claire told me the truth. Maybe I didn't *want* to believe it," she cooed as the first few tears leaked down her face. "But I see it, now. It's your eyes. You have his kind eyes. *My Niko.*" Helena sobbed the name as she held his cheek in her hand.

"Mommy, why are you crying?" The little girl said, Nick shuttered slightly at the sound of her sweet voice, and when he saw the girl wasn't wearing a medical mask, Nick's eyes leaked a tear down his cheek. Helena softly wiped it away and looked lovingly into his eyes.

"I'm not him," Nick softly confessed as he looked down at Bella. Avoiding Helena's eyes. She gently grabbed Nick's chin and forced him to look at her.

"Maybe not," she said with a smile. "*My* husband would know better than to argue with me. You *are* him." She said with an air of finality. "You are."

"We're all ready to go," Evan called to them after he tossed the child-sized prisoner cart to the side of the lane like it disgusted him.

"We should go," Nick said gently pushing Helena to the back of the prisoner cart. Nick moved in beside Helena and helped her into the back with Bella in her arms. "Get in," he said to Evan who moved with surprising quickness as he lifted his bulk into the back. The poor cart jounced on its wheels as the big man settled his weight to the floor.

Nick moved around and hopped into the driver's seat and pulled the cart out into the lane.

He followed the flow of traffic as he circled around the level and approached the checkpoint before the vehicle lift of the central pillar. Nick swerved into the open lane to pass the vehicles waiting in the queue and tried to look bored as he approached the guards working the checkpoint. Nick waved cooly at the stationed guards, and was waved through into the central pillar of the stack by the guard who first noticed his approach. Nick quickly turned off the lane soon after and moved into the vehicle lift. Nick parked in the assigned spot between a maintenance cart and a large transport cart.

Nick pulled out his datapad while he watched as the lift started to fill with the other vehicles.

"Athena? The second this lift starts moving, they're going to know where we are." Nick hissed quietly and stared at the screen.

I'm working on it.

"Work faster," Nick said and looked up as the last couple transport carts moved into the front of the lift. "This goddamn lift is filling up quick."

Ahead of him, in the last spot left on the lift, a produce delivery truck expertly backed into the spot like the operator had been doing it his whole life. Then the wide steel barriers began to slowly close in from the sides. They had maybe twenty more seconds before the lift would ping the ID chip of everyone in the lift. *Come on, Athena!* Nick growled inside his head as he felt his ability to escape slowly closing in around them.

An idea flashed into his mind on how Nick could hijack the lift. If he connected his datapad to the lift's diagnostic connector and put the lift into *test* mode, then he should be able to manually operate the lift from his datapad. There would be a few safety lockouts he would have to override, because the lift would exceed the weight limits for a functional test, but Nick suddenly had a whole slew of operational and diagnostic codes he could use to override the lift's safety features at his disposal in the back of his mind.

Of course, all that would take time. And as soon as the alarm rings, this lift will start filling up with guards from all sides. Nick only had so many bullets.

"Goddamnit!" Nick cursed and reached for his sidearm. He was just about to exit the cart when a loud series of clicks erupted around him and the lift slowly started to rise Stack Four's central pillar. Nick let out an exasperated sigh and fell back into his seat just as his datapad pinged again.

Keep your panties on. I'm hip deep in the bureaucracy of the megastructure's computer system. Fucking thing is a nightmare to navigate. I switched their IDs with someone else's. You shouldn't have any other problems as long as you keep your head down.

Nick let his head fall back to the headrest and took in a deep breath and let it out. If Athena was telling the truth, he had a clear path from here to the secret lift inside the central stack. He just had to cross over the causeway to the central pillar and he would be home free. Nick looked down at the datapad in his hand when it pinged again.

You did good. You know, there's room for one more on that ship... If you're interested.

A part of him *was* interested. A part of him desperately wanted to escape with Lena and Bella, to leave this corporate monstrosity in their wake and begin a new life with Nikoli's family. To take this new start the universe was giving him.

"I'm not him," Nick said remorsefully remembering the first moment he opened his eyes as this new person. As Nick Jones. He wasn't Nikoli anymore. He was so much more, and at the same time, so incredibly lacking when he compared himself to the man whose life flooded into his memories. "You're right. They won't be safe if I'm near them. Malum will tear this system apart looking for me." Nick Jones was special. The only way Nikoli's family could be safe was if Malum didn't have a reason to look for them. The only way that would happen was if he already had what he wanted. Nick had a sneaking suspicion that Lucien was about to lose his ship. So, that just left him. And after today, Lucien would probably need a bargaining chip. "You'll keep them safe, won't you Athena?"

You have my word.

Nick nodded solemnly. It would have to do. Nick knew there wouldn't be any guarantees once those two were out of his sight. They would have a chance. A chance at something better. Helena would have a chance to live in peace and watch Bella grow up into the woman Nikoli always knew she would be, if only she had another chance at life. Well, now she did. They both did. Nick wouldn't ruin it by trying to include himself in it. Inside him, the whimpering man was silent. He knew the score. He knew that the path Nick had set out for them was the right one. It's not what either of them wanted to do, but letting the girls live their lives was something he had to do. For them. *Maybe not forever,* Nick told himself as a consolation. *But for right now, it's for the best.*

Nick arrived at their destination forty minutes after he left Special Projects. He couldn't say he was tired, but there was a definite weariness he felt inside. Like he had been running too fast for too long and his body was beginning to feel the strain. His right bicep still ached horribly, but Nick was happy the mobility had returned for the most part. Considering the damage the knife did to it, Nick should just be happy he didn't bleed to death getting to this point.

He parked the cart at the side of the vehicle lane on the edge of the commercial district and the food court. According to the datapad, they had to navigate the alleys and work their way towards the pillar of the central stack. Nick kept his datapad in his hand as he exited and moved to the back of the cart to open the rear doors for his passengers.

"How is she?" Nick nodded towards the child in Helena's arm. Nikoli's little monster.

"She's scared," Helena said with some sympathy. "She doesn't know what's going on."

"We'll be there soon," Evan chimed in with an optimism that made Nick cringe. "We just have to go down these alleys." Nick was pleased when Evan went on to explain he had already scouted the entranceway to this magical lift well ahead of time.

Evan led the way through the alleys and brought them to a dead-end that was cluttered with trash. The large black man calmly walked up to the side of the alley and moved a pile of debris to the side. Nick was surprised to find a small metallic keypad hidden behind the trash. He watched Helena as she bounced Bella in his arms and said soft words into her ear to calm the child.

"Just one sec," Evan said absently as he punched in a ten-digit code into the keypad. "There we go."

A section of the wall at the dead-end parted and revealed a sparsely-lit and dusty corridor. Nick led the girls into the hallway and waited for Evan to close the corridor's entrance behind them. Nick walked forward towards a bend ahead of them with the girls by his side and Evan in front. There ahead of them was the lift's entrance.

Just beyond the powered armored suit that was standing guard.

There was nowhere to go, Evan had walked them blindly around the bend and out into clear view of the guard.

"Jones?!" A familiar voice came over the suit's external speaker. *The Colonel!?* "What are you doing here?" Soldado asked with obvious surprise.

"Colonel?"

"The Butcher fucking betrayed us, didn't he?" Evan questioned the man with venom.

"No," Soldado said reassuringly. "I can't pin this one on him. That fat fuck actually paid me a goddamn fortune to look the other way. So much, in fact, I couldn't resist seeing what it was that was so important as to pay me that many credits." *This is bad,* Nick thought to himself as the Colonel confessed his crimes. There was only one reason for someone to feel confident enough to confess their sins, because they were sure they would get away with them.

"You work for Castille?" Evan asked with a shocked cadence. Apparently, this was news to him also.

"When the price is right," Soldado said with some amusement and shrugged his bulky, armored arms.

"He's not going to like this," Evan warned smugly. "Usually when he pays someone to do something, he expects it done." Nick rolled his eyes at the man's feeble attempt to intimidate the man. Evan didn't know who he was dealing with. If Soldado was here, he already made up his mind what he was going to do. Nick wasn't surprised at all when the powered armor in front of them chuckled humorlessly.

"You dimwit," Soldado scolded Evan. "The only reason *The Butcher* still exists is because I allow it. What I'm going to do is kill you." Soldado pointed towards Evan. "Arrest you." He then pointed at Nick. "And those two will go to the highest bidder." Soldado's finger pointed at Helena and Nick growled out his next breath. "Whether that's Castille or Malum, I don't really care."

"Get out of the way," Nick said sternly. It was a hollow threat. Even with the large black man with the metal arms at his side, and a .50 caliber handgun on his hip. Nick didn't like their chances. But there was little else they could do except face the monstrosity in front of them. *Maybe, we can distract him long enough for the girls to get to the lift?* Nick pondered the idea. It could work.

Before Nick could work out a strategy, Evan bolted forward yelling a deep-throated war cry with his fist raised.

"What the-," Nick said stunned by the man's impulsiveness.

"Evan, no!" Helena cried out from behind him.

They watched helpless as Evan charged the towering powered armor and roared as he threw his mighty metal fist at Soldado's face.

Which the man nimbly caught it in midair.

Evan, undeterred by the major setback, threw his other fist at the man just to have it snatched up just as easily. Evan looked up into the cold, blackened visor as a chuckle emanated from it.

"That's cute," Soldado said thoroughly unimpressed.

Evan wasn't done though.

"Surprise motherfucker!" Evan yelled and then lightning arched out from his hands.

Nick couldn't believe his eyes. Evan's metallic hands, that were currently fully enveloped inside Soldado's fists, began to shoot out blue lightning that arched out across Soldado's armored forearms. The whole armored suit convulsed in front of Evan for a full five seconds before something blew in Evan's arms and smoke started pouring out from the elbow joints. Nick wasn't focused on that though.

He was looking at the freshly depowered suit of armor.

"Go!" Nick shoved Helena forward and the two of them ran for the lift.

"A little help here," Evan cried out nervously as he tried dumbly to pull himself away from the motionless armor's grasp. "My arms are blown." Nick could see the man was using his shoulder to try and tug his fists free.

They had mere seconds before that suit would reboot from the power overload.

"Get to the lift!" Nick yelled at Helena and madly pointed to the lift door behind the frozen behemoth

Helena held Bella tight to her chest and ran past the depowered suit of armor that was still holding onto Evan's hands. Nick rushed up to the black man's side and viciously chopped his hand down, freeing his hand. Which promptly fell limply to Evan's side. Nick then moved to the other one and repeated the process.

"Run!" Nick commanded and pushed the large man towards the lift door that Helena had just opened.

With his useless arms swinging by his side, Evan ran for the lift door like his life depended on it. Nick followed closely behind but dread bloomed as the looming figure behind him suddenly moved.

"Where do you think you're going?" Nick heard Soldado's voice call out to him from behind before a large hand descended upon his shoulder, clamping down on it like a vice.

The next instant Nick was flying through the air.

Nick landed hard on the floor and used the momentum to roll up into a shooter's stance. He came up facing down the corridor towards Soldado, just as he turned the armored suit towards the lift. *No!* Nick screamed in his head as he saw the Colonel take a step towards Nikoli's family.

BAM!

Nick pulled the heavy .50 caliber pistol from its holster and shot Soldado behind the knee, right where Eve had shot him earlier. Soldado cried out in shock as the bullet punched into the joint and buckled it.

"Go!" Nick yelled at the top of his lungs as he bolted towards the Colonel. "Go! Go!" He waved madly at Helena to leave as Soldado was recovering from the first shot. Nick ran up to the powered armor and jammed the barrel of the pistol into the knee joint from behind.

BAM!

This time the knee folded and Soldado dropped onto it with a cry of pain that rang out into the corridor. Nick glanced towards the lift and its occupants.

"Go!" He screamed again and was rewarded when the lift's door began to whisper to a close.

Then Soldado turned sharply, swept his massive arm backwards, and caught Nick in the side. Nick heard his ribs break like twigs before he was violently thrown to the side. He struck the corridor wall painfully, bounced off and crashed to the ground. Nick couldn't breathe for the longest time, and when he finally could, he coughed out a glob of blood that splattered against the floor.

"You little asshole," Nick heard Soldado hiss behind him. Nick groaned as fire spread all over his body as he struggled to raise himself up to his hands and knees. When he did, Soldado stood beside him, towering over Nick in his powered armor. He looked to Soldado's feet and saw blood running down the man's leg. "You're going to pay for that."

Nick looked up at him and smiled contently with his bloodied teeth. He had accomplished his mission. There was nothing the man could do to him now.

"Do your worst," Nick wheezed painfully and spit a red glob of spittle onto the man's boot.

Nick didn't feel the next blow. Well, he did. Nick didn't feel the pain from it, though. He wasn't conscious long enough for that.

CHAPTER 21

Eve

The G.H.S John Taylor, the Mormon freighter bound for the Jovian planets, was ascending into the heavens. Its drive plume gave the ship the appearance of a rising star against the dull red Martian sky. The ship was named after some ancient prophet from the Mormon Order. G.H.S stood for God's Holy Ship. Eve took that as a good omen. Eve was out of the digital landscape by then, but her splice found the surveillance footage of Helena, Bella, and Evan boarding the ship. Castille had come through, just like Eve hoped he would and made the handoff to the Mormons. Eve trusted the Mormon Order. It was hard not to trust people who believed it was their holy mission in the system to do God's work. *God's work* being whatever the Mormon High Table says it was. Thankfully, freeing people from the Corporation was still pretty high on that list. Eve suspected that they just liked sticking it to the Corporation whenever they could. Eve couldn't argue with that.

That part of her mission was done.

Eve felt sorry for Jones, though. As Oberon prophesized, Nick was apprehended and taken into custody. It was part of the long game Oberon was playing. Eve didn't know that part of the plan. Her interest in Jones ended the second his family walked into that lift. It was kind of shitty. Jones took a leap of faith in Eve, and now she was ordered to leave him twisting in the wind. *He knew what he was getting himself into,* Eve told herself. It was true. Nick was a soldier. Albeit, one for The Corporation, but Oberon made sure that Nick Jones had the right mindset for his new role in the system. He understood the importance of sacrifice. Didn't make it any easier for Eve though.

She hated to leave a man behind.

Eve stood in Ares' powered suit after she reconfigured it to her frame. Even though the air she breathed was thoroughly recycled, and the suit was frozen inside an ice cube for centuries, it still smelt like *him*. Like Thomas. It caused her to pause when she first recognized the faint aroma of old leather and whisky, but she breathed in the scent deeply when she did. She took that as another good omen. She was tickled by the thought that some part of Thomas would be with her for this next part. Eve flexed her fist at her side as she stood in front of the sleek angles of the nose, and planned out the next ten minutes.

You will have your vengeance.

Eve moved towards the open gangway up into the passenger compartment. She had loaded and secured Thomas' remains, scrubbed the Special Projects mainframe of any and all data relating to Nick Jones, the Motherbot, and Hera. All aspects of her mission were complete. By now, the subroutines Eve installed in the Port Authority, and Corporate mainframes should be kicking in and blaring radiation alarms all over the Shipping and Receiving level. Evacuation protocols should be enacted and filtering people into various shelters around the level. She could have also hacked the equipment lift in the section, and gone through all the tedium of moving the ship in the lift. That would take time, though. The trip to the surface alone would take over a half hour. Nevermind the effort required to load the ship into the lift.

Eve was on the clock.

Outside the section, Lucien Malum was practically losing his mind. He ordered an industrial laser shipped down to the section after it became clear that the firewall around the section wasn't coming down anytime soon, and the door wouldn't be opened with a computer. Currently, a squad of techs were hurrying around the large laser getting it ready to fire. Eve knew those blast doors wouldn't last long after that laser was turned on.

Eve cycled the gangway closed and walked into the cockpit. She eased herself into the pilot's chair and moved it forward towards the controls. Eve flipped the Master switch, the controls around her immediately came to life and the holographic heads-up display winked into life all around her.

Eve was avoiding this part.

"Hera?" Eve quietly called out to ship's AI as she ran through the pre-flight checklist. "Hera, are you there?" She heard a crackling sort of static from the cockpits speakers that was reminiscent of weak sobs.

"Athena?" Her weak voice asked with a rising hope. "Is it *really* you?"

"Yes, Hera. It's me." More crackling static sobs came. *This isn't good,* Eve thought to herself. In her experience, Hera developed bit of Thomas's personality in that she was stoic, stern, and sometimes downright bitchy. She didn't even know the AI's could weep, and it broke her heart to find out.

"He's dead. Dead. I killed him. It was me," Hera wailed. "I was supposed to protect him. I didn't, I couldn't. I tried so hard, Athena. I wanted him to survive *so* badly."

"I know," Eve cooed, feeling a familiar sting in her own eyes.

"They hurt me, Athena. They *burned* me. Burned me up completely, but not before I heard Thomas screaming inside me. Oh, Athena! I loved him so much." Eve reached out and placed her hand on the ship's canopy. Thomas had often referred to Hera as *Mother* because of her doting nature, much to Hera's chagrin. Hearing the ship's cries now, Eve felt it. She felt the raw maternal pain of a mother who had lost her child. "And now he's gone."

Tears leaked down Eve's face inside the armor. With no way to wipe them from her face she was forced to just try to blink them away.

"Hera? Do you know where we are?" Eve asked trying to steer the conversation away from Thomas. They didn't have time to grieve right now. Besides, Hera had been grieving for centuries. It was time to snap her out of it.

"I'm in *Hell*," Hera sneered weakly. "They're going to take me apart, Athena! They're going to tear me down until I'm nothing more than parts on the floor. I deserve it. I do! I failed him. I shouldn't be allowed to function anymore. What's the point? Thomas is dead. What's a ship without a pilot?" Eve hated to hear the ship say the words, because Eve once said similar words to herself at one point. *What am I without Thomas? How can I go on without him?*

"No, you're on Mars. Inside the Corporate megastructure."

"What!?" Hera growled. *Oh! She* did not *like that!*

"Hera, pull yourself together. Check it yourself." Eve had no doubt Hera had already confirmed her location before she continued. "I'm here to take you home. Oberon has a new pilot for you."

"I don't *want* a new pilot." Hera said sternly. "I *want* Thomas."

"Me too," Eve said softly. "Me too. Regardless of that, I'm here to take you home. And I was thinking on our way out we can get some payback."

"Payback?" Hera asked with a child-like optimism.

"For what they did to Thomas. And for you and me." Around her, the ship shuttered.

"Yes!" Hera said with a sinister excitement. "I want them to pay. I want them to hurt like they hurt us."

"Well, okay then." Eve then switched gears. "But I need to know that your head is in the game, Hera. I need to know you're *fully* functional." Soldiers had the term *battle-ready* to communicate their readiness for combat. AIs had *fully-functional*. "Or else I have to shut you down. I don't want to do that. You deserve to be a part of this too. But I need to know, *right now*, if you're up to it." There was a pause.

"I'm fully functional, Athena."

"Perfect. Pull up the layout of the section we're in and find me the most direct route out of the megastructure." Eve finished her hasty pre-flight just as the cutting laser team was pushing the staff back away from the door to the entrance of Special Projects.

Time was running short.

"The most direct path is the vehicle lift to the Shipping level," Hera said with some annoyance before adding, "obviously." Eve just sighed.

"No, it's not." Eve corrected the AI as she fired up the ship's reactor. A high-pitched whine erupted from the back but quickly died away to nothingness as the reactor primed up to operational levels. The reactor mass probably had another thousand years before it degraded to uselessness. "There's a reason you're called *Lancers*. While you're at it, find me a nice safe spot on the Caldera's lid as well."

"I see," Hera said with quiet amusement. "Charging Zeus." The Zeus laser was a high intensity beam laser that could burn a hole in a large ship at close range. Its compartment was under the nose. Hera opened the bay door and dropped the emitter. "There." Eve saw the red dot Hera had put on the HUD. It was just a few degrees off the nose. Perfect.

"Tell me Hera," Eve said as she lit the ship's boosters in the back. She didn't dare use the main drive. While, it was tempting to vaporize the entire level, the loss of life would be catastrophic. "How prepared was Thomas for the *peace summit*?"

"I'm fully armed, Athena." Eve was as happy to hear the news as Hera sounded, when she gave it.

"Well, why don't we kick this pig," Eve said while opening the thrust vents at the bottom of the craft. The hydraulic lifts holding the ship up, flew to the sides from the thrust and crashed loudly into the walls of the hangers. Eve slowly turned the hovering craft until it was lined up with the red dot.

"And leave it squealing from the feeling," Hera finished the saying that was a favorite of Thomas' before it fired the Zeus laser. Almost immediately the wall in the distance flared a bright red and started to droop slightly.

That's when Eve kicked the throttle.

The ship punched through the skin of the megastructure and burst forth into the black interior of the volcano. Only the position lights of the stacks could be seen within the interior. Instantly, Hera shifted the view out the canopy to night-vision and the landscape in front of her was suddenly visible in varying shades of green. Eve kept the throttle to a minimum as she maneuvered the ship to the outer wall of the volcano.

When she looked back, the megastructure rose above the caldera's floor like bony fingers trying to escape a grave. Eve traced the central pillar up to the mouth of the volcano and the Shipping and Receiving level. To the extreme side of the level, near the mouth of the volcano on the north side, was Hera's waypoint.

"That's spot's not under some populated area, right?" Eve asked, testing Hera. "Because we're here to fuck up a lot of their shit, but I'm not interested in killing a whole bunch of people." It was a fine line to walk *inside* the megastructure. But outside, was a different story. There were tons of anti-aircraft guns, anti-ship torpedo batteries, short- and long-range radar stations, and unmanned orbital relay stations. Outside, there were a lot of things she could destroy.

She just had to get there.

"Please," Hera said dismissively. "I'm not *that* far gone. I, too, want them to pay, but I, too, do not wish for innocent people to perish. *That* spot doesn't have a living person within five hundred meters of it, and there are at least two blast doors sealing off *that* spot from the rest of the level's air supply. Satisfied?"

"Very," Eve said. She moved the control sticks, and started the slow vertical ascent towards the waypoint at the top of the volcano. "Fire the laser."

With a splash of molten metal, Hera burst out of the volcano like a bullet and rocketed into the sky. Eve cut the engines, unfolded the wings of the craft and just rode the scant Martian winds in the upper atmosphere. *God, I miss flying in an atmosphere,* Eve thought to herself as she sailed listlessly above the volcano.

It couldn't last though.

"Athena, I have multiple defensive batteries targeting us all over Olympus Mons." Hera was quick to inform her and she pinged each of their locations on the HUD. Eve nimbly rolled the craft over and looked down upon the volcano and its collection of red dots.

Seventy-four.

That's not insubstantial, Eve thought playfully as she looked down upon it. Staying inverted Eve spread the wings wide and caught the draft coming off the volcano's side and rode it to an even higher altitude.

"Unidentified craft," A very irate voice came over her communication system. "Unidentified craft. This is Corporate Air Command. You have been deemed an enemy combatant for your numerous violations against The Corporation. You have been ordered to power down all weapons systems, and hand over the operational codes for your craft immediately." *He sounds mad,* Eve smiled as she lazily wafted on the air currents high above the volcano's mouth, almost taunting them. "Failure to comply immediately and you *will* be fired upon, and we *will* blow you out of the sky."

"Hera? Would you care to respond?"

"I'D LIKE TO SEE YOU FUCKING TRY!" Hera roared over the comms and readied the countermeasures.

An instant later the sky was filled with magnetic-flak rounds, torpedoes, and guided missiles.

"Jesus Christ, Hera!" Eve laughed as she pointed the nose of the craft towards the volcano and punched the throttle.

Instantly 5G's worth of thrust slammed her back as the craft dived towards the volcano, leaving a sonic boom in her wake parting the scattering of blue clouds that were around her. Eve tweaked the control stick in her right hand and expertly rolled, weaved, and threaded the craft through the field of flak rounds. One advantage she had over the anti-aircraft guns was that Hera's hull wasn't magnetic, so most of them sailed right by before the proximity sensor could explode the round.

The torpedoes and missiles were another story.

Eve didn't waver in her direction. She rocketed straight down towards the top of the volcano and watched as the heavy ordinance flew by without detonating because they couldn't cross the minimum threshold to arm their warheads before Eve passed them.

"They're turning," Hera warned a heartbeat later

"Decoy drones," Eve called out as she inched the controls to the side and the ship wildly banked down the side of the volcano. The craft's speed kicked up dust and small rocks in its wake as it sped down the side of the volcano and through the crossfire from the AA guns. The drones from the belly of the craft shot down and each sought out its locked target before it embedded itself into the defensive batteries she was buzzing passed.

The decoy drone replicated Hera's radar signature and suddenly the missiles and torpedoes didn't have one target to track, it had a dozen. Eleven of them were stationary, which made them much easier to hit. The heavy ordinance prioritized the stationary target and started slamming into them behind her. The missile sent a fiery dust plume high in the sky, but the anti-ship torpedoes detonated on the ground and the blast wave shook Hera as the entire area behind her lit up with each impact.

"Hera! Fire at will. Light'em up." Eve called out as she banked the craft at the bottom of the volcano at did a tight loop around the wide base of the volcano. Hera lit up the missile and torpedo installations first and fired a series of omni-directional missiles that shot out from Hera's back like mortar rounds and spun in the air before the rockets fired and the tiny missiles flew straight towards their targets, leaving white smoke tendrils in their wake. Eve bounced and dipped Hera wildly over the Martian landscape as flak rounds punched into the ground all around her. Eve left a giant red dust plume in her wake as she circled the volcano, dodging the flak rounds while Hera fired off another batch of missiles as she went.

"Flares," Eve barked as she jumped the craft back into the sky just as the next series of missiles and torpedoes shot out from the skin of the volcano.

Eve didn't bother rushing them like before, she assumed the safeties have been removed from the heavy ordinance that was currently flying towards her. Hera waited until Eve banked away from the oncoming ordinance before it released the flares in her wake. Eve heard the explosions behind her from the missile impacts as she rolled the craft and dove back towards the ground.

Unfortunately, the torpedoes weren't so easily fooled.

"We have three torpedoes closing in fast behind us. Should I use the point-defence cannons?" Hera asked calmly. The craft was equipped with two small rotary guns that were stored in separate bays that were located on the ship's rear, close to the rear stabilizer, and another one located on the underbelly. Hera could use those guns to shoot down enemy ordinance.

But where's the fun in that?

"Do you doubt me, Hera?" Eve tried to sound playful as the G-forces slammed her back into her seat as she sharply banked to the right. The comment came out sounding more like a growl.

There! Eve glanced towards the ground and spied the deep, narrow canyon at the northern edge of the volcano's base. She folded the wings back as she rolled the craft in a wide arch before angling the nose towards the canyon and the craft plummeted towards the ground. Hera fired off another batch of missiles just as Eve bobbed, weaved, and rolled away from the flak rounds on her way towards the canyon. She checked the threat detection system. It was lit up like a Christmas tree, and noticed that the three torpedoes were a thousand feet back and closing fast. The low-yield nuclear warhead had a 100-meter proximity sensor. So, she had time.

But not much.

Eve eased up on the throttle just before she dropped below the Martian landscape and entered the canyon with the wings folded back like a traditional fighter. The instant she disappeared into the canyon the flak ceased exploding behind her. Eve kept an eye on the threat detection system as she eased off the throttle and snaked her way through the canyon.

There's a big difference between atmospheric missiles and torpedoes. Missiles relied on rockets for propulsion, so they were incredibly fast right off the bat, topping out at their maximum speed in no time at all. Their gyroscopic guidance system and small maneuvering flaps at the front and rear of the missile made them more agile than most ships. *Most* ships. But they were dumb as dirt. Whereas torpedoes used a satellite-assisted guidance system that was fueled by a powerful CPU, torpedoes used a standard jet engine and had wings similar to regular fighter craft. Unlike the missile, the longer a torpedo was in the air, the faster it got, but it had a much slower build up time. Eve could outfly a single missile, or trick it into attacking a flare, but torpedoes were the relentless seekers in the sky. They mercilessly tracked down its target until eventually engulfing it in a nuclear fireball. The torpedoes closing in behind her in the canyon were sophisticated enough to easily traverse the canyon's twisting route.

But not smart enough to figure out it probably shouldn't get too close.

Eve let the trio of heavy ordinance behind her close in to about three hundred meters. Behind her, in Hera's wake, dust, debris, and small rocks were pulled off from the canyon's wall as she rocketed past. Eve pictured all that debris being sucked into the massive intake at the bottom of the torpedo. As if on cue, Hera spoke up a moment later.

"Splash one." Eve made small adjustments on the controls as she shifted and swerved through the tight canyon and waited for the others to follow suit. "Splash two," Hera informed her a second later. "We're running out of canyon, Eve."

"I'm aware," Eve quickly said as she eyed the canyon walls slowly closing in on their sides. "When we come out of this canyon we're heading straight for that fucking volcano again," Eve said with some venom. "Pick your targets well ahead of time so we're not shooting at the same targets on our way up the side. When we get to the top, drop a mine on that radar tower."

"Gladly," Hera said before quickly adding, "Splash three."

Eve banked the craft around a tight corner and saw where the canyon closed in ahead. She pointed the nose out of the canyon and punched the throttle until the afterburners kicked in and shot them forward. Eve rolled so that she was inverted and exited the canyon, tightly dropping the ship low to the ground before she rolled it over again.

The flak fire started up again and the shells exploded closely behind them while Eve moved towards the side of the volcano. Hera was already firing another batch of omni-directional missiles towards the various missile and torpedo batteries that dotted the landscape up the western side of the giant volcano. Hera pinged her targets and highlighted them with green dots, leaving the red ones for Eve as she rolled into the sky.

Then a flak round struck Hera.

It struck the fuselage just before the wing on the right side, dangerously close to the intake. The craft jumped weirdly in the air. Eve dropped the throttle and rolled the craft into a short dive before she pushed it to seventy-five percent and felt the sudden thrust compress her chest.

"Hera?" Eve called out.

"Don't worry about it," Hera said without missing a beat and said nothing further.

So, Eve didn't worry about it.

"Let's see how you fuckers like this," Eve growled as her crosshairs drifted towards her first target.

Eve pressed the trigger on the control stick.

The shrill sound of the 30mm rotary cannon spinning up erupted through the cabin a heartbeat before the depleted-uranium shells were spat out at a rate of a thousand rounds a second. Eve used short bursts as she snaked her way towards the volcano at literal neck breaking speeds as she took out her targets at the bottom of the volcano first. The craft shot towards the base of the volcano and Eve pitched the craft up the side an instant before they would impact it. Proximity warnings flashed all around the sides of her vision as Eve navigated the chaotic topography of the volcano on her way up the side.

The flak fire ceased almost immediately. She was far too close to the surface of the volcano for those. She cruised up the side of the biggest volcano in the solar system and weaved around the various rocky outcroppings, and the numerous black plumes of smoke from the ruined defensive batteries as she searched for her targets. Eve took out the ones she could using short bursts of the cannon, and was rewarded by briefly witnessing the armor-piercing rounds shred the gun emplacement apart before she zipped by. The one where she couldn't find a shot she simply buzzed them and let the destructive turbulence in her wake do the job for her.

Eve struggled to breathe as the G-forces pressed in on her chest. A normal person would have blacked out a long time ago but she could take it. This was another one of the many gifts the nanomachines provided her. She could only dream of piloting a craft like this, in this manner, before the Motherbot had been implanted in her. Flying this fast, and this close to the ground, where one minute slip of the control in any way would be her doom. Eve should be terrified at the velocity she was operating at, but she found it exhilarating.

Better than sex, in fact.

Eve rolled the craft just as she crested the top of the volcano and exposed the underbelly. Hera had a fraction of a second to deploy the magnetic mine before they were past the radar installation on the far corner of the volcano's lid, In true AI fashion, Hera hit her mark perfectly. Eve's wake carried the rising debris from the explosion even higher into the sky, as the shockwave rattled the craft around her.

In an instant, Eve was at the upper limits of Mars' atmosphere. Around her, the dull red sky started to give way to the blackness of space. *This isn't going to feel great,* Eve thought before she cut the engines and used the maneuvering thrusters to flip the ship while its momentum still carried them into space. It was a standard *flip-and-burn maneuver,* it was standard practise to begin a large ship's deceleration burn. But it was never meant to be used with fighter-crafts, because such a maneuver would be lethal to the pilot. It was a little trick Eve had developed over the centuries. She sucked in a deep lungful of air.

"Athena? What are you-," Hera started to say but Eve didn't hear the rest of the question.

Apparently, Hera was unfamiliar with the maneuver.

Eve waited the half second until the nose was pointing towards the volcano again then she punched the throttle until the afterburners roared behind her. It felt like a large cargo container had slammed into her chest and pinned her against her seat with enough force to painfully compress her ribs. Twenty G's slammed into Eve's body as she reversed her momentum in an instant and dropped out of the sky with enough force to push her eyeballs deeper into her skull. Eve struggled to see the red dots in front of her as she lined them up to the gun reticle and fired short bursts from the wing-mounted cannons. Behind her, Eve miraculously picked out the sounds of Hera launching more missiles. And not to be outdone, Eve queued up the surface missiles from the weapons bay on the underbelly, and fired one after another at her own targets.

Eve dropped from the sky and rained hellfire down upon the outer shell of the corporate megastructure. She let the air out of her lungs in a low growl that rose to a hate-filled, guttural war cry that erupted from her for a full second before she tweaked the controls and banked down the side of the smoking exterior of the corporate megastructure. She dumped the throttle and let the afterburner die away as she tore a destructive path with the gale-force winds she pulled in her wave. The scant Martian atmosphere somewhat lessened the effect. If Eve had done this trick in the denser atmosphere of Earth, the external temperatures would have shot up over a thousand degree and Eve would have torn whole chunks out of the volcano's surface and sent debris flying for miles.

As it was, Eve leveled out at the bottom of the volcano and shot out twenty miles from the volcano before she banked the craft into the sky and waited for the anti-aircraft fire to begin anew once the back-up systems kicked in.

But it never came.

Eve lazily circled the volcano for a full thirty seconds before Hera spoke up.

"They are no longer targeting us," the AI stated coldly.

"Maybe they learned their lesson," Eve said smugly, even though she was still catching her breath. She circled to the south-east from the volcano.

She knew better though. Right now, inside that volcano, there were a whole host of military personnel that was shitting themselves. The megastructure's external defensive network was the culmination of centuries of work. They built the expansive network of installations, upgraded them over the years, redesigned them to the best of their ability before the next generation came along and slowly rebuilt, and redesigned the whole thing all over again. Olympus Mons was the impenetrable fortress of The Corporation that nobody dared approach without permission or risk being ripped apart by the flak cannons, blown to pieces by the advanced missile systems, or reduced to atoms by the nuclear warheads of the torpedoes. Eve had just stolen a fighter craft from inside the megastructure, and promptly shit all over their defences, leaving the majority of the network a smoldering ruin. Inside the megastructure, Eve imagined that the military personnel were losing their minds trying to figure out what to do next while numerous military accountants were trying to calculate the damage for their reports. Eve knew what The Corporation would do.

It was the same thing they always did when a problem presented itself. They threw people at it without a care for their lives.

Eve imagined that all over the monstrous volcano's exterior, the launch tubes that weren't damaged or obstructed were opening up.

"I have bogies in the air, Athena. *Numerous* bogies." Hera didn't have to say anything. Eve could see the fighter crafts being spit out of the volcano's sides like spores from an intrusive fungus.

Fuck sakes, Eve thought bitterly as she opened the comms channel to the megastructure's defensive command.

"Listen, guys. I don't mind blowing up unmanned installations. Shit, I could do that all day," Eve said lightly. "But I really don't want to kill any pilots today. Why don't we call it a day and go our separate ways?"

The Corporate response was quick.

"Unidentified craft," a voice said coldly over the line. "You have been ordered to power down your weapon systems, and hand over operational control of your craft. Continued resistance will result in your destruction."

Eve closed the channel. *Fuckers!*

"That sounded like a threat," Hera said over the intercom like she was titillated by the prospect. Eve was less excited.

"Hera, open a comm channel to those fighters," Eve commanded. She watched two fighter squadrons form into two separate spearhead formations and slowly move into position on her tail as she lazily cruised around the Olympus Mons.

"Done."

"Guys," Eve said harshly. "Let's not do this. I was fucking around. I'll just leave," Eve offered pleasantly, trying to make it sound like the easiest thing in the universe. "Just let me go and we don't have to do anything we'll both regret."

"You fucked with the wrong people," an angry voice said from the channel before Eve's threat detection system lit up as each of the fighters got a weapon's lock on Hera.

"We got missiles in the air!" Hera warned suddenly.

"No!" Eve growled before she closed the channel. "*You* fucked with the wrong person."

Arrogant assholes, Eve cursed inside her head as she backed away from the volcano and tried to gain some distance between herself and the fighter squadrons.

Martian fighter crafts were more akin to gliders in Eve's opinion. The scant Martian atmosphere forced designers to make some unfortunate concessions in their fighter designs. These aircraft were made with lightweight materials and had thin, wide wings that stretched out to the sides. They had probably the most advanced jet engines ever created, but with the meager Martian atmosphere, they were severely underpowered. In Eve's opinion they were hardly fighters because they moved in the sky like fat swans. They did have one thing going for them.

They had missiles.

"Countermeasures are ready," Hera chimed in.

"Hera, can you jam their targeting systems?"

"*All* of them?!" Hera exclaimed with shock. Currently there were two dozen ships in the air. It was a big ask. "I wouldn't be able to do it for long," Hera said apologetically. "There's just too *many* of them."

"I just need three seconds," Eve said as she dumped six sensor drones into the sky before she banked away from them, forcing the multitude of missiles rocketing towards her to change course. *Jesus!* There were still forty-two missiles tracking her. Six had already impacted with the sensor drones she left behind in her wake. Eve had seconds before she would have to actively evade them.

"I can do three seconds," Hera said with a renewed confidence.

"I let you know when. Until then, feel free to shoot anything that gets within one hundred meters of us." Eve dropped another batch of sensor drones and quickly banked back to the southeast, towards the flat expanse of dusty terrain of Gordii Fossae. Eve waited for the proximity alarm before she rolled the craft, dropped it out of the sky and raced towards the ground with the missiles in hot pursuit.

With the maneuvering thrusters, Hera was impossibly agile within the Martian atmosphere, whereas the missiles had wide fins at the front and back of the ordinance that moved independently of each other. Eve was more maneuverable, but not by much. Each turn gained her an inch on the front runners, but the missiles in the back of the group would easily adjust to Eve's new path and marginally gain on her. Eve moved towards the wide, flat plateau of Gordii Fossae and banked the craft towards the ground and leveled out 25 meters above the Martian landscape. In her wake, a plume of fine, iron-rich dust particles rocketed into the sky just as the missiles started raining down around her. Hera fired the PDC gun mounted on her back and spat out short bursts. Behind her, explosions were sounding off as Hera starting picking off the missiles that got too close. Eve banked left sharply, all the while the altitude warning was flashing red in the corner of her HUD. At this height, the tip of the wing cut through the air mere feet above the ground. Eve banked in the opposite direction just as a score of missiles punched into the ground to her side and promptly exploded. Hera shook around her and shrapnel sprayed her armor but she continued to fire short bursts as Eve deployed the second last batch of sensor drones into the air behind her before she banked away from them hard enough to steal the wind from her lungs. The drones were destroyed almost the same instant that they went active and Hera's backside was sprayed with more shrapnel.

But it gave them room to move.

Eve fired the nose thruster while banking back towards the fighter squadron, which was still flying confidently at a presumed safe distance behind her. The craft drifted in the air in a tight circle, back towards the squadron.

"Jam them now, Hera!" Eve barked as the nose lined up to the unaware squadron. Eve didn't wait for a response. She trusted Hera.

The afterburner flared, and melted the Martian landscape to glass before it shot the craft into the sky. Inside Ares' armor, one of Eve's ribs broke as the G-forces punched into her painfully. Medical alarms flashed in the HUD that Eve didn't pay any attention to. The taste of copper in her mouth was harder to ignore, but she managed it as she rocketed towards the tight fighter formation. In her blurred vision she saw the formation begin to slowly part.

But it was too late.

Hera hit the fighter squadron doing in excess of Mach 10 after she shot out from the dust cover Eve had created. At that speed, Eve could circumnavigate Mars in under two hours. She couldn't read the air speed display, though. Blood had started to leak in from the sides of her eyes from burst capillaries. The nanomachines were madly working to repair the damage to her body as Eve dumped the throttle and let her speed bleed down to a reasonable level. She didn't need to see the damage in her wake. Eve just knew.

"How many Hera?" Eve wheezed painfully. Eve imagined the destructive turbulence in her wake ripping the wings right off the fighters as easily as she could rip the wings off a fly.

"Out of the twenty-four fighter craft, eighteen have been rendered inoperable." Hera waited a moment before she told Eve what she really wanted to know. "None have ejected thus far."

Eve's vision cleared a moment later and she banked so she could see the fighter squadron out the side. Eve looked just in time to see the ruined remains of the fighters tumble into the giant dust cloud she had created. The rest of the squadron were scrambling clumsily in the air to regain control of their crafts.

They were sitting ducks down there.

"Okay, Hera." Eve looked away and sighed heavily as she thought about the eighteen souls that were falling to their end. "That's enough. Transmit our ID before anybody else gets hurt over this." *It was necessary,* Eve told herself. It was a show of force, a display to let the fighter pilots know exactly how outmatched they really were. Eve told herself it saved lives in the end. *Eighteen,* she thought remorsefully.

I would have killed them all, Eve imagined Thomas saying in that deep, warm sounding voice of his. Eve didn't doubt it. Thomas would have cracked that volcano wide open avenging her death, killed every pilot who dared share the sky with him, and then destroyed any ship in orbit who tried to stop him from leaving. Deep down, Eve *wanted* to do that. But the problem with living forever is that you have to share that time with the choices you made along the way. Eve has already made that mistake dozens of times before.

It was time to stop.

"Transmitting now." Eve waited a full second for the megastructure to comprehend their dilemma before she opened a channel.

"Tower, this is *Athena*," Eve said sternly. "Of The *Council*." Again, Eve gave them a full second for it to sink in. "I am in the process of retrieving one of *our* ships, that one of your own was so kind to store for us inside your volcano. Please be sure the convey my deepest gratitude to Lucien Malum for not only finding *our* lost ship, but also for transporting it to his facility inside the megastructure for safe keeping. Again, he really went above and beyond for us there," Eve said with great mirth. She didn't mind throwing that guy under the bus, it was a perk actually. *That's for Helena and Bella, you asshole!* "Anyway, sorry for the *confusion* earlier. I was having *radio troubles*," Eve said with an utterly unconvincing cadence. "But everything seems to be working okay now." She looked out over the side and down toward the volcano just as the giant dust cloud she created miles away started to form in around its base.

"Yes." A different voice came on the channel. It was a deep, scratchy voice that hinted towards age and experience. Eve could hear the suppressed rage in his tone. "*Athena*. We have received and acknowledged your ship's ID. Welcome to Mars. It is most regrettable to hear about your sudden communication problems, but we are *thrilled* to hear there will be no further *misunderstandings* concerning your intent. Please accept our humble fighter crafts to escort you to the upper atmosphere where we have provided you with an unobstructed flight plan out of Mars's magnetosphere." There was a short pause before the sandpaper voice started up again. "Be advised, any, and I mean *any*, deviation from that course will be considered an act of aggression against The Corporation and will be dealt with swiftly."

Eve rolled her eyes.

"I have received the information packet from tower control," Hera said quietly.

"That is so considerate of you, tower. But I think your pilots have been through enough for one day. I should be able to manage quite well on my own, thank you. Please be advised, my AI is acting up and seems to respond adversely to anyone locking in on my ship. To be safe, maybe keep your distance and keep local weapon systems powered down until I'm gone to avoid any further *regrettable* actions."

"Excuse me?!" Hera protested loudly over the intercom. Eve just shushed her like she would a child.

"Understood, Athena. Safe travels. Tower out."

"Have a wonderful rest of your day, guys. Athena out." Eve banked the craft away from the volcano and started on the flight path that would lead her out of the atmosphere. "Let's go home, Hera."

CHAPTER 22

Lucien

Tap-tap-tap.

Lucien huffed as he struggled to keep up with the Special Operation's Liaison Officer as he escorted Lucien to the holding cells. Lucien wanted to come sooner. Hell, he wanted to race up here the second he found out where Jones was being held, but these past three days had been the worst three days of his entire life.

He wasn't alone in that regard, either.

The megastructure had suffered its most grievous and destructive attack in its entire history. Lucien's suspicions about The Council had been correct. He couldn't prove it, though. The surveillance footage from inside his section had been scrubbed from the mainframe, along with his research data. Staff members and guards alike reported nothing out of the ordinary at the time of the alarm. As far as anyone knew, that goddamn ship just flew itself out of Lucien's section. It flew itself around the interior of the megastructure's volcano before it promptly flew through fifty feet of steel and popped through the Shipping and Receiving level like it was made of paper, before raining hell down on the exterior.

Lucien had exactly two leads.

One, was Melissa Linson, who was a part of Bryce Cailleanach's team. She wasn't present at the head count at the emergency muster point outside of the section, and eyewitness accounts put her *inside* the section at the time of the radiation alarm. She was seen evacuating people near Cattivo's lab, which she shouldn't be doing because that's not her job. Stranger still, three hours after the attack, Melissa Linson was discovered bound in her apartment. When questioned, *this* Melissa Linson claimed to have been attacked in the early morning. The *real* Melissa Linson was stunned, bound and left in her apartment. She never even made it the section that day. She provided investigators with a description of the woman, but no profile matching that description was in the Corporate Registry. So, whoever that woman was, she was basically wandering around the megastructure undetected and untracked, like a ghost. Which was impossible.

The other was Jones.

He had exited the section shortly after the blast doors closed, apparently grievously injured according to the other staff members who watched as he assaulted the guard contingent's commanding officer before running off. How Jones found how about the requisition order he put out on his former wife and child, Lucien didn't know, but the man left a trail of unconscious and broken bodies in his wake as he tore through the megastructure to reach her. When Lucien first heard about it, he blamed the malignant personality profile. Some defect that simply drove the man over the edge. But that was before Lucien found out about the G.H.S John Taylor. The Mormon Collective's transport freighter that moved goods and passengers back and forth to the Jovian mining colonies. As far as The Corporation was concerned, Helena and Bella were still nestled comfortably on level forty of Stack Four. But when a team of guards went to apprehend the woman, they found that Helena's ID tag brought them to an elderly dark-skinned man, and the daughter's ID tag belonged to his dog. Lucien watched the video. He saw Nikoli Jonlesky's wife and daughter board G.H.S John Taylor with another unknown black man with metal arms. The man wore the uniform of a student, but again, no corporate profile could be found. Lucien struggled at first in seeing the correlation between Jones's breakdown and the theft of the Council ship, but Lucien didn't believe in coincidences. He couldn't understand how Jones could orchestrate smuggling his wife and child out in such an elaborate way, at exactly the right time, all on his own. While being closely monitored by Lucien's team.

Unfortunately, the Boards of Chairs didn't believe in coincidences either.

Lucien received the summons to appear in front of the Board of Review to explain his, and his section's alleged involvement in the recent *terrorist attack*. At least, that's how he was going to spin it. The truth would bury him, but he might not even have a choice in the matter. If one of those committee members recommended an audit, that could be a real problem for him. Lucien had plenty of *off-the-books* projects in William's service that he would rather not be brought into the light. In the summons, to Lucien's shock and horror, it spelled out the allegations against him, and presented him with a recording from the Council member that implicated him.

By name!

Lucien didn't know about any of that. He knew Cattivo's lab was a smoldering ruin with a jagged hole in the one wall big enough to drive a tram through. The ship was missing, along with the powered armor, the few remains of the pilot, and every single scrap of data they had collected on all of it. And he knew that the exterior of Olympus Mons, the symbol of their corporate superiority, was a smoking ruin with a damage estimate in the high trillions.

And his newly acquired section was at the center of it all.

"Right through here, sir." The Liaison Officer quickly moved to the side of the large door and cycled it open just in time for Lucien to walk through the threshold into the waiting area.

"Where is he?" Lucien growled to the Liaison Officer when he came to the security desk of the Special Operations section. The clean-cut guard behind the desk regarded Lucien professionally and was about to answer his question before the other man interjected.

"We'll just get you signed in, and issue you a visitor's permit," The officer said while grinning like an idiot and nodded down towards the datapad the guard behind the desk was sliding across the table. Lucien picked it up and started filling out the short form while the Officer continued to prattle on. "Then I can take you into the holding area where the prisoner is being held."

Goddamnit, Lucien cursed inside his head as he filled out the form with the two idiot Special Operations personnel looking dumbly at him. If Jones had been apprehended by the regular security service, then Lucien would have been able to get him released by now. But the Special Operations people had been throwing red-tape in Lucien's way every since Jones was taken into custody. He suspected Soldado's involvement but Lucien couldn't figure out to what end.

"Fine, here." Lucien slide the datapad with its completed form back to the guard behind the desk. "Can we get on with this, now?" He looked to the Officer at his side with an annoyed expression. "I have a million other things to do today."

"I completely understand, sir." The officer's expression saddened slightly while he still held that stupid grin on his face. "It will just be another moment to process the visitor request and issue you the special permit. Once we're all set,

I'll take you through the door over there." The Liaison Officer motioned to a heavy metal door at the other end of the room. "And take you right into the holding area."

"*You'll* take me?" Lucien frowned at the man. "I'm an *executive*, I don't need to be escorted everywhere like a child." To Lucien's frustration the man just grinned wider.

"The Colonel's orders, sir. VIPs get *special treatment*," he said it like Lucien should be excited to have the large framed man shadowing him everywhere he went. Lucien snorted dismissively at that as the guard behind the desk looked up to his comrade and nodded his head. "Okay, the temporary permit has been added to your profile, and we're all good-to-go, sir. If you'll just follow me." The Liaison officer didn't wait for a reply before he turned sharply and walked towards the imposing-looking door in the corner.

Once the officer was at the door, it buzzed loudly. He reached out for the knob and promptly pulled the door open for Lucien to enter. *Tap-tap-tap.* Lucien moved through the door and up to another guard that was behind a similar desk as the first one. The guard sat tall in his seat and looked at Lucien dispassionately as he approached.

"Nick Jones," Lucien said promptly. Lucien ground his teeth when the guard behind the desk ignored him and looked to the Liaison Officer that was stepping up behind him. The officer nodded twice slowly, the entire time maintaining the stupid, affable grin on his face. Lucien was beginning to dislike him because of that grin.

"Cell six," the guard behind the desk said while looking to the Liaison Officer like Lucien wasn't standing there in a custom-made, pearl-colored suit.

Lucien didn't wait for the Liaison officer to show him the way. The holding area was such that anyone with a working set of eyes and a functioning brain would be able to easily navigate it. It was a single, wide hallway that led further down another sixty feet. On each side, were six-by-eight-foot holding cells with synthetic glass fronts for easy viewing. The cells themselves had all the comforts required by the corporation. A toilet, a sink, a bed, and a desk occupied the sterile-looking cell. Each made of poured concrete so they were impossible to move or damage in any way. Each reinforced glass front housed a door that slid open and a service hatch on the side for the prisoner's meals.

Lucien made his way down the hallway. The cell numbers were stencilled on the top corner of the glass. Jones's was about halfway down on the left hand side. He was laying on the concrete bed on his back with his hands folded behind his head. Like some daydreaming pre-schooler.

"Do you know someone named Athena?" He asked as soon as he recognized Jones's form on the bed. Lucien, of course, was more than aware of the Council member, but wanted to see Jones's reaction to the question. Jones just lazily turned his head and looked at him with a predatory gaze.

"She's a girl I know," he said with little enthusiasm while looking at him coldly. "She kicked my ass. Twice." He inexplicably chuckled warmly. "And I think we're friends," he said the last part like he was unsure of it. *Friends?!* Lucien just sneered at him.

"Did you know she is a Council member?"

"She might have mentioned it to me," he said with a smile as he lifted himself up and moved his legs over the side of the concrete bed and sat there looking at him. "Or I might have found that part out on my own. I'm not sure. I've had a lot of disturbing revelations lately."

"Do you think this is funny?"

"A little bit, yeah."

"Open that fucking cell!" Lucien barked to the Liaison Officer. He grabbed his cane by the shaft and gripped it tightly.

"I don't think that's a good idea, sir." The officer said, his affable smile slipping from his face.

"What?" Lucien almost challenged the man to disobey him again.

"You should listen to the man, *Lucien*," Jones said wickedly and almost growled his name.

"What the fuck did you just call me?" he peered back into the cell and looked at Jones with a mixture of rage and surprise.

"Lucien," he said again with some amusement. "I said you should listen to that guy." Jones just looked at him for a moment as he raised his large frame off the bed with ease and moved towards the reinforced glass front of the cell. "You killed a man," he went on to say and Lucien looked nervously to the officer beside him.

"I did no such thing," he protested angrily. Jones just smiled at him.

"Sure, you did. You might not have killed his body, but you tried to erase his life all the same," Nick said and gently brought his index finger up to tap the side of his head. "He's up here, though. And he's *not* happy to see you at all. If this door were to open," Nick said looming in front of him. "I might just have to beat you to death. And there's nobody within a hundred meters of this place that could stop me from *ending* you."

Lucien looked at the heated look of contained rage on Jones's face and instantly knew the corporate fail-safes Sanders installed into his personality profile had utterly failed to take hold. Just like that, Lucien found himself in a position where he might lose another project.

"You should be thanking me. I made you into something *special*. Into someone that could make a difference in this conflict. If it wasn't for me-."

Jones punched the solid glass door soundly. The sudden motion followed by the sound of the impact made Lucien flinch away.

"You took everything from Nikoli Jonlesky, and threw me into his body! You put me into his head, and he's in here with me now," Nick fumed and tapped the side of his head again. "Crying and wailing about the wife and daughter that *you took from him*!"

"I can fix that," Lucien shot back. Nick just laughed.

"I'm going to see you dead. I don't know when or how, but I'm going to kill you for what you did to Nikoli." Lucien switched gears. He wasn't about to stand here and be threatened by some *experiment*.

"You better change your tune real quick, mister. You might find it very stimulating to stand behind that door and sling your threats, but there's one thing that might have slipped your fractured mind. I am the only thing standing between you and termination. Because that's what happens to *abandoned experiments*, they're *terminated*." To Lucien's frustration, Jones just chuckled again. Lucien was so agitated he didn't even notice the buzzing sound in the distance.

"Yeah, well," Jones said dismissively. "I might have secured myself a better deal, actually."

"There is no better deal available to you than termination." That's when Lucien heard a gruff voice he recognized.

"You can't just terminate Corporate citizens, Lucien." Soldado strode noisily down the hall. Lucien could see that the man wore a medical brace on one of his knees, but it didn't hamper his stride in the least. "You should know that," the old soldier said with some disappointment.

What's going on here? Lucien wondered bitterly as he watched the Colonel approached. The Liaison loudly clicked his heels together and stood at rigid attention with a sharp salute that remained in place until the Colonel stopped beside Lucien.

"You are dismissed, Corporal." Soldado gave the Liaison Officer a quick salute.

"Sir!" The Liaison officer stamped his one foot down loudly on the ground before he turned abruptly on his heels and marched off.

"Nice to see you again, Lucien."

"What are you playing at Soldado?" Lucien asked warily. "Jones is an unregistered entity. He's an experimental prototype. *My* experimental prototype. He is under my purview. So, I can do whatever I want with him." Soldado nodded sympathetically.

"That may have been the case, *once*, but it appears some things have changed without your knowledge." Soldado offered him the datapad in his hand. Lucien took it and read what was displayed on the screen.

It was Nick Jones's Corporate profile.

What the fuck?! Lucien screamed inside his head as he quickly scanned the profile. *This is impossible!* Somebody had registered Nick Jones as an official Corporate citizen. Lucien grit his teeth painfully when he noticed Jones's parents were listed as F. U. Lucien

"This is obviously fake!" Lucien hissed and handed the datapad back to Soldado.

"Maybe so," the Colonel said lightheartedly. "But it's in the Corporate Registry, so as far as anyone cares, it's legit. Which means our boy here," Soldado began and pointed towards Jones smug frame in the cell. "Is a full-blown Corporate citizen, and it entitled to *all* rights and privileges bestowed upon regular *registered* citizens. So, no terminations without a fair trial. However, as it worked out, there won't be a trial." Lucien was speechless by this point. "Nick here has agreed to an incredibly generous plea agreement authorized by the Judicial section." Soldado couldn't help the smile that spread across his face. "He is going to spend five years on the Brig on Deimos for his crimes, and afterwards, he is coming to work for me. *Full-time.*

Nick already signed a ten-year contract with Special Operations. Hell, I even gave him a signing bonus."

"*You* did this!" Lucien angrily accused the Colonel and used his cane to motion towards the datapad. The Colonel chuckled and shrugged.

"I couldn't do *that* even if I wanted to. I can't explain it, but I might as well take advantage of it. You're welcome to contest it, however you can, Lucien. But for the time being at least, it appears Jones here is under my jurisdiction. Until that changes, you will schedule appointments if you wish to visit *my* prisoners," Soldado looked at him severely before he said his final words. "Good day." Lucien couldn't believe what he was hearing.

"Are you fucking excusing me?" He asked with raging indignation.

"You can be excused, Lucien, or I can have you removed," Soldado said coldly before he loudly snapped his fingers. Instantly the beefy guard behind the desk shot up from his chair. "The choice is yours." Lucien fumed for a full second before answering.

"Un-*fucking*-believable!" Lucien hissed red-faced before looking back to Jones. "This isn't over!" Lucien turned to walk away.

Tap-tap-tap.

"You better pray it is. If not, I'll be the last person you ever see, asshole." Jones calmly threatened behind him.

Tap-tap-tap.

***

"Honestly, darling, how bad could it really be?" Leslie asked while she poured them some drinks from the modest bar in Lucien's office. A gin martini for him, and she poured two fingers of bourbon for herself. "It's not like they have any actual evidence that links you to this Athena person," she tried to sound reassuring as she set the frail-looking martini glass in front of him.

"Fuck!" Lucien cursed loudly, exasperated. "You didn't hear that goddamn recording. That bitch *personally* thanked me for everything I supposedly did for her." He took an angry sip from his drink. "And that was after she tore through the Corporation's air defences like it was a goddamn joke! Eighty-nine trillion credits in damage," Lucien said the number with disbelief. "That cunt did eighty-nine trillion credits in damage with that fucking ship in less than five minutes. *Eighty-nine trillion*! If I get saddled with that debt, I'll be ruined." Lucien rubbed his hand over the stubble on his head and took another sip. "Ruined!"

"The Board of Review won't transfer that debt to you," Leslie casually waved off the concern.

"What makes you so sure, Leslie?" Bowers looked at him slightly amused.

"Because if they did, then The Corporation wouldn't be able to file a grievance with the UN. After all, you can't charge for the same expense twice." *The UN?* Lucien hadn't considered The Corporation using the United Nations to try and resolve the matter. *That's brilliant.* Lucien took another sip and listened intently as Leslie continued. "From what I hear, the Board of Chairs is chomping at the bit they're so excited to bring this before the UN. They have the clerks in the Central Administration Bureau working double shifts to file all the paperwork in order to get the matter brought forward at the next general assembly. They'll probably grill you for a few more sessions to get as much information out of you as they can, but there's nothing linking you to the actual attack. You know this."

"But the recording from Athena," Lucien cut in.

"Pure conjecture," Leslie scoffed. "Lucien, darling, you worry too much. The facts as everyone understands it are that you found an artifact of *unknown* origin, you brought it back to your lab to study it, and it was stolen out from under you. It's not particularly flattering, but every shred of evidence that points to the contrary has been erased. As long as you keep your wits about you, I don't see how they can prove you knew beforehand that it was a Council ship. And if you didn't know that, how could you possibly know that they would come for it?" Leslie smiled like she had just solved all his problems. Lucien grimaced bitterly.

"So, my defence is I'm a fucking idiot. Great."

"There are worse things than being foolish, my dear. Like being demoted. Or fired," Leslie coolly warned him before waving her hand in front of herself again. "But like I said, your problem isn't with the Board of Review. It's the Research and Development Board. Those piranhas will never let you forget this unfortunate business." Leslie took a thoughtful sip from her drink, and pondered his dilemma for a moment more before continuing. "They'll probably vote to give you a leadership review, and suspend your budget until after the review period. They might even ban you from Board meetings until after it's over as well. *And* once you've cleared that, proposing any future increases to your budget will be an uphill climb, but if you keep your nose clean, and keep your head down, you should be able to get out from under this mishap in less than a decade."

"And what happens when that simple leadership review turns into a full-blown section audit?" Lucien asked sourly. Mainly because he knew Leslie Bowers would tell him the hard truth, even when he didn't want to hear it.

"Well, if that happens, you better have your house in order. All your little *side projects* will have to be abandoned." Leslie knew all about Lucien's plans to transfer Ernst's mind into a brand-new cybernetic body until he could gestate his new cloned body. Both of those projects were still in their infancy, and each was strictly prohibited.

"Shit," Lucien growled before he drained his drink and placed the delicate glass back onto his desk. He had a sudden urge to fling the frail martini glass against the wall and watch it smash into a thousand jagged pieces.

"Oh relax," Leslie said with some humor as she set down her glass and reached over the desk to retrieve his. "I highly doubt the Board will vote for a full-blown audit," Bowers said with soft reassurance as she mixed him another drink with a seductive grace. On any other day, Lucien would find that very alluring, but his mind was elsewhere at the moment.

"Oh, Leslie, this is not the time to be coy. If you know something, tell me. I'm fucking drowning over here." Leslie just chuckled slightly.

"I do enjoy watching men suffer," she said absently and with some humor. "And I'm not suggesting that I know anything specific. But let's be honest, none of the Directors on that Board want to see one of their own audited, because it makes it all the more likely that the Chairman will order other sections audited. Everyone like to maintain the illusion that everything is business as usual. For most of them, the leadership review is enough of a humiliation, which is all they really want." Leslie refilled his glass and delicately dropped two olives into it before she slowly stirred the drink as she looked at him lovingly. "To see you knocked down a peg. They see you're not like William was. You can't be controlled as easily, because your ability far exceeds their own, and they know it. Half of those board members are afraid of you, and the other half want to *be* you." Leslie tapped the metal stir stick once against the glass's rim before she dropped it on the bar's top. She deeply swayed her hips as she wafted across the floor and deposited his drink in front of him. "Most of them probably would vote against an audit just to avoid your wrath." Leslie slowly sank herself down into one of the two chairs in front of his desk. In the chair Ernst normally sat in. "Lastly, I doubt they'd order a review because there's nobody left to replace you. We've pretty much cleared the field of available candidates." Lucien took a sip of his drink and looked at Leslie over the rim.

"What about you?" He asked with a sly grin. Leslie just smiled.

"But then who would run Energy Development once we get rid of Fred Johnson?" She shot back innocently.

They both shared a gentle laugh at that and tipped their glasses to each other.

"As much as I want to make that happen for you, Leslie." Lucien's expression dropped. "I've got nothing." He shook his head slowly. "All my research, everything we learned about that ship, the nanomachines, and the stupid powered suit of armor are all gone. Even the useless projects William was working on was lost. All that's left is an empty mainframe, a skeleton crew of semi-competent lab workers and researchers, and a repair bill that might hit a billion credits. Fuck!" Lucien angrily shook his head before he took another drink.

"First, we'll get this mishap behind us." Bowers looked at him with gentle confidence. "Then we'll focus on the future." It was Leslie's turn to look at him over the rim of her glass. "On a different note. Lucien, when was the last time you slept?" She asked and looked at him suspiciously. "You look like shit."

"It has been a couple days," Lucien said with some shame. He had been putting out figurative and literal fires ever since those idiots bombed his section a lifetime ago. The neurocaine patches had been keeping him going, but Lucien felt he was getting to the end of that particular rope as well. "I've just been so damned busy."

"Well, thankfully, you now have an abundance of free time on your hands." Leslie looked at him with genuine concern. "Take a couple days to focus on yourself. Hell, take a month. It will take that long to complete the repairs to your section anyway. Get that lovely mane of yours regrown, and get that disagreeable limp taken care of."

"Is it really that bad?" Lucien asked lightheartedly because he was afraid of the truth. But Leslie wasn't.

"You've been hobbling around here like an angry troll for over a week. Rest. It's the best thing you can do for your section right now." Leslie looked at him severely. "After all, it's not the ship, or the seas on which it sails, it's the captain that determines the success of the voyage." She gave him a knowing look and held it for a moment before Lucien relented.

"You're right," he sighed. "I haven't been myself lately. I have been working non-stop trying to avoid the next catastrophe, without the knowledge of what it might be."

"And it came anyway. So, all that effort was wasted," Leslie said coldly. "You should have been preparing for the inevitable."

"Excuse me?"

"All this time you've been whining about an attack that *you knew* was coming, and yet you did nothing to prepare for it." Bowers held up her hand and started ticking off her fingers. "You didn't back-up your research to an external source. You could have moved the ship to another section. You could have trusted me with it. Then, if it was stolen from Energy Development, we could have used that against Johnson. I can't even explain the rationale of keeping the armor in the same location as the ship. *Or* the remains of the pilot." Leslie then dropped her hands in disappointment. "Honestly, Lucien, you were practically baiting The Council the steal it all from you." Lucien groaned loudly.

"You're right," he admitted because there was nothing left to be said. "You're right. I guess I didn't honestly believe they could get to us here. We're at the bottom of the megastructure, *for Christ's sakes*. I can't even fathom the lengths the woman would have had to go to just to get down here." He shook his head in disbelief while Leslie just chuckled softly in her seat.

"Typical male hubris," she said with bitter amusement. "Never underestimate a *determined* woman." Leslie smiled, and Lucien tipped his glass to her.

"*That*, I shall never do again."

"I hope so. You've already done it *twice*." Lucien raised his eyebrow at that. "If you trusted me enough to tell me everything, I could have counselled you on this earlier, and helped you avoid certain missteps. I could have helped you turn your inevitable misfortune, into *our* good luck. But no," Bowers gently scolded him. Lucien nodded his head as she did, she was right after all. You couldn't deny her that. "You wanted this partnership, and I have all my cards on the table, but you're keeping things from me. Makes me wonder what kind of partnership this really is," Leslie said with a questioning look.

"As I've said, a mistake I will not repeat." Lucien tried to give Leslie a reassuring smile. It was hard given what was just said. He still felt bitterly stung over the recent events. It was hard not to.

Then a knock came from the office door.

"Is this a bad time?" Bryce Cailleanach asked sheepishly at the door. Lucien noted that he was holding something in his hand.

"What are y-," Lucien started to say, rather harshly, before Leslie sharply interrupted him.

"*I* invited him. Jesus, Lucien! He's your Assistant Director. He *should* be here," Leslie said in that gentle, scolding tone of hers. Lucien initially flinched from the comment. *No, Ernst should be here,* he thought on reflex.

But Ernst was in a coma.

Lucien looked at Leslie who just returned his angry gaze with a challenging one of her own. In the end, Lucien took in a deep breath and let it out.

"You're right," he said to Leslie again. He turned to Bryce, who looked like he was strongly considering escaping the whole situation. "Bryce," he regarded the man warmly. Which Cailleanach clearly wasn't ready for. "I owe you an apology." Lucien rose out of his chair and strode over to the man.

Tap-tap-tap.

"What?" Bryce said with utter shock, and maybe a hint of fear. "No, sir. You don't owe me anything." Lucien noted that the man was wearing a finely tailored suit, it was a flattering color for Cailleanach's palate.

"Nonsense!" Lucien waved off the comment. Cailleanach jumped away from the sudden movement. "I've been horrible to you. Please, come in. Have a drink with us." Lucien ushered the man into his office with a soft pat on the back, that again, Bryce shied away from. "What can I get you to drink?"

"Oh, I couldn't possibly," Bryce couldn't even finish the sentence.

"I insist," Lucien motioned to the empty seat in front of Lucien's desk. He looked to Leslie, who gave him the slightest nods of approval. "Vodka, I believe, right?" He asked as he made his way to the bar.

Tap-tap-tap.

"If you're offering, yes. Please." Bryce looked apologetically towards Bowers. "I hope I'm not interrupting anything."

"Well," Bowers said playfully. "Lucien was telling me how he should have taken my council earlier, and if he had, he would have avoided a lot of his current heartaches."

"Oh?" Bryce responded nervously, mostly because he probably thought he had to. Lucien knew he didn't really want Cailleanach here, but at the same time, Leslie was right. He should be here. Lucien chose him to fill in until Ernst was back on his feet, but never actually treated the man like *his* assistant. That was because of Lucien's shortcoming, not Cailleanach's. Bryce was a competent researcher, and would probably make a fine executive, given the right mentorship.

"Indeed," Lucien called back as he picked the best crystal glass for Bryce's drink. "And Leslie here was tutoring me in the ways of good leadership, while gently reminding me my recent series of unfortunate events could have been much worse." Lucien finished pouring two fingers of the finest vodka the Corporate distilleries had ever produced, and walked it over to Bryce's seat, handing the man his glass with a warm smile.

"Yes! Which makes the good news I wanted to tell you-,"

"Right! Before the meeting," Lucien wagged his finger at Bryce. "You had said there was something you needed to talk to me about. Again, I am sorry for pushing you aside like that." Lucien nodded towards the man. "You're my assistant. You shouldn't have to come and beg me for a moment of my time. Everything has been so chaotic around here, and if I'm being honest, I'm still used to seeing Doctor Cattivo by my side." Lucien paused at his chair and looked mournfully at his two guests for a full second, before he wiped the expression from his face and replaced it with a warm smile. "What did you want to tell me?" Lucien set his drink off to the side and folded his hands on the desk and gave Bryce his full attention.

Cailleanach placed the object that he was carrying in his hands on the desk without saying another word.

He didn't have to. Lucien recognized the strange light-absorbing material.

"Jesus Christ, Bryce." Lucien stared at the small, flat square for a moment before he reached out and picked it up. It was lighter than he assumed it would be. "You managed to cut a piece of the ship's hull off. That's fantastic!" Lucien looked to Leslie with renewed energy. Bowers smiled and let her expression say it all. *I told you.*

He must have kept the sample in his own lab, Lucien thought to himself as he looked at the small charcoal-colored plate in his hand with awe. It wasn't much. It was just a fraction of what he could have learned from that ship, but it was something. It was something he could use to keep the wolves from his door. *It wasn't a total loss.*

"No," Bryce said sharply, which caused both himself and Bowers to look at him. "I didn't remove that from the Council's ship." He pointed to the small plate in Lucien's hand. Lucien felt a curse boiling up inside him but then Cailleanach smiled widely. "I made it."

"You what?" Leslie asked, suddenly interested in the conversation.

"I made it," he said again, louder this time. "In my lab." Cailleanach sat taller in his seat and took a cautious sip of his drink. Lucien watched the man wrinkle his nose a bit at it. He just regarded Bryce with sudden suspicion.

"You made this *before* the attack?" Lucien asked with muted optimism. His heart skipped a beat when Bryce's smile widened.

"A couple years back," Bryce said with a new found confidence. "Special Materials updated the mainframe and I lost month's worth of work." Bryce paused to take another sip before he looked to both of them. "Since then, I've backed-up my work to an external drive." Cailleannach reached in between the twenty-four carat buttons of his shirt, and slowly pulled out a small drive that was the size of Lucien's two fingers put together. It swung freely at the end of a silver chain. "I produced *that* sample," he continued and pointed to the ebony plate in Lucien's hand, that seemed to suck the light into its depths. "This morning."

"Fucking hell, Bryce!" Leslie exclaimed loudly and then chuckled. Lucien looked wide-eyed at the man. He was speechless.

"I have all the material data I collected. The complete external scan of the ship, with the thrust profiles, a rough schematic of the atmospheric booster design as well as the main drive, and I have some of the relevant data from the other areas too." Bryce tucked the drive back into his shirt. "In short, I have everything you *need*." Bryce took a large sip of his drink, shuttered slightly and then dropped the bomb. "But it's not going to be free."

Lucien didn't hesitate.

"Name it."

"For starters, I'm staying on as your Assistant Director, even *after* Doctor Cattivo returns to work. No offence to the good doctor. He's a brilliant scientist, and a good man, but he's not an *executive*. If he was, he would have secured his patron's success the way *I* have."

"Done," Lucien promptly said as soon as Cailleanach gave him the chance.

"*And*," he continued. "You're going to help me take the directorship of Special Materials from that asshole, Adler." Bryce looked at Lucien with wicked intent.

"Agreed." Lucien nodded once, rose from his seat, and offered his martini glass to Cailleanach. Bryce eagerly rose off his chair and touched his glass to Lucien's. "Welcome to the inner circle."

"Thank you, sir." Bryce said obediently and returned to his seat, grinning.

"You see!" Leslie said and patted Bryce on the back. "You surround yourself with skilled, competent people, but you don't use them to their full potential. I'll tell you again, you bring us in, trust us as we trust you, and we will deliver Research and Development to you on a fucking platter, Lucien."

He looked at both of them for a full second. Lucien didn't see competitors, or even executives. He saw loyal generals in his army.

"I don't know what to say," Lucien said looking at Bryce. "I have completely underestimated both my enemies *and* my allies. I have been a fool." Lucien looked to both of them with a sad expression. They each had delivered Lucien out of the fire when they could have just as easily let him burn.

"You have," Leslie said lightly. "But we forgive you." Cailleanach eagerly nodded his agreement to the statement.

"If I may, sir? I have a few thoughts on the Jones dilemma." Bryce spoke up after. Lucien looked at him and opened his hands. "Please."

"Well, as I understand it, you wish to have the man back under your control?" Lucien nodded. "Well, seems to me you'd never be able to do that by holding his former family over his head. He'll just hate you for that." *He already does,* Lucien quipped inside his head. "But if you were to offer him something he couldn't find anywhere else? You could use that to bring him back into the fold." That piqued Lucien's interest.

"What did you have in mind, Bryce?" Leslie asked that question for him.

"Vengeance," he said quickly and paused for the concept to linger in the air. "With the data I've collected I believe I can replicate the Council ship, structurally. It won't be as good, but it will be scores above what we are currently using for atmospheric fighter craft. Plus, with Bowers' help I think we can fit it with a reactor powerful enough to equip it with a main drive." Bryce had the room's attention at that point. A dual role fighter craft that functioned as well in space as it did in an atmosphere was a technology that was just beyond the Corporation's grasp. Until now. "The best part is, I can make a ship that has an identical ship profile to the one that attacked us. We could use that to attack Ceres station in a two-fold operation. One goal would be to frame The Council for the attack. At the very least, we could discredit The Council. We could make it look like they have a rogue member amongst them. At the same time, we kill the Jonleskys, and when Jones finds out The Council is responsible for the death of his family,

I imagine he'll come to us looking for his revenge. Once we get him back into the lab, we make sure he doesn't leave it until we've learned everything about the nanobots that we can."

"And what about Soldado?" Leslie asked with a serious look on her face. "He's not just going to roll over and let us have him back."

"Jones's contract doesn't start until *after* his prison term. That gives us five years. It's not a lot of time," Cailleanach admitted with a shrug. "But it's doable."

Lucien was silent for a moment, thinking over Cailleanach's idea.

"Bryce, that's fucking genius," Lucien said in a low appreciative voice.

"There's one problem, though. I can build the ship, but the pilot is another matter entirely. From my analysis of the attack from the satellite footage, the operator of that Council ship was enduring enough G-forces to reduce a normal person to paste. Like, *literal* paste. I calculated the G-force on one maneuver in particular, it was *twenty* G's! No human could survive that. For context, at twenty G's, the average pilot's body would suddenly weigh over thirty-five hundred pounds. So, Like I said, I can make the ship, but I don't know how we would be able to fly it convincingly enough for people to believe it's a Council member inside the cockpit." Bryce looked around the room sympathetically.

Lucien just smiled as he thought of the cybernetic body he was building for Ernst.

"Actually, Bryce, I think Cattivo might be able to help us with that."

The End...For now.

Don't forget to check out my other books.

Ronin of the Dead

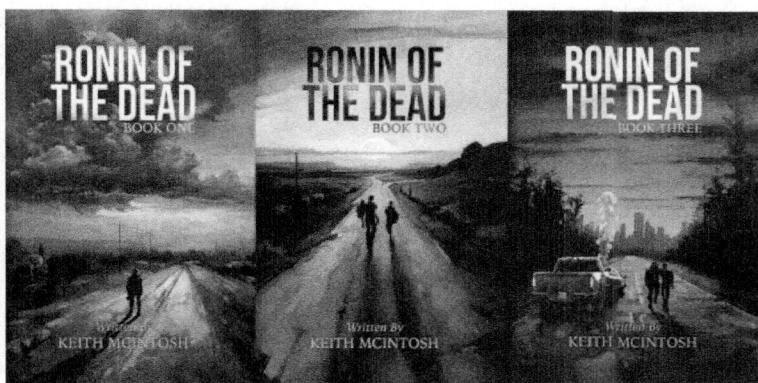

Book One Book Two Book Three

Available on Amazon and Kindle Unlimited.

Printed in Great Britain
by Amazon